FROM THE DESK OF
ADAM RAPP

D1627108

Dear Reader,

Twelve years ago I received a package in the mail from my aunt Roberta, who is one of my mother's eight sisters. My mother, Mary Lee Rapp, the oldest of thirteen children in a Scotch-Irish, Catholic family, grew up in Elmira, New York, and later in central Illinois. She passed away from cancer in 1997, at the age of fifty-five, and the package from Roberta, which arrived fourteen years after my mother's death, was a simple shoebox containing keepsakes that had been left to me. (Roberta was my mother's power of attorney, and it took her a while to distribute my mother's few possessions.) One of the items inside the shoebox was a laminated ID, my mother's badge at Stateville Correctional, a maximum-security prison where she was working as a nurse toward the end of her life. At the time I didn't pay close attention to it.

Growing up in Joliet, Illinois, in the '70s and early '80s could be scary. A once-vibrant steel town, Joliet was rampant with crime after the industry dried up. The gangs on the east side were in full force. Joliet became known as a bit of a murder capital. And the specter of the serial killer John Wayne Gacy, who was arrested in December 1978, felt like it had crept all the way down to our city, about forty minutes south of Gacy's home in suburban Chicago.

As an adult I've been both fascinated and troubled by Gacy, but it wasn't until some years after receiving my mother's effects that I took a closer look at her ID badge—a simple photo of her, citing her job title (Nurse)—and noticed the issue date of January 1994. Stateville Correctional was also where executions in Illinois were carried out, and that meant my mother (who retired the following year because of complications from her illness) was still employed at Stateville at the time of Gacy's execution, in May 1994. After digging further, I learned that she was on duty May 9, the day leading up to Gacy's scheduled lethal injection. Though there is no definitive proof, I also discovered that she was likely the nurse who performed his last physical before his execution. She never shared this information with me or my siblings.

Prior to working at the prison, my mother was, by turns, a pediatric nurse, a Head Start nurse, and a stage mom (my brother, Anthony, was a child actor). As the oldest of thirteen, she helped her mother raise many of her brothers and sisters. She spent her life devoted to children. She raised three kids by herself on a nurse's salary. She never drank, didn't smoke, hardly ever cursed, and was an avid Catholic for much of her life. After making that connection between her and John Wayne Gacy, I became intrigued by a simple, decent woman's proximity to such horrendous violence. In an awful coincidence, it turns out that she was also friends with one of the eight nurses killed in Chicago in 1966 by Richard Speck, in a crime often considered to be the country's first random mass murder. (My mother graduated from the University of Chicago's nursing program the year before the murders.)

The novel sprang from this unnerving confluence. I wanted to honor my mother's life, and I wanted to examine how a seemingly normal family—a good, hardworking, lower-middle-class family—can be in relationship to this very scary part of America. Today we have school shooters. We are a country beset by serial killers, who are often middle-aged white men. These characters are walking through our neighborhoods, they're taking communion in our churches, and they're even sitting down for dinner with us in our homes. They are in our midst, in plain sight, and yet somehow obscured.

When I pictured my mother ministering to Gacy, I couldn't shake this notion. It haunted me and still does. And that's why I had to write this novel.

WOLF AT THE TABLE

ALSO BY ADAM RAPP

NOVELS
The Year of Endless Sorrows
Know Your Beholder

SELECTED PLAYS

Animals and Plants	*Kindness*
Stone Cold Dead Serious	*The Metal Children*
Blackbird	*Ghosts in the Cottonwoods*
Red Light Winter	*The Hallway Trilogy*
Bingo with the Indians	*Dreams of Flying Dreams of Falling*
American Sligo	*The Sound Inside*

NOVELS FOR YOUNG ADULTS

Missing the Piano	*Under the Wolf, Under the Dog*
The Buffalo Tree	*Punkzilla*
The Copper Elephant	*The Children and the Wolves*
Little Chicago	*Decelerate Blue*
33 Snowfish	*Fum*

GRAPHIC NOVEL
Ball Peen Hammer

WOLF AT THE TABLE

A NOVEL

ADAM RAPP

LITTLE, BROWN AND COMPANY
New York Boston London

Little, Brown and Company
Hachette Book Group
1290 Avenue of the Americas, New York, NY 10104
littlebrown.com

First Edition: March 2024

Little, Brown and Company is a division of Hachette Book Group, Inc. The Little, Brown name and logo are trademarks of Hachette Book Group, Inc.

The publisher is not responsible for websites (or their content) that are not owned by the publisher.

The Hachette Speakers Bureau provides a wide range of authors for speaking events. To find out more, go to hachettespeakersbureau.com or email hachettespeakers@hbgusa.com.

Little, Brown and Company books may be purchased in bulk for business, educational, or promotional use. For information, please contact your local bookseller or the Hachette Book Group Special Markets Department at special.markets@hbgusa.com.

ISBN 978-0-316-43416-4
LCCN [tk]

10 9 8 7 6 5 4 3 2 1

LSC-C

Printed in the United States of America

TK

AMERICANA

All the houses are red or green,
with bright yellow roofs.
Birds sing full-throated
in the fruit-laden trees.
Shiny cars line the streets.
But when the sea of night
rolls in from the east
to cover the continent,
over the foothills and factories
and the deep rivers
overflowing with rain,
the men and women
sitting in hot rooms
with tightly drawn drapes
turn off their televisions
and pull down the sheets
and lie side by side in silence
wondering who will save them
from death, and why, and what
it is they're waiting for
if not that, even as an ark,
white as moonlight,
crosses the horizon carrying
the people who escaped a flood
in some distant town.

—Nicholas Christopher

PART ONE

1

ELMIRA, NEW YORK
AUGUST 19, 1951

MYRA LEE

ON A STIFLINGLY HOT early Sunday evening—the third Sunday of August—a young girl in a red-and-white plaid gingham dress sits in the corner booth of Kylie's Diner and Bakery in downtown Elmira, New York, reading a novel. Her long dark hair is pulled back and away from her face with a simple white ribbon. Her calves and shins are spotted with calamine lotion, where the region's mosquitoes, notoriously insatiable at this time of year, have had their way with her. Her eyes are on the gray side of hazel—her pupils full and wondrous—and she rarely blinks while scanning her author's sentences, which seem to unspool across and down the page like meticulously arranged, magical black thread.

The reader's name is Myra Lee Larkin and she is in love with the story's narrator, a restless, opinionated, at times foul-mouthed young man named Holden, who, at sixteen, has just run away from his boarding school in Agerstown, Pennsylvania, a fictional town that Myra imagines being located due south of Elmira, just on the other side of the state line. Holden has been expelled and leaves on a Saturday, after a football game with a rival academy, just before Christmas break, rather than on the following Wednesday, the official beginning of winter recess, when his parents are expecting him. After an awkward visit with the only professor whom he felt obliged to bid farewell, Holden takes a train to New York City. As he peers out the window of the eastern Pennsylvania landscape, while his train hurtles toward Manhattan, there is the sense that his life will be forever changed. Myra Lee Larkin briefly peers out the small window beside her booth, hoping that her life will someday include similar adventure.

There are three others seated in the small chromium-trimmed diner. Two booths in front of Myra an old man looks down at a plate of scrambled eggs as if it will provide a solution to the quandary of his life, while in the booth closest to the entrance sits a plump, overly made-up woman whose hair is arranged like a swirling pastry. At the counter slouches a handsome older blond boy smoking a cigarette and drinking a cup of coffee.

Myra holds the book with her thin, pale hands as if clutching a thing that should never be dropped, so transfixed that she isn't even aware of the black fly buzzing around her food. She'll often order a grilled cheese sandwich and a malted milk, which she pays for with her weekly allowance. She can always read up to fifteen or twenty pages during her visit to the diner. Myra tries her best not to read too quickly, but sometimes the words start to tumble and the voice of her narrator gallops in her head as if to overwhelm her and she has to force her eyes away from the page to calm herself.

At thirteen, she is the oldest of the six Larkin children and her mother always grants her this free time after five o'clock mass as long as she's home by 7:15 sharp to help with her baby brother, Archie. Following the service she makes a beeline west toward the little diner in her white saddle shoes, which, after re-soling, will be handed down to her sister Fiona, who will be twelve in October, only sixteen months younger than Myra but two grades behind her in school. Myra can't flee the church parking lot fast enough. She even holds her breath so she won't inhale the gravel dust.

Her mother has no idea that her daughter is reading this purportedly scandalous novel, which has been secreted into a makeshift cardboard slot rigged with duct tape to the underside of the table at this booth. The head waitress, Ethel, with her Jean Kent hair and knowing eyes, has become a kind of shepherd to the book's safekeeping. Last Sunday the corner booth was already occupied by a pair of Irish nuns, who drank cup after cup of coffee, but Ethel made sure to deliver the book to Myra—under the plate containing her usual grilled cheese deluxe—with a conspiratorial wink. Myra always makes sure to tip Ethel at least a quarter.

For the past few weeks, Myra has been composing letters to Holden in her diary. In her looping, careful penmanship she dutifully writes to him about Elmira; about its long winters and insufferable summers and the rotten-egg stink of the Chemung River and her dream of someday going to New York City. She's even sketched a few pictures for him: her tall mother with her thick nest of black hair and the Larkins' Siamese cat, Frank, and the bedroom desk where she does her homework (and composes letters to him) and her brother Alec with his crooked bangs and mischievous dark eyes. Myra has never considered herself to be much of an artist, but she likes to draw, and more than that, she likes to share the images of her life with Holden. Although the letters will, of course, never be sent or receive a response, for her they feel as real as anything she's ever sealed in a stamped envelope and delivered to the post office.

She looks up from her book to find the blond boy from the counter sitting across from her. In the novel, Holden's train has just pulled into Penn Station and Myra is anxious to know what happens next. She doesn't want to put the book down but elects to do so out of politeness.

"You gonna eat that?" the boy says, pointing to her grilled cheese sandwich.

Myra hadn't even noticed him walk over and she's a little shocked by his sudden proximity. And by his handsomeness. He has light blue eyes and a strong chin and his hair is parted on the side in the style of Montgomery Clift. Myra has never seen this boy before, certainly not at Holy Family Jr. High, at church, or anywhere else in Elmira for that matter. He wears a short-sleeved plaid shirt and tan trousers.

"I'd be happy to help you out," he offers, still staring at her plate.

She nods and he takes half of the grilled cheese and bites into it. The muscles in his jaws dance and pulse. He breathes noisily through his nose. She pushes her malted milk toward him and he gulps from it. He thanks her and wipes his mouth with the back of his hand. Unlike other boys his age, who usually have pimples or blemishes where they've nicked themselves shaving, his skin is clear.

"What are you reading?" he asks.

Myra shows him the novel's spine.

"Interesting title," he says. "What's it about?"

"This boy who's running away from his boarding school," she says. "Well, he actually got kicked out for failing four subjects, but he's leaving before he's supposed to. He's pretty confused but there's something about him."

"Everyone's always running from something," the boy says. "You live around here?"

"I live over on Maple Avenue," she says, "which is about a mile and a half from here."

"I'm not familiar with that part of town," the boy says. "What's your name?"

Myra has a momentary instinct to lie and offer one of her sisters' names but for some reason she can't. "Myra," she says, in a voice that sounds strange and faraway.

"Pleased to meet you, Myra. I'm Mickey." He reaches across the table and extends his hand.

She accepts it and they shake in a businesslike manner. His hand is strong and calloused and there are little soft blond hairs sprouting along his wrist and forearm. Myra is struck by how safe his hand makes her feel. After retracting hers, she takes a bite out of the other half of the grilled cheese and drinks from the malted milk, just to have something to do.

"I'll bet you've lived in Elmira your whole life," the boy says. "Ever been anywhere else?"

"I've been to Niagara Falls," she says. "And two summers ago we went to go visit my Aunt Grace up in Buffalo. Do you travel?"

"Oh, I love traveling," he says. "I've been all over the country.

I've seen the Grand Canyon, the Mojave Desert, and the Pacific Ocean. I've even been to Washington State."

"Where are you from?"

"I'm originally from a small town in Oklahoma," he replies, "but I consider myself to be a genuine citizen of the world."

Ethel appears at the booth. "Your check, honey," she says. She scribbles on her pad and drops the check on the table. Myra thanks her and opens her pocketbook.

"Yours is over on the counter," Ethel tells the boy.

"Thank you," he says.

Ethel stands there, smiling, her arms folded, until he takes the hint, excusing himself and heading back to the counter, where he reaches into his front pocket, produces a few coins, and drops them beside his coffee cup.

"Was he being funny with you?" Ethel quietly asks through the side of her mouth.

"No," Myra says, "he's nice."

The older boy opens the door to exit the diner. "Have a good evening, ladies," he calls over his shoulder.

A FEW BLOCKS AFTER Myra begins the mile-and-a-half journey home it starts to pour. The crickets were loud on her way into church, and the rain comes as no surprise. The raindrops, as big and round as coins, splat on the sidewalk. Myra shelters under the awning of the Fanny Farmer Candy Store, which is currently closed. She knows she should keep walking or she won't make it home on time to help her mother with Archie but she stays put, hoping the storm will pass.

Moments later a yellow Chevy Bel Air with whitewall tires and Pennsylvania license plates pulls up beside her. The boy from the diner is at the wheel.

He lowers the window. "Looks like you could use a ride," he says.

Myra hesitates. Something tightens the bones in her chest. The rain is really coming down now.

"This storm's only gonna get worse," the boy says.

The color of his car brings out the blond in his hair. Even in the dim, overcast light his eyes seem so blue.

Myra's bladder feels weak, as if she could go right there in front of the candy store. "Okay," she hears herself say. She emerges from under the awning and jogs around to the passenger's side.

Myra has never gotten this kind of attention from any boy, let alone an older, handsome high school boy. During the seventh grade she would often catch Ralph Namie, a quiet eighth grader with the unfortunate, unformed face of a scarecrow, staring at her in the cafeteria, but that's about it. One of her girlfriends, Emily Kerr, has already started messing around with boys. She even talks about going all the way with a high school sophomore named Charles Wilkes. But to Myra that kind of thing still seems a long ways off.

Her new friend drives nonchalantly, with one hand on the wheel and the other in his lap. The Bel Air's windshield wipers squeal across the glass.

"Where to?" the boy asks.

"Home," she says and directs him toward Maple Avenue.

It usually takes her thirty minutes to walk; by car it should take only five or ten. They pass by the houses of Elmira, many of which are thin, two-story, colorless homes jammed together, their flat roofs a bit lopsided. But after a half mile or so they happen upon a series of vast, palatial Victorians with their conical attic dormers and wide lots.

"Are you in high school?" Myra finally asks.

"Me?" the boys replies. "I'm past all that."

She asks how old he is and he tells her that he's nineteen. "Are you enrolled in college?" she says.

No, he says, he already has a job.

"Doing what?" she asks.

"I play right field for the New York Yankees," he says.

"You're on the *Yankees*?" Myra practically squawks.

"Scout's honor," he says.

She wants to believe him but it just seems so improbable. In the car on the way to church Myra heard about the Yankees' day game. As the Larkins pulled into the parking lot of St. John the Baptist, the radio announcer was reporting the results.

"Didn't you have a game today?" she asks.

"We did have a game," Mickey says. "Got our tails kicked in by the Philadelphia Athletics. Fifteen to one. Right in Yankee Stadium, too, in front of the home crowd. It was downright embarrassing."

"How did you get up to Elmira so fast?"

"Oh, I'm not with the team right now," he says.

"Why not?"

"They sent me back down to the minor leagues in July. I fell into a bit of a batting slump so I got demoted. I had to report to their Triple-A affiliate to work the kinks out."

Myra is simply amazed.

"I love playing the outfield," he continues. "One of my favorite things to do before a game—before I head into the locker room to put my uniform on—is to take my shoes and socks off and walk barefoot through the grass of Yankee Stadium. They mow it so perfectly and you can feel a softness coming up between your toes. But you can also feel a wildness, too. All the secrets of the earth hidden in the soil."

Myra imagines him walking through the outfield grass in Yankee Stadium, holding his shoes and socks, the cuffs of his trousers rolled up to his calves.

"I'm s'posed to be in Kansas City but I got a coupla days off so I thought I'd take a drive, clear my head. I love this part of the country."

Myra directs him to turn left onto Maple Avenue. "It's only four more blocks," she says.

They are quiet for the rest of the drive. The rain has thinned but there is a roll of thunder. Myra can't quite believe she's getting a ride home from a genuine New York Yankee. Who would believe her? When they arrive at her house the boy pulls the car over on the other side of the street and shifts into park. As the Bel Air idles Myra can feel him looking at her. It's as if she's being leered at by an animal and she knows she should be afraid but she feels strangely calm. She's already late, but not by more than a few minutes. If she were smart she would get out of the car and go inside and help her mother, but she finds herself unwilling to move.

"I like talking to you," Mickey finally says.

Myra's cheeks fill with heat.

"Do you like talking to me?" he asks.

"Yes," she hears herself say.

"Would you like to continue our conversation?" he says.

"Okay," she replies. "But my mother might come out here if she sees me in your car."

"Where should we go?" he asks.

She tells him about a nearby park and the boy shifts the car into gear and five minutes later they enter a large green dotted with trees. He parks under a weeping willow, whose heavy, soaked catkins graze the windshield. After Mickey turns the engine off Myra's senses sharpen. She can smell the car's leather upholstery, its rich, nutmeggy calfskin. The cool ozone from the storm slips in through the crack in her window. The rain has settled into a steady simmer.

Mickey turns the radio on to Patti Page's "The Tennessee Waltz."

> *I was dancing with my darling to the Tennessee waltz*
> *When an old friend I happened to see . . .*

It might be the saddest, most romantic song Myra has ever heard.

"How old are you?" Mickey finally asks.

"I just turned thirteen in June," she says.

"June what?"

"June fifteenth," she says. "I'm a Gemini."

"I was an October baby," Mickey says. "October twentieth."

"That makes you a Libra," Myra says.

"What exactly is a Libra?" he says.

"In astrology it represents the scales of justice."

"So that makes me a weight-measuring device?" he says. "How boring. I'd rather be a lion or a fish."

They laugh and their laughter seems to mix well with the lilt of Patti Page's voice.

From his pocket Mickey produces a ball of Dubble Bubble chewing gum, its purple wrapping wrinkled, and offers it to Myra.

"Oh, no thank you," she says.

He sets the gum on the dash in front of her. "In case you change your mind," he says. After a silence he adds, "You're very pretty, Myra. I know that might be rude of me to say."

She thanks him, feeling the heat again in her cheeks, which she has to resist hiding with her hands.

"I don't meet many girls like you," he says.

"Oh, I don't believe that," she says. "I'm not much to look at."

"You are, though," he says. "Those eyes of yours could do a lot of damage. Are they gray or green?"

"My mother says they're hazel."

"I noticed them as soon as I came over to your booth."

Myra bites her lower lip to keep from smiling. She wishes she could somehow make her hazel eyes surge and put him under a deep spell.

"Do you have brothers and sisters?" he asks.

"Three sisters and two brothers," she replies. "I'm the oldest."

"Such a large family," he says. He seems to consider something, intensely, for a moment and then, under his breath, adds, "Too large," and shakes his head.

"Too large for what?" Myra asks.

"Oh, I don't mean nothin' by it," he says. "It just seems like it would be a lot to manage."

"It is," Myra says. "My sister Joan is mentally handicapped. She can dry the dishes but she's not allowed near the silverware. Her mind is quite stunted. And I have a baby brother now, too, so my mother relies on me to help with the others."

"How old is your baby brother?"

"Two months. A June baby, like me. His name is Archibald. We call him Archie. He can be very fussy but he quiets down after Mother feeds him."

The new song on the radio is Perry Como's "Hoop-Dee-Doo." The rain hitting the passenger's side window seems to be momentarily in cahoots with the song's jaunty polka rhythm.

"Tell me all their names," Mickey says.

"Fiona, Alec, Joan, Lexy, and Archie. That's everyone, in order. Sometimes Alec calls Joan 'The Bullfrog.' He can be mean."

"And you're Myra," he says, smiling.

"The oldest," she says.

His smile makes her imagine him brushing his teeth, washing his face, combing his hair, even peeing in the toilet. She shoves these images from her mind.

Another car enters the park and wheels past the Bel Air. Mickey watches the car keenly for a moment, craning his neck. He even rolls down the window partway. It's still light out, but darker than usual because of the rain.

After he rolls the window back up he says, "Lincoln Cosmopolitan."

"You like cars?" Myra asks.

"I do," he says. "I prefer Chevrolet to Lincoln, though."

"Yours is lovely," Myra says, immediately embarrassed by her flattery. The words feel clumsy to her, as if she uttered them through a loose tooth.

Mickey doesn't acknowledge the compliment and the two of them are quiet again. Only Perry Como on the radio. Myra feels a strange peace sitting with this older boy in his car. Might they drive away together? Might he take her back to Kansas City with him?

"Can I give you a picture?" he finally says.

"Of what?" she asks.

"Of me," he says.

"…Okay," Myra hears herself say, doing her best to hide her excitement. Her teeth nearly begin to chatter.

Mickey reaches into his back pocket and produces a billfold, from which he removes a small snapshot. He unfolds the black-and-white photo and hands it to her. Myra smooths it out on her lap. Staring back at her is a boy in military uniform. He has taken a knee. His right hand clutches the snout of a rifle whose stock has been driven into the dirt. The boy wears camouflage fatigues and a combat helmet and he's smiling proudly.

"That's you?" Myra asks.

"It sure is," he says. "Over in Osan, Korea."

"It's a lovely picture."

"I want you to have it."

She thanks him and secrets it away in her pocketbook. After she snaps it shut he asks her for a picture.

"I don't have any with me," Myra says.

"Will you send me one?"

"You'll have to give me your address."

"Just send it to me at Yankee Stadium."

"What's your last name?" she asks.

"Mantle," the boy says. "On the envelope just write 'Mickey Mantle, in care of Yankee Stadium, the Bronx, New York.'"

When he drops Myra off in front of her house he gives her a silver dollar.

"What's this for?" Myra asks.

"For being you," the boy says. "I'm tempted to flip it but I've already made my decision."

"About what?" she says.

"About you," he says, and winks at her.

She kisses him goodbye on the cheek. As she walks into her house she can still taste the faint salty tang of his skin.

"You're thirty-five minutes late," Ava Larkin tells her daughter as she enters the kitchen. Ava is rinsing a rag in the sink.

Myra looks at the clock over the stove and it's true. "I got caught in the rain," she lies.

"That's a poor excuse," her mother says. "Archie's running a fever," she adds, squeezing the water out of the rag. "I need you to make him a cold bath."

"Yes, ma'am."

At two months old, Myra's baby brother still possesses the bald, wrinkled face of a stunned elderly police officer. Following church services, Ava likes to mill about the parking lot with the other mothers, baby Archie on her hip. Myra's three other sisters—Fiona, Joan, and Lexy—will busy themselves picking dandelions in St. John the Baptist's front lawn. Fiona dutifully marshals four-year-old Lexy, keeping her close, while the heavyset, mentally slow Joan, who just turned seven, is content to stay in one place. Often she'll happily sit cross-legged and stare at the church's ancient sugar maple as if it will someday bestow upon her a great secret.

Ava and the other mothers will gather around their Packards and Hudsons and Plymouth Cranbrooks and gossip about the teachers at Holy Family Jr. High School, especially Sister Rose, who's far too pretty to be a nun, and the water level of the Chemung River, and President Truman's sourpuss wife, Bess, and the troops in South Korea, and how Steve and Myrtle McCrae's boy, Cotter, just landed in Busan, and the Soviet Union and their dastardly atomic bomb, and the recent lightning storm that felled the Blubaughs' maple tree over on South Magee Street, and how at least two gallons of whole milk from Houch's Dairy went bad, and what about the new salesman at Triangle Shoes, doesn't he look exactly like that handsome detective character from *Where the Sidewalk Ends*, Dana Andrews? They talk and smile and smoke their Old Golds, somehow indifferent to the hovering gnats.

At nearly 6'3", Myra's mother looms over her children like a creature in a fable. Donald Larkin, a head shorter than his wife, often stands beside her like some dutiful, ever-ready attendant. At thirty-two, despite having already given birth to six children, Ava is still slender and pretty, with rich, youthful skin, and only a few strands of gray shooting through her bootblack hair. Myra admires her mother's beauty, her steady poise, her physical strength.

In the upstairs bathtub, after Myra fills the baby's basin with cold water, she brings it down to the kitchen, where her mother is at the counter next to the icebox, cleaning the mess between Archie's legs.

"Next Sunday there will be no free time following mass," Ava tells her. "You'll remain at the church with your sisters. You can mix with the other children in the lawn and keep an eye on Joan."

Myra nods. The disappointment of having that hour taken from her feels like a blow to the backs of her legs. How will she read her book? Holden's train has just arrived at Penn Station and anything could happen. The thought of not having that time with him almost makes her sick, but she knows better than to argue.

Archie's legs swim out as her mother wipes up the greenish, foul-smelling muck. Myra grabs a clean diaper from the compartment below the silverware drawer and sets it beside the basin.

"I need to be able to rely on you," her mother tells her, unfolding the diaper.

"Yes, ma'am," Myra says.

"I don't enjoy taking your privileges away."

"Yes, ma'am," Myra repeats.

"You have to set the proper example for your sisters. I'm not sure if there's much hope for Alec, but Fiona and Lexy have a real chance and they look to you."

Myra is struck that her mother never includes Joan in these talks about her siblings. It's as if Joan is not quite a person, or worse yet, as if she's something unnamable and heavy that must be transported from room to room in order for the Larkins to survive, like some huge bag of sand that, if not continuously moved, will eventually fall through the weakening floorboards and take everything with it.

Back in her bedroom Myra finds a strip of her seventh-grade class photos. She scissors one of them away, sure to trim the edges just so. She thinks she looks naive, like a little girl, slightly stunned by the flashbulb, as if the photographer had sneaked up on her. But her smile is okay—nice, even—and it's the only recent photo she has. She writes a short note, folds it in half, slips the photograph into the crease, and seals it in an envelope, which she addresses to

Mickey Mantle, care of Yankee Stadium, the Bronx, New York, NY, 10451, just as he instructed. She licks a stamp and affixes it to the upper-right corner. She'll mail it first thing tomorrow, following her morning chores.

After that she opens her diary and tapes the silver dollar onto a new page. Under it she writes the following letter:

Sunday, August 19th, 1951

Dear Holden,

> *Today I met a boy at the diner. He was very handsome and polite. His name is Mickey and he's a professional baseball player who is an outfielder for the New York Yankees and he also fought in the Korean conflict. He has blond hair and blue eyes. He gave me a silver dollar, which I've taped to the page above. He also gave me a picture of himself from when he was in the Army. He is so young to have accomplished so much. I think if you met him you'd like him. You might even be friends. I know how you prefer polite people to those who are cruel or rude, like your annoying dormitory neighbor, Robert Ackley. Mickey is very polite. He even gave me a ride home in the rain. He has a very nice yellow car.*
>
> *Other noteworthy news is that my baby brother, Archie, is sick with a fever. My mother was angry with me because I was late coming home, so I won't be able to go to the diner next week. I will miss you.*
>
> *I'm sure Archie will be fine. Babies get sick all the time.*
>
> *In closing I want to write that I consider this to be a special day and I'm glad that I could share it with you.*
>
> *Yours Sincerely,*
> *Myra Lee Larkin*

* * *

DURING DINNER, VERY LITTLE is said. Everyone is concerned about Archie, whose fever hasn't broken. Ava has placed him in his bassinet, which is parked beside her, at the foot of the table. There are cucumber slices arranged on his naked torso. When Lexy asks her mother why there are cucumbers on him, Ava tells her that they help to draw the fever out.

Fiona picks at her meatloaf and Joan seems to be arranging her peas as if to protect them from the rest of the food on her plate. At the head of the table, her father eats with a slow intensity, his eyes cast down. Myra waits for any cue from her mother that will signal she needs help. The smallest look can send her into the kitchen for more salt, napkins, or a clean fork. Alec still hasn't come home from who knows what—his only friend Roman's house? throwing rocks off a bridge?—and no one seems interested in mentioning it.

A portrait of Jesus hangs on the wall above the dining room table. It's been in that spot for as long as Myra can remember. Jesus's golden hair is wavy, his brown eyes deep and kind and round. Sometimes Alec will tilt the frame so it looks crooked. Ava will correct it without comment or, apparently, suspicion. Tonight Jesus looks different. His face, usually imbued with benevolence, seems beset by mischief, as if he's harboring a naughty joke he's just overheard.

Archie makes very little sound, only a chirp here and there. Ava keeps dipping her napkin in her water glass and dabbing at his forehead. She quietly sings to him:

> *Give me oil in my lamp, keep me burning*
> *Give me oil in my lamp, I pray*
> *Give me oil in my lamp, keep me burning*
> *Keep me burning till the break of day*

Myra's mother has a beautiful voice. She sings in the choir at church and often gets a solo during the Christmas recital. Joan stops eating and stares at her, entranced. Lexy joins in with the singing, not quite forming some of the words, and warbling other shapeless vowels, as if under a spell.

> *Sing hosanna! Sing hosanna!*
> *Sing hosanna to the King of Kings!*
> *Sing hosanna! Sing hosanna!*
> *Sing hosanna to the King...*

AFTER DINNER MYRA GOES into her father's study, where Donald sits in his plaid recliner, smoking a pipe and reading the *Star-Gazette*. Beside him, his old Philco Cathedral Radio reports the news.

> *More than a hundred people are dead from a hurricane in Jamaica...*
> *Reds threaten the U.N. with annihilation...*
> *Major battles erupt on the Korean front...*

Myra's father is a machinist at the tool-and-die in nearby Horseheads. He's a year younger than Myra's mother and speaks so infrequently that many Elmirans believe the war—specifically his difficult time in the Hürtgen Forest—took his voice away. He's more apt to talk at home, especially after dinner, when he sits by the radio with his pipe and newspaper. Myra can sometimes coax entire sentences out of him—quiet, careful half-sentences, really—but she looks forward to these few minutes with her father, who, except for Sunday mass, rarely changes out of his olive drab, gabardine work clothes. He can be seen in the Larkins' driveway nearly every Saturday morning, polishing the Chrysler's engine with vinegar.

"Come sit," he tells Myra, who perches on an old dining room chair that squeaks, the only other one in the room.

Donald's study is a glorified alcove, really, with a window and the two chairs and a floor lamp and the radio handsomely centered on a cherrywood side table. All of this is arranged on a small rope rug made fuzzy by their cat's claws. Myra thinks her father loves the radio almost as much as his car.

The pipe smoke smells like plums and pepper. Her father is starting to go gray at the temples. Myra has always considered him handsome, though his tired expression obscures it. There are deep lines in his forehead that appear as if engraved. He sometimes works more than sixty hours a week. His hands, pale and calloused, are large for his size.

He draws on his pipe and sets the newspaper down.

"Do you know anything about Mickey Mantle?" Myra asks.

Her father rarely misses a game. The Yankees are his favorite team and he prefers to listen to them on the radio to watching them on the television set. Joan will often come sit on the floor beside him and he'll give her the foul ball he caught at Yankee Stadium when he was a boy. He caught it with his bare hands and wrote the date on it in black ink: *July 5, 1930*. He keeps the ball on a small saucer next to the radio. During the Yankee broadcasts, Joan will rotate it in her hands and rock back and forth hypnotically.

"Mantle's that young hotshot rookie who can really run," Donald says. "Got sent down to the minor leagues last month. I think they got plans for him to take over in center after DiMaggio retires."

"He fought in Korea, right?"

"I believe he had some sort of medical condition that may have prevented him from serving. But I couldn't tell you for sure."

Her father returns to puffing on his pipe. This is the most he's spoken in weeks. Sometimes Myra wonders if he's been issued an allotment of words. Once he reaches that number he'll fall silent again.

"What's got you so interested in Mickey Mantle?" her father asks.

"I overheard some people talking about him at the diner," Myra says.

She rarely veers from the truth, and is surprised at the little thrill she feels lying to her father. It's like sneaking a bite of a Hershey bar during mass. She will be confirmed in the spring. What will these white lies mean then? She imagines that the process of getting closer to God might feel like having her hair aggressively braided.

"He certainly had a fast start," Donald offers. "At the beginning of the season Stengel had him leading off a bunch. Not sure why they demoted the kid. I think he was hitting around two-seventy."

Myra's mother enters the study, holding the baby. "His fever's gotten worse," she announces. "We need to take him to the hospital."

Her expression is pinched. It frightens Myra to see her this worried.

"I'll drive," her father says, putting his pipe down and snuffing it with his bare thumb in the standing ashtray. He turns off the radio and heads toward the kitchen for the car keys.

"Keep Lexy's fingers out of her mouth," Myra's mother tells her. "Don't let Joan near the electrical outlet in the living room. When Alec gets home please ask him to take the trash to the curb. And make sure Fiona empties the litter box."

Myra nods sharply, obediently, at the instructions.

"And what's gotten into you, anyway?"

"Nothing," Myra says.

"You seem strange. You have a dreamy look about you. I noticed it at dinner."

"I don't feel strange."

"Myra seems a little funny, doesn't she?" her mother calls to her father.

"Seems okay to me," he replies from the hallway.

"Did you smoke a cigarette or something?"

"No, ma'am."

"Donald, did you give her your pipe?"

Her father laughs.

While holding Archie, her mother leans down toward her. Archie's face is pink and inflamed. His eyes look swollen shut. His fingers are so small they seem more suited to a species of amphibian.

"Let me smell your breath," her mother says.

Myra breathes on her.

"Clean your teeth," she says, rearing back with Archie and lifting him onto her hip. "Your breath smells sour."

A TENSE HOUR PASSES. The rain keeps coming. There is a leak in the kitchen and Myra places an iron pot on the floor to catch the drip.

Later, Myra is sitting on the sofa with Fiona and Lexy. They are watching *The Colgate Comedy Hour* on the new Zenith Porthole that their father bought in the spring, although he has hardly ever watched it. Fiona, the sole Larkin redhead, picks at the mosquito bites on her knees. In her new glasses she looks smart and overly serious. She's never been a particularly good student but now at least she looks like one. Going against her mother's orders, Myra lets Lexy suck her fingers because it keeps her quiet. She tells her that her teeth are going to go buck and leaves it at that. Joan is on the floor, a few feet away, sitting cross-legged in her nightgown, having already taken a bath. During a lull in the rain, Myra went into the backyard and caught a lighting bug for her. It's trapped under a mason jar now, on top of a saucer, crawling about, its light pulsing. Joan is rapt. The girls are anxious about Archie, the living room air thick with worry.

During a commercial break a pretty nurse in a white hat praises Palm Olive soap and all the good things that it's doing for her skin. Her hair is so shiny it looks as if it's been painted. Myra wonders if she'll ever be able to get her hair to look that silky. She likes the uniform a nurse gets to wear. It's like a nun's, but more appealing.

There has been no word from Myra's parents when Alec finally enters the house, around 9:30, and tries to sneak past the living room. He is poorly concealing something with a handkerchief. Myra stops him halfway up the stairs. His thick black bangs settle crookedly on his forehead.

"What's that?" Myra asks.

"Nothing," he replies.

His movements are shifty and it seems he doesn't know what to do with his free hand, which keeps twitching. He won't look his sister in the eye.

"You're stealing again," she says.

"I'm not."

Alec is always coming home with strange things: pocketknives and fishing lures and packets of baseball cards. Once he had a salt-shaker. Myra walks up the steps and snatches the object out of his hand: it's a tortoiseshell shoehorn. The handkerchief falls to the steps.

"Whose is that?" she says.

"Father Oates gave it to me."

"Liar."

"I'm not lying. I did him a favor."

"What kind of favor?"

"I helped him with the vestments."

"Thief."

"Just let me go to my room."

She pushes the shoehorn toward him and he takes it. Then she bends down and picks up the handkerchief. It's monogrammed *N.P.* "You stole this, too," she says.

"I found it," he says. "Someone left it in the pews."

"Mom and Dad took Archie to the hospital," she tells him, handing him the handkerchief. "He's running a fever. You're supposed to take the trash to the curb."

"Okay," Alec says.

"You're home late, by the way," Myra adds.

"You were late, too," he counters. "I saw you in that car earlier."

"What car?"

"That yellow car with the whitewall tires. You were with that boy. Right in front of the house. He dropped you off."

Myra is speechless. How could Alec have seen that? That was a couple of hours ago. Why would he be spying on his own house?

Alec turns and heads up to his room with the shoehorn.

"Don't forget about the garbage," Myra calls after him.

He doesn't respond. His door opens and closes and that's that.

When Myra returns to the sofa, Fiona and Lexy are laughing at the television. All the heavy worry in the room has seemingly lifted. Dean Martin is trying to teach Jerry Lewis the proper way to ask a woman to dance. Jerry Lewis throws his body this way and that. His arms fly out absurdly. His legs twist and shuffle as if he's made of rubber. The live TV audience howls with laughter. He couldn't be more hilarious.

Lexy's laugh is infectious. At four she's the second-youngest Larkin and once she starts laughing she can't seem to stop, which makes Fiona, who's otherwise been quiet, laugh as well. Lexy has a galaxy of blond hair that appears to expand when she's happy. Still spellbound by her firefly, Joan seems immune to all the fun. She laughs only at Alec, especially when he teases her, not understanding his cruelty.

Eventually, Frank, their gray Siamese cat, joins the three girls on the sofa. He's most fond of Fiona and purrs loudly while she pets him.

"Frank, you're such a bad boy," Fiona says, stroking the cat. "So, so bad…"

The sound of the front door opening and closing reaches them above the TV laughter and moments later their father enters the living room. His eyes are tired and the rain has pasted a few stray strands of his brown hair to his forehead. He simply looks at his four daughters. The television scores the tense silence. Jerry Lewis is producing a sound through his mouth like an airplane dive-bombing to the earth and the audience can't get enough.

"Where's Mom?" Fiona asks.

"She'll be staying overnight at the hospital," their father replies. "Archie's still running a fever."

"What's wrong with baby Archie?" Lexy asks, her pure, tiny voice cutting through the din of the television.

"They don't know, sweetheart," he answers, wiping his forehead with a handkerchief. "It might be the flu." He dabs the rain off his face. "I'm going to bed," he adds. "I have to work tomorrow." He tells Myra to look after her sisters and to make sure that Joan uses the toilet before bed.

After he closes the door to their parents' first-floor bedroom, Myra turns off the television and herds her sisters up the stairs. As she often does, she supervises while they get ready for bed. She sits on the edge of the bathtub while Joan uses the toilet.

"Did you say goodbye to the firefly," she asks her, trying to take her sister's mind off her task. Whenever Myra catches a firefly for Joan she lets her little sister release it in the backyard.

"I said goodbye," Joan says, "I did."

"Did it light up when it flew away?"

Joan nods and smiles.

"That was her saying goodbye," Myra says.

Sometimes when Joan smiles it makes Myra sad. It's as if she smiles only when prompted by the lift at the end of a question. Maybe to Joan certain words are no different from notes played on a woodwind.

After the toilet, Myra helps Joan wash her face and hands and brush her teeth. Joan shares a room with Fiona and Lexy at the end of the hall. They each have their own twin bed. Myra says the Lord's Prayer for Joan, then tucks her in and kisses her gently on the forehead, just as their mother does. She can hear Fiona sniffling across the room. Myra moves to her and sits at the edge of her bed.

"Don't cry," she tells her, removing her glasses. "Archie's gonna be all right."

"But his cheeks were so hot," Fiona says. "Didn't you feel them?"

"I'm sure he'll be home tomorrow," Myra offers. Though Fiona will be twelve soon, when she cries she seems much younger. "Did you clean Frank's litter box?" Myra asks her.

Fiona shakes her head. "I forgot," she says.

"I'll do it," Myra assures her.

She places Fiona's glasses on the bedside stand, then moves on to Lexy, who is already asleep. Her small bed is under the window, but the blade of moonlight that usually cuts across her figure is absent tonight. Lexy has fallen asleep with her fingers in her mouth. Her bed is like a drug, Myra thinks. As soon as she climbs into it she is rendered unconscious in a matter of breaths, as if her pillow is laced with gas. Her blond hair has completely obscured her face and she breathes through it while sucking her fingers like some blessed sea creature with gills. Lately Lexy has been declaring that she wants to be a ballerina. Where this comes from is anyone's guess. Myra sometimes wonders if Lexy dreams of other worlds far away from Elmira, worlds populated by ballerinas and elves and talking creatures. Myra gently extracts Lexy's fingers from her mouth. Lexy doesn't even stir. How is it possible that the youngest Larkin girl sleeps the soundest?

After Myra cleans Frank's litter box, down in the mudroom, she comes back upstairs and finally changes into her nightgown and washes her face and brushes her teeth. In the mirror her reflection is old and haggard, and she thinks, *I'm thirteen, not thirty.* She tries to smile like she did in her class photo—the one she put in that envelope for Mickey Mantle—but something tugs downward at the corners of her lips. She tries again, really forcing herself, but her mouth just looks like a wound that hasn't healed properly.

As she walks down the hall toward her bedroom she stops before Alec's door and sets her ear against it. She hears nothing. What is he doing in there? Plotting something? Sometimes she fears he will hurt Joan in the middle of the night. He likes to play tricks on her when she's not looking. He'll switch her silverware so that she'll have two spoons. Or he'll hide her fork under a serving tray and delight in her confusion. Myra believes he possesses a cruel streak that has yet to be fully realized—that he might be capable of truly terrible things—and this frightens her.

IN THE MIDDLE OF the night, the neighborhood erupts with the squawks of sirens. Myra is awakened from a deep sleep.

In her nightgown and slippers, she sneaks across the hall, pads down the stairs, and moves to her parents' room, just off the living room, where she can hear her father snoring. She opens the door onto their separate twin beds. Her mother's is empty, neatly made. Is she still at the hospital? Her father sleeps in a white T-shirt and pajama bottoms, his covers half off the bed, his body twisted into itself. Myra shuts the door. Her father's snore is animal-like, almost violent.

In the mudroom she grabs his denim work coat, slips through the front door, and walks barefoot down Maple Avenue toward the spinning police lights. It's still raining. Several people from the neighborhood are gathered in front of the Mulerts' Victorian, whose wraparound porch is congested with policemen, firefighters, and emergency professionals, their harsh white uniforms flashing in the dark. An ambulance is parked on the front lawn, its back doors flung open. The sirens have ceased, but a lone revolving blue light atop a patrol car still casts an orbiting light across the scene.

Myra recognizes Mrs. Schwarber, who is smoking a cigarette, her hair in pink rollers. She lives four houses down, with her dentist husband, Ron, and their three kids. With her makeup removed she looks washed-out and pitiful. Another woman whom Myra doesn't recognize holds an umbrella above the two of them. The women mutter to each other, gossiping. Mrs. Schwarber smokes like a man, pinching her cigarette between her thumb and forefinger, shifting from foot to foot.

A policeman spots Myra and tells her she should go home. She nods to him and then hides behind a fat man in a brown housecoat who is telling another man that Bob and Bonnie Mulert, and their eleven-year-old daughter, Marie, were murdered in their sleep.

As if on cue, the bodies are brought out on stretchers, their figures covered with white linens through which faint bloodstains have seeped. The shape of Marie's body makes her seem smaller on the stretcher, like a doll. Two men carry each stretcher, one in the front and one in the back. They are all dressed in white except for a fireman at the helm of the stretcher containing the biggest figure, which is probably Mr. Mulert. Myra has the distinct feeling that these men are transporting furniture, not bodies. That's a coffee table on the fireman's stretcher, she thinks. And a sideboard and a small standing clock on the other two.

The Mulerts' dog, a black Lab named Sheila, whimpers and circles the stretchers. At least the killer had mercy on the dog, Myra thinks. Or maybe Sheila escaped? Now who will take care of her? One of the firemen grabs the dog's collar and kneels to speak to her.

The fat man in the brown housecoat is offering more grisly details: their throats were cut; some thirty stab wounds were discovered on each body. With so many stab wounds, Myra wonders, what would happen to the eyes, the cheeks, the chest and stomach... the thighs...the feet...? This would certainly explain the blood-stains expanding through the white linens. Did they have to wrap the bodies before putting them on the stretchers? Did they have to stuff each wound with cotton?

Myra tries to imagine how one could cut three throats, in succession. She's seen her father cut a deer's throat with a bowie knife. They'd gone camping up in Canastota and she'd been awakened by a gunshot. Donald Larkin had killed a deer not even fifty feet from their campsite. Myra came out of her tent and watched her father sever the deer's throat.

"You have to bleed it," he explained to her in the early-morning light, still wearing his olive drab work uniform from the night before.

He'd propped his hunting rifle against the tree from which he'd strung up the deer with rope, upside down. The deer's eyes were open. its tongue lolling out of its mouth.

"Otherwise the meat'll go bad," he added.

Myra was fascinated by her father's quick, fluid movements. It suddenly made so much sense. He was a veteran, after all. He knew weapons. It was a ballet of the hands. Surgical, without emotion. Myra sometimes wondered how many Germans her father had killed in the war. He'd fought in the Battle of the Hürtgen Forest, only seven years ago. Like many men from the area, he'd volunteered. Tens of thousands of American soldiers died in that battle. Myra remembers her father's return. She was almost seven then. Fiona was five, and Alec, already a troublemaker, was four. There had been a brief celebration at the Elks Club with cake and punch and colorful bunting and little American flags on all the tables and a live polka band. But then her father had to stay in the Veterans Hospital up in Bath for three weeks before moving back into the house. When they finally let him come home his movements were slow and careful. It took him several minutes to tie his shoes. He didn't speak for weeks. But then one day he did. He simply said, "Good morning," and everything seemed to click back into place. He returned to work at the tool-and-die in Horseheads and all was right in the world.

Clouds of gnats convulse in the revolving police light. Myra can feel the cool damp grass between her toes. The rain still hasn't ceased and many of the onlookers shield their heads with newspapers or shopper leaflets. Myra spots Alec near the back of the crowd, his black hair twisted wild. He isn't wearing his nightclothes, but, rather, a pair of his school uniform trousers and a white undershirt. He is barefoot, standing on his tiptoes, trying to look over the shoulders of a woman in front of him. He is only ten, but he suddenly looks like a much older version of himself. A pickpocket on the make.

Myra and Alec meet eyes and then she moves to him. "Alec Christopher, you should be in bed."

"So should you," he counters. His breath is sweet and gamy, his teeth filmy because he never brushes.

"Go home and wash your face and clean your teeth," Myra says.

"Don't tell me what to do."

Mr. Fessenden, the retired grocer with gauzy hair, cradles a cane in the crook of his elbow as he speaks to two policemen. He wears seersucker shorts and has pale, hairless legs that look like they would break easily. His shins are so white they almost look fake.

Mr. Fessenden tells the policemen that he saw someone enter the Mulerts' home earlier that night. It was a young man, perhaps nineteen or twenty. He was wearing a plaid, short-sleeved shirt and tan trousers. He had blond hair, which he wore parted on the side, and possessed an athletic build. "A genuine towhead," Mr. Fessenden adds.

Myra feels suddenly lightheaded. She can't help but think of the boy from the diner: his keen blue eyes and clean skin, his pronounced Adam's apple, the golden-blond hair parted on the side.

"I took him for a relative," Mr. Fessenden continues. "The way he just walked up onto their porch and opened the front door. I didn't think anything of it."

One of the policemen asks him if he noticed him carrying anything that looked like a weapon and if he saw the boy leave.

"I didn't see no weapon," he replies. "And I didn't see him leave."

Myra feels Alec's eyes on her like a pair of stag beetles boring into the back of her neck. Vengeful. Judging her. She's always wondered where his dark eyes came from. Their mother's are blue. Their father's, gray. Fiona's are green. Lexy and Joan's are blue like their mother's. But Alec's eyes are so dark they're almost black. It's as if he came from somewhere else. Like they found him in a forest.

Myra pivots to him. Before she can warn him about the trouble he'll be in if he doesn't go home immediately, he says, "You should tell 'em about his car." His soaked hair makes him seem sinful and ghoulish.

Myra would like to strike him thirty times, actually, like the killer with his knife, from the crown of his dirty, unwashed head down to his filthy ankles, and she turns her right hand into a fist and presses it against her thigh. Although she has never struck one of her siblings, if there weren't so many people around she would let Alec have it, but instead she quells the impulse to punch him in the face.

"You're going to hell," Myra tells him.

The words seethe through her teeth like a hated medicinal broth. She is surprised at how much she loathes her brother at this moment.

And then, just like that, his nose starts to bleed from both nostrils.

"Your nose," she adds evenly.

Alec's face goes soft. The tough snarl has disappeared. He brings his hand to his upper lip, dabs at the blood, stares at his fingertips, and strides backwards three or four steps, plugging his nose, then pivots and jogs toward home.

Myra turns back to the scene. The final stretcher is getting loaded into the ambulance. The bloodstains are grotesque now but she can't look away. Three days before her thirteenth birthday she got her first menstrual period while she was walking to her world history class. A tearing sensation inside and then a liquid loosening. Her mother had never told her anything about it. It just came like an unwanted, angry letter in the mail, and there was so much blood. Myra thought she was dying of some awful disease. The Holy Family Jr. High School nurse, Mrs. Honiotis, was helpful and gave her a feminine napkin, two aspirin, and a pair of padded underwear. She also offered a cursory explanation of the menstrual process; why the blood is shed and how it prepares the uterus for conception. After that Myra thought she would feel a kinship with Mrs. Honiotis but she found that she avoided her. Whenever Myra passed her in the hallway she felt only shame.

There is so much blood in a body, Myra thinks. An ocean of it. But it's mostly hidden. And so deep within. We only see it when there is violence and suffering. When Lexy was born, Myra's mother bled so much it was as if she'd been slaughtered like an animal. She went into labor right there in the house—going to the hospital was out of the question. Afterward, they had to re-sand and re-varnish the floorboards in the downstairs bedroom. The mattress had to be replaced. They even had to repaint one of the walls.

Finally, one of the attendants closes the back doors to the ambulance. When it pulls away, another policeman orders people to return to their homes.

Myra wonders if she should tell him about the yellow Bel Air, about its whitewall tires and Pennsylvania license plates.

"Go on home, everyone," the policeman says sternly. "Go on home and get out of this rain. There's nothing more to see."

2

NIAGARA FALLS, NEW YORK
AUGUST 26, 1964

ALEC

B Y TEN O'CLOCK IT was already 80 degrees and Alec Larkin had had enough. His supervisor, a stork-shaped man called Ned Shipley, caught him sitting in the shade and promptly fired him. The apple picking always began at 8:00 a.m. sharp and there wasn't ever a break until 10:30. At the height of the season, after climbing down and emptying a pouch of apples (around forty-five pounds of fruit) into your bin, you were allowed to stand by your ladder for a few breaths before heading back up, but sitting down simply wasn't acceptable, especially sitting down so arrogantly in the shade, behind the shed where they store the ladders, of all places. And the fact that Alec had taken his shoes and socks off was even more disrespectful and he knew it.

"That's it, Larkin," Ned told him in his oddly high voice, drumming one of his maddening mathematical patterns on his clipboard. "Go pack up your things."

Alec lives in Bunk 7, a cinderblock cabin with a cement floor and fluorescent tube lighting that made his flesh look green and cadaver-like. He shares it with twin Negroes from Orlando, Florida, Torris and Terrace Pinchback. There are ten of these cabins, each of which houses between two and five workers. The workers wake together, wash together in the communal latrine, eat their meals together, and pick apples together, all day, every day, with optional weekend shifts. Although the money is decent, it has seemed like the kind of life Alec always imagined one suffered through in the Army, or, worse yet, on a prison work farm.

The only female on the premises is the owner's daughter, a quiet, sixteen-year-old blond with thin pale arms who is so pretty it makes Alec's hands ache just to look at her. She sometimes picks apples on Saturdays and Alec will head into the orchard with his burlap shoulder sack, just so he can catch a glimpse of her. He rarely gets much picking done on these weekend mornings, filling at most a sack or two. He'll mostly smoke cigarettes and set and reset his ladder, within view of the girl, who hardly ever looks his way.

It's the final week of August, a Wednesday, and now Alec Larkin's future prospects are dwindling faster than he would care to admit. The black flies were particularly nasty this morning, not to mention a pair of crows and an unusually aggressive grackle that kept slashing the apples. Alec had come to Blackman Homestead Farm in early July and his first few weeks were promising. He was filling between eight and nine bins a day, but he never did much better than that. The good pickers could fill ten; the great ones, twelve. The Pinchback brothers have filled ten bins every single day since they were hired in mid-June. A skinny Mexican known only as "Flaco" filled fourteen one day. And he did it in 97-degree heat. Flaco uses both hands with equal dexterity and doesn't ever seem to tire and his agility on the ladder could rival a circus performer's. But Alec's hands are average, if not slow, and they have a tendency to shake, sacrificing time. His numbers, which Ned Shipley marks on his clipboard after every shift, have been getting progressively worse. He filled only four bins on Tuesday, and five the day before that.

Back at the barracks Alec changes out of his sour-smelling work clothes, packs his few possessions into his father's green Army-issued duffel bag, and then sits on his bunk waiting for Ned. If he wasn't owed money, he'd just take off. The last thing Alec needs is another lecture from the bastard.

Alec looks over at the Pinchbacks' meticulous bunks. The brothers wake every morning at least an hour before breakfast, make their beds, and kneel together in prayer. Alec rarely even attends breakfast. He hasn't done up his bed properly in over a month. And since he left Elmira, three years ago, he hasn't prayed once.

There is a knock on the hollow front door and Ned enters, ducking his head. "You packed up?" he asks.

"My work clothes are on the hook over there," Alec says. "You're prolly gonna want to burn 'em."

Ned makes a note of the work clothes on his clipboard and drums on it briefly. Starlings and robins can be heard chattering in the orchard. "So do I need to explain myself?" he finally says. "Cause I can."

"Save it," Alec says, though he knows Ned won't be able to help himself. The bastard can't just fire you, he has to pour vinegar on the wound.

"It don't make no sense to me," Ned launches in. "You got a good build. You're young. What are you, twenty-one, twenty-two?"

"Twenty-three."

"Twenty-three years old. You know how many bins I was fillin' when I was twenty-three?"

"I'm sure a lot," Alec says.

"You're damn right it was a lot, and I was proud of it."

"Well, you're a proud man."

"I hate to say it, Larkin, but you're lazy."

"I know."

"You know."

"Yeah, I'm as lazy as a fat man, I hear it every day."

"Well, why don't you do somethin' about it?"

"Like what?"

"Work harder?"

From his clipboard Ned hands Alec an unsealed manila envelope. Inside is forty-five dollars in cash.

"That's it?" Alec says, thumbing through the cash.

"I'm afraid so."

"I was expecting around eighty."

"Well, that's what's owed to you. We can go through the particulars if you want."

"Nothing would make you happier, I'm sure."

Ned wipes his face with a soiled bandana, wedges the clipboard under an arm, and folds the bandana in fourths. "What are you gonna do next?"

"Not pick apples," Alec says.

Ned laughs and wipes his forehead again. "I know a guy who buffs floors over in Rochester," he offers, surprisingly. "Uses one of those oscillating machines. The work is spottier—it's only a few times a week—but he's always lookin' for an extra body."

"Not interested," Alec says. The little cinderblock room seems to have suddenly gotten hotter, and he thinks of how at night the Pinchback twins sleep with wet rags on their stomachs. He can feel Ned watching him, judging him.

"You know what, Larkin? You're not a bad guy."

"You already said I was lazy."

Ned repeats the ritual of wedging the clipboard under his arm, unfolding the bandana, and wiping his face. He also dabs the back of his neck this time, then stuffs the bandana in his back pocket. "You need me to call you a cab?"

"I'll walk," Alec says.

"Suit yourself." Ned goes over and grabs Alec's work clothes off the hook. "You want this?" he says, proffering the burlap sack with Blackman Homestead Farm logo on it.

"Am I supposed to turn it into a pillow?"

"You could keep your essentials in it. Your laundry."

"No thanks," Alec says.

"Well, good luck to you, Larkin." Ned stuffs Alec's work clothes into the sack and extends his hand.

Alec hesitates, but accepts it and they shake.

"You might want to figure out how to steady those hands," Ned says on his way out.

After Ned leaves, Alec can't help but stare at his hands. There were some afternoons in early August when they shook so bad he had to practically talk to them so he wouldn't drop the apples. Dropping apples could get you fired faster than low bin rates. There was something wrong with him, Alec knew. Something truly, truly wrong.

On his way out of the orchard Alec spots the Pinchback brothers. They are high on their ladders, picking from neighboring apple trees, their shirts off and their sinewy arms rippling in the sun. It's incredible how unfazed they are by the sheer boredom of the job, how they seem to be immune to the black flies and the hornets and the mosquitoes. They drop fruit into their sacks with such thoughtless, even-keeled consistency, it's as if they're in a trance. Even though Alec spent many nights talking to them in the dark about baseball and Dionne Warwick's magic eyes and what her voice does to you in "Walk on By" and the girls in the South versus Northern girls and the difference between Ava Larkin and Edmonia Pinchback's meatloaf—despite these conversations—Alec doesn't bother saying goodbye to them. He simply walks off the farm with his father's duffel bag hoisted onto his shoulder and doesn't look back.

LATER ALEC IS SITTING at the Niagara Hotel bar waiting for Duke Foster.

Duke is his father's age. They met several weeks ago at a small saloon near Oakwood Cemetery. They were both belly-up to the bar, and both drinking whiskey. After Duke chipped at the silence with a comment about the pleasures of Kentucky bourbon versus scotch, which according to him leaves an aftertaste of liquified cat shit, he invited Alec to shoot pool and then loaded the jukebox with quarters and chose every Elvis song on the machine while they racked several rounds of eight ball and alternated buying rounds of beers. Duke then invited Alec over to his dimly lit SRO down by the Erie Canal. The little apartment smelled of unwashed feet and Vitalis hair tonic. The two men drank an entire fifth of Old Crow out of coffee mugs and listened to Eddie Fisher records on Duke's Magnavox automatic turntable—purportedly his only legitimate possession besides his car—until they both passed out.

Alec woke up in Duke's twin bed late the next morning, with

the sickly smell of the canal ebbing in through the window. Duke was on the other side of the small room, stretched out in an old synthetic leather recliner riddled with cigarette burns, snoring thunderously. Alec, a rangy 6'2" and heavier than he looks, was impressed that Duke had apparently been able to lift him into his bed, and even more impressed that he hadn't been robbed or in any way taken advantage of. A bond was formed that night and Alec believes that Duke has looked out for him in the intervening weeks.

Duke drives a bottle-green Pontiac Bonneville hardtop and claims to have bedded more women than Sean Connery, although he'll admit that most of them weigh more than 007. He claims to prefer his ladies larger than he is, and it can't be easy to find them, given that Duke Foster is a massive, broad-shouldered, barrel-chested man with a size fourteen foot and an enormous leonine head. He likes to feel as if he's getting smothered by his lovers, he tells Alec.

"It makes me have to fight for my life," he explained to Alec over "Turn Back the Hands of Time." "It's sorta like drowning. But there's no water in your lungs and you get to come. And then you get to smoke a cigarette and kick her fat ass out of bed. Triumph all around."

Duke Foster styles his hair in the legendary Elvis pompadour and has worn the same orange Hawaiian shirt bearing a pattern of guitars and pineapples every time Alec has met him. During their long first night of acquaintanceship, when Alec asked Duke what he did for a living, Duke said that he was currently dabbling in scrap metal. He'd also spent two long years installing drywall down in New London, Connecticut. And in the late '50s, for "several lost months in Detroit," he'd toiled as a "deeply uncertified electrician," whatever that meant.

On the television mounted over the hotel bar, the evening news reports on the upcoming election. At the Democratic Convention in Atlantic City, New Jersey, Lyndon Johnson has been officially nominated for president and is ahead of Arizona Republican Senator Barry Goldwater in the polls. In sports, the Yankees were shut out by the Washington Nationals, 2–0. Buster Narum limited the Yankees' offense to five scattered hits and their superstar sluggers, Mickey Mantle and Roger Maris, went a combined 0–5 at the plate.

Duke enters the bar with an unlit cigarette dancing between his lips. Despite the heat he wears a long black duster over the orange Hawaiian shirt, loose, paint-splattered white pants, and suede moccasins that look like they might slip off his giant naked feet at any moment.

"So how much they give you?" Duke asks, drawing on his cigarette.

Alec had called him from a payphone as soon as he got into town and told him about getting fired.

"Forty-five bucks," Alec says. "Stingy bastards."

"You're prolly lucky you got *that*," Duke says. He grabs the stool next to Alec and orders Old Crow on the rocks and a can of Highlander. "For both of us," he tells he bartender.

One of the first things Alec noticed about Duke was the plague of nicotine stains rimming his enormous, calloused fingers. Beyond the orange Hawaiian shirt, he dresses himself as if he's grabbing things out of random piles in the dark, but he always shaves, which gives his face a surprisingly clean and youthful look. His eyes, however, seem beset by an ancient curse, like they long ago saw too much for one man's life.

"Well, look at it this way," Duke says. "No more goddamn black flies. You might dream of picking apples for the rest of your life but you won't ever have to deal with those flies again."

The bartender delivers their drinks and Duke and Alec clink glasses.

"Here's to gettin' away with shit from here on out," Duke says.

Alec downs his entire tumbler of Old Crow and Duke immediately orders him another. He then taps out a cigarette from his pack of Pall Malls and Alec takes it. The bartender slides Alec's new drink to him and lights their cigarettes. In the last year or so Alec has become the kind of smoker who bums them from everyone else, which Duke calls a catfish smoker. A bottom-feeder. Alec rarely buys a pack, especially if he knows he's going to be drinking with Duke.

"So what now?" Duke says. "Back to Elmira?"

"I'd rather go to hell," Alec says.

"Well, you're likely headin' there anyway," Duke says, laughing, exposing his short, crooked teeth.

Alec laughs as well. Since he's been hanging around Duke he is well aware that he's been taking on his mannerisms. The curl of his wrist and the slight squint of his left eye while he draws on a cigarette. His insouciant comfort with extended silences. The way he lets the ice cubes gently clink against his teeth before drinking his bourbon. His surprising tendency toward humor rather than bitterness. And his laugh, which never exceeds three or four descending reports, like a horn player at the back of the stage making fun of a flat joke.

"I may have a quick fix for you," Duke says after a silence. "Of the financial persuasion."

Duke goes on to tell Alec that he is aware of an establishment, a couple hundred miles east, in Frankfort, New York, where he can easily get his hands on at least three thousand dollars cash. The place is a variety store whose proprietor is a near-deaf lady, close to seventy, who lives by herself, above the shop. The money is hidden in cigar boxes, somewhere in the shop. A security gate protects the storefront, but there's also a back entrance.

"How do I figure into it?" Alec says.

"Just ride along," Duke says. "Be my Tonto. It's a three-hours-plus drive. You can help me stay awake. We can do state capitals, list all the presidents, name every part of the female anatomy."

The last crime Alec committed was the one that drove him from Elmira. He got caught stealing the offertory money from St. John the Baptist. Father Oates, who had mentored him from his acolyte days all the way though his two years as head altar boy, walked in on him in the rectory, dumping the third of four offertory baskets into the same green duffel bag that is currently resting at his feet. Although Father Oates decided against pressing formal charges, he did tell Ava and Donald Larkin about the incident, and consequently, Ava, in front of his younger sisters, Joan and Lexy, asked Alec to leave the following morning. Alec was nineteen at the time, and hadn't accomplished much since he'd graduated high school. There was talk of him enlisting in the Army, but he could never seem to get around to it. His grades were too poor for college and he wasn't interested in a trade school. As far as Ava and Donald Larkin saw it, the church theft was unforgivable.

After that Alec spent a year and a half up in Buffalo, living with his aunt Ruth, working odd jobs, which included hoisting tar shingles for a roofing company, washing dishes at a boarding school cafeteria, and tamping down asphalt for a road construction crew. Nothing ever lasted more than a few weeks because he couldn't take the physical labor. When he bounced out of Buffalo, the job he liked the most was fishing golf balls from water traps at a country club in Freehold, New York, where he managed to stay employed for an entire summer. He'd wear high rubber waders, a diving mask, and snorkel, and set off into each pond brandishing a fishing net as if he were searching for a legendary pearl oyster. He earned a quarter per ball, each of which he scrubbed clean. The golf course would then resell these balls by the bucketload to club members at their driving range. Sometimes Alec made as much as thirty dollars a day and for the last few weeks he was even asked to work in the clubhouse, where he bussed tables and occasionally got tipped a five-dollar bill for helping some old drunk shuffle to the bathroom. He loved that golf course: its slow pace and clean, manicured greens; all the rich men in their soft clothes the color of Neapolitan ice cream; the smell of freshly clipped grass; the big, fuzzy, muscular bees vectoring along the fairways; everything bathed in sunlight. But the summer season terminated at the end of August and by Labor Day he was out looking for another job.

"When were you planning on heading to Frankfort?" Alec asks.

"After another round or two of these," Duke says, knocking back his bourbon and ordering another. He is already well into his third cigarette. "If we make good time, we'll get the thing done before dawn. I'll split whatever I get fifty-fifty with you."

"How do you plan on getting in the back door?" Alec asks.

"I have the key," Duke replies.

BY MIDNIGHT THEY'RE LOADED into Duke's Bonneville, heading east on Interstate 90. For the first hour they drive with the windows down. The radio blares Roy Orbison and the Beach Boys and Dean Martin and the Beatles and Martha and the Vandellas. When they reach Batavia it starts to rain. They roll the windows up and Duke triggers the wipers and lowers the volume of the radio.

Alec is suddenly overwhelmed by the sentiment that Duke has *chosen* him for the adventure. Adventure, yes. He can't quite classify it as a crime because nothing's happened yet. Duke has taken him under his wing. He trusts me, Alec thinks. There was never anyone like this in Elmira, only a few priests who had a hard time keeping their hands off him until he grew big enough to be a physical threat. There was an English teacher at Holy Family—Mr. Clarke—who would ask Alec to stay after class now and then to check in on how he was doing. During second quarter of his sophomore year they read *The Adventures of Huckleberry Finn*, which remains the only book Alec has read cover to cover; he was more vocal than usual during class discussions. Mr. Clarke tried to engage Alec. Did he ever get around to reading the new British novel by William Golding, *Lord of the Flies*? He might even like Jack London's *White Fang*. But Mr. Clarke's literary overtures didn't quite catch on. It was still reading, after all, and reading beyond what was required in class. Alec was always eager to get to his next period.

And then there was Alec's father, who was too quiet, too remote. Donald Larkin seemed to always prefer his daughters to his only living son. Once, when Alec was fourteen, his father took him to a Yankees game. He hardly uttered a word to him during the long drive down to the Bronx, mostly smoking his pipe and listening to the radio. After the third inning Alec went to the bathroom. On the way back he found a full beer abandoned near the concession stand and guzzled it. Then he found another, half-full, and drank that, too. By the time Alec returned to his seat, way up in the left-field grandstand, he was drunk, but his father, obsessed with his score-card, never noticed. In the seventh inning, when the Yankee left fielder, Mickey Mantle, hit his second homer of the game, his father released a high-pitched sound that Alec had never heard come out of his father's mouth before. It almost shocked him, as he realized it was the first time he'd witnessed his father express anything close to a thrill. If the sound had been made in the dark one might have thought a woman had been knifed.

It wasn't that his father didn't reach out, in his way. He'd invite Alec to go fishing with him up on Lake Ontario or dove hunting in Pennsylvania. He even tried to teach him how to make copper etch-ings at his little shop table in the back of the garage. Alec simply wasn't interested. He wanted to be around his friends, smoking and drinking and riding around in cars, chasing girls over by Quarry Farm.

In Duke Alec has found someone he can genuinely look up to. He's his own man. He sets his own rules, lives by his own clock. Duke doesn't even wear a watch! Alec looks forward to spending time with him at the bar and listening to records with him and driving around Niagara Falls, going from watering hole to watering hole; those long Saturday nights that never seemed to end. They even slept with the same woman once. Her name was Becky and she was so fat they had to do it on the floor. Duke went first. Alec waited in the hall and listened to their whooping and panting and Becky's squeals of ecstasy. When it was Alec's turn, Duke didn't even bother leaving the little apartment. He simply sat in his recliner, shirtless, and smoked a cigarette, staring out the window. Alec was struck by the long, sloping appendectomy scar across Duke's abdomen, a kind of grotesque smile. When it was all over, Alec had to help Becky off the floor and she almost pulled his shoulder out of its socket. Duke gave her twenty dollars and even though Becky wasn't a prostitute she accepted the money.

"It smells like fuckin' horses and trout in here," Duke proclaimed after Becky left.

They couldn't stop laughing for ten solid minutes.

In a town called Victor they stop for gas at a rare twenty-four-hour service station. While Duke fills the tank, Alec cleans the windshield. The remains of dead bugs are stunning.

"It's amazing we didn't swallow any of those," Duke says. Alec laughs and Duke looks about for a moment, then peers up at the sky as if in contemplation. "If we pull this thing off tonight," he says, "do me one favor." He finishes pumping and screws the gas cap back on.

"Okay," Alec says, wiping the squeegee. "What?"

"Use the money for somethin' worthwhile," Duke says, setting a cigarette between his lips.

"Like donate it to the blind?"

"No, just don't spend it all on bourbon. That's the harebrained thing I would do. Sock it away. Put it toward…I don't know what I'm sayin'…" He trails off. "You're a young, good-lookin' kid," he continues, exhaling smoke, "and you got a decent heart. You still got a chance to do somethin' positive in this shit-stained world."

Coming from Duke, this fatherly advice is surprising—no, astonishing—and Alec likes it.

They stop in Utica, a town ten miles west of Frankfort. It's past three in the morning now. Duke knocks on the door of a small white clapboard house with a tarpaper roof and a lopsided, add-on front porch that looks as if would slide into oblivion if not for the retired icebox and the stack of used tires anchoring it to the earth. A young woman answers the door. She has red hair—a darker shade than his sister Fiona's—with long bangs swept to the side, a light dusting of freckles across the bridge of her nose, and the prettiest gray eyes Alec has ever encountered. She wears cutoff blue jeans and an old white tank top. Her feet are bare. Without a word she and Duke embrace for a long time. Alec peers into the house and can see clear into the kitchen, where the refrigerator has been left open, with only a quart of milk and a box of baking soda visible on a shelf.

"This is Alec," Duke says, breaking from the hug. "Alec, Nan."

"Hey," Nan says.

"Hey," Alec echoes.

Nan lets them in and they sit at her small kitchen table, its nickel surface scarred with faint knife streaks. After Nan shuts the refrigerator door, she removes an ice tray from the freezer, pops free a few cubes into a clear plastic tumbler, pours a Jim Beam over them, and hands the tumbler to Duke as if she's done this a hundred times before.

"He'll have the same," Duke tells her.

After she fixes Alec's drink he thanks her and she sits on her ankle in the empty chair. Duke just stares at her and smiles. Alec has known Duke's grins to be laced with irony or disgust or a caustic knowing, but this one seems to be filled with love; this one is pure, untainted.

"How's the little fella?" Duke finally asks, his usual booming voice cut in half.

"Loud and selfish and completely spoiled," Nan says. "I put him down again about an hour ago."

Over the kitchen table hangs a framed needlepoint of a clown with red balloons in his cheeks. Somehow the clown's expression reminds Alec of the portrait of Christ in the Larkin dining room back in Elmira. He imagines his mother serving dinner to Lexy, Joan, and his father. Lexy is a junior in high school now. She and Joan are the last two Larkin children living at home, held there like hostages under hypnosis, their mother's voice melodically binding them to those rooms filled with the Son of God and all that high-gloss mahogany furniture. Fiona moved to New York City two years ago and Myra is in Chicago. Alec hears about his sisters from Myra, whom he'll occasionally call when he's drunk or broke or feeling lonely.

"What brings you into town?" Nan asks Duke.

"We were just passing through," he replies. "I'm gonna head up to Canada for a bit, see what's happenin' in Montreal, or Magog."

This is the first time Alec's heard any mention Canada. He figures it's Duke's cover story for what they're about to do in Frankfort.

"How's the back?" Nan asks.

"The back's fine. Pretty stiff in the morning but after a hot shower it loosens up. Lately it's my goddamn ankles." He drinks and to Alec adds, "Don't get old. It hurts too much."

"You're not old until you're fifty," Nan jokes.

"Well," Duke says, "I feel like I'm damn near sixty."

"You still got that good face."

"Tell that to my liver," Duke says, and excuses himself to the bathroom. Disembarking from his chair is a three-part move with accompanying grunts, at least one of which is real.

When Alec is left alone with Nan he does his best not to stare at her.

"How long you known Jerry?" she asks.

The name Jerry shocks Alec, like swallowing a mouthful of curdled milk, but he manages not to betray his surprise. "Coupla months," he says. *Jerry? Who the hell is Jerry?*

"You met him on a job?"

"At a bar," Alec says.

"That doesn't surprise me."

"Yeah, we tie one on now and then."

"He obviously likes you. He usually doesn't like anyone."

"Why wouldn't he?" Alec offers.

Nan laughs. Alec likes the sound of her laugh so much he has to stare at the table so as not to lose his train of thought. And her smile is sweet. Sometimes a woman's smile will ruin her face. Alec has always thought that his sister Fiona suffers from this problem. She's pretty enough, but whenever she smiles she reveals short, imperfect teeth. It looks like something is dissolving in her mouth.

"He's not really going to Canada, is he?" Nan says.

"I honestly couldn't tell you," Alec says.

Jerry. Alec wonders how many other names he uses. Is there a different one for each person he meets? Or a small assortment he chooses from based on how it might suit whatever fool he encounters? Or is Duke simply a recent, self-appointed nickname?

"And what about you?" Nan asks.

"I don't have any plans at the moment," Alec replies.

"Just along for the ride?"

"For now, I suppose."

"What are you, twenty-one?" she asks.

"Twenty-three."

"What do you do for work?"

"I was picking apples at an orchard near Niagara Falls but I just got laid off."

"Are you from Niagara Falls?"

"I'm originally from Elmira."

"Big family?"

"Four sisters," Alec says. "I had a brother, too, but he died when he was a baby."

"I can't even fathom that," she says. "Are you the oldest?"

"Third oldest," he says. "My sister Myra has me by almost three years, my sister Fiona by a year and a half."

"Are you Spanish?"

"No," Alec says.

"You look like you could be," Nan says, "with those dark eyes and that hair. But European Spanish, not Mexican Spanish. You're too tall to be Mexican."

"My dad's Irish and my mom's Scottish and German."

"What's your last name?"

"Larkin."

"Alec Larkin," she says.

When he hears her say his name he has the sensation that his head has momentarily floated away from his body; it's drifting toward the ceiling and if there were a hole in it, his head would just keep going, up into the night sky. He would like to say her full name but he doesn't know it. Instead, he asks her if she has any siblings.

"It's only me," she says. "As far as I know, at least, though my dad had a lotta fun."

"Where is he?" Alec asks.

"Dead," she says. "Some big machine fell on him in a gravel pit."

"Sorry," Alec says. "What about your mother?"

"What about my mother? What about *your* mother?" Nan quips.

"My mother's taller than most men," Alec replies. "And more Catholic than the Pope. Still sings in the choir at St. John the Baptist. I wasn't good enough for her."

"My mother lives on a houseboat in Knoxville, Tennessee," Nan says. She reaches across the table and seizes his tumbler.

"Really?" Alec says.

"No. She lives on the other side of town with a three-hundred-pound man who thinks a big spaceship's gonna come down and take the saved away to some planet with American currency and air conditioning."

"I'd like to see that planet," Alec says.

"Plus they're nudists," Nan adds. "So I tend to keep my distance."

Alec takes his tumbler back, drinks from it, and chews an ice cube. "How old are you?" he asks.

"Too young to be sittin' around an eat-in kitchen, flattening my own ass," she says. "Twenty-four."

"You're pretty skinny for just having a kid."

She laughs. He knows it was a stupid thing to say, but she seems more charmed than upset.

"You shoulda seen me nine months pregnant," she says. "Nursing takes the weight off."

Alec thinks she's taking about nursing as a profession and imagines her in a white uniform with the hat and the soft shoes. "My sister Myra just finished nursing school at the University of Chicago," he offers.

"Nursing the baby," Nan explains, laughing again.

"Right," he says. "Feeding."

After he drinks another mouthful of Jim Beam he asks her what she does for a living. She tells him she'd been going to beautician school but had to put it on hold after she had her son.

"Where's the father?" he asks.

"Not where his lady and his little boy are."

"He ran off on you?"

"Like a gazelle on one of those nature shows."

"What's his name?"

"Drew."

"Drew," Alec echoes. Uttering the man's name makes him feel vengeful, like some character in a movie who has to come up with a plan.

"Why," Nan says, "you gonna go hunt him down?"

"Maybe," Alec jokes.

"Well, he's about six-foot-three, two hundred pounds. Light brown hair, blue eyes. Big rangy bastard, kinda like you, but not as skinny. I could try and sketch him for you."

"You don't have a snapshot?" Alec jokes again.

"I tore 'em all up."

Nan reaches across the table again and takes another drink from his bourbon. Her eyes have such a hold on him that he can feel it in his throat. With each look they share, it feels as if she's stealing a little bit of his oxygen.

"Why are your hands shakin'?" she asks.

"I don't know," he says. "Sometimes they just shake on their own. They always have."

"Restless heart," she says.

He shows her his hands, palms up. "The only time they don't shake is when they're holding cash."

She draws her fingers across his palms and the gesture nearly pulverizes him. It's witchy, but good witchy. It feels like he's coming apart. She's turning him to sawdust.

Duke returns from the bathroom cradling the baby, who wears a bulging diaper and a look of wonder on his face.

"Say hello to Drew," Duke says to Alec.

"Hey, Drew."

"Drew, this is Alec. My one true friend in this world."

Drew has big blue eyes and he might be the quietest baby Alec's ever seen. For a moment he thinks he might be deaf.

"How old?" Alec asks.

"Four-and-a-half months," Nan replies. "This heat makes his face puffy. I keep a fan going in his room."

"His face is perfect," Duke says. "It's a perfect little face." Drew clasps onto Duke's pinkie. "What a grip you have," Duke says. "Soon you'll be swingin' a hammer."

With his tiny wrinkled hand Drew paws at Duke's nose, then his mouth, his chin.

"Am I wrong to assume your spineless daddy ain't comin' back anytime soon?" Duke murmurs sweetly.

"I stopped waitin' up for him a few weeks back," Nan says.

"Has he even called?" Duke asks her.

"No."

Duke takes a seat at the kitchen table and bounces Drew on his knee a few times and the baby promptly starts wailing. The noise is incredible, like some Midwestern tornado siren that's gotten stuck. Nan takes the baby from Duke and holds him to her breasts. He is immediately quieted and Alec is astonished by her power over the child. She doesn't even need to feed him; the proximity of her flesh has rendered him dumb. Is it a smell? Or something else? The drunkenness of anticipating warm milk? Did Alec's mother have this power over him? Ava Larkin, that tall, righteous, God-fearing bitch.

Alec notices another dusting of freckles along Nan's collarbone, her shoulders. He longs to cradle one of her bare feet in his hands.

During a lull, a wave of cicadas surges. A sadness seems to have passed over Duke's face.

"I'm gonna go change his diaper and put him back down," Nan says, hoisting Drew onto her shoulder. She gets up and walks toward the hall with him.

As they pass by Alec, he can smell the baby's mess. A door opens and closes. Moments later, faint calliope music can be heard.

"Drew's father disappeared a month after the baby was born," Duke explains. "Cowardly fuck."

"Did you know him?"

"Yeah, I knew him," Duke says. "He's my son."

The idea of Duke having a son is so startling to Alec that he has to resist the need to sit on the floor. Duke's never mentioned any kids. Alec has always imagined him entirely singular, unattached to anything or anyone.

"Do you know where he is?" Alec asks.

"If I did I'd be there with a cattle prong."

Nan returns and sits. She's tied her hair back. She exhales and dabs at the sweat from her forehead with the back of her hand.

"Full-time job," Duke says.

"Yep," Nan agrees, "but minus the salary."

She asks Duke for a cigarette and he produces his pack of Pall Malls and taps one out for her. She uses the stovetop to light it and draws from it heavily. The calliope music continues wheedling from the baby's room.

"Here," Duke says, and pushes a hefty wad of cash toward Nan.

It's folded in half and secured with a rubber band. Alec can't decipher the amount, but it seems to be all twenties. It's probably more money than he's made the entire summer.

"That should help get you over the hump."

"I don't know what I'd do without you," Nan says, squeezing Duke's forearm.

The calliope music fades and is replaced by the cicadas, whose incessant throbbing seems more organized now, as if they're closing in on the house.

"We better head out," Duke says to Alec.

Alec gets up from the table. When Nan also rises he is seized by the desire to make every moment count. Their farewell has to be movie-like.

On the front porch, Nan and Duke hug again. This one goes on longer than their first. Duke clearly loves the mother of his grandson. Alec has walked to the car, allowing them privacy, though he can see Nan kiss Duke's cheek.

"You gotta get this porch fixed," Duke says. "Someone's gonna sprain their ankle."

She thanks him again for the money.

As Duke walks away, Nan remains on the porch, the light from her living room window casting her figure in silhouette. She looks spectral, only half there, a perfect ghost.

Just before they load into the Bonneville, Nan raises her hand and waves goodbye to Alec. Their farewell should've been more intimate. The disappointment settles in his jaw. He would have liked a few words and a hug. He even felt a pang of jealousy during her embrace with Duke, like a faint blow to the kidneys. He raises his hand and waves back. Then Nan pivots and goes into the house.

In the car Duke doesn't turn the radio on. For several minutes he seems remote, inaccessible.

Alec asks him if everything's okay.

"Everything's fine," he says. "I just love the hell outta that little boy."

A QUARTER OF AN hour later they arrive in Frankfort. It's after 4:00 a.m. in the small town and all but the traffic lights are off. The variety store is outfitted with a metal security gate, just as Duke described. Above the store is an apartment with three windows, whose curtains are drawn.

Duke parks across the street and kills the engine. "You stay put," he says. "Only come and get me if you see any lights go on in her place."

Duke disembarks form the Bonneville and calmly walks around to the back, not sneaking, not ducking, as if he's about to enter his own house.

Alec can't stop thinking about Nan. About sitting across from her in her little kitchen with the needlepoint picture of that clown high on the wall. Her thin wrists and fingers. Her red hair and freckled skin. The ease with which she carried her infant son down the hall...

A light above the store flicks on. It's the second window. Alec watches it for several breaths before registering what Duke had tasked him to do. Now another window is illuminated—the one on the far right. Alec gets out of the car and jogs across the street and around the back of the store. Loose change jingles in his pockets and he throws the coins into the unmown grass at the side of the store. But for some reason he halts at the back door, unable to go through it. Feeling the acute need to urinate, he unzips and relieves himself against the cement foundation. His urine smells like ammonia and Jim Beam and he realizes he's hardly had a thing to eat all day.

By the time he finally enters the back of the shop, things have already gone too far. The overcrowded variety store has been completely ransacked. Vintage clothes and books and knickknacks are strewn everywhere. The cash register is wide-open and empty and the shelves under the main display case have been pillaged. The old lady from upstairs is pleading with Duke. She has thin white hair and pale, translucent skin and wears a cream-colored terrycloth housecoat bearing a floral pattern. She is trying to stop Duke from hunting through the bottom of another display that showcases belt buckles, turquoise rings, leather wallets.

The old lady tries to grab him around the neck, from behind. Duke turns, seizes her by the shoulders, and flings her away from him like an unwanted, crazed cat. She crashes against a standing radiator, falls into a heap, and cries out. Duke grabs a brass bookend and brings the heavy, sharp object down onto her head repeatedly. After the third blow her skull empties onto the floor and an arc of blood sprays onto a Virgin Mary statue dressed with many colorful beaded necklaces.

Unseen by either of them, Alec turns and exits through the back door and runs as fast as he can to the Bonneville. It feels as if his legs have been pulled off and haphazardly put back on. He flings himself into the driver's side. He could leave. All he has to do is turn the key, which Duke left in the ignition. Just turn the key, Alec thinks. Turn it! But he can't. Instead he wrests himself out of the car and shuffles over to the passenger's side. His ankles have been pulled off too—pulled off and reattached—and he almost falls twice. He manages to open the passenger's side door and gets back in. His hands are shaking so bad he has to sit on them. He feels like he might vomit. He opens the door and leans his head out and retches, but nothing comes up.

Moments later Duke is walking toward the car from behind the shop with several cigar boxes stacked up against his vast torso, somehow keeping them in place with his chin. He hip-checks the passenger's side door shut, then sets the boxes down and calmly walks around the front of the car and grabs the keys from the ignition. He heads to the trunk, opens and closes it, and returns holding three Dutch Masters cigar boxes.

"There's around a grand in each of those," Duke says, shutting the driver's side door and handing Alec the three cigar boxes.

Alec opens one and simply stares at the cash, which is neatly arranged in tight stacks of twenties and tens. "What about your cut?" he says.

"I just put four of those in the trunk." Duke starts the engine and they drive away.

Frankfort blurs by Alec's window. A gas station. A pawnshop. A church with a white steeple. This is a town where things like this happen, Alec thinks. A man drives three hours in the middle of the night and robs an old lady and bashes her skull in.

"Where are we goin'?" Alec finally asks.

"Bus station," Duke says. "We have to split up."

"Are you gettin' on a bus?" Alec asks.

"No," Duke says, "you are."

When they arrive at a stoplight Alec asks Duke where he got the key to the back of the variety store.

"I've always had it," Duke replies. "I used to live with the old lady who owns the place."

"She rented you a room?"

"Somethin' like that," Duke says. "Here," he adds, handing Alec a handkerchief. "Your nose..."

Alec brings the handkerchief to his nostrils, which are gushing blood. Since he was a kid, his nose has always bled easily, especially at the sight of anything disturbing. Once when he was a boy, the next-door neighbor, Mrs. Kaminski, accidentally backed her Plymouth over her poodle, Skipper, whose skull popped like a plastic bag. Alec and his sister Myra saw the whole thing. Alec's nose immediately started bleeding. He's reminded of the night the Mulerts were murdered in their home, and the same thing happened to him then, and Myra noticed and the shame sent him jogging back to the house, plugging his nose as he ran.

When they finally arrive in the parking lot of a small bus terminal, Duke shifts the car into park, taps out a cigarette, and lights it. "My advice would be to head west," he tells Alec, exhaling.

"Where are you gonna go?"

"Far away from here," Duke says. "It's better if you don't know. And if I were you I'd stuff that money in the bottom of your duffel bag," Duke adds.

"Okay," Alec hears himself say.

"Do it, then," Duke says.

Alec opens his father's duffel bag, removes a blob of unfolded, yeasty smelling clothes, packs the three cigar boxes, re-stuffs the clothes, and secures the top.

"Maybe try the Midwest," Duke says. "People are nice there."

Alec gets out of the car with the duffel bag and closes the door.

Through the open window, Duke adds, "And remember what I said to you earlier. About bein' smart with that money."

Duke pulls away. Alec watches the Bonneville until it turns left at the next intersection. The engine fades and is overtaken by cicadas.

Inside the small bus terminal a large, standing fan oscillates with a sound louder than a lawn mower. There is only one other person in the waiting area: a young kid in a military uniform who's fallen asleep with his face in his hands. The attendant behind the fiberglass ticket booth is watching a small black-and-white TV. A re-run of *Bonanza*. Lorne Greene looks like an apparition, like some damned, minor ghost trapped forever on the Ponderosa. The clock high on the wall says that it's almost 4:00 a.m.

"When's the next bus?" Alec asks the attendant, who is covered with a gluey film of sweat.

"Thirty-five minutes," he replies, fanning himself with a bus schedule.

"Where's it going?" Alec asks.

"New York City."

Alec hoists his duffel bag onto his shoulder and asks if there are any buses heading west. The attendant tells him that the next west-bound bus departs at 6:00 a.m.

"How far west does it go?" Alec asks.

"It'll take you all the way to California if that's what you're lookin' for," the attendant says. "You want one of these?" He proffers the bus schedule he's been using to fan himself.

"No thanks," Alec says, and heads back outside, where even in the dark the heat rises out of the asphalt as if by its own will. Walking in it is like wading through a warm pond. Everything on this side of the state wants to slow you down. It's as if the night gives nature permission.

Alec can't shake the images from the variety shop: the old lady's body crashing into the radiator; then Duke or Jerry or whatever the hell his name is staving her head in with that brass bookend; her skull opening up like a cantaloupe; that arc of blood spraying against the Virgin Mary statue...Alec finds that he is weeping, that the grotesque images have awakened a fragility, some child-like weakness. It's the sound he used to produce when he sang in the choir as a boy. Warm air sluices into his mouth and down his throat and almost chokes him. Although his nose has stopped bleeding he's still clutching Duke's blood-soaked handkerchief. He blows a gout of bloody snot into his bare hand and wipes it with the handkerchief.

The cicadas surge feverishly. There's a relentless trance in their song. It's as if they're trying to keep you in one place, Alec thinks, to stop you from moving forward, so they can eventually take over.

He digs in his duffel bag and opens one of the cigar boxes. This is a moment, he realizes. You only get a few of these, maybe two or three in a lifetime. It's like a door rising out of the earth, the simplest of doors, wooden, with a tarnished brass knob. You either grab hold of it, turn the knob, and walk through the fucking thing, or you don't. Should he call the police and turn Duke in? Should he get rid of the money?

Alec goes back inside the terminal and from the attendant he purchases a one-way ticket to Los Angeles. As he parts with the cash his hands tremble so intensely he can feel a rattling in his elbows.

A few hours later, just before dawn, Alec boards a westbound Greyhound whose final destination is Los Angeles, California. There are two others on the bus—a pair of older, mannish nuns in black-and-white habits, sitting beside each other, just behind the driver. One of them is clutching a rosary, the other is reading a paperback. They seem bemused by their own tranquility, a seemingly permanent mild form of joy afforded them by the Holy Spirit, no doubt. They smile at Alec as he passes them with his father's duffel bag hoisted on his shoulder. Alec tries to return a smile but his face doesn't seem to be working properly.

The heat has finally lifted a bit and the bus lurches through the modest neighborhoods of Utica and toward Interstate 90. The dawn, blue as a goat's eye, is starting to climb up the eastern horizon. Through his lowered window Alec can hear birds chattering. Just like that, the cicadas are gone, replaced by the shrieks of crows, skylarks, and swallows, repetitive and maddening, but Alec is comforted by the fact that he has over three thousand dollars to his name.

3

ELMIRA, NEW YORK
DECEMBER 24, 1965

LEXY

"WAKE UP, SLEEPYHEAD," ED says, pulling his station wagon into the Larkins' driveway.

Lexy feels his soft full lips on her forehead. He shaved that morning and his smooth face smells of English Leather. The three-and-a-half-hour drive from Poughkeepsie has left a taste in her mouth. She wants a Coke, which she most certainly won't find here, as her mother has always frowned upon carbonated soft drinks. The best thing she'll get from the Larkin refrigerator is a glass of whole milk or a serving of her mother's virginal holiday eggnog.

Lexy met Ed at a mixer in New Haven, back in early September. He is from the Upper West Side of Manhattan. They made eyes across the Dwight Hall ballroom as the Whiffenpoofs, Yale's elite glee club, sang Cole Porter's "Miss Otis Regrets." Before the end of the final chorus, the lanky, broad-shouldered, 6'5" junior, who resembled a young Gregory Peck, had sidled up to her. Without saying a word, Ed offered his hand and Lexy took it. By New Haven standards it was an unusually warm September evening and they wound up taking a walk through campus. She loved his voice, his slow, loping gait, and the ease with which he moved.

Before she boarded the bus back to Poughkeepsie, they shared a chaste kiss at the threshold of the New Haven Green, then spent nearly every day of the following week talking on the telephone about how they couldn't wait to see each other again, which happened the next weekend, when Ed drove his '58 Ford Country Squire station wagon two hours north to the Vassar campus, a trip he's repeated each weekend since.

Lexy's first few weeks at Vassar were nothing less than thrilling. She quickly established herself as the star freshman on the volleyball club and she's grown particularly fascinated by a twentieth-century literature course, which introduced her to the haunting Albert Camus novel *The Stranger.* She's been carrying the slim book around in her purse and often rereads early sections, casting herself as Meursault's girlfriend, Marie, imagining them making love, swimming in the Mediterranean, walking through the sun-soaked streets of Algiers, eating in the cafés, and riding the trolly cars. Although she's always gotten along just fine with her mother, Lexy's time away has made her feel like an adult (finally!), with real freedoms. Beyond keeping her side of her dorm room picked up there are no chores. And she hasn't gone to church a single time since she's been at school; it's been almost four months of unencumbered Sundays. When she was home for Thanksgiving she lied to her mother, assuring her that she hasn't missed mass.

As Lexy and Ed approach the house with their weekend bags, it begins to snow. The flakes seem almost synthetic as they descend through the floodlight attached to the garage.

"Right on cue," Ed says of the snow.

The trees of the neighborhood, looming bare and arthritic, take on a sudden luster. The dead leaves on the colorless lawn are silvered anew in their misshapen drifts. Leaves this late into the year suggests that her father's arthritis has gotten worse. Maybe she'll ask Ed if he'll offer to do some raking. It would certainly impress her mother. The ancient sycamore—the tree Lexy and her siblings climbed and ran around and read beneath for years—looks thin and blighted, as if it survived a bombing. The old tire swing hangs from it like an afterthought.

Inside the house it is warm and smells like cooking: ham and stewed mustard greens and her mother's famous cheesy garlic butter rolls and something cinnamon. Ava Larkin has no doubt been at it all day and the promise of the Christmas Eve feast gnaws at Lexy's stomach.

"It smells extraordinary in here," Ed says.

"Wait till you taste it," Lexy says. "My mother's cooking secrets go back to the Old Testament."

In the foyer they shed their coats and hang them on the few available pegs along the wall. Lexy removes her red wool beret and stuffs it in the pocket of her coat. She peers into the living room, where Joan sits in front of the television on the old, oval rope rug. The glow from the TV makes her face appear lifeless, sallow. Even from the foyer Lexy can see that Joan has gotten heavier. From certain angles, in certain lights, she looks like one of the many over-weight middle-aged men in the neighborhood. As soon as Joan sees Lexy, she stands and bounds toward her, surprisingly light on her feet. During their embrace Lexy is shocked by Joan's weight, the concentrated density of her body.

"Hi, Joan," Ed says to Joan, who hides her face in Lexy's baby-blue cashmere sweater, which was an early Christmas gift from Ed. "It's nice to finally meet you."

Joan peaks out at him. "I'm going to watch *Rudolph the Red-Nosed Reindeer*," she tells him, still holding on to her sister. "There's a snow monster and a lumberjack and an elf who wants to be a den-tist. Fiona is coming with a boy named Sky. Myra's in the kitchen with Mother."

"Is Dad around?" Lexy asks, curling a strand of Joan's hair behind her ear.

"He's at the grocery store," she says. She peeks at Ed again, who sends her a winning smile, when causes her to completely buries her face in Lexy's sweater.

"What about Alec?" Lexy says.

"Myra says he's in Kansas being a nincompoop. Will you please kiss my head?"

Lexy kisses her sister on her forehead, which inspires a grin so unabashed that it causes Ed to laugh.

"Lexy has magic kisses," Joan tells Ed, and then turns and bounds back to the living room.

She plops down in front of the behemoth Magnavox Console color TV, whose volume has been turned down. Two years ago, after his beloved Zenith Porthole's picture slipped off-center, Donald splurged for the combination television-phonograph-radio. The enormous entertainment system seems to take up more floorspace than the sofa. It is dense, indestructible, a thing to be ridden into battle. On-screen is a commercial for the new white Ford Thunderbird featuring a sunroof and many automotive refinements. Joan is instantly transfixed by the ad's smooth images. Her thumb is in her mouth, a habit she has carried past her twenty-first birthday. With her free hand Joan kneads at the edge of the rope rug as if it might cause *Rudolph the Red-Nosed Reindeer* to appear on the screen sooner than its *TV Guide* listing.

"That's some tree," Ed says, nodding toward the corner of the living room, where the Larkins' Christmas tree pulses with blinking lights and colored ornaments and looping strands of popcorn.

Lexy takes his hand and leads him toward it. It excites her to feel his large wide palm, its warmth, its strength. Ed is her first lover. They've spent the past few days in a motel room in Poughkeepsie, making love and drinking peach schnapps and taking hot baths together. Lexy told her mother it was a mandatory volleyball tournament that kept her on campus until today and Ava seemed to accept the lie without suspicion.

"Is that Mickey Rooney?" Ed asks, pointing to the angel at the top of the tree.

Lexy laughs. The familiar angel, with its vast feathered wings, seems too large for this tree, which is almost a foot smaller than usual. Every year, since Lexy can remember, her father drives up to his brother's nursery in the Catskills the week after Thanksgiving and cuts down a Douglas fir. It used to be one of the big family outings where they would all vote on the perfect tree, drink hot cider, and chase each other through the snow, but now her father goes alone.

Up close, the angel seems mildly amused, as if hoarding a dirty secret.

A smattering of presents has already been arranged under the tree. Per the Larkin tradition, the majority of gifts will be sneaked into place while everyone's asleep.

Lexy reaches into her weekend bag and sets her small wrapped offerings among the others: a Vassar collector pen for Myra; a leather-bound diary for Fiona; a Mickey Mantle bobbing-head doll for Joan: a pair of wool socks for her father; a knitted scarf for her mother.

"It smells like oranges," Ed says, leaning toward the tree.

Lexy stands beside him, lightly grazing his exposed forearm with her fingers. In the motel room, she explored his body in ways she never thought possible; her hands touched hidden places, primitive parts of the flesh where carnality and pleasure wait to be coaxed from the body. It briefly thrills her to think of those long slow hours of sex and sleep. They used protection, of course, and despite all the pleasures they shared, this special time with Ed wasn't completely devoid of a wheedling Catholic guilt that seemed to faintly ring in her left ear each time she excused herself to use the bathroom. The only thing that made it go away was when she turned the light off so she couldn't see her reflection in the medicine-chest mirror.

She picks off a few pieces of stringed popcorn from the tree and tosses a couple of them into her mouth. The other she places the other one in the center of Ed's large hand.

"Go on," she dares him.

"Billy goat," Ed teases, then slips the popcorn into his mouth and chews.

"Rebel," Lexy teases back, easing her thigh into his groin.

During dinner Christmas music drifts in from the living room.

Fiona and her shaggy-headed boyfriend, Sky, are seated across from each other. They arrived in a tan '59 Bonneville convertible with many rust splotches. Lexy is seated to the left of Sky, who sports a butterscotch threadbare corduroy suit and a black Kinks concert T-shirt. His pale blue eyes are keen, intelligent. His wild nest of brown hair smells of clove cigarettes and some sort of musky oil. To Sky's right is Joan, who has grown so shy since Lexy's arrival that she wonders if her sister has been sedated.

On the other side of the table, opposite Lexy, seated right to left, are Myra, Fiona, and Ed, who has changed into a collared shirt and a crew neck sweater. Fiona wears a thin mustard-yellow turtle-neck with brown and red stripes. She is not wearing a bra and Lexy can't help but notice her nipples pressing through the thin Polyester fabric. She's certain that Ed can see them as well. A class move by her sister, forever the provocateur, always trying to make people notice her. She arrived with a bad cough — she says it's hardly any-thing — and Ava has asked her to please cough into her napkin or the crook of her elbow.

Kitty-corner from Lexy sits Myra, who wears a simple red car-digan sweater over a white blouse. A thin gold crucifix rests between her collarbones. Lexy has always thought Myra to possess the kind of beauty that takes hold of one's gaze after a third or fourth glance, a beauty that slowly, almost imperceptibly, gains strength and never weakens. Without question Myra is the most consistent of her three sisters, the one who will outlast everyone else with her slow, steady demeanor and quiet confidence.

At opposite ends of the Larkins' ancient, claw-foot mahog-any table are her mother, seated near the archway leading into the kitchen, flanked by Joan and Myra, and her father, positioned before the five-pound ham with his back to the living room, near Lexy and Ed. Her father is wearing light blue shirtsleeves with a festive plaid V-neck sweater vest and a knit tie. His hair has been combed neatly, with its precise, customary side part. Her mother has changed into a long skirt and a green sweater. The recently refurbished portrait of Christ looms over her right shoulder, as if her conspirer.

During grace, which is led by her father, Lexy steals a glance at Ed, who meets her gaze. While everyone else's eyes are closed she mouths the words "I want you." Ed smiles and closes his eyes. She will sneak into Alec's room when everyone is asleep. They have not discussed it but this is her plan.

After grace, steaming serving dishes are passed around while her father carves thick slices of ham onto another plate. His hands are worse than they were during Thanksgiving, trembling as he grips the knife and fork. Though his expression is steady, the knobs of his jaw pulse ever so slightly. He's learned how to clench his teeth and not give too much away. At forty-seven, he's only recently started to go gray at the temples and there are very few lines at the corners of his eyes. In high school Lexy's girlfriends all had crushes on him. His gnarled, afflicted hands are the one thing that belies his age.

After Fiona's plate lands in front of her, she coughs fiercely into her napkin and clears her throat. She and Lexy meet eyes. They've hardly said a word to each other since Fiona arrived with Sky.

"Anyone heard from Alec?" Fiona asks, her eyes still locked on Lexy, her voice husky, dehydrated.

Fiona has been, without a doubt, the most freely sexual of Lexy's siblings. She was far more adventurous than the other girls in Elmira, losing her virginity to a college boy when she was sixteen. His name was Rusty Bales. He was a sophomore at Syracuse University and during spring break he'd picked her up at the restaurant where she was hostessing in nearby Corning. She didn't come home for an entire weekend. Worried that her daughter had been kidnapped, Ava Larkin called the police and that Sunday she even filed a missing person's report, but then Fiona showed up at evening mass as if nothing had happened. The following week in school, the rumor about Fiona and Rusty Bales spread through the cafeteria like the flu, and far from refuting it, Fiona defiantly owned up to it. Her girlfriends stopped speaking to her and between classes students started calling her a slut and a whore and a hussy. But the ridicule seemed only to embolden her. If anything her autonomy grew fiercer. She's the only Larkin sister who would dare to attend Christmas Eve dinner braless. Lexy would never admit it to Fiona, but she has always admired the way her sister dresses and wears her makeup, although tonight her eyes are naked. She looks younger, thinner than normal.

"Myra says he's in Kansas," their mother says of Alec's whereabouts, heaping a large serving spoon of greens onto Joan's plate.

"He got a job working road construction," Myra says from the other side of the table.

"You talked to him?" Lexy asks.

"He calls Myra whenever he's drunk or needs money," Fiona says.

"Fiona," their mother warns, cutting Joan's ham into small squares.

Fiona smiles to herself and shakes her head as Sky sends her a look of admonishment across the table and mouths the word "STOP." Through the chaos of Sky's hair Lexy can see that his left ear is pierced, though he doesn't wear an earring. The piercing has been torn through the lobe. She wonders if this is an affectation, part of his renegade costume. She imagines him ripping his own earring out, first staring in the mirror, counting to three, and then yanking.

"It's good that he's working," her mother says, tending to her own plate now.

"I told him he was invited to Christmas," Myra says. "That Mom and Dad said it was okay."

"You said he could come home?" Fiona says to their mother, as if in disbelief.

"We did," she says. "Your father and I talked it through and we think it's been long enough."

"He sounded good," Myra says. "He likes his job. He's renting an apartment, near Wichita."

Something passes over Fiona's face. She seems suddenly far away. Her mouth goes slack and her eyes slide a bit. Is it regret? Lexy wonders. A memory? Is she jealous of Alec's unexpected clemency? Or is it some unexpressed feeling for her only living brother?

When their mother rises and exits to the kitchen, Fiona seizes one of the dinner rolls from Ed's plate and tosses it across the table at the mysterious Sky, who catches it, sets it beside a pile of greens, and then second-guesses himself and winds up offering it back across the table to Ed, a preemptive armistice.

"You have it," Ed says. "But thank you."

The subject of Alec—the unspoken shame and sadness of his life—seems to have cast a heavy silence over the table. The Chicago Symphony Orchestra's rendition of "Silent Night" floats in from the living room. Lexy can feel Fiona's eyes on her again. She looks across the table and sure enough she's staring at her.

"What?" Lexy says.

"Nothing," Fiona quips.

"Why do you keep staring at me?"

"How's school?" Myra asks Lexy, clearly trying to be a buffer.

"It's good," Lexy says.

"Have you thought about a major yet?" Myra asks.

"I'm considering economics."

"God," Fiona says. "Why?"

"*Gosh*," their mother says, reentering the dining room with her mother's crystal decanter of red wine, one of the Larkins' few beloved heirlooms. "Or *good grief*."

"Good grief, why?" Fiona says without missing a beat.

"There's something certain about numbers," Lexy says.

"She means money," Fiona says.

Their mother hands the decanter of wine to Fiona. "Please pass this down to your father."

"Why not accounting?" Fiona says, handing the decanter to Ed, who in turn gives it to Donald.

"Because accounting is just a lot of adding and subtracting," Lexy replies. "Economics is more than that."

"How so?" Fiona says.

"Accounting doesn't necessarily deal with the marketplace. Or the politics of business."

"She'll be on Wall Street in no time," Fiona says to Sky, who smiles politely but doesn't take the bait.

"She's reading an interesting novel," Ed offers, a clear attempt to steer the subject away from Lexy's potential career.

Myra takes it up. "What book?" she asks.

"*The Stranger*," Lexy says.

"*Ooh*," Fiona says, "*Camus*. Do you like it?"

"I do," Lexy says.

"What about it do you like?" Fiona asks.

"I don't know. The main character isn't like anyone I've ever met."

"*Meursault*," Fiona says with an exaggerated French accent. "The Algerian enigma."

"You've read it?" Myra says to Fiona.

"'How had I failed to recognize that nothing was more important than an execution; that, viewed from one angle, it's the only thing that can genuinely interest a man?'" Fiona says, quoting the lines effortlessly. "My favorite part is where the chaplain asks him if he's seen the face of God in the wall of his cell and Meursault admits that he's been looking at the wall for months and waiting for a face to emerge and it wasn't the face of God he'd hoped to see, but the face of his girlfriend."

"Is he spiritually deviant?" their mother asks.

"I think he finds the idea of God to be absurd," Fiona says.

"Or indifferent," Lexy says.

"Do you find the idea of God to be absurd?" their mother asks Fiona.

"I don't know," Fiona answers. "The jury's still out on that one."

"And what about you?" their mother asks Lexy.

Lexy can't answer. It's as if there's a fishhook caught in her lip. She's never expressed such things in front of her mother.

"What does he do to get himself sent to prison?" Myra asks, rescuing Lexy.

"He kills an Arab man on the beach," Lexy says, thawing from her brief freeze. "He shoots him in self-defense."

"The first bullet is in self-defense," Fiona says. "But then he unloads his revolver. He shoots him four more times."

"That sounds grisly," their mother says.

"Why does he shoot him more than once?" Myra asks.

"It's not entirely clear," Sky offers out of nowhere.

It's the first time Lexy has heard him speak, and his voice is surprisingly gentle, not at all what she expected. Everyone turns to him.

"And I don't think the action is meant to be easily interpreted," he adds. "It's implied that the jury ultimately finds him guilty because he didn't openly mourn at his mother's funeral. Even though there's probably not enough evidence to suggest that it was a blatantly malicious act and *not* one committed in self-defense."

Lexy is struck by the ease with which the words leave Sky's mouth.

"In the end," he continues, "he's sentenced to death. I think what Camus is getting at is the indifference of the state."

"And God," Fiona adds.

"Not to mention the stupidity of the courts," Lexy says.

"The folly of the justice system," Sky says, nodding in agreement.

"Folly," Fiona says. "Exactly."

"Did you study the book in school?" Myra asks Sky.

"I never finished school," he says.

"So you came to these conclusions on your own?" Lexy asks.

"More or less," he says.

Their mother, letting the comment on God's indifference pass unremarked, rises and helps Joan scoot her chair closer to the table, presumably so she won't spill any more food in her lap. "And what do you do for work?" she asks Sky.

"I'm actually between jobs at the moment," he says, swiping a strand of hair away from his forehead. "I was plastering walls for a few months but that gig ended. There's lots of buildings getting renovated in the city, though, so I like my chances of finding something else soon."

"He's an amazing artist," Fiona says. "His paintings are like dreams. He's self-taught. Like all the best painters."

"Do you live in the city?" Lexy asks.

"He rents a loft in Soho," Fiona says.

"With a few friends," Sky says. "We're sort of a collective."

"Interesting," their mother says. Lexy notices her share a look with her father, who raises an eyebrow.

"There are six of us," Sky explains about his roommates. "We pool our resources, give what we can to the rent, the electric bill, food."

"They're all extraordinarily talented," Fiona says. "One guy makes sculptures out of bicycle parts he finds all around the city."

"And are *you* part of this collective, too?" their mother asks Fiona.

"Fiona's been helping me stretch canvases," Sky says. "And learning how to mix paints."

"Are you living there as well?" their mother asks.

"I am," Fiona says.

Lexy watches their mother cast a look down the table toward their father again, who meets her eyes, though this time his expression reveals very little.

"And last month you were in Washington?" their mother says to Fiona, pouring herself a glass of wine from the decanter that's been making its way around the table.

"Only for a few days," Fiona says.

"Is that why you couldn't come home for Thanksgiving?" Lexy says. "Because of the protests?"

"I'm here now, aren't I?" Fiona says.

"We're glad you're here," their mother says. "And we're glad to meet you, too, Sky."

"Thank you for having me," Sky says. "I've heard so much about all of you."

"Eat your greens," their mother says to Fiona, who complies by gently stabbing a forkful of them.

Fiona then coughs into her napkin. Three sharp, ragged hacks that sound painful.

"Have you seen anyone about that?" Myra asks her.

"It sounds like bronchitis," Lexy says.

"Are you a doctor now?" Fiona says. "I'm fine. I get this every winter. It'll go away."

"Myra, what do you think?" says their mother, who has designated Myra the expert for all ailments ever since she went to nursing school.

"Do you have a fever?" Myra asks Fiona.

Their mother rises and places her hand on Fiona's forehead. "You are a little warm," she says, then exits to the kitchen.

"It doesn't sound good," Myra says. "You best get your rest. And drink plenty of liquids. Do you have any way of sitting in a steamy shower?"

Fiona shakes her head. "Not at the moment," she says.

"There's a shower upstairs," Lexy says.

"I'd be wasting water," Fiona retorts.

Lexy imagines her sister bathing in Sky's Soho communal loft, some paint-splattered industrial sink designed for the scrubbing of machine parts, the water rusty and septic-looking, then imagines her not bathing for days on end, her feet discolored and fungal, her scalp rampant with lice.

Their mother returns with two aspirin. "Take those," she says.

Fiona puts them in her mouth and swallows them dry.

There is a brief silence, scored by the clinking of utensils on plates and the Christmas music. One song ends and the radio host announces another offering from the Chicago Symphony Orchestra. "O Little Town of Bethlehem," he says in his silky baritone.

Lexy glances across at Ed, who takes a drink of wine and wipes his mouth with his napkin. He's been so quiet. She was so excited for everyone to meet her tall, handsome boyfriend. She thought he'd be fielding a litany of questions, but Sky appears to be the one who's captured the family's interest.

"You were protesting the war?" their father asks Sky from his end of the table.

Everyone stops eating and turns to him. It's the first time he's spoken since he said grace. He's fixed his gaze on Sky, his large gray eyes expectant, unblinking.

"Yes, sir," Sky says, "we were protesting Vietnam."

"You don't agree with it," their father says.

"I'm afraid not. And I mean no disrespect, Mr. Larkin. Fiona told me how you served."

"Do you not love your country?" their father asks.

"I do love it, sir. Very much. That's precisely why Fiona and I went to Washington." Sky seems to take a moment to gather his thoughts. He dabs at his mouth with his napkin and continues: "Like many others I feel like we're not over there for the right reasons. It's none of our business."

"But stopping the spread of communism *is* our business," their father says.

"Thousands of lives are being lost," Sky gently counters. "So many people are suffering. Women and children. I just don't see the point."

"Everyone's entitled to their opinion," their mother says.

"If it means anything," Sky continues, "my father also served in World War Two. He was a gunnery sergeant in the Marines. He fought in Iwo Jima and I admire him very much."

"How does he feel about you protesting?" their father asks.

"In all honesty, it's complicated," Sky says. "We haven't spoken in a few years."

"I'm sorry to hear that," their mother says.

"His dad wanted him to go into the family business," Fiona says. "Back in Wisconsin."

"What kind of business?" Myra asks.

"Medical supplies," Sky says.

"But he's a painter," Fiona declares to the entire table. "It's what he's been put on the earth to do. And his work is extraordinary. He recently finished a large canvas of a rainforest. When you stand before it you can almost smell the air. You can practically hear the insects. You can sense the creatures lurking behind the trees. It feels like you're truly part of it. It's as if the painting has imagined *you*."

"It sounds so vivid," Myra offers.

"Mr. Larkin," Sky says, "I honestly don't know what my father would say about my protesting."

Their father nods and returns to his plate. Earlier in the evening, when he entered the house with the groceries, he kissed Lexy on the cheek and said hello to Ed and shook his hand in a respectful, businesslike fashion, but to Lexy his actions seemed somehow muted. There was something quietly despairing about the manner in which he removed his coat and carried the bag of groceries into the kitchen. At Thanksgiving Lexy noticed a seed of ache that had formed between his eyes, and is still there tonight.

After a silence, their mother fills her wine glass and says, "How's the ham, everyone?"

"Delicious," Ed says.

"Really good," Sky adds.

"Well, there's plenty more," she offers. "Don't be shy."

"What about you, Ed?" Fiona says, twirling her own fork in a vortex of mashed potatoes.

Lexy is relieved. Now it's his time to shine. Finally.

"What would you like to know?" Ed says.

"What are your interests?" Fiona asks him, performing extreme politeness, really articulating her consonants.

"I'm majoring in education," he says, "with a minor in psychology. I'd like to someday teach high school and maybe coach basketball."

At last Lexy glimpses her opening. "He's on the varsity at Yale," she brags. "He's their second-leading scorer.

"Wow," Fiona says. "Yale."

"Could I trouble you for another slice of ham?" Ed says to Myra, passing his plate to Fiona, who hands it along.

Is he dodging the spotlight? Lexy wonders. She didn't expect him to be so shy.

"No trouble at all," Myra says. She uses the serving fork to place another slice of ham on his plate and passes it back down the table.

"Did you go to school?" Ed asks Fiona. Lexy detects the slightest bit of derision in his voice.

"She started at the College of Saint Rose up in Albany," Lexy says, "but she came home after a semester."

"I had mononucleosis," Fiona says.

"She dropped out," Lexy counters.

"I was bedridden for a month!"

Lexy casts her silverware onto her plate and leans into the table. "Fiona's problem is that she can't decide if she's an artist or a revolutionary." A rush of adrenaline heats her face. "One minute she's silk-screening anti-apartheid T-shirts in some stranger's attic in New Jersey, and then before you know it she's living with a half-baked nudist, quote-unquote *photographer* from Peekskill, supposedly employed as his quote-unquote *assistant*—whatever that means." The words are tumbling out of her mouth now, her cheeks aflame. "*And* after that didn't work out she found a job sweeping floors at some community food co-op on the Lower East Side of Manhattan, but of course that didn't last either—I guess that broom just got too heavy for her—and a month later she's growing out her armpit hair and protesting the war in Washington." She locks eyes with Fiona. "Pick a lane and stick to it, you might actually get somewhere!"

"Lexy, come on now," Myra says after absorbing a grave look from their mother, who has kept her composure since the argument started.

Lexy can barely raise her eyes now. Their father is staring at his plate as if the ham will provide a solution.

Fiona's face, bone-white, is utterly still. Her green eyes look pinned, feral. But then she seemingly regains herself. "Lexy suddenly has opinions," she starts, speaking directly to Ed, "because she's going to some fancy liberal arts college. Because she's reading *Camus*." Her head pivots sharply to Lexy. "Maybe I'll pick the most *upstanding lane*, like you. A lot of fun that must be, playing by the rules, being the Model Young American Daughter. You really must get off on the pursuit of perfection, you stuck-up priss!" Her face is also pink now, inflamed. She turns back to Ed. "Although I doubt she has any idea what getting off feels like!" She gulps her wine and goes right back at Lexy. "And Graham wasn't a nudist, he was *comfortable with his body*! And he didn't live in *Peekskill*, he lived in *Katonah*! And just for the record, his photographs have been featured in *magazines*!"

"Take a shower—you stink!" Lexy lashes back.

"I smell *real*, you phony!"

"You smell like a goat!" Lexy seethes. She can feel herself baring her incisors. The heat from her face has moved down her neck. Her ears are on fire.

"And you smell as dull as that cashmere sweater you're wearing! Who do you think you are—Jackie O?"

"Put a bra on, Sheena!"

"*Girls!*" their mother finally cries, rocketing out of her chair. Her height is towering, almost capital in its magnificence. "That's enough!" she says.

Only the Christmas music from the living room. A children's choir singing "The Little Drummer Boy."

Joan drops her fork onto her plate, brings her fists to her eyes, and starts to cry, without sound, in a way that makes it look like her face is trapped inside a plastic bag. Her features are ghoulish, contorting in on themselves.

Fiona turns away and unleashes a coughing fit into her hands. Lexy takes pleasure imagining her sister plagued with some horrible respiratory infection, expelling puddles of brown phlegm.

"Go get her book," Ava says to Myra, who scoots her chair away from the table and heads for the stairs.

Fiona coughs a few more times, then brings her napkin to her mouth, pivoting away from the table.

Still standing, their mother shakes her head. "For Godsakes it's the first time we've all been together in over a year." She looks to Fiona, to Lexy. "Can you two at least *try* to get along? ...Fiona Marie, I'm talking to you!"

Fiona turns her head, gives their mother her profile.

"Is it that hard?" their mother says.

Their father reaches under the table and gently squeezes

Lexy's leg. These small moments of affection from him are few and far between and she is always surprised at how desperately she needs them. Although she and her father rarely speak, her love for him is absolute, and despite his quiet demeanor, she knows it's mutual. She can feel Ed watching her but she can't possibly look up. She bites the inside of her cheek to stop herself from crying. Her lower lip always betrays her. If she could only freeze her fucking lower lip!

The music continues to drift in from the living room, now with "Joy to the World" by the Philadelphia Symphony Orchestra. Lexy casts her gaze past Sky to Joan, whose cheeks have gone blotchy. Their mother is standing behind her, stroking her back. Since she was little, Joan has been prone to spells of hyperventilating.

"Easy now," their mother tells Joan. "Just breathe . . ."

Lexy can feel Fiona staring at her, gloating like a sated pig.

"Excuse me," Lexy says, and sets her napkin on her plate and pushes away from the table.

When she enters the kitchen, Myra is speaking quietly into the telephone.

"Okay," Myra says. "Everyone is thinking about you. Hang in there. Merry Christmas." She hangs up the phone and turns. Under her arm she is holding Joan's sketch pad and pencil box.

"Alec?" Lexy says.

Myra nods.

"Where is he?"

"He wouldn't say."

"He wanted money again?"

Myra nods once more and asks her not to tell the others.

"Why do you protect him?" Lexy asks.

"I don't know," Myra says. "I guess because no one else believes in him."

"But you do."

"I want to," Myra says. "I really do."

* * *

IN THE MIDDLE OF the night, a few hours after the family has returned from midnight mass at St. John the Baptist, Lexy sneaks across the upstairs hall and enters Alec's room. When she opens her robe to Ed, he sits up in the twin bed so quickly it's as if he is seeing beyond this world for the first time. He reaches for one of her breasts and Lexy falls on him. They cling and stroke and taste each other. It has started to snow again and moonlight spills in through the window, silvering their figures. Making love in the house she grew up in — in her brother's room, no less — feels dirty, like they're being spied on through the keyhole; or worse yet, it's as if Alec himself is hiding in the closet.

Before Alec was banished from the house, she walked in on him masturbating in the garage. He must've been fifteen or sixteen. It was the height of summer and the heat that day was extraordinary. As instructed by their mother, Lexy had entered the garage to retrieve a metal basin to fill with ice. Alec was in the corner, his figure in profile, masturbating with a milk bottle stuffed with canned tuna. The two opened cans of StarKist were on the floor next to his feet, along with one of the can openers from the kitchen. The smell was unmistakable. She watched him, frozen there, for what felt like a full minute. Needless to say, she never returned to their mother with the metal basin, and she could never bring herself to eat tuna fish again.

Now, Ed burrows between her legs. And then they switch positions and she moves over him. His body is slim, hairless. She traces the faint, raised segment of his appendectomy scar, which travels to his hip, his groin. She takes him in her hand, then in her mouth. He releases a moan and she forces her hand over his face. He bites her fingers and they nearly explode with laughter, driving their faces into the lone pillow. They regain their composure for a few breaths and almost lose it again. Lexy whispers to him that above all else they have to be quiet. The restraint is thrilling. When she uses her hand to bring Ed to orgasm, Lexy covers his mouth with her other hand again and he makes a noise that sounds like someone being smothered.

Afterwards Lexy heads down to warm some of her mother's

eggnog. As she descends the stairs—on her tiptoes, so as not to make them creak—she overhears Fiona asking their father for money. From the stairs, there in the dark, she can see into the living room, where he is arranging presents under the tree. Fiona is standing behind him, still in her turtleneck and blue velvet pants, her arms crossed. Their father leans back on his haunches and removes his wallet. He reaches into it and offers her a twenty-dollar bill.

"That's it?" Fiona says. She stares at the twenty-dollar bill in her hand. "But what about rent and groceries? What if I need medication for this cough?"

Their father gives her another twenty. Fiona just shakes her head, indignant, staring at the money.

"We've given you plenty this year," their father says. "You need to start figuring things out on your own."

Fiona turns and storms out of the living room, crossing into the dining room and then the kitchen. Lexy can hear her open the basement door, followed by her descending footfalls. She remains sitting on the stairs, watching her father, who has resumed arranging the presents under the tree. Now two sets of muted footfalls can be heard ascending the basement steps and moments later Fiona and Sky cross through the dining room and the living room and then they're in the foyer opening the door and exiting the house. Sky is carrying Fiona's red suitcase that she inherited from Myra, and they don't even stop to say farewell to her father on their way out.

Lexy descends the stairs and through the living room window can see them get into Sky's Bonneville, parked behind Ed's station wagon. Sky sets the red suitcase in the backseat, shuts the door, then clears snow off the windshield with his bare hand and does the same to the driver's side mirror. Fiona coughs loudly, spits phlegm into the snow, enters the passenger's side, and slams the door shut. Sky gets in the driver's side. The car starts with a roar and backs out of the driveway, thick gray exhaust billowing from the tailpipe.

Her father, seated on the floor before the Christmas tree, turns and sees Lexy.

"They just left," Lexy tells him.

"I guess they did," he says, as if they are merely two strangers who used the Larkin driveway to back in and turn their car around. In typical fashion he clearly doesn't want to talk about it. "Can't sleep?" he asks.

"Classic Christmas Eve insomnia," she offers, approaching him. "You'd think I'd have grown out of it by now."

Next to her father lies a large box of candy canes, each one individually wrapped in plastic. The surprise Christmas-morning candy canes decorating the tree are a longstanding family tradition, Santa's little personal flourish for the Larkins.

Lexy sits on the floor beside her father. "Don't you ever get bored of this?" she asks, rubbing her eyes.

"I actually like it," he says. "My own little ritual. It's surprisingly calming...Your mother makes dinner all day and I stay up all night handling this."

"You've always been a good team."

Her father busies himself fixing a string of lights that have been shorting out, unplugging them from the wall socket and untwisting a section of the line. All those years of working in the factory have turned his hands beastly. They are large and veinous and slow, some of his knuckles misshapen, one of his pinkies oddly bent.

Lexy realizes that she is naked under her robe, still wet between her legs. She makes sure that her sash is secured. "I think I need some air," she says. "I might take a walk."

"Would you like some company?"

"No, but thanks," she says. "I know you have a lot to do."

"Well, it's cold out there. Be sure to bundle up."

Lexy rises and kisses the crown of her father's head, which smells of burning leaves and paraffin oil, the odor of the hair dressing he has long used. "Merry Christmas, Daddy," she says.

"Merry Christmas."

In the foyer she wraps herself in Ed's overcoat, dons her red wool beret and Myra's plaid tartan scarf, and slips into Joan's rubber boots. When she's home she always finds herself wearing everyone else's clothes.

Outside the sky is clear and the stars are bright. The snow has finally stopped. Its hide, stretched across the neighborhood yards, is so pristine and unbroken that it looks like snow from a fable.

At the end of the driveway one of the aluminum garbage cans has fallen over and the lid is off. Among the loose garbage Lexy spots a brown postal box addressed to her mother. The box is decorated with a festive velvet red bow and little frills of silver ribbon. Lexy can't help but open it. Inside she finds a small rectangular Tupperware receptacle containing what appears to be some sort of chocolate pudding. She cracks the lid and the smell of human feces makes her gag. She drops the container in the snow and turns away, retching twice and then a third time. Nothing comes up. After catching her breath she squats in the snow and snaps the container shut.

Taped to its underside, she notices now, is a black-and-white postcard with a church. Lexy removes the postcard, studies it. The church boasts a large steeple, piercing a clear, cloudless sky. In the foreground is a small fenced-in graveyard. The caption identifies it as Holy Trinity Catholic Church in Trinity, Indiana. On the other side of the postcard, in blue ballpoint ink, it reads:

Merry Christmas, Mother.
Love, Alec

Her brother's imperfect handwriting is all too familiar. Alec's penmanship was always malformed, as if he was forced to use his left hand. At school his teachers often criticized him for his poor penmanship. What a horrible thing to do, Lexy thinks. What's wrong with him? She collects the Tupperware along with the rest of the garbage and stuffs it all back into the can, which she stands beside the other one, then secures the lid.

Along Maple Avenue lit Christmas trees glow softly in the darkened living room windows, appearing ghostly, spectral. Lexy approaches the house where the Mulerts were murdered fourteen years ago. Even though she was only four at the time she can recall the dark feeling in Elmira, as if infected clouds had permanently gathered over her hometown; how everyone in her neighborhood seemed to be hiding behind the drapes of their living rooms. The police never caught the killer. The Mulerts' house has been repainted battleship-gray with white trim. A widower lives there now, a thin Jewish man named Mort Abelman whose wife died in her sleep back in August, just before Lexy left for Vassar. Mr. Abelman is a retired diamond merchant and purportedly looks after some unfathomable number of cats.

In Joan's boots Lexy tromps through the snow along the edge of the property and slips between the evergreen hedges. Through a crack in the curtains she can glimpse Mr. Abelman sitting in a wool recliner, staring at some unseen object, seemingly lost in thought. Is he an insomniac? Lexy wonders. Forever stunned awake by grief or regret or some combination of the two? Sure enough, there are a number of cats—seven, eight, nine of them?—lounging on the furniture and an enormous gray tabby curled into Mr. Abelman's lap. Some believe the spirit of his dead wife possessed the giant cat, which her mother says follows Mr. Abelman around, from room to room.

Do the dead ever leave us? Lexy wonders. She thinks of her baby brother, Archie, who died at the hospital the morning following the murders, his little body glistening, the fever having turned his flesh a strange coral color. As a four-year-old Lexy thought the Holy Spirit had entered the baby, that he would burst into flames like some character from a Bible story in Sunday school. Is Archie's spirit still alive in their house somewhere? Did his soul cling to her mother's hair as she was leaving the hospital that early dawn? Lexy imagines Archie's infant soul like a thin, clear membrane, fine as spider silk, floating from room to room, hovering above her mother while she sleeps.

Lexy turns and looks back along Maple at the Larkin house, which for all the years she can remember has contained the totality of her family's joys and sufferings. She recalls her mother and father slow-dancing one night in the living room to Perry Como's

"Dream Along With Me." Everyone was supposed to be asleep, but Lexy stood at the top of the stairs and watched as her father leaned his head on her mother's taller shoulder, her long thin hand curled around the back of his head, their figures almost infinitesimally swaying back and forth. And then she sees Myra soundlessly weeping at the kitchen table after receiving her acceptance letter to the University of Chicago's nursing program. Their mother stood behind her with her hand on her back as Myra cried tears of joy. And then there was the awful night during dinner when Alec got up from his chair, took two long strides, and drove his fist into the wall next to the portrait of Christ. The picture frame jumped its nail and crashed to the floor. One of its joints cracked like a femur. Alec ran out of the house without his jacket and didn't return for two days. Lexy imagines Joan sitting cross-legged in their mother's rhubarb patch, staring at the lightning bugs she'd trapped in a mason jar, mesmerized for hours, blissfully unafraid of the dark. And the time Fiona came home drunk out of her mind and stripped off her clothes and sauntered naked all throughout the downstairs rooms, shouting, "For joy! For joy! For joy!" Fiona shrieked with laughter as their father tackled her onto the sofa and wrapped her with one of their mother's patchwork quilts.

The old house with all of its dark, sturdy furniture; its wooden floors in need of new varnish; the rattling stove and the loud refrigerator; the dank stone basement with the long, crooked shelf of jars crammed with her mother's rhubarb preserves, countless jars going on seemingly for infinity; the narrow bedrooms and thick walls; the leaky sinks and incessantly gurgling downstairs toilet; the scarred wood in the attic where the termites feasted; all the keepsakes hidden in boxes—innumerable boxes filled with photo albums and yearbooks and tax records and report cards and forgotten school projects and reams of old magazines; a house of silences and outbursts; a house that has endured blizzards and hailstorms and nor'easters; a house whose windows have been cracked by confused birds colliding with their own reflections, whose thin panes have been loosened by the wind; a house now half-asleep like some forgotten ship anchored at sea.

The lights are off except for a faint glow downstairs, where her father is no doubt still arranging the presents just so and placing the last few candy canes on the tree.

Her mother will die in this house. The thought takes hold of Lexy like someone grabbing her by the backs of her arms. She sees her mother lying on the living room floor, an elbow twisted oddly over her head, her clear blue eyes wide open like the stunned, permanent eyes of a porcelain doll. She imagines her entire family dying in the house, one by one: her father stumbling against a wall, grabbing for the furniture, going to a knee and pitching forward onto the rope rug; Alec having his heart stop while scampering downstairs, gripping the long wooden banister, sitting down in the middle of the stairs, pawing at his chest, his black eyes going still in their sockets; Fiona tumbling down the basement steps, crying out to God or cursing the Devil, her skull cracking open like a melon; Myra expiring elegantly on the front porch while sitting on one of the rattan chairs, her hands folded on one knee, hummingbirds darting about the sugar-water feeders as her final breath exits her lungs; Joan choking to death on crackers and jam that she sneaked into her room from the pantry, her lips clotted shut with blueberries...

And then Lexy sees herself falling off the roof in the late spring and breaking her neck. Days later her body is discovered by a neighbor boy looking for an errant baseball. He finds her in the lilac bushes, ants in her nostrils, stag beetles nesting in her blond hair, her limbs jutting clownishly. She feels a twinge in the vertebrae at the top of her neck. The final Larkin, dead. Yes, that old house with its brick chimney and its sagging front porch and its steep ancient roof in need of repair will outlast them all.

4

CHICAGO, ILLINOIS
JULY 13, 1966

MYRA LEE

I'T'S THE SECOND WEDNESDAY of July and at 9:00 a.m. it's already 87 degrees and verging on 90 percent humidity. By the time the sluggish Lake Michigan breeze reaches the small, coin-operated laundromat on the corner of 100th Street and South Bensley Avenue, here on the South Side, it offers little, if any, relief. The air feels like some warm gelatinous ointment that's been applied to the skin. The sky looks sickly and green.

Myra Lee Larkin has carted nearly half her body weight in dirty clothes two blocks from her small apartment on South Yates Avenue to the laundromat, where the Negroes work slowly, rhythmically, methodically folding and separating clothes, and wait for their loads to dry with a grave, enduring patience. Some smoke mentholated cigarettes, others thumb through magazines. One woman deals herself a hand of solitaire on a portable TV dinner table. The laundromat's air conditioner has broken down and a large metal fan blows noisily from a corner of the room.

Most of the clothes that Myra digs out of the nylon bag lining her rectangular wire cart belong to Fiona, who moved in with her on Sunday. After a desperate middle-of-the-night collect call, her sister had showed up a couple of days later on the rear wooden fire escape of Myra's apartment building, lugging her bulging, thoroughly scuffed red Samsonite Pullman suitcase—a piece of luggage that Myra had handed down to her a few years ago—and an impossibly bloated black garbage bag full of clothes. When Myra had seen her standing at her back entrance she couldn't believe how skinny and exhausted her sister was. Fiona was wearing skin-tight, peach polyester pants, a knit tank top with a stained rainbow on the front, and a pair of dirty men's tennis shoes that looked three sizes too big. Her hair was an unwashed, haphazard mess, her shoulders were slumped, and the expression on her face said it all: New York City had had its way with her.

Ever since her boyfriend, Sky, had kicked her out of his Soho loft not long after Christmas, Fiona had been living in and around Greenwich Village, making experimental theater with an all-female ensemble who called themselves the Early Westside Widows. The Widows performed exclusively at Caffe Cino, a small storefront arts space on Cornelia Street, in the heart of the West Village. For the past six months, since her breakup, Fiona had been working her way up in the company, maintaining costumes and making coffee for productions with titles like *Why Holiana's Dress Won't Stay On* and *The Madness of Lady Bobcat*. She eventually landed a small part in a short play called *The Walrus and the Lost Queen*, for which she got to puppeteer a pair of giant papier-mâché walrus tusks. There were promises of actual speaking roles after that—new members had to put in their time, after all—but by the end of June Fiona had had enough. She'd been sleeping on whatever couch she would land on and eating exclusively at the theater company's biweekly potlucks, whose offerings invariably consisted of vegetarian chili, cornbread, and some sort of soggy, improvised tossed salad. In the spring, for a little over a month, she'd managed to hold down a job as a clerk at a used bookstore on St. Mark's Place, but she was fired after missing back-to-back shifts because of her theater company duties. Improbably, she'd also suffered another broken heart at the hands of a person named Dido about whose gender Myra is still confused. After receiving that desperate phone call, Myra had wired Fiona enough money to cover a train ticket, a couple of meals, and cab fare. Two days later she arrived in Chicago.

The bursting garbage bag contains mostly costume pieces that

Fiona pillaged from her theater company: flaring bellbottom jeans, men's trousers, an assortment of colorful halter tops and blouses, striped business shirts, pencil skirts, several pairs of overalls, and a large wash-and-dry business suit. Also in the bag are various, cheap, bric-a-brac costume jewelry pieces, which Myra carefully separates onto a towel on top of one of the narrow folding counters. Fiona has assured Myra that she plans to sell the clothes and costume jewelry to a Milwaukee Avenue thrift store that she heard about from the Widows' head costume designer. Fiona has promised Myra that whatever she gets for her spoils will be put toward the rent.

The washing machine in Myra's building has been broken going on three weeks and for the past two Wednesdays she's been forced to use the Jeffrey Manor neighborhood laundromat. Wednesday is her only day off from the hospital. Despite the early hour, she's already cleaned her bathroom and done her food shopping and dropped off a letter to her parents at the post office. The bimonthly letter contained the usual update about life at Saint Francis Hospital, reports of the endless Chicago heatwave, and news of Fiona's arrival. Until the phone call, her sister's whereabouts had been unknown since the ill-fated Christmas Eve in Elmira.

Regarding her sister, Myra kept things simple: *Fiona is alive and well and under my care.* She didn't bother mentioning Fiona's unkempt hair, her thinness, her generally unhealthy disposition, or the mysterious person who broke her heart for a second time, a character even more mysterious than her painter ex-boyfriend, Sky. Those grisly details would only send their mother into an apoplectic rage. Ava Larkin might hire a U.S. marshal to come detain Fiona and drag her back to Elmira.

As Myra is separating lights from darks and placing pieces of the cheap jewelry onto the towel, a tall, thin, gangly man in a yellowing T-shirt and faded blue jeans sidles into the laundromat. At a glance, Myra can see that he has a pale, horsy but oddly handsome face, and like everyone else in the world on this insufferably hot morning, his exposed flesh is covered with a film of sweat. He sports greased-back, long brown hair and wears black cowboy boots. His sleepy eyes seem out of sync with a greedy, full mouth. He doesn't appear to be at all uncomfortable in the mostly Negro laundromat.

He approaches the counter, produces a crumpled dollar from his jeans pocket, and requests change. The attendant hands him four quarters and works the kinks out of the dollar bill while the white man turns and surveys the place, visoring a hand over his eyes as if he's looking out over a vast, sunny meadow. Myra casts her glance back down to her laundry. The two Negro women folding clothes on either side of her seem indifferent to the strange white man, but Myra can't help herself, and as soon as she picks her head up again and they meet eyes, he steps toward her. As he draws closer, he unleashes a mischievous, rubbery smile, working a wad of chewing gum. His long jaw slips this way and that. He somehow finagles his way between Myra and one of the Negro women, who moves her pile of clothes down the counter.

"That's a lotta clothes," he says.

His spearmint gum fails to neutralize the smells of Nicotine and beer and sandwich baloney that are on his breath. His cheeks are marked with faint measles scars, his eyes grayish-blue and as bald as a shark's.

Myra doesn't respond.

"Husband's?" he mumbles, pointing to a pair of overalls. His fingers are long and white. His nails, filthy.

"No," Myra says.

"Boyfriend's?"

"I've combined loads with my sister."

"She as skinny as you are?" he asks.

Despite the crudeness of his question, Myra can feel herself blushing. He has a slow, sloppy way of speaking. None of his words quite get completed; their consonants fall away like corners of a pastry. And his movements are almost comical in their languor. His body seems to be governed by an almost defiant nonchalance. He leans and lists, bending like a cheap plastic comb.

"You could prolly eat a whole plate of pancakes and you wouldn't get no fatter," he says. "What's your name—Julie?"

Myra focuses on her clothes. Surely he will just go away if she folds them with the right kind of intention.

"Mona," he says.

She creates a pile of two folded towels, separates it from the clothes.

"No, no, no, wait," he says, closing his eyes and bringing his fingertips to his forehead, a pose of mock divination. "Margaret."

She shakes her head.

"Dang," he says, "I straight up thought it was Margaret."

"Well, it's not," Myra says.

"But I got the M right, ain't it?"

Myra reaches into the garbage bag and removes three faux-silver bangles, knotted to each other with string, and then a pair of cat-eyed glasses with a beaded retainer. She adds the bangles and a set of toy rings to the pile on the towel.

"Maybe I'll just call you Margaret anyway. Or Maggie. Want summa this, Maggie?" he says, producing a stick of chewing gum wrapped in foil. There is something perverse about offering this individual piece apart from its pack, as if he found it on the sidewalk.

"No, thank you," Myra says, folding another towel.

"What's your sign?" he asks. "I'll bet you're a Virgo."

The Negro woman on Myra's right looks at her. A warning? Maybe she knows something about this man? Does he come into this laundromat often? Does he always get a dollar in change and find his way to the lone white girl?

"You don't gotta answer that," he says. "Why would you?"

Myra finishes with the towel and grabs another.

"You prolly live around here," he continues. "I'll bet you live right down the street."

Despite the heat, a chill passes over Myra's shoulders. The tops of her arms turn to gooseflesh.

After the woman playing solitaire complains loudly, the counter attendant reaches over and changes the fan to a faster setting.

"Thank you, Levon," the woman calls to him.

The dryers behind Myra churn and tumble.

The strange man jingles his quarters in his hand. "So, Maggie," he says.

"What?" she says, doing her best to avoid the dull white of his eyes, almost yellow like the stains on his T-shirt.

"I just like saying your name. Maggie, Maggie, Maggie."

Now the Negro woman on her left also sends Myra a look. She is lighter-skinned, younger than the woman on her right. This warning is sharper. The woman stops folding her clothes. She doesn't blink.

"Come get a drink with me," the man says. "Get outta this god-forsaken heatwave?"

"I'm afraid I have too much to do," Myra says.

"We all have stuff to do. Stuff to do and things to get over and appointments to make. Ain't that right?" he says to the woman on Myra's left, the one who's just sent her the look.

The woman just shakes her head and unfurls a flat white sheet.

"I could change your life," the man says to Myra.

"Is that so?" Myra says.

"Yes, ma'am. You know why?"

"Why?"

"Because I'm a remarkable individual."

"I wasn't aware that my life needed changing," Myra says.

"But every life needs a little excitement now and then. What do you do, anyway?"

"I'm a nurse," she says, and immediately wonders, with genuine perplexity, why on earth she's telling this strange, unnerving man about her life. Maybe it will somehow make him go away? Maybe he'll get bored with how normal she is?

"Of course you're a nurse," he says. "I can just picture you in the little white uniform, with the hat and the shoes. There's a buncha nurses around here. Nurses galore. It's such a wonderful profession. All that care."

Now he's smoking a cigarette. Myra has no idea where it came from or when or how he lit it. He offers her one. She shakes her head.

"What kinda nurse are you?" he asks.

"Pediatrics."

"So you work with old people."

"Children," she says, correcting him.

"Children and their wicked games," he says obliquely. "I know what pediatrics is," he adds. "I was just playin'."

Myra unearths a pair of jeans, shakes them out, begins folding them on the counter.

"As far as I'm concerned children and old people are pretty much part of the same filthy category," he says. "Always crappin' their pants, bellyachin' about this and that."

Myra is about to fold a pair of Fiona's underwear but thinks better of it and stuffs them back into the pile. Instead she begins pairing her white nursing socks.

"You know," he says after exhaling smoke toward the ceiling, "you remind me a lot of my little sister." He leans close to her. She can smell his unwashed hair, the odor coming off his scalp. Like chicken fat left in the pan. "Come on, come get a drink with me," he whispers into her ear. His breath again, barely sweetened by the chewing gum, its foulness festering underneath.

Just as his nose grazes Myra's cheek, a young, shirtless Negro boy runs into the laundromat and starts shouting at full volume. "They got Truvoy!" he cries. With his arrival comes the sound of thunder, rich, seemingly right overhead.

The woman to Myra's right—the older, darker-skinned woman—stops folding clothes and squares her body to the boy. "Where?" she shouts.

"They cuffed him over by the liberry and put him in a paddy wagon!"

"What'd he do?" the woman asks.

"He didn't do nothin'!" the boy cries. "We was just walkin' along."

The woman, though heavyset, runs out of the laundromat with surprising speed, leaving nearly two loads of unfolded clothes on the countertop. The other patrons follow her out with their eyes, then return to their games and paperbacks and makeshift fans.

"This heat is makin' everybody crazy," the man says.

"I suppose it is," Myra says.

"Specially the niggers," he whispers.

The ease with which he uses this word in a South Side laundromat shocks Myra. She digs out a pair of wrinkled polyester men's slacks, starts to fold them even though they haven't been washed yet. The gooseflesh on her arms is starting to migrate toward the small of her back. She feels clumsy and dumb.

"Shit-cago's startin' to feel like Dallas," he offers. "You ever been to Dallas?"

"No," Myra says.

After the men's slacks she absentmindedly grabs a pair of boy's pajama bottoms off the Negro woman's pile and begins folding them. They are light blue and patterned with baseballs.

"Dallas heat hangs on you," he says. "You wear it around like some old suit jacket you can't never take off. Gets that way as early as June and doesn't let up till the middle of September. But it keeps you skinny."

And then the sound of rain comes, and through the storefront window Myra can see sheets of it slanting down, almost biblical in its volume.

"Rain, rain, go away," the man says. "At least it'll get some of the filth off the streets."

Myra notices a tattoo on the top of his right forearm: BORN TO RAISE HELL. He catches her looking at it and squeezes his fist, making the tendons jump. The tattoo dances a bit. Myra looks away.

"So how 'bout that drink?" he says, taking another drag on his cigarette.

"I don't drink," Myra says.

"Not even a Shirley fuckin' Temple?"

"No, thank you."

"Or a Coca-Cola with a goddamn cherry?"

"No, thank you," she repeats.

"Suit yourself," the man says. "Can't say I didn't try."

Myra can feel him drawing even closer to her. He presses up

against her hip. He's all bones and cartilage. No fat, very little muscle. Lean like a yard tool.

"You should be flattered," he says quietly. "But you know what you can do with your flattery?"

She can feel his erection now, boring into her side, just under her ribs.

"You can go fuck yourself in the cunt with it. You ain't no better than me."

Myra pushes him away and turns his direction, preparing to say that she never said she was better than him or anyone else for that matter, but before she can get the words out he flicks his cigarette at her. The filtered end bounces off her throat and the cigarette lands on the floor. A speck of its burning ember stings her forearm and she brushes it away without breaking eye contact with the man. If she looks away he will do something worse, she is sure of it.

He holds his stare, his pale eyes bearing only a pinprick of pupil, like the eyes of some preternatural half-raptor, and then, finally, he blinks, breaking the spell, and begins backing away in long, surprisingly swift strides. His grin is grotesque and promiscuous, as if he's smiling through a mouthful of half-melted chocolates. Just before he reaches the entrance he pulls a stack of clothes off a folding counter, sending them tumbling to the floor. And then he's off in a jaunt, striding across the storefront and disappearing into the deluge pummeling South Bensley Avenue.

The girl who'd been folding the stack of clothes the man toppled — a thin pregnant Negro with her hair arranged in a colorful scarf — simply looks down at the pile and shakes her head, her hands on her hips. The counter attendant jogs to her aid. The woman playing solitaire pushes her portable TV dinner tray aside, stands in a multi-part move, hikes up her shorts, and also helps.

Myra steps on the man's still-burning cigarette, snuffing it out. "Should we call the police?" she asks the woman to her left.

"What are they gonna do?" she replies.

Myra returns to folding the abandoned laundry belonging to

the heavyset Negro woman who ran out after Truvoy. She separates everything carefully: T-shirts, underwear, bras, socks, trousers.

In less than a minute business returns to normal. Someone has turned on the radio. The broadcast can be heard cutting through the noise of the fan. The White Sox, having just returned from losing five straight to the Red Sox in Boston, including two double-headers, will host the Cleveland Indians starting tomorrow. The reeling Cubs, who are also off, will begin an away series with the Pittsburgh Pirates tomorrow.

The woman with the TV dinner tray sits again, gathers her scattered cards, and deals herself another hand of solitaire.

WHEN MYRA GETS HOME, drenched from the downpour, Fiona is still asleep on her calico pullout sofa. Of course she slept through the storm. She could always sleep through anything. A cheap, plastic oscillating fan blows over her body. Her sister sleeps only in her underwear, with no bra, on top of one of their mother's patchwork quilts.. In the Larkin Family, if Ava gives you one of her quilts it's a sure sign that you've made it in the world. Myra has one and so does Lexy, who received hers the previous fall when she left for Vassar.

Fiona's breasts, Myra notes with a little jealousy, are like a pair of perfectly sculpted melons, round and full, their nipples prominent, pale. She has let her armpit hair grow, though there are only two wisps, faint as tea stains. Her sister really has turned into a full-fledged bohemian. A beatnik. Even though she has stopped taking care of herself Fiona is still far prettier than most, Myra thinks, as she dries her arms with a dish towel. She then pulls the clean clothes out of her wire cart and begins stacking them on the kitchen table. If her sister would only get herself a decent haircut and shave those armpits and stop dressing as if she's some itinerant circus performer. Her auburn eyelashes are thick, absurdly lustrous. She sleeps like an epileptic after a fit, her breath tainting the room despite the fan.

Myra goes to the refrigerator, pours herself a glass of lukewarm orange juice. Even household appliances are struggling amid this heatwave.

"You already did the laundry?" Fiona calls from the sofa, her voice dreamy, dehydrated.

"I did," Myra says.

"Isn't it supposed to be your day off?"

"It is," Myra says. "Every Wednesday."

"You're like a machine."

"I figured it wouldn't be too crowded. Who would want to wait for their clothes to tumble dry in this heat? The storm's barely cooled things off."

"It stormed?" Fiona says, oblivious.

"It's raining cats and dogs out there," Myra says.

Fiona sits up without bothering to cover herself. She claws at her collarbone with one hand, rubs her eyes with the other. "You sure you don't have a cat?" she asks, claiming she's allergic, even though she spent most of her youth around the various Larkin cats.

"Pets aren't allowed in the building," Myra says. "It's probably the wool sofa. If you put that top sheet over the back of it like I said, you wouldn't even feel it. You should take a shower," Myra says.

"You can smell me from the goddamn kitchen?"

"It'll make you feel better," Myra says.

Myra suddenly realizes she's brought the Negro woman's laundry home with her.

"The Moroccans drink hot tea in this weather," Fiona says.

Her voice is low and mannish. She takes pleasure in the sound of her speaking voice, Myra thinks, as if every syllable is part of a meal in which she luxuriates. She is plagued by the narcissism of the actress. In the few days they've spent together, Myra has noticed how Fiona constantly finds her likeness in every mirror, in any reflective surface at all. Last night at dinner she even caught Fiona staring into her soup spoon. It's odd that she can be simultaneously so self-obsessed and hygienically lazy.

"It's supposed to lower your body temperature," Fiona adds about the Moroccan's hot-tea theory. "Did you know goats live in the trees in Morocco? Apparently they literally stand in them like they're waiting for their picture to be taken."

"Why do you know so much about Morocco?"

"Dido lived there for a year. She survived this major earthquake in Agadir that killed fifteen thousand people."

Dido again. Is she French? Myra wonders. Greek? The name alone sounds more like a concept than a person. Like a silly dance performed under a broomstick. Myra is starting to imagine some sort of African chieftess in handmade sandals. Impossibly dark and tall. Thin as a birch tree. "I thought you didn't want to talk about Dido," she says.

"You're right," Fiona says. "That's the last time I'll mention her name, I promise."

"But it *is* a her," Myra says.

"You're worried I'm a lesbian."

"Do I seem worried?"

"You're always worried," Fiona says. "But when you're *really* worried that little seam appears between your eyebrows. It runs in the family."

"We get it from Dad," Myra says. "You don't have it yet."

"Trust me, I have it in other places," Fiona says.

Myra separates the folded towels and sets them on the counter. "So you're bisexual," she says after a lull.

"Must we use labels? He's a can of corn. She's a can of green beans."

"How many women have you slept with?" Myra asks.

"Many."

"And men?"

"Probably not as many. Or maybe more. But recently I find men less appealing. Please don't tell Mom. She'll make another patchwork quilt. That woman transforms her Catholic angst into some of the finest quilts in America."

"And Dad smokes his pipe." Myra opens the refrigerator and removes a green University of Chicago T-shirt, which she keeps chilled for hot days. She tosses it to Fiona, who catches it. "It'll cool you off," Myra offers.

"No one in New York had air-conditioning, either," Fiona says. "To cool off we'd go hang out at the Woolworths in Times Square."

Fiona's pallor is striking. She is ghost-like. Even from the living room her pale green eyes have a feral intensity. Surviving in New York has obviously sharpened their gaze.

The rain slows a bit, but continues rolling down the kitchen window.

"Come help me put these away," Myra says, pointing to the piles of clean laundry she's stacked on the kitchen table.

Fiona nods and feeds her arms into the refrigerated University of Chicago T-shirt. When she walks over she does so on her toes. Her sister has always moved in this feline manner. Faint tufts of pubic hair creep out the sides of her underwear. Myra and Alec got the dark hair and Myra has always been a little jealous of Fiona and Lexy, and even Joan, whose brown hair always turns honey-blond in the summer.

On the wall above the kitchen table hangs a small wooden crucifix. Christ's eyes are closed, the look on his face one of pained benevolence.

"Still going to church?" Fiona asks, gesturing toward the crucifix.

"Not as often as I should," Myra says. "I work Sundays so it makes it tough."

"Myra Lee Larkin, the lapsed Catholic."

"I haven't lapsed," she says.

"She's just taking a pause, folks. An ellipsis of faith...I haven't been to church since I left Elmira."

Which was four years ago, thinks Myra, who received an early-morning phone call from her incensed mother that day. It was just after 6:00 a.m. Chicago time. Fiona had left in the middle of the night. There was a note on the refrigerator:

Mom and Dad,
I had to leave.
Love,
Fiona

"Nine words!" her mother cried into the phone to Myra. "That's all she had for us? Nine words?!"

After high school, and Fiona's short-lived stint in college, their mother had tasked her with looking after Joan, who'd been growing more and more erratic and dependent on supervision. Although Fiona had gotten decent grades in high school and posted surprisingly strong test scores, she agreed to attend the College of Saint Rose, in Albany, which was their mother's first choice because of its strong Roman Catholic background. Fiona was more interested in going to Wesleyan, in Middletown, Connecticut, but it was far too progressive for their mother. At the College of Saint Rose, Fiona dropped out after just a semester. While it was true that she'd contracted mononucleosis, it was also clear that she had no real interest in higher education. Her brief time in Albany was beset by too many late nights and a poor attendance record. She'd always dreamed of being an actress, a secret that only Myra knew. Their mother has always considered the arts to be a frivolous waste of time. She wanted her children to be teachers or social workers or healthcare professionals. She is proud of Myra's nursing career. Fiona, however, was someone who would sneak-read Shakespeare and Chekhov and even Arthur Miller. She would hide the published playscripts under her mattress so their mother wouldn't find them. Since she didn't have a job, caring for Joan became Fiona's contribution to the household, her way of earning her keep. Eventually the arrangement became unbearable, and how could it not? Helping a teenage girl to the toilet, putting her to bed, helping her tie her shoes, cutting her food for her like a child, the constant marshaling away from electric outlets and wasps' nests, guiding her along the safest path all day long like some oversized low-flying helium balloon. It would drive anyone crazy, especially a young woman who'd just graduated high school and thought she had her whole life ahead of her.

"Maybe later you can go try and sell some of those," Myra says, pointing to her sister's pile of costumes. "I used fabric softener, so it should all smell nice."

Fiona puts a pair of overalls to her nose. "Like a spring meadow," she says, and begins inspecting and refolding the clothes. "Do you ever talk to Alec?" she asks.

"I spoke to him a few weeks ago," Myra says. "He's still in Kansas. Some town south of Wichita."

"He needed money?" Fiona asks, without even a shred of self-awareness.

Myra lets it pass. "No, he just wanted to talk," she says.

"When I was still at home he would hit up Mom and Dad at least once a week."

"He always ends up crying into the phone," Myra says. "He had a job working on a loading dock at some furniture store but got himself fired."

"What'd he steal this time?"

"A leather armchair. He said they told him he could have it— that they set him up."

"Once a thief always a thief," Fiona says.

"I told him he could come stay here if he needed a place."

"You sure you want to do that?"

"He's our only brother, Fiona."

"After you went off to nursing school, do you know how many times he stole from me?"

"I'm taking you in, aren't I?"

"But I'm not a thief. I'm just desperate."

"You stole these clothes," Myra says.

"They owed me."

"The pot calling the kettle."

"Alec will steal the hinges off your fucking doors if you let him stay here."

"New York's made you cynical."

Fiona opens the fridge, simply stands in front of it.

"Don't do that too much," Myra says. "It ends up being a cheap thrill. You feel worse afterwards."

"You'd think the rain would at least cool things off a little."

Fiona continues standing there. Myra can't stop looking at her, this character she's become. A transient. A half-naked bohemian. The refrigerator light silvers her sweaty flesh. She seems lost within herself. How does a girl suddenly become remote in her own life? Myra wonders. Fiona is like a damp fallen leaf clinging to a window. How is it possible that someone as pretty and interesting as her sister fades into the background of every room she finds herself in? And an aspiring actress, no less? It must be terrible for her to have to eavesdrop on every encounter because she's no longer the focal point.

Fiona shuts the refrigerator door and returns to her pile of clothes. "You're gonna wind up taking us all in," she says, refolding a pair of white carpenter's overalls. "Alec, me, eventually Lexy. You'll have to buy another pullout sofa."

"I have a feeling Lexy's going to be just fine on her own," Myra says. "You were awful to her at Christmas, by the way."

"I just wanted to see what she was made of. What that froofy fucking school was doing to her."

"Here," Myra says, proffering a pair of cutoff shorts, "put these on."

Fiona legs into them and stares down at her thighs. "I'm getting fat."

"I was going to say just the opposite."

Fiona looks at the backs of her calves. "I need to shave," she says.

"I was going to suggest that," Myra says. "There's an extra razor in the medicine chest." Myra unknots the towel containing the costume jewelry, starts arranging the items in rows.

"What about Mom and Dad?" Fiona asks. "Are they okay?"

"They're as good as can be expected. Dad's been having a hard time. The diabetes, his hands. He hates taking the arthritis medication because it upsets his stomach."

"Poor, quiet Donald."

"They worry about you," Myra says.

Fiona stops refolding her stolen clothes and sits in one of the two mismatched chairs. It's gotten even hotter and the fan seems to be making it worse rather than better. Myra sits as well. She can feel the humidity sticking to her skin. Discs of sweat grab at the cotton fabric of her blouse.

"You should give them a call," Myra says. "Or write to them."

"Dear Mom and Dad, it's Fiona—remember me? Don't worry, I'm fine. I don't have syphilis and I'm not necessarily a lesbian."

"Just let them know you're alive and breathing."

This remark, Myra can tell, unlocks something in Fiona, who unexpectedly and offhandedly begins telling her how she'd been flirting with the idea of killing herself. She'd been carrying around a prescription bottle of Quaaludes. She'd even considered the idea of asphyxiating herself with a plastic bag over her head and "floating" to death in a warm bath. Apparently the warm body-temperature water can trick the brain into thinking it's in a safe, womb-like space, so you never go into shock and you pass out before you drown. It's like going to sleep and drifting away, Fiona says, talking about suicide like she's considering having a picnic lunch in the park.

It's all so morbid, Myra thinks. So terribly narcissistic and morbid.

"If you hadn't accepted my collect call I'm not sure I'd be here," Fiona adds.

Myra considers the loss of her oldest sister, the notion of Fiona being in the world one moment—sitting on a dirty mattress on the floor in some impossibly small room in New York City, chipped paint on the wall, a wilted plant on the windowsill, traffic roaring across the avenue below—and then her sudden absence. The story of Fiona Larkin consumed so quickly, absorbed by the earth's invisible gases. Myra feels a pang in her kidneys, a twinge of regret. If she were to lose Fiona this feeling could be endless. She leans over and hugs her sister, who allows it, going slack in her arms.

"You do still want to be here, though, right?" Myra says.

"I think I do," Fiona says. "For now, at least."

Myra squares Fiona's shoulders, then nudges her chin up with a soft fist. Fiona instinctively sits up straighter. This is something their mother used to do when she would catch her children slouching at the dinner table.

"This person whose name we're no longer mentioning must've really done a number on you," Myra says.

Fiona doesn't respond. The wound must be deep.

"And where are those pills now?" Myra asks.

"I flushed them down the toilet."

"When?"

"Before I boarded my train," she says. "At Grand Central Station."

Myra takes her sister's hand, squeezes it, then rises to make them tomato and cream cheese sandwiches.

AN HOUR LATER THE rain finally ceases. On the way back from returning books to the library, Myra passes by the second-floor laundry room, where a young man is trying to make sense of the washing machine. He is clutching two large handfuls of clothes and staring at the coin slot, confused.

"It's broken," Myra offers from the hallway.

The man turns to her, his fists filled with socks, T-shirts, under-wear, a green washcloth.

"There's a laundromat two blocks away," she adds. "I just did a few loads earlier this morning. There's no air-conditioning but if you can stand the heat it's a decent alternative."

The man thanks her. He has light brown hair, not quite blond, parted on the side, almost a military cut, and a clean-shaven face.

"And you shouldn't mix that washcloth in with those whites," Myra adds. "It'll turn them all green."

He places the clothes in a plastic laundry basket on top of the dryer. "I didn't even realize that was in there," he says of the washcloth.

"I do it all the time," Myra says.

He wears a T-shirt with UNITED STATES MILITARY ACADEMY embossed on the front, matching shorts, and clean white sneakers. He has big gray eyes, not unlike her father's.

"Are you new in the building?" Myra asks, still hovering at the threshold of the laundry room.

"Moved in yesterday," he says. He's just driven down from northern Wisconsin this past weekend, he tells her. He's running out of clothes and thought maybe he could get a load done, but apparently it's not in the cards today.

The man grabs his laundry basket and joins Myra in the hallway. Up close he's taller than she expected, around six feet, broad in the shoulders. He smells faintly of sweat and suntan lotion, like he's spent the day at the beach.

"West Point," she says, pointing to his T-shirt.

"It's my laundry day shirt," he explains.

"I'm originally from Elmira, New York," Myra offers. "We used to drive past West Point on our way to visit my aunt in Connecticut."

"No kidding," he says.

"I live upstairs, on the third floor," she says.

He tells her that he lives at the end of the hall and Myra walks with him toward his door. He is slightly bow-legged and walks with a purpose. Although he's coming from Wisconsin, he says, he's originally from Chicago, and grew up on the North Side, in Rogers Park.

"So you're back home," Myra offers.

"Sort of," he says. This fall he plans to give it another shot at school. Illinois Teachers College.

"Good for you," Myra says.

They arrive in front of his apartment and he sets the laundry basket down and produces a key from the front pocket of his shorts. His movements are swift, graceful. Myra thinks he might be a tennis player. He keys into the lock and opens the door.

Myra feels a sudden burst of adrenaline surge in her wrists. "I'm Myra," she says. "Myra Larkin. Three-F."

"Denny," he says. "Denny Happ."

"Nice to meet you, Denny."

"You, too," he says.

Through his open doorway Myra can see that, aside from a small dinette table, a pair of matching chairs, and a few boxes on the floor, his apartment is pretty empty. Nothing on the walls. Not even a sofa. Spartan to say the least. Myra knows she should continue toward the stairwell but she's not ready to leave.

"I'd invite you in," Denny says, "but there's not much of a breeze. I think they accidentally painted the windows shut. I left a note with the super but I haven't heard back from him yet."

"Do you have a fan?"

"They were all sold out at the Woolworths," he says.

Myra feels another rush of adrenaline. "Would you like to have dinner with me later?" she hears herself say. The words gush forth like something she wasn't supposed to swallow and must spit back out. She's never been this forward with a man. "It would be me and my sister," she continues. "I was going to make lemon chicken with rice."

"Oh," he says, clearly surprised by the invitation.

"Lemon chicken," she repeats. "Rice, probably some sort of vegetable. Do you have any allergies?"

"I'm allergic to cauliflower," he says.

"What happens if you eat cauliflower?"

"I get gout," he says. "In my ankle. Cauliflower, lobster, sea scallops. I'd feel silly imposing on you and your sister."

"You wouldn't be imposing at all. We'd welcome the company. It's probably not much cooler than your apartment but at least I can open the windows. And we have a fan."

"I wish I had something to offer," he says.

"Just bring yourself. Seven thirty. First apartment off the third-floor stairwell."

Denny thanks her and picks up his basket of laundry and goes into the apartment. The door closes behind him, practically in Myra's face. It's a blunt farewell, awkward to say the least, but she's thrilled nonetheless, and heads upstairs.

Myra spends the next hour cleaning the kitchen, scouring the bathroom, and helping Fiona organize her things in the living room. Cooking the meal makes everything even hotter so Myra sets up the fan in the kitchen. The heavy air moves through the apartment like wavering, invisible blankets. Despite the heavy rainstorm it's still hot. Barefoot, Myra can feel the heat rising up through the floorboards, penetrating the arches of her feet.

She can't even remember the last time she cooked for a man.

AROUND SIX O'CLOCK, FIONA finally showers. She towels off in the living room while Myra is pulling the chicken out of the oven. Fiona's body is perfect, Myra thinks, watching her from the kitchen. As she dries her hair, Fiona hums to herself. Myra notices that she has shaved her armpits.

Once all the food is prepared Myra showers herself and fixes her hair with barrettes. She wears a cream blouse, blue cotton pants, and a gold necklace with a simple cross.

"Don't wear that," Fiona says, pointing to the necklace. He'll think you're Catholic."

"I am Catholic," Myra says, "and so are you."

"He'll think you're a virgin."

Myra doesn't respond, starts setting the table.

"Are you still a fucking virgin?" Fiona asks.

"No," Myra protests. When she lies she always feels like one of her incisors is going loose.

During her final year of nursing school there was one man — a boy, really. He was an undergraduate math major named Paul Griparis. He had a handsome face but was still built like a teenager, all long, smooth, soft limbs. He was virtually hairless, not yet fully formed, like he was made of melon. He would joke to Myra about it, calling himself the "Latest Bloomer in North America." They dated for not quite a month. Their relationship — if you could call it that — consisted mostly of post-library meals and walks along Navy Pier. They even screwed around a few times in Paul's dorm room, but when it came to sex, Myra was put off by his small, spindly hands and an unfortunate body odor that reminded her of her mother's liverwurst and mustard sandwiches.

She'd only touched him on the outside of his pants once and it did thrill her. His surprisingly large erection pulsed through his trousers and into her hand, and as long as she held her hand there, gripping this manifestation of his desire the way one might a roll of coins or a can of lima beans, she could feel herself taking pleasure in her sudden power over him. She felt like she could lead him around campus this way, as if he were an animal who'd misbehaved. At one point he chirped like a dolphin. Myra had hoped for a groan from the lower register. The above-average handsome math major from right there in Melrose Park seemed suddenly drunk and stupid and obsequious and Myra felt herself falling into this transaction, wondering if he would reciprocate in some way. Part of her wanted to go further, she really did; something inside her started to give way to the act. She even imagined putting her mouth on him, on the erection hidden in his pants, but she simply couldn't figure out how to take the necessary steps. She couldn't instruct herself as how to free him from his various layers—the belt and the trousers and then his underwear for Godsakes—and he ruined even the possibility of it by continuing to make those awful dolphin noises.

A few days after another abortive attempt at sex, in a surprising move, Paul Griparis wound up breaking up with Myra, calling her frigid. "You're too pretty to be frigid," he told her outside the library where they'd spent so many hours together.

Myra actually apologized and wished him luck—yes, luck, as if he were about to set forth on an epic snowshoeing expedition.

DENNY HAPP ARRIVES AT 7:30 sharp wearing linen navy trousers, a white button-down shirt with the sleeves rolled up to his elbows, and tennis shoes with no socks. He carries a small paper grocery sack, from which he removes three oranges. "I stopped by the market," he says. "I got grapes, too, if you'd prefer those. They're downstairs."

"Oranges are perfect," Myra says, taking them from him and placing them in a small enamel colander on the counter.

"Your place is so nice," Denny says.

She tells him that it's taken her the better part of six years to make it feel like home; before that, she'd lived in the small town-house around the corner, on East 100th Street, with several other nursing students, but once she graduated she had to leave. Her friend Gloria, she says, is still living in the nurses' townhouse. Gloria, twenty-two, is six years younger than Myra. They met last year at an Illinois Nurses Association event and became fast friends. She tells Denny how they'll often spend their days off at Lake Michigan, picnicking on the beach. "We're planning on going to the Indiana Sand Dunes this weekend," she adds. "I managed to get this Saturday free."

"I'll bet it's nice to have a friend so close by," Denny says.

Myra is so excited that she's forgotten to offer him anything to drink. She's already uncorked one of two bottles of chardonnay. The other one, owing to the underperforming refrigerator, is on ice in the bathtub. Before she can mention the wine, Fiona enters the kitchen wearing a baby-blue halter top and white majorette shorts, which make her legs look long and coltish. Myra introduces them. When Denny takes her hand Fiona ever so slightly arches her back and rises on her toes as if she's performing in some nineteenth-century drawing room drama.

Urged by Fiona, Myra replaced her gold crucifix with a necklace of colorful glass beads. She suddenly feels silly wearing the stolen costume jewelry. She starts to stuff the beads under the neck of her blouse but Fiona grabs her wrist.

"Leave it and pour some wine," she tells Myra.

They all sit at Myra's round kitchen table and over the first glass of chardonnay they talk about Fiona's recent arrival from New York City.

"How do you like it so far?" Denny asks her.

"It's hot," Fiona says. "Not that New York isn't. Chicago's cleaner than I expected. You definitely have that going for you."

Denny tells them that even though he spent nearly a year and a half at West Point—a mere fifty miles north of New York City—he never visited. For holiday leaves he would take the train from Peekskill to Grand Central Station and then another overnight express to Chicago but the stop in New York was only to change trains; he never actually ventured into the Big Apple.

"How did you like West Point?" Myra asks. She imagines him wearing the gray-blue uniform. In high school she used to see pictures of cadets in the Elmira newspaper when they would cover the Army-Navy football game. They all looked so clean-cut, so American, so full of pride and promise.

"I was only enrolled there for three terms," Denny says. "Not quite three terms, actually."

"Why didn't you finish?" Fiona asks.

"I got injured about six weeks into my Yuck year." Off Fiona's confused expression he adds, "Yuck means sophomore. Yuck or Yearling. First year you're a Plebe, then a Yuck, then a Cow, then a Firstie. Don't ask me how they came up with all of that."

"Sounds like a game children play," Fiona says. "I see a bunch of blindfolded four-year-olds in the middle of a pasture holding beanbags and ping-pong balls."

"You're not that far off," Denny says. "Maybe add a Springfield rifle and a few sabers."

"What kind of injury did you sustain?" Myra asks.

Denny explains that he was on the track-and-field team and messed up his knee in the triple jump, tearing his meniscus. "After surgery," he says, "they put me on crutches and I had to join the walking wounded. That's a detail of cadets who can't march or participate in drill. It's the last thing you want to happen to you at West Point, especially as an underclassman. Things went downhill pretty quickly after that."

"You dropped out?" Fiona presses.

"I was discharged," Denny says matter-of-factly. "That's the official term for it."

Myra senses something underneath his composed report. Is it disappointment? Grief? Bitterness? She shoots a look at Fiona and shakes her head sharply, once, a blunt exhortation to cease this line of questioning. Fiona smiles demurely and drinks her wine.

"Mickey Mantle also had bad knees," Myra says. She exits to

the living room and returns with a baseball card secured in Lucite, which she hands to Denny. "That's his rookie card. My father gave me that for my sixteenth birthday," she says. "Mantle is his favorite player." She doesn't tell Denny about her brief brush with him when she was a young girl; how she met him at the diner in Elmira and how he drove her home in the rain; how he gave her his picture.

"He's a great player," Denny says, and passes back the collector card.

Myra returns it to the living room, then comes back to the kitchen table and begins serving the lemon chicken and rice.

"What were you doing in New York?" Denny asks Fiona.

"She was acting," Myra says.

"Actually I *wasn't* acting," Fiona says. "I was mostly mending costumes and handing out mimeographed programs at the front of house. I was *supposed* to be acting."

"She was involved with an experimental theater company," Myra explains. "And she was starting to perform in their shows."

"If you count playing a pair of walrus tusks."

"But bigger roles were coming," Myra says. "Please help yourself," she urges Denny, pointing to the asparagus.

Denny serves himself as Fiona tops off his wine, then hers, then Myra's. Fiona playfully nods toward Myra's wine glass, encouraging her to drink. Myra takes a modest mouthful, swallows. She's never been much of a drinker and she can already feel it going to her head.

Fiona pushes away from the table, pads in bare feet over to Myra's phonograph, and puts a record on. Moments later, Simon & Garfunkel's "The Sound of Silence" plays.

Hello darkness, my old friend...

"Music to eat to," Fiona says, returning to the table. "It was either Simon and Garfunkel or that god-awful John Denver."

"Hey, I like John Denver," Denny says.

"Yikes," Fiona says, cutting into a piece of chicken.

"What's wrong with John Denver?" Myra asks.

"Nothing if you like sexless boobs."

"I don't think he's sexless," Myra says.

"That box of Quaker Oats over there has more sex appeal than John Denver," Fiona says. And then to Denny: "Isn't he sexless?"

"I wouldn't be the one to ask."

"Practically all of his songs are about women," Myra says.

"That's true," Denny says. "There's that song 'Ann.' And 'Darcy Farrow.'"

"And what about 'Blues My Naughty Sweetie Gives to Me'?" Myra adds. "If that song doesn't have sex appeal I don't know what does."

Fiona shakes her head. "If you pulled his pants down you'd probably find a weird light switch or some such thing."

Myra laughs, and Denny follows. His smile is bright and brings out his cheekbones, as well as a pair of surprising dimples.

"A light switch," Fiona says, in love with her own humor, "or what do you call those things on a radio?"

"An antenna?" Myra says.

"A dial," Denny says, still laughing.

"A goddamn dick dial!" Fiona cries.

They all laugh for a solid minute. Myra has the sensation that her face is expanding. Her teeth feel huge.

During "Leaves That Are Green" Myra realizes that she's eaten nearly half her plate. She needs to slow down. She breathes, takes another gulp of wine.

"What singers do you like?" Denny asks Fiona, who is holding a stalk of asparagus between her fingers as if she might use it to conduct a children's choir.

"I like the Association," Fiona says, biting into the asparagus, chewing. "The Rolling Stones. The Kinks. Dirty rock-and-roll. And you?" she asks, swallowing. "Beyond the sexless genius of John Denver, of course."

"I like lots of stuff," Denny says. "The Beatles, the Beach Boys, the Byrds."

"Just to name the Bs," Fiona says with a smirk. "But who's *weird* that you like? I want *weird*."

"The Beach Boys are pretty weird," Denny says.

"I think they're weird, too," Myra says. "All those spooky harmonies."

"But the Beach Boys sound exactly how you *expect* them to sound," Fiona says, grabbing another stalk of asparagus with her fingers. "What about someone like Crispian St. Peters? He *looks* normal with the haircut and all, but he's *weird*. And he *sings* weird."

"My sister likes it when you can't judge a book by its cover," Myra says.

"Oh, you're a weirdo, too," Fiona retorts, chewing, swallowing, gulping wine in a flurry of effortless movements.

Her thin pale hands are beautiful, Myra thinks, even with their bitten-down nails. Fiona got the hands of a pianist, whereas her own hands are knobby and mannish, like the hands of a plumber.

"She's just more organized than all the other weirdos," Fiona continues to Denny. "This chicken is really good, by the way. Might even be better than Mom's."

"That's rare high praise," Myra says to Denny.

"The chicken really is very good," Denny agrees, holding up a forkful. "The sauce is delicious."

During a lull in the conversation "Blessed" plays. Myra can feel herself bobbing to the rollicking drums. She takes pleasure in watching Denny eat. He is well-mannered, dutiful with his napkin. He cuts his chicken with his knife and then sets it down and passes his fork from his left to right hand before skewering it and delivering it evenly to his mouth. His movements are agile, noiseless. He never scrapes his plate or bangs his utensils on the table. They obviously taught him well at West Point. As he chews with his mouth closed his jaw pulses and his nostrils flare just a bit. His face thrills Myra. She wants to nudge her chair closer to his, to refold his napkin or serve him another helping of chicken, but she knows this would be too forward. Instead she swallows another mouthful of wine.

Fiona says something about how "Blessed" is an anti-faith song, how "god" with a small *g* is the same as "man" with a small *m*, how in her opinion Jesus was nothing more than the equivalent of a really talented electric guitarist with salon-fresh hair. Like a white Jimi Hendrix, if he actually *was* white, he meaning Jesus, who was probably a lot darker-skinned than they'd have us believe. "It's a song for all the fallen Catholics," she adds.

During the warbling guitar intro to "Kathy's Song" Myra imagines walking with Denny hand in hand down Michigan Avenue. Ontario Street…Ohio Street…Grand Avenue. She pictures them stopping along the storefronts and picking out things they might buy. Clothes for the colder seasons. Matching wool coats to help them survive the Chicago winter; scarves to guard them against the brutal Lake Michigan winds. Paul Simon's voice carries so much promise.

"Would you like more chicken?" Myra asks Denny, and before he can answer, she serves him the remaining breast, smothering it with rice and sauce.

"I hear it's expensive to live in New York City," Denny says to Fiona.

"You're telling me," Fiona says. "Most of the girls in the theater company were living on Mommy and Daddy's dime."

And here you are living off me, Myra thinks. You little freeloader. You charmer. But she pushes the thoughts from her head.

"They just raised the subway fare from fifteen to twenty cents," Fiona continues. "Twenty cents to ride the fucking subway."

"Hey," Myra says.

"Hey, what?" Fiona says.

"Language."

"Language, my ass. I'm twenty-six years old." Fiona takes a drink of wine, which spills onto her chin. She wipes it away and, without the least bit of self-consciousness, sucks it off her fingers. Her manners have gotten even worse than they were at Christmas. "All I'm saying is New York's too expensive for regular people," she adds.

"Maybe you're not regular," Myra says.

"Oh, I'm regular. Apparently I'm as regular as a bowl of corn-flakes. That's why I couldn't get any of the good roles."

"She's a beautiful girl," Myra tells Denny. "I keep telling her all she has to do is get a decent haircut."

"And meet a man from Des Moines and get married and have babies and get our initials stenciled on the garage door? Fun."

"Is it just the two of you?" Denny asks.

"We have two other sisters and a brother," Myra says.

"Myra, Fiona, Alec, Joan, and Lexy." Fiona fires off the names as though spitting watermelon seeds into a jar. "There was also Archie but he died when he was a baby."

"Rheumatic fever," Myra adds. "He was only two months old."

"Sorry to hear that," Denny says.

"Are you from a large family?" Fiona asks.

"I have two half-siblings. A brother and a sister. They're both much older. They live in Skokie."

"So you were alone a lot," Fiona says.

"You could say that."

"I'm a big fan of the lone wolf," Fiona says.

During another silence, Denny seems to contract within himself. Myra fears he is losing interest. Of what she thinks of as the three normal Larkin sisters, she's always considered herself the ugly one. There's Lexy with her height and her blond hair and blue eyes and perfect skin, and Fiona with her striking green eyes and red hair and provocative personality. Myra sees herself as so plain, with her brown hair and unremarkable face, her hazel eyes always hidden behind her glasses, her average figure, her large hands.

The phonograph needle crackles in the dead wax of the record, and Myra realizes that the first side of *Sounds of Silence* has ended. She excuses herself to the living room to flip the record. She hears her sister ask Denny how long he's lived in the building.

"Just a few days," he replies.

"He lives on the second floor," Myra says from the living room, setting the needle on the side B lead-in.

"Down the hall from the laundry room," Denny adds.

"He's getting his degree from Illinois Teachers College," Myra says as she returns to the table, happy to dispense this knowledge Fiona doesn't possess.

"I start in the fall."

"Where'd you go to high school?" Myra asks.

"Senn," he says. "Here in Chicago."

"That's up on the North Side," Myra says. "Sometimes I pass it on my way to work."

Denny asks Myra where she works and she tells him she's a pediatrics nurse at Saint Francis Hospital in Evanston.

"A pediatrics nurse," he says, "I'm impressed."

"Anyone ever tell you that you look like Robert Redford?" Fiona says. She's siting higher on her chair now, directly facing Denny, her legs tucked under her. "You could be his brother," she adds.

"I'm afraid I don't know who Robert Redford is," Denny replies.

Fiona's pupils are wondrous and rabbit-like, dwarfing their green irises. My sister, the beautiful unkempt bunny, Myra thinks. Is she drunk? Or has her shift away from lethargy this evening been inspired by the simple fact that she has an audience? Only an hour ago she was shuffling around the apartment half-naked, drifty and hopeless, flaunting her unshaved armpits.

"He stars in that film *Inside Daisy Clover*," Fiona tells Denny.

"He's very handsome," Myra adds, which causes Denny to smile, revealing those dimples again. But the smile is quickly over-taken by surprising color in his cheeks; the flattery is making him uncomfortable.

"You really could be his brother," Fiona insists.

Ironically, during "A Most Peculiar Man," the subject turns to their father, who Fiona also thinks bears a resemblance to Redford.

"Dad's the lost, sad, old, unsmiling version of him," Fiona says. "With darker hair."

"Donald Larkin is the last man in the world who would think he's handsome," Myra adds. She goes on to tell Denny about her father: the young soldier who survived the Hürtgen Forest; the quiet World War II veteran turned machinist; the devoted Yankees fan; the dutiful, churchgoing husband.

"You know he voted for Goldwater?" Fiona says

"But Dad's always been a Republican," Myra says.

"But he doesn't even think about the candidates. He just votes along party lines."

"And you don't do that?" Myra says to her sister, pouring more wine into Denny's glass.

"If there was a worthy Republican candidate I'd vote for him," Fiona says, seizing the wine bottle from her sister. She fills her glass nearly to the rim, then tops off Myra's, finishing the bottle. "Or her."

"And who *did* you vote for in this last election?" Myra asks Fiona.

"I couldn't bear the thought of Johnson coming back."

"So what'd you do?" Denny chimes in.

"I wrote someone in."

"Who?" Myra asks.

"Burt Lancaster."

Denny releases a sound that could be construed as scorn.

"Are you scoffing at me?" Fiona says playfully. "Burt Lancaster played a general in *Seven Days in May*. He probably knows more about leadership than LBJ and Barry Goldwater combined."

"Playing a general doesn't qualify a person to be president," Myra says. "It doesn't even qualify that person to be a general."

"What is anybody really qualified to do?" Fiona counters. "I'm no pastry chef but I can bake a cake. You read the directions, mix some stuff in a bowl, preheat the oven, and pop it in, what's so hard about that?"

Fiona, forever the contrarian. Is she just saying these things or does she really believe them? Myra wonders. Is this the same girl who used to sing all the hymns in church? The same girl who believed in Santa Claus until she was thirteen? The same girl who was so afraid of thunderstorms that she'd hide in her bedroom closet?

"Roy Orbison would've been a great president, too," Fiona adds. "He could just sing all of our country's problems away." She turns to her sister. "Myra's a Democrat but she keeps her apartment like a Republican."

To prevent herself from saying anything, Myra drinks a mouthful of wine.

"And what about you?" Fiona says to Denny. "Who did you vote for?"

"I didn't vote in the last election," he says.

"Why not?"

"I was in the hospital," Denny offers, setting his fork down and looking at his plate.

"The knee again?" Myra says.

"No, it wasn't the knee," he says. "My knee was fine."

His right hand gathers into a fist. For the first time Myra notices his high school class ring, its bright blue stone. She can make out the word "SENN" engraved along the setting. Little blond hairs sprout across the tops of his fingers, his wrist.

"The handsome hospital," Fiona says mischievously.

The air around the small table seems to have thickened. The storm should have cooled off the apartment by now, but it simply hasn't. And the fan is useless. The wine bottle is empty. "April Come She Will," Myra's favorite song on the album, came and went. She can hardly recall a verse. Denny continues looking down. A blue vein, faint as faded ink, pulses near his temple.

"Should I go get the other bottle of wine?" Myra says. She has to be at work at 7:00 a.m. tomorrow and doesn't even want to think about how early she'll have to get up to shower and iron her uniform and clean her white shoes and make breakfast and take the bus to the elevated train and then walk several blocks to Saint Francis Hospital in Evanston. But she won't be able to sleep much anyway because of the heat. Another glass of wine or two will likely help her doze off.

"Definitely get more wine," Fiona says.

Myra takes the corkscrew into the bathroom and opens the other bottle of chardonnay, which has been soaking in what is now lukewarm bathwater. The cork breaks and it takes her far too long to wrest the last quarter-inch or so from the neck of the bottle.

When Myra reenters the kitchen Fiona is sitting in Denny's lap. The Simon & Garfunkel record is skipping in the gutter, faintly popping with each revolution. A cool current of rage rises in her throat but she swallows hard and places the wine bottle on the table. She thinks she might be sick. Fiona is peeling one of the oranges that Denny brought to dinner. She dotes on him as if he were a king. Myra fills her sister's glass and passes it to her. Fiona sets the half-peeled orange on the table, takes a healthy slug of wine and then offers her glass to Denny.

"No, thanks," he says. "I better not."

Myra fills her own glass, takes a mouthful, forces it down.

Still on his lap, Fiona tries to get Denny to drink from her glass.

He turns away, smiling. "I've had too much already, I really have," he says.

His eyes are gray and large and sad. Myra can feel the ache he carries, like a suitcase of unwanted books. She longs to unburden him, to hold his face in her hands.

He gently nudges Fiona off his lap and stands. "I should go," he says. "Tomorrow's Thursday. I have so much to get done. Myra, thank you for dinner."

"It was my pleasure," she says.

Denny stands there another moment, meeting Myra's eyes, then exits. The door closes behind him. Gone, just like that. A pair of unpeeled oranges sits at the edge of the kitchen table.

Myra walks over to the skipping record player, finally lifts the needle, and turns it off. From the living room she glares at Fiona.

"What?" Fiona says.

"After everything I've done for you," Myra says. She can't think of a time she's ever been angrier with her sister.

"Oh, please," Fiona says. "Was he not fair game? He was clearly interested in me."

"Because you were throwing yourself at him! Do you have any dignity at all?"

"Now there's a word."

"I thought you were a lesbian," Myra says, knowing as the word leaves her mouth that it's a cheap, hollow blow.

"Well, tonight I wasn't," Fiona says, and backs into the living room, where she collapses onto the sofa, her legs spread, her chin tucked into her neck.

"You're drunk," Myra says.

"And you should be too." Fiona stares at her sister for a long moment, then unleashes a long, hectoring laugh. "Myra Lee Larkin, always the good girl," she says through the laughter. "You're twenty-eight years old. Have you ever done a bad thing in your fucking life?"

Myra doesn't respond. She reaches over for Fiona's glass of wine, downs nearly the whole thing.

"I was in an orgy in New York," Fiona continues, "with five other people. One of them was a sixty-year-old man. And one of them was blind."

"And look where it's gotten you," Myra says, though even with what she knows of her sister she is a little shocked at the admission.

"I fucking loved it," Fiona says.

Myra could throttle her. The impulse twitches in her wrists. She's never physically fought with Fiona. Growing up, Myra was her protector, always defending her from school bullies. But now Myra could seize the ungrateful opportunist by the throat, she really could. Instead, she turns and starts to clean up. As she's clearing the table she drops the serving dish of lemon chicken. Clumps of rice and sauce spill onto the floor.

"If you're so crazy about him go dock on his goddamn noor," Fiona says, sinking further into the sofa cushions.

"You can't even speak," Myra says, using a wet sponge to clean up the mess. "This is all just a game to you, isn't it? Everything's one big lark."

But Fiona doesn't reply because she's passed out. She begins snoring loudly.

Myra crosses to her in the living room and rolls her onto her side, off the sofa and into the overstuffed chair. She removes the sofa cushions and pulls out the convertible bed, then manages to get Fiona situated back on the pullout mattress, whose fitted sheet barely clings to its opposite corners.

"Stay on your left side," Myra says.

Fiona smacks her lips.

"Can you hear me, Fiona? If you're going to be sick please try and make it to the bathroom, okay?"

Fiona nods and a bemused look passes over her. She indeed possesses a beautiful face. Those lustrous lashes. Those lips. That perfect, unsullied chin. How could Denny have resisted her?

After Myra finishes cleaning the kitchen, she gulps yet another glass of wine, forcing it down as if it's medicine, then heads down to the second floor and knocks on Denny's door. It's late now—well past midnight.

"Myra," Denny says after he opens the door. He's wearing boxer shorts and a white T-shirt. His calves are so muscular.

"Were you sleeping?" she says.

"No," he says. "I was awake."

"I can't sleep either," she says. She knows she is drunk. Her face feels lopsided, her tongue bloated. Each word is large in her mouth.

"Come in," Denny says. He closes the door behind her and turns the deadbolt. "I managed to pry one of the windows open," he says.

And before he can get out another word Myra has come around to face him and forces her mouth onto his. She can taste the salt from his sweat, the peppermint from his toothpaste. Less than a minute later they have traveled into his dark bedroom, their faces still joined, their bodies moving as if by their own intelligence, and fall onto a full-sized mattress laid out on the floor. The sheet is quickly dispatched to the corner, along with their clothes, and they make love clumsily, with a kind of gentle, animal will.

This first time hurts more than Myra thought it would, but it is also magical. Tears of joy stream from her eyes. When he is inside her she feels as if she is also inside him. She loses herself completely. She has the sense that she has been turned into something finer than dust. She is pollen. She is the absolute, indivisible particles of love. A kind of vapor. She can make out shapes, sounds, the muscles in his back, the combined spice of their breath, the heavy pulse in his lower abdomen, the swollen horn of him coming into her...

When it is over Denny curls into a ball, as if somehow bereft. Myra arranges herself around his broad back and shoulders, comforting him, and in doing so discovers a thick scar between his upper left bicep and his armpit. He is covering it with his right hand, as if guarding it. Myra pries his fingers loose and gently grazes the scar with her fingertips. It is grisly, raised. Denny allows her to touch it. He is a child, lost. It seems as if he's forgotten who he is, what they just shared.

"What happened here?" Myra whispers, still touching the scar.

Denny makes no response except to cover the scar with his hand.

Not wanting to push things, Myra simply continues embracing him and he allows it. She has never felt anything like this for anyone. Denny Happ will become her destiny, the end of everything she was before him. The beginning of everything new that will happen to her. She knows this with a certainty as powerful as the streaks of blood marking the mattress ticking. Even now she can feel his semen inside her, its warm, sluicing inevitability.

Myra wakes with the troubled sense that something terrible has happened. She overslept! It's past 9:00 a.m. She's two hours late for work! Denny is sound asleep, breathing deeply. Even in slumber his beauty astounds her. Morning light from the bare window silvers the edges of his body. Aside from her one question about his scar, they have said nothing to each other since she entered his apartment. Her groin is sore and achy. It is a pleasurable ache, though. She is no longer a virgin.

Myra gets out of bed, quietly dresses, finds a pen and writes a note on the back of a torn packing slip, which she leaves on the kitchen table.

> *Denny,*
> *Thank you for a lovely night.*
> *I had to leave for work. I didn't want to wake you.*
> *Myra*

Holding her sneakers, she exits through his back door, which opens onto the building's wooden fire escape. Even through the morning sunshine the flashing blue and red of police lights are visible on the wall of another apartment building in the alleyway. Out on East 100th Street, an ambulance and two police cars are parked before an area cordoned off with yellow tape. It appears that all the yellow tape has been arranged in front of the nurses' townhouse where Myra used to live. She is troubled by the scene but she simply doesn't have time to stand there and watch.

Myra returns to her apartment to find Fiona sleeping on the pullout, still turned onto her left side, just as she'd left her, her face bemused, guiltless. She calls her boss, Mrs. Denton, the head nurse, and lies about the power going out in her building, how it caused her to sleep through her alarm. The second lie in less than twenty-four hours. Will they start piling up? Will they cause more teeth to start going loose?

Mrs. Denton is stern but understands. "Get here as soon as you can," she says.

As she prepares for work, while listening to the radio, Myra learns that late last night eight young nursing candidates were tortured and murdered after returning home to their townhouse on 2319 East 100th Street. One of the victims is Myra's friend, Gloria Davy, with whom she was planning on taking a trip to the Indiana Dunes this weekend. The thought of Gloria being dead knocks the wind out of her. Myra has to sit. She lowers herself all the way down on the linoleum floor.

* * *

WHILE ABOARD HER NORTHBOUND bus that will drop her at the elevated train stop, Myra can't quite fathom the truth of the murders. How could one person commit so many atrocities? Did the nurses fight back? Myra has always known Gloria to be tough and self-sufficient. She wouldn't back down without a fight. She grew up in Chicago, after all. Did the murderer have a gun? A knife? Did he drug them?

On the elevated train Myra is lucky to find a seat. She tries to let her mind go blank, to not think about Gloria or her sister or everything that happened the previous evening with Denny, for that matter. It's simply too much to hold in her head. Instead, she closes her eyes and begins humming to herself. It's the Simon & Garfunkel song she longed to hear during dinner, "April Come She Will." Myra wonders why they decided to only sing about six of the twelve months, April through September. What's the significance of this? She finds herself quietly singing aloud the July section of the song:

> *July, she will fly*
> *And give no warning to her flight*

It's July 14th, after all. She probes the song's poetry. *July, she will fly*. Is there a secret meaning in its spare lyrical arrangement? A puzzle? Is she, Myra Lee Larkin, hidden somewhere in the shadows of this song?

As her train clatters past Wrigley Field, Myra realizes that she's wearing her white nursing uniform and holding her RN cap in her lap. She can feel other commuters' eyes on her. Do they know about the murders? she wonders. Do they think she's playing some cruel joke, donning a nurse's uniform on public transportation after such horrible, tragic news? They all hate her, no doubt. She does her best to keep her eyes cast down. She can't bear the thought of anyone confronting her.

Myra briefly peers up at a man who is reading the sports section of the *Chicago Tribune*. He breaks from the newspaper, peers directly at her. His jowly face has the consistency of Spam, with broken blood vessels spidering across a bulbous, carbuncular nose. Myra looks down. For the rest of the commute she will fix her gaze on her lap.

A FEW HOURS LATER, in the fourth-floor lounge of the pediatrics ward of Saint Francis Hospital, while Myra is gathered in front of the large console color television with several other nurses and orderlies, an anchorman on the local news reports to the greater Chicagoland area that more information has come out about the murders. It turns out that Myra's friend, Gloria, was also raped. The killer had raped and then strangled her, and then stabbed her several times. Something goes slack inside Myra and she has to sit on a chair, which she nearly misses. It takes a moment for her to catch her breath. Gloria's family must be devastated. How will they survive this terrible day?

The one piece of good news about the grisly murders is that there was a survivor at the nurses' residence at 2319 East 100th Street, a young woman named Corazon Amurao, who managed to keep hidden under her bed while a man tortured and murdered eight other nursing students. One time while visiting Gloria at the townhouse, Myra met Corazon. She remembers that Corazon didn't drink alcohol. She was very pretty and very Catholic. They talked about possibly attending mass together at St. Joseph Parish up in Back of the Yards. At that point it had been weeks since Myra had gone to confession and she felt guilty. She had been slipping, as her mother would say.

According to the anchorman, Corazon Amurao, one of the three Filipino exchange students who lived at the residence, described the still-at-large killer to police authorities as being tall and white, with measles scars marking his cheeks, greasy, brown, slicked-back hair worn in the style of Elvis Presley, and a distinctive

BORN TO RAISE HELL tattoo crudely rendered in the pale flesh of his upper right forearm.

BORN TO RAISE HELL.

Myra tries to push from her mind the familiar tattoo, which belonged to that strange man who was so crude to her at the laundromat. Is this the same man who raped and killed Gloria? Is that possible? She feels as if she will be sick and forces herself to swallow.

As the news report continues Myra finds herself clinging to images of her time with Denny: his shoulders poised over her; his bare bedroom window, that perfect rain-flecked square of moonlight; the look on his face as he entered her; how surprisingly inevitable their conjoined flesh felt; the peace she experienced after the act; the deep, intense care she felt for him while they embraced.

5

SALEM, MASSACHUSETTS
FALL 1970

FIONA

Dearest Myra,

It's hard to believe it's been years since we last spoke. I'm not writing to ask for money, or for your help in any way, so please don't tear this up. Please keep reading.

So much has happened since Chicago. New York and Chicago are two chapters in my life I wish I could erase, or somehow re-write, but the ink has dried on all that and I'm afraid I'll have to live with those shameful months for the rest of my days. You taking me in was incredibly charitable. As Mother would say, you were a Saint and I know I showed you zero appreciation. If anything I was a belligerent, unappreciative mess. For those two months you fed me, got me back on my feet, put up with my lack of hygiene (your poor sofa!) and you never asked for anything in return. And for all of this I will always be grateful.

St. Myra, the Patron Saint of Charitable Works for Awful Siblings.

After I left your apartment, I took the money from the clothes (and the money I stole from your purse), and I boarded a Greyhound bus heading for Milwaukee, where I got a job in the cafeteria of a boys Military Academy in Delafield, Wisconsin of all places. Apparently the St. John's campus is an exact replica of West Point, with little castle-like buildings made of stone. (Denny might have flashbacks!) The cafeteria gig didn't last long and there's no need to go into detail about that. Let's just say I got involved with one of the teachers there — a young English teacher (younger than me — he was 24) named Perry — and he was married and I sort of got involved with his wife too. (Her name was Eden. They were high school sweethearts from Kenosha and they both had such perfect skin!) And then things got particularly ugly and three months later I was on another bus, this time heading to Detroit, where I got a got another job in the food service industry, this time at Wayne State University, but it was the middle of winter and I came down with a terrible bronchitis — I nearly coughed up a lung — and I missed almost a month of work. Well, understandably, I didn't have a job when I got my health back. As I was gathering my things and walking away from campus I happened upon a bulletin board with a simple index card that was very humbly advertising an opportunity to work as a farmhand in Massachusetts, so I called the number and three hours later I was on yet another Greyhound, this time heading east.

Many, many hours later I was greeted at a small bus station in northeast Massachusetts by two women wearing white bonnets. And that's when everything changed.

For these last few years I've been living with a community of women on a working farm. The farm is set on ten acres, half of which are dedicated to agriculture. There is an old clapboard house and a converted barn. There is a former corn crib where various chores are done. There is also a fishpond, a majestic willow tree, three chocolate Labs, innumerable cats, more hummingbirds than you could imagine in the spring and summer (Mother would be jealous!), and an old white, swaybacked spotted mare that sleeps standing up.

We don't believe in Time in the classic sense. We believe in seasons, however. And weather, of course. Weather is truer than the news, after all.

As I write this it is the fall, probably somewhere between late September and mid-October. Whether my birthday has passed, I'm not entirely sure. If it has, I am thirty-one. The leaves are amazing here. So many stunning shades of reds, oranges, golds. There are forty-eight Sisters and we come from all over the country. Three are from Galveston, Texas. One is from McCall, Idaho. One girl is even from Ghana, Africa. Sister Laine is from Canastota, New York, which, as you know, is only a couple of hours north of Elmira. Laine and I are very close. (Yes, "very close" is code for what you think it is.) You would like her a lot. She's tall like Mother (although not quite that tall!), has sparkling blue eyes and long blond hair. She was in her second year of graduate school at Brown (she was getting her Master's in Anthropology), when she came to the Farm. Laine and I wear matching bonnets, which signifies that we choose to be identified as a couple. Our leader, Mother Emily, would like to Join us after the first snowfall. Joining is sort of like a marriage ceremony. I know Dad and Mother will have simultaneous strokes when they hear about this. And I'm fine with you telling them, by the way. It's all going to come out eventually anyway. I can just see Mother's face now. Her beauty drawn in by those severe lines of judgment. Her quiet bitterness squeezing her eyes closer together.

I think about you and Alec often. Myra, I know that you'll always be fine. You always were fine. So steady,

*so independent, so reliable. And now that you've found
someone, your life is even more solid. A happy life has
always been in the cards for you. It's been your fate since
you were little. But Alec is a different story. Poor Alec.
There is something lost about him. Something loose
in his center. It's not so much that he's a thief and a
liar; there's something subtler going on. Even though I
haven't seen him in years I get the sense that he's fading
away; that each city or town he flees to (and eventually
from) keeps some residue of him. The more Alec runs,
the more of him gets rubbed away, bit by bit, layer by
layer. Soon his skin will barely be able to contain him
and his insides will spill out into the streets and dribble
down some curbside drain. He will eventually dissolve
into vapor, into nothingness. I don't know where he came
from, Myra. Maybe it's the dark eyes and olive skin.
Sometimes I wonder if Mother found him in a parking
lot and faked her third pregnancy.*

    *As far as the other Larkins are concerned I don't
think much about Lexy. Like you, she will be fine.
She'll wind up a lawyer or a doctor or maybe even a
U.S. Senator. She'll live in a four-story house that will
survive tornadoes. She'll have three kids and a husband
who calls her "Babe" and pats her on the rump when
she walks by him holding a casserole. She'll become a
vigorous hiker. Once a year she'll climb to the top of some
impossible summit and declare something triumphant
in another language. And she'll love every minute of her
life.*

    *Joan I spend even less time thinking about. By the
time I left Elmira she was becoming more inconvenient
than a piece of faulty furniture. And before my escape
I was bearing the brunt of that inconvenience. I wish
Dad and Mother would move her to the home up in
Watertown. It would be better off for everyone. The idea*

of it doesn't sadden me. Joan would probably feel normal for the first time in her life. She'd probably actually make a friend or two.

If this happened Joan would be at a "Home," I'd be on a "Farm," and Alec would be "Nowhere." It sounds like a children's board game. Roll some dice, spin an arrow, and watch the Larkins clodhop around the colored squares, searching for whatever it is we're all searching for.

But back to my life on the Farm.

We are not a religious community, although there is optional prayer before meals and we are allowed to read religious texts if we so choose. There are former Catholics, practicing Catholics, five Jews, a handful of agnostic girls, an older atheist Greek woman, a black Muslim from Baltimore, and even a Mormon from Utah. The focus here is agriculture, feminine strength, kindness, and sustaining a way of life that is independent of the American grid. We make our own clothes. We build our own furniture. We pasteurize our own milk. There are goats and cows and chickens. There is a Sister who can even fix a car. She probably knows more about an eight-cylinder engine than Dad.

The truth is that, regarding "Faith," I'm not sure what I believe anymore. The invasion of Cambodia, Richard Nixon, the Beatles breaking up, famine, the assassination of MLK. How could a just and thoughtful God allow this kind of stuff to go on? What is there to believe in anymore? Our tax dollars are robbed to fleece the pockets of plutocrats in Washington. All those ancient little men with dandruff and hairy ears move our money around without our knowledge. Money that pays for wars that nobody wants. Money that fattens their personal bank accounts.

In short, the Farm makes sense to me. Our

simplicity. Our reliance on shared labor and kindness. Our mission of agriculture and self-sustenance.

I should also tell you that we shed our last names on the Farm. I no longer identify as Fiona Grace Larkin. I am simply Fiona. Or Sister Fiona. Like a nun! How ironic, right? The fallen Catholic turns out to be called Sister Fiona. The trappings of one's family name can only prevent one from reaching one's full potential. And I'm not talking corporate potential. Or consumer potential. I'm talking human being potential. The potential for empathy. The potential for forgiveness. The potential for really listening to others. The potential for caring.

We farm. We work. We tend the meadows. There is singing. (We do love the Beatles! Although there is a small contingent of Sisters who are desperately smitten with the dreary Carpenters—yuck!) We swim naked in an ancient lake not even two miles away where there are loons and salamanders and giant turtles. We walk there in homemade sandals.

There are children here as well, who are taught by two Sisters who used to be public school teachers. The classroom is in the back of the barn. There are no textbooks. Just knowledge being shared. The children learn to read and think and use math.

And there is one man, simply known as David, who visits us during our ovulation cycles. If we so choose we can have sex with David. He sires our children. David is very gentle and quiet. He reminds me of Dad in more ways than I can articulate. He fought in Vietnam and has a damaged leg, but he believes in Peace now and he's very generous (he helps us with the cows) and seems utterly committed to our mission.

I'm sorry for the way I left Chicago. I was in a bad, self-involved place. I trust that you and Denny survived my ugly behavior. He seemed like a good guy and you deserve someone like him. Someone who will love you and take care of you.

I hope you will accept this bonnet as a token of my love for you. Sister Elsa made it. It's the same color as your eyes when you wear that green sweater that you've had since high school. When you look at it please know that you're often in my thoughts. I'm not leaving a return address — it's against Farm policy to disclose our home — but I will continue to write.

Love,
Fiona

6

CHICAGO, ILLINOIS
JANUARY 21, 1973

ALEC

THERE'S A YOUNG CATHOLIC priest on the bus who won't stop talking about God. Father Bryce is his name and his unblemished, clean-shaven face keeps reminding Alec of a newborn's soft, immaculate ass. The priest, who says he was originally from South Dakota but has been living in Boone, Iowa, boarded the Greyhound back in Des Moines and took the seat next to Alec.

Father Bryce gives off a quiet, confident wisdom that belies his age, which Alec guesses to be around twenty-five. Alec is now thirty-one but everyone he meets thinks he's ten years younger, and whenever he shows people his driver's license it seems to inspire an odd reaction. In Kansas, with the intent of appearing older, he experimented with facial hair, but it grew in sparingly and he thought the patchy, meandering beard—if you could even call it that—made him look like someone who was vitamin deficient. A weakling. Like one of those guys who got punched in the face a lot as a child. When a woman who worked at a pharmacy asked him if he was anemic and tried to sell him iron supplements, he wound up shaving everything off that same night.

Until accepting his new assignment, Father Bryce says, he ran the youth ministry at Sacred Heart Church, back in Boone. It is precisely this—his blatant, unsullied youth—that repulses Alec, perhaps because it's a reminder of how far from the realm of innocence Alec now finds himself. He's been called a freeloader, a con

143

artist, a kleptomaniac. At least two former employers, not to mention his own family, have referred to him as a cold-blooded criminal. He's also been called flaky, shiftless, and stupid.

Within minutes of the priest introducing himself, Alec decided he was one of those unfortunate men who seem never to have completed puberty. There is something not fully formed about his face. The full lips and tiny nose and delicate cheekbones and soft, hairless chin are altogether incongruous with the rich, radio host's baritone of his speaking voice. The man has strawberry-blond hair, a little lighter than Fiona's, and clear blue eyes whose pupils seem to dilate every time he utters the word "God" or some variation of it. Like Alec, Father Bryce will be getting off the bus in Chicago, but will then transfer to another Greyhound for some ninety more miles north, where he'll be joining the faculty of a Catholic elementary school in Milwaukee. The bitter cold doesn't seem to bother this priest one bit. He's not wearing his wool coat and watch cap, which he stowed with his bags on the overhead rack. Unlike many others aboard the bus, he isn't even wearing so much as a scarf or sweater, only his black collarino shirt with the little white tab and black pants. Perhaps the Holy Spirit is keeping him warm. God's sultry, omnipotent breath.

Alec, on the other hand, is fucking freezing. Even though he's wearing long johns underneath a pair of blue jeans and a bulky, wool sweater over a thermal undershirt and has buttoned his navy peacoat up to his chin, he can't seem to get warm. He isn't wearing socks, which doesn't help matters.

It's January 21st—a Sunday—and over the bus radio a congested news reporter is prattling on about it being the coldest day of the year, with an expected high of 13 degrees and a wind chill factor of -20.

"I don't meet many nonbelievers," Father Bryce starts in again.

Alec has been indulging the priest in conversation for almost three hours.

"At least none who are so hospitable," he adds.

Since Des Moines Alec has been politely answering a litany of questions whose subjects have ranged from growing up Catholic to the agriculture in western Nebraska, the most recent place he'd washed up. Just outside Davenport, when the Greyhound pulled over to refuel, Alec got off the bus with his bag and smoked two cigarettes and bought a candy bar out of the vending machine. When he reboarded he changed seats, passing Father Bryce and finding an empty one near the back left of the bus, but the priest hunted him down and took a new seat, directly across the aisle.

The priests back in Elmira loved the altar boys and acolytes. It was easy to avoid the handsy ones who couldn't help themselves, like ancient Father Oates, with his drunken, puffy eyes and yellow teeth, and Father Nickel, who was always pulling the younger boys onto his lap as if they were kittens he was peeling off the drapes. It was the quieter, more remote priests you had to watch out for. Father Farrell, for instance, who would often happen upon Alec in the vestry while he was hanging up his cassock. Father Farrell would close the door and watch Alec dress and ask him questions about his relationship to God and whether his schoolwork was progressing and what he thought of Father Oates's sermon. Throughout these talks, Father Farrell would draw progressively nearer, almost imperceptibly so, and there would inevitably be a hug, which would lead to Father Farrell's heavy, cadaver-like hands traveling up to Alec's shoulders, where they would begin kneading at the tense muscles at the sides of his neck—*Do you like that?*—and then the hands would continue down his spine, toward his waist, where they would loop back around and gather in front of Alec's corduroy slacks. Alec would watch the knobs of Father Ferrell's wrists toggle back and forth as he undid Alec's leather belt—the one his mother had given him for his twelfth birthday. As Father Farrell genuflected before Alec, there was the familiar, potatoey smell rising off his thick black vestments, the flash of one of his hairy ears, with its surprising thatch of short, dark thistles, his sour, peaty breath, and the drifts of dandruff on his shoulders.

Alec had vowed that he would never trust a priest again, especially a goddamn Catholic one.

As the bus trundles along Interstate 80, ribbons of snow flare across the highway's blighted, salt-rimed pavement. Beyond the shoulder, power lines dip and swoop along a low iron sky. The flat barren farmlands of western Illinois seem to fade into infinity. The occasional silo or corrugated corncrib punctuates the landscape here and there. The faraway farmhouses look like toy dwellings that some whimsical Midwestern giant has pulled out of a bag and haphazardly forced into the earth.

Alec looks over at Father Bryce, who, shockingly, has fallen asleep. Finally he'll have some peace and quiet.

As he stares out his window, however, he has the uneasy sense that he isn't journeying toward a better, more promising future, but merely migrating from one horizontal, cursed place to another. In Ogallala the landscape had been so shapeless and boring he feared it would eventually drive him mad. There were remote places beyond the town, out in the deserted flatlands, where he would have sworn he could see the earth bulging on its axis. Miles and miles of endless fields interrupted here and there by a trio of radio towers, or a tall, lone weathervane. A sea of harvested wheat. A freight train far off on the horizon, as infinitesimal as a column of ants. Those parts of western Nebraska could make you feel small and dumb and unremarkable.

At least in Chicago there will be skyscrapers. There will be big public parks and baseball stadiums and the elevated train and sandy beaches along the shores of Lake Michigan and thousands of new women.

Alec left Nebraska because of a woman. Her name is Emma Flahive and he loved her as much as he's ever loved anyone or anything but things got complicated after she told him she was pregnant with his child. Alec was working for Emma's father, Kerwood Flahive, who had a successful moving company. He'd changed his ways and become a hard, reliable worker and had been put on Kerwood's biggest, best-paying truck in less than two months.

Within a few weeks of meeting Emma, he found himself parked with her out in the flatlands and Emma gave herself to him in the backseat of her father's green '69 Bonneville. There was something about her innocence and the way she looked at him that made Alec start to believe he actually had some good left in him. He hadn't felt that way about himself for as long as he could remember. Taking her virginity was as easy as unwrapping a birthday gift. Alec knew he was her first and as he spilled himself inside her she clung to his flesh as if she were about to fall backwards into an endless chasm. The fingernail marks on his flanks took a month to heal. Emma, twenty-two, was on the pill, without her parents' knowledge, but it failed. Somehow, whatever sexual brew they'd created was too potent and spoiled its contraceptive magic.

Alec had first met Emma in the front yard of the Flahives' big Tudor house in North Platte, where he was washing the moving truck for extra money. Emma, who was enrolled in secretary school and still living at home, came outside to offer Alec a glass of lemonade and from that moment on they couldn't bear not being around each other.

As soon as Kerwood Flahive found out that his only daughter was pregnant, he told Alec in no uncertain terms that he needed to marry her and Alec in turn said he would. He meant it, too, convincing himself that he would follow through on his promise and start a family with this perfect girl from an upstanding family. Yet as the reality set in, he began to panic. Kerwood had given Alec and his daughter enough money to put a down payment on a small ranch house in nearby Stapleton and he even co-signed the mortgage. During the mandatory inspection, as the man leading it took Alec and Emma and Kerwood through the various empty chambers of the house, Alec could feel a shift taking hold. There was something all too real about the unfinished basement's water softener and the gas boiler and the fuse box. About the talk of fireproof asbestos insulation and the newly glazed windows and Emma's almost erotic astonishment at the state-of-the-art kitchen appliances, how she trailed her fingertips across the brushed-steel surface of the refrigerator. All this doting on an empty house made him sick to his stomach. He excused himself to the master bathroom, where he dry-heaved into the toilet several times.

That night Kerwood and his wife, Bridget, took their daughter and future son-in-law to dinner at a local steakhouse, where they celebrated Alec and Emma's new home. They ate filet mignon and whipped potatoes prepared in goose fat and his future father-in-law picked up the check and Alec had the genuine sense that he was being welcomed into the Flahive family. During dinner Kerwood even brought up the possibility of promoting Alec to lead man of one of his moving trucks, which would be a nice bump in salary. Emma kept her left hand on her belly throughout the evening, as if bestowing a gentle benediction on their unborn child.

But much later that night, when Alec couldn't sleep, he used the public payphone on the floor of his SRO in downtown Ogallala to call his sister in Chicago and ask if he could come stay with her. He didn't mention Emma or the new house or his unborn child. He simply told her he needed a change of scenery; that he'd grown tired of Nebraska and that he'd heard so many good things about Chicago. Although Myra seemed initially cautious, after a few minutes she said that he could come stay with her and her husband, Denny, as long as he didn't mind sleeping on the convertible sofa. Alec's four-year-old nephew, Ronan, whom he's never met, sleeps in the other bedroom, he learned. The only caveat, which Myra insisted on, was that he get a job and find a place to live. She would give him as long as he needed, but he had to make a real effort. Of course he would, Alec promised her. And he wouldn't mind sleeping on the convertible sofa, he wouldn't mind that one bit, he'd said. He'd slept on much worse, after all. Once he slept on a urine-soaked shipping pallet. He looked forward to reconnecting with his oldest sister. It had been over a decade since they'd seen each other.

Alec left Emma in the middle of the night with a canvas gym bag containing his few belongings. He slept fitfully on a bench at the back of the Greyhound station. As soon as the sun came up he found himself hiding in one of the stalls in the men's bathroom. He had over four hours to kill and couldn't shake the fear that Kerwood Flahive might come bounding into the station looking for him. But lucky for Alec, that didn't happen. In the late morning, with the crisp Nebraska air cold in his lungs, he finally boarded the eastbound Greyhound.

"How much longer?" Alec suddenly hears.

Father Bryce is awake again.

"A couple hours," Alec tells him.

Father Bryce nods and rubs his eyes. He turns in his seat so that his back is up against the window. He is directly facing Alec now. "You never mentioned what's bringing you to Chicago," the priest says.

"I'm going to visit my sister."

"How long will you be staying?"

"Indefinitely," Alec says.

"Can I ask you something?" the priest asks.

"As long as it's not math-related," Alec says.

The priest chuckles, revealing perfect little guinea pig teeth. "Are you in some kind of trouble?" he asks.

Alec turns away and inhales sharply but he can't bring himself to exhale in front of this man. He fears it will come out as what it is: exasperation. He forces himself to swallow the frustration as if it's a spoonful of salt. Will it be two more hours of this benevolent third-degree? He moved all the way to the rear of the bus—boldly walking right past this fucking priest—to reclaim his privacy. He even took this unwanted seat near the bathroom, from which the smell of piss wafts almost continuously. Why can't this man take a hint?

"If there's anything you need to confess," Father Bryce continues gently, "I'm here for you."

"You'll give me communion, too?" Alec jokes.

"Well, it is Sunday," Father Bryce says. "I often travel with the host just in case."

"I left Ogallala because I got a girl pregnant," Alec hears himself say.

A woman two seats in front of him turns around to look at him. She has a swollen, blotchy face with inflamed slits for eyes. Probably another nosy, righteous Catholic.

"Turn around and mind your business," he says to her.

She scoffs, clearly appalled by his rudeness, but does turn around, shaking her head.

Since his time in Niagara Falls, Alec has found that he takes pleasure in being cruel to women. This tendency ceased with Emma, or so he thought. He treated her like she was royalty. He was a gentleman at all times. He opened doors for her and made sure she always felt safe and secure. He doted on her. But here he was, being mean to another woman.

"So you're fleeing," the priest says, bringing them back to the subject of Ogallala.

"It's one of the few things I'm actually good at," Alec says. "If there was a profession for it I'd be in luck. Alec Larkin, Professional Fleer, take my card."

The priest smiles. "Did you say goodbye to her?"

"Now that would've taken guts," Alec says.

Father Bryce rubs his pale hands together and then looks at his right palm as if considering a piece of scripture he has written there. "What was her name?" he asks.

"Emma," Alec says, and the sound of his own voice uttering her name lances his ribs with shame, the pain so real it's all he can do to avoid clutching his torso.

"Can you talk about why you decided to leave?"

"I needed a new scene," Alec says. "There was too much pressure there." He goes on to tell the priest about Kerwood Flahive and the new house and the gifted mortgage.

"Were you going to marry Emma?"

"That was the plan," Alec says.

He turns to his window and presses his forehead to the cold, damp glass. There's a furniture delivery scheduled on Tuesday at the house that he and Emma were to live in. Emma's mother took Alec and Emma to a showroom where they picked out a sofa, two matching armchairs, a dining room table, and a sideboard. Kerwood's three top men would be delivering everything with great care. They would "white glove" it for the young couple.

"What are your plans for Chicago?" the priest asks.

"Get a job," Alec says. "Find a place to live. Start over. My sister's gonna let me crash on her sofa till I get situated." Under further questioning, he offers that his sister lives with her husband and their little boy, Ronan.

"So you're an uncle," Father Bryce says, pushing the silver lining.

"I s'pose I should bring him a present," Alec says. "A box of caramel corn or something."

"I'm confident that a young boy meeting his uncle for the first time will be a fine enough gift. Or"—the priest opens the latches of his briefcase and reaches into it—"you could give him this." He proffers a Holy Bible, bound in black leather.

It seems to hover in the middle of the aisle magically, until Alec finally takes it. He holds it in his lap. Its weight is surprising, its density a portent. "This isn't new," he says, studying its weathered spine and softened corners. "Father David Bryce," he says, reading aloud the name on the inside flap, embossed in goldleaf. "For some reason, I thought your first name was Bryce," he adds.

"I'm one of those unlucky people with two first names," the priest says.

"This was a gift," Alec says, pointing at the embossing.

"It was from my mentor and it's been with me for a long time. And now it's yours to give to your nephew."

Alec flips through it. A faint odor of frankincense rises from its pages. Sometimes Alec thinks he can still catch the ancient, familiar scent lingering in his clothes, even in clothes he didn't start wearing until well past the time he'd served as an altar boy. Perhaps the smells of church penetrate the oils in your skin and never leave you?

Alec thanks him and sets the Bible on the empty seat beside him. He imagines giving it to his nephew and pictures the boy hurling it across the room like a football.

Then they are quiet for a while. The bus downshifts as they enter the city limits of Joliet, Illinois.

"Is there anything else you'd like to share with me?" Father Bryce asks.

Alec sincerely considers the question, its clear invitation for a confession. He's been a part of so many minor and not-so-minor crimes that he wouldn't know where to begin. He has witnessed a man murder an old woman in her novelty shop. He has stolen money from his hometown church and office furniture off the end of a loading dock in Manhattan, Kansas, and in Omaha, from the passenger's side of the car, he watched an ex-con named Virgil Roundtree hot-wire a mint-condition '68 Cadillac DeVille, which he and Roundtree then drove down to the Texas panhandle and sold to a used-car lot for three grand, and then two days later he helped Roundtree rip out copper pipes from the walls of a vacant condominium complex in Little Rock, Arkansas, and sell the pipes as scrap to a metal yard. He has cheated on several young women, taken money from their purses and rings and necklaces and earrings from their jewelry boxes and sold them to pawnshops and gold dealers. And when he broke these young women's hearts he took pleasure in their humiliation, telling them that they were stupid or fat or that they didn't know what they were doing in bed or that they smelled bad. He drinks too much and sometimes sleeps all day. Besides for his one brief season of genuine hard work with Kerwin Flahive's moving company, he is horribly, horribly lazy. When anyone extends a kindness to him he never bothers to reciprocate or even thank the person. His selfishness has no limits. He hasn't spoken to his parents in over ten years. From his sister he knows that his father is diabetic now and he couldn't care less. He was even invited home for Christmas Eve a few years back and he let the invitation disappear in his mind as easily as a phone number he didn't care to memorize. There is so much Alec could unload on this priest.

"No," he says finally. "Nothing."

WHEN THEY ARRIVE IN Chicago it starts to snow. It's late afternoon and the sky is dim, like dirty mopwater. The air west of Lake Michigan and south of the bend in the Chicago River is alive with small, stinging flakes that whirl about like confused, whitewashed gnats. Newspapers and debris whip across Randolph Street in mini cyclones. At the station the light has gone out in the big Greyhound Bus sign. As they pass under it and into the subterranean depot, the sign rattles on the corner of the enormous granite building to which it's attached. What they say about Chicago is obviously true, Alec thinks: the wind here is no joke.

The bus parks in the giant cement lot below the station. Over the PA the driver welcomes everyone to Chicago, the Windy City, home of the Bears, the White Sox, the Bulls, and the Cubs. A few people near the front clap and cheer. For Alec, standing up takes a second, as if all these hours on the bus have aged him. His knees are stiff. His back and hips ache. His neck feels like somebody punched it. He manages to wedge Father Bryce's Bible into his already over-stuffed gym bag and disembarks with his fellow passengers, who appear to be just as used up by the journey. The smell of halitosis and unwashed bodies is almost sickening.

Alec doesn't look behind him, for fear that he will have to reengage with the priest. On the escalator leading up to the main level he keeps his eyes front. But inside the bustling terminal there Father Bryce is, jogging toward him.

The priest offers a piece of paper containing the phone number where he'll be staying in Milwaukee. "Call me if you need any-thing," he says, a bit out of breath. He is thick in the hips, almost heavyset from the waist down. "Even if you just want to talk."

Alec thanks him, accepting the piece of paper and stuffing it into the front pocket of his jeans.

Over the PA, Sammy Davis Jr.'s "The Candy Man" is inter-rupted by the terminal dispatcher announcing the gate assignment for the Milwaukee-bound bus.

"That's me," Father Bryce says. He extends his hand and they shake. "God bless you, Alec."

"You, too, Father," Alec says.

As soon as the priest is gone, Alec makes his way over to a bank of public payphones, where a long-haired, bearded veteran is sitting cross-legged, holding a sign in his lap.

SHOULDA DIED IN KHE SANH
SORRY CHARLIE
HELP FEED A HUNGRY VETERAN

It looks like the man's green Army jacket is consuming him, as if the beleaguered being trapped within it is the jacket's unsuspecting host. He asks Alec for a cigarette, and Alec apologizes, telling him he ran out back in Davenport.

The man's throat is covered in scars that look like melted candle wax. "God bless," he says to Alec.

Two blessings within the span of a few minutes. Something must be up. Maybe he'll get lucky with some Windy City girl?

"Stay warm tonight," the vet says. His voice is a wheezing, creaking screen door in need of oil.

When Alec spoke to Myra he told her he'd take a cab to her apartment, which is up on North Hoyne Avenue. He still has eighty-four dollars in his wallet, but he feels the need to be extra frugal. Maybe it's all the snow swirling across the large street-facing windows.

At the payphones he dials Myra's number. On the other end it rings several times. He turns back to take in the terminal. People are so bundled up it seems strange. They wear parkas over jackets, with wool hats and scarves covering their faces as if they are awaiting an inescapable punishment. Even the two police officers standing over by the waiting area appear doomed. When no one answers at Myra's place, Alec hangs up.

In the center of the terminal, at the circular kiosk, a man with well-groomed, lubricated hair, parted on the side, is studying Alec. He has intense, unblinking gray eyes, and a clean-shaven, portly face. He wears a white painter's jacket too thin for the weather and baggy canvas carpenter's pants. He looks like a man who scoops ice cream, improbably out of time and season.

"You lost?" the man asks Alec.

"No," he says.

"You act like you are."

"I'm in Chicago and this is the Greyhound station," Alec says. "If I'm somewhere else please tell me."

"You need a ride someplace?"

"You got a cab?"

"I got a *car*. It's got gas in it and the heat works. Where you goin'?"

Alec wouldn't normally engage with an odd stranger so easily but this portly guy seems harmless enough. "Forty-two hundred..."—he can't make out his own handwriting scrawled into his left palm—"something Hoyne."

"*North* Hoyne," the man says. "Twenty minutes from here. Up near Lane Tech."

"What's that?" Alec asks.

"Fancy high school," the man says. "The guy from *I Dream of Jeannie* went there. The buddy, Roger. Anyway, I'll charge you two bucks." He produces a pack of chewing gum and takes out a stick, undoes the foil, and pops it into his mouth. He offers the gum to Alec. "Spearmint," he says.

"No, thanks," Alec says.

"Visitin' family?" the man says.

"My sister."

"Well, all the cabbies are full up right now. The snow, the elements. It's comin' down out there like it's the end of days."

Alec again looks out at the big windows facing Randolph Street, where the snow is diagonal.

"You ain't gonna beat two bucks," the man says. "Where you comin' in from, anyway?"

"Ogallala, Nebraska," Alec says.

"Flattest land in the world," the man says.

"Can't argue with that," Alec says.

"I spent a buncha time in Iowa. I thought *that* part of the country was flat. Nebraska makes Iowa look like San Francisco. What's your name?"

ADAM RAPP

Alec's first impulse is to make something up—why should he surrender his name so easily?—but something about the snow slanting across the big bus-station windows, the pure dread of it, causes him to opt for sincerity. "Alec," he hears himself tell the man.

"Nice to meet you, Alec. I'm Jack."

They shake hands. Jack's is small and tense and stronger than it looks. It could be the hand of a science teacher.

They exit up the long escalators leading to the street level. Jack politely yields at the foot of the escalator and lets Alec go ahead of him.

During the four-block walk to Jack's car, the snow is almost blinding. The wind skirls between the buildings like a hungry animal left on a hill. Alec pulls up the collar of his peacoat and squints hard as the snow pelts his eyelashes and forehead.

"Is the snow always this crazy here?" he shouts.

"This ain't even half of it," Jack replies, seemingly immune. He's not even wearing a hat. "In about two hours it'll feel like Siberia." He offers to carry Alec's gym bag but Alec declines the offer.

At one intersection they have to wait for back-to-back salt trucks to clear the street before they can cross. Alec's naked toes are starting to go numb in his sneakers and he hops back and forth. Jack, on the other hand, doesn't even have his jacket zipped all the way to the top. They continue walking south on Clark, shuffling past City Hall, leaning into the icy wind as though adventurers on some epic expedition.

"I got good heat in my car!" Jack shouts as they turn onto Madison Street. "But it'll take a minute to kick in!"

His burgundy Pontiac LeMans looks like a police cruiser. It's in good shape, with no rust, though a hide of snow has blanketed its roof and hood. Jack opens the passenger's side door and Alec slides in clutching his gym bag.

"Watch your fingers," Jack says, slamming the door shut. For the next few minutes he employs a plastic scraping tool on the windshield.

The inside of the car smells clean, like disinfectant. Alec has the strange sense that he should be in the backseat, that sitting beside this man is somehow too informal. Jack works efficiently on the wind-shield, his hands bare, definitely a veteran of these snowstorms. When at last he gets in and slams the driver's side door, the glove compartment pops open and a blue police light tumbles into Alec's lap.

"Are you a cop?" Alec asks, holding the domed light.

"Not in a million years," Jack says, taking it from him. "I got that in case I ever have to make a citizen's arrest."

"Huh," Alec says, truly surprised.

"Say I'm drivin' along in my neighborhood and I see some bozo smashin' the window of a parked car," he explains. "Or I'm cruisin' along up in Rogers Park and one of those Southside niggers snatches some poor lady's purse. You never know when your community might need you."

"Have you ever had to use it?" Alec asks.

"Not yet," Jack says. "But this city's got more than its fair share of racial problems. You got the niggers and the skinheads. Mexican gangs, Irish gangs. The Eye-talians, whathaveyou." He pushes the police light back into the glove compartment and forces it shut. "Let's fire this up and get you warm."

The drive north is slow-going. Jack tells Alec his strategy to use side streets, citing the bumper-to-bumper congestion on Lake Shore Drive. It takes several blocks for the heat to kick in but once it does, Alec is finally warm.

Still thrown by the police light, he asks Jack what he does for a living.

Jack tells Alec that he has his own contracting business, with a crew of eight guys. He hangs dry wall, installs bathrooms, and does some basic carpentry too.

"So this cab-service thing is on the side?"

"Side job, yeah. I pop into the Greyhound station coupla times a week. Specially when the weather's bad. Earn a few extra dollars. Make a new friend here and there."

They are silent for several minutes. Alec can feel his toes thawing. He's about to see his sister and the thought makes him nervous. Although he and Myra were never good friends growing up, at times he felt a genuine closeness between them. But he also had the sense that she could see through him. Whenever he lied to their mother, which was often, Myra would try to get him to come clean—to take responsibility for scratching up their father's Chrysler, or admit to throwing one of their cats off the roof. She was forever half-protecting him and half-admonishing him, and as much as he hated the latter, he's always been grateful for the former. Somehow he can hardly believe that Myra is actually married, much less that she has a kid. He has no idea what her husband is like. And now he's an uncle of all things. He doesn't even know how an uncle is supposed to behave.

Jack pulls the car over beside a building with Myra's address on it and shifts into park. "Here we are," he says, peering through the windshield. "Nice neighborhood."

Alec looks out at the brick apartment buildings. The street is glutted with parked cars and half-shoveled snow drifts.

"By the way," Jack says, "any chance you're lookin' for a job?"

"I am, actually," Alec says.

Jack tells him that he might have a spot opening up on his crew and gives him a white business card. Printed on it, in simple capital letters, is PDM CONTRACTING, with the telephone number below it. "Stands for Painting, Decorating, and Maintenance," Jack says. "After you get settled, ring me up."

"I will," Alec says, and produces two dollars from his wallet.

"You keep that," Jack says. He then tells Alec that he'll wait for him, just to make sure he gets in okay. "I'd hate to leave you hangin' in this cold. Just come back down and give me a thumbs-up."

Alec thanks him and exits the car with his gym bag.

Myra's apartment is on the third floor. Per his sister's instructions, he finds the key under that mat and lets himself in. Nobody's home but she's left a note on the kitchen table:

Alec Christopher,

Welcome to Chicago!

*Make yourself at home. Please excuse the mess. I had to go
pick up Ronan from the sitter's. Denny should be home by 8.
If you want to take a nap I put out clean sheets and a comforter on the sofa. There's potato salad and cold cuts in the
fridge. See you soon.*

Love,
Myra

Seeing his middle name in Myra's salutation makes him feel
young and stupid. He looks around the small apartment. In the living room there is a wool calico sofa, not unlike the one in the living
room back in Elmira. It's the convertible, no doubt, the one he'll be
sleeping on. It'll be itchy, hot. The sheets and comforter are neatly
folded on top of a pillow. A television set is poised on a stand, and
beside it, a stout, wide bookcase filled with books.

The wall over the bookcase features framed photographs of
the Larkins. There is a portrait of Alec's father just before he left
for the war. He is wearing his dress greens and has a crew cut. He
appears to be proud and hopeful. He's even smiling. Alec can see
Myra's eyes in his. In another photo, his mother is standing beside
the upright piano, which was in their living room in Elmira. She's
maybe thirty—just younger than Alec is now—and smiling
demurely, with downcast eyes, as if she's keeping a secret. She's
wearing a light-colored dress, a matching pillbox hat, white gloves.
He remembers it being one of her favorite church outfits. There is a
white vase of lilacs on the hood of the piano. Ava looks tall and shy
and unaware of her power, which is shocking to Alec. He's always
only known her to be dominant and direct; she never turned away
from anything. Beside this photo of their mother is Fiona's senior
class portrait. Her pale eyes seem to surge through the glass. She
wears a sneaky smile, as if hiding a lit cigarette just outside the
frame. Her white Catholic school blouse isn't buttoned all the way
up to her neck and the loose collar exposes her collarbone. Directly

under Fiona's senior picture, in a small gunmetal frame, is a snapshot of Joan. She's mid-laugh, bowled over on the living room floor, hugging Frank, the Larkins' Siamese cat. She's wearing her bumblebee Halloween costume, her face ecstatic. Poor dumb Joan. He was always cruel to her, sometimes viciously so, and yet she still loved him. And then there's Lexy, elegant and mature in her high school senior color portrait. Her long blond hair and blue eyes and high cheekbones make her seem like a pageant girl. Even in this simple photo her expression exudes an intelligence.

There's also a baby picture of his nephew, Ronan, a bald little wrinkled newborn wrapped in a baby blue blanket, and Myra's wedding photo from the ceremony back in Elmira that Alec couldn't bring himself to attend. Myra, who is wearing makeup, which is rare for her, is beautiful in her white wedding dress—genuinely happy—and Denny is dashing in his tuxedo. The priest—one he's never seen before, a tall, bony man with a sharp nose—looks on benevolently. The shame of missing her wedding makes his side ache. Her new last name sounds like a drawer slamming shut: *Happ*.

And then there's Alec's photo. He sits atop a picnic table on the banks of the Chemung River, holding a fishing pole, a coffee can of earthworms set beside him. He is maybe eleven or twelve. He is struck by his own black hair and dark eyes, forever the family imposter. He's wearing cutoff jeans and a white T-shirt. A streak of dirt mars his face and he's smiling for the camera. He doesn't recall having this picture taken and he wonders who was holding the camera. Probably Myra, who had a small Minolta point-and-shoot that she would experiment with now and then. It's the smallest photo on the wall, even smaller than Joan's.

On top of the bookcase are a few knickknacks: a figurine of an angel; a small potted cactus; two ticket stubs from Wrigley Field; and a Mickey Mantle baseball card preserved in fiberglass. Mantle is wearing the navy-blue Yankees cap and holding a yellow bat over his right shoulder and looking off at something in the distance. There is something slightly ominous about his gaze, as if he is watching a wild animal that has sneaked into the stadium. Alec flips the card over. It's from 1952, Mantle's rookie season, and it's likely worth thousands. Almost without thinking of it he slides the card into a pocket of his peacoat.

The floor is overrun with toys. There are wooden blocks and plastic baseballs, a child's leather infielder's glove, and a half-finished coloring-book figure of a cowboy on a TV dinner tray. In the corner, an inflatable Bozo the Clown plastic punching bag. On the coffee table, a vast collection of plastic army figures arranged in two small battalions. Although Alec has never met his nephew, he knows that Ronan was given his baby brother Archie's middle name. He briefly recalls little Archie Larkin, the newborn who died in infancy, barely a smudge in Alec's memory.

The sight of Ronan's toys and his shoes and especially his small clothes neatly folded and arranged in a laundry basket—the checkered underwear and red corduroy trousers and the Casper the Friendly Ghost T-shirt—sets a panic in Alec. He heads into the kitchen, where he encounters more evidence of this child: boxes of breakfast cereal and colorful plastic bowls drying in the rack beside the sink and the alphabet magnets on the refrigerator door, the letters L-O-V-E affixed to the four corners of a Polaroid featuring Myra, Denny, and little Ronan on the steps of the Shedd Aquarium. *October 19th, 1972, Ronan's 4th Birthday* is written on the bottom white panel. Alec recognizes his sister's elegant handwriting, for which she was endlessly praised in grade school. The boy looks happy, squinting because of the bright sun. He's wearing a blue Chicago Cubs T-shirt. Alec can't help but think of the child he is supposed to have with Emma, the life he's just abandoned back in Ogallala. Will it be a boy or a girl? Will it be born with Alec's black hair, or the strawberry blond of Emma's? He sees the baby being born, the crown of its head emerging between Emma's legs, then a shoulder, then a small withered lobster claw instead of an arm. Alec's heartbeat quickens and the tip of his tongue starts to go numb. He can't stand being there for another second. He strides across the apartment, almost tripping over a plastic baseball bat, punting it into the wall. He drops his gym bag and has to re-shoulder it. He opens the door and closes it behind him, locks it, returns the key to its place under the mat, and scampers down the three flights of stairs, taking them two at a time.

As he's passing through the building's narrow foyer, a man entering the building stops him. He's bundled in a parka with a fur-lined hood, which he pulls back from his head. "Hey," he says to Alec.

"Yeah?" Alec says.

"You're Myra's brother."

Alec recognizes the man from the Polaroid on Myra's refrigerator door. Even though the man's face is wind-chapped and his nose is running, Alec can see that it's Myra's husband. He resembles a tired movie actor.

"I'm Denny," the man says. "Denny Happ." He removes a wool glove and offers his hand.

Alec is momentarily speechless. It feels as if he has a sunflower seed caught in his throat.

"Alec, right?"

Alec takes Denny's hand and they shake. Alec is struck by its warmth, its strength.

"Sorry I'm late," Denny continues, releasing his hand. "I had a terrible time finding a parking spot. Our street gets really congested on Sunday nights."

"I'm not Alec," Alec finally stammers.

"Oh," Denny says. "You're not?"

"My name's Jack," Alec says.

"But you look just like my wife's brother."

"I'm Jack," Alec repeats, pulling the business card out of the pocket of his jeans. His gym bag slips off his shoulder again. This time he catches it in the crook of his elbow. He shows the business card to Denny, who takes it from him. "You need any work done on your apartment?" Alec says. "We do drywall, painting, plumbing."

"Our superintendent handles repairs," Denny says. He studies Alec, squinting. "You really are the spitting image of my wife's brother," he adds. "I could show you a family photo. You sure you're not Alec Larkin?"

"I don't know what to tell you," Alec says. "I can only be who I am."

"Well, sorry to bother you," Denny says.

Alec can feel Denny's eyes still on him as he exits the building. Outside he's assaulted by the freezing wind. And relieved to see Jack's Pontiac still idling in front of Myra's building, clouds spewing from its exhaust.

"Nobody's home," Alec says, getting back in the car.

"Then I'm glad I waited," Jack says. "You're liable to get frostbite in this tundra."

Alec asks Jack if he can take him to a motel but Jack protests.

"Don't go blowin' your money on some careless motel," he says. "They'll overcharge you, hit you up for a buncha godforsaken hidden fees. Come stay at my place. I'm just out in Norwood. Get yourself a home-cooked meal. I think my wife's makin' pork chops tonight. We'll give you a warm bed and a proper Chicago welcome."

"I'd hate to be an inconvenience," Alec says.

"Baloney," Jack says, and puts the car into gear and starts the windshield wipers. "Warm bed, home cookin', that's where it's at. In the mornin' I'll run you back down here to your sister's place."

During the drive to Jack's house, Alec realizes that he left Myra's apartment with the Mickey Mantle rookie card. He can feel the corner of its protective case in the pocket of his peacoat.

Jack offers Alec another stick of chewing gum and Alec accepts.

"So what's your story?" Jack says.

"No story, really," Alec says. "I'm just tryin' to find my next — I don't know — chapter, or adventure, whatever you call it."

"The *reason*," Jack says. "The *grand reason*."

"I guess."

"You religious?"

"Hell no," Alec says.

"I usually go along to church with my wife," Jack says. "For the visuals."

"The visuals?" Alec says.

"It looks good," Jack says. "Throw on a pair of trousers, buff up the wingtips. Glad-hand it with Father McQuaid. I don't take much from the sermon, though. Way I see it, the world is the world. No amount of science or religion or championship baseball's gonna change things. You're always gonna have war. You're always gonna have famine. Old ladies with blue rinse in their hair. Astronauts floatin' around in the atmosphere. Mariachi bands and Godzilla movies. We're all here for barely a blip—same as the chickens and the termites—and if there really is a God he clearly ain't payin' no attention."

After another silence, Jack asks Alec what kind of job experience he has. Alec tells him about his stint picking apples near Niagara Falls, his recent gig on Kerwood Flahive's moving truck, and the summer he tamped down asphalt on a road-construction crew in Topeka, Kansas.

"So you clearly been a laborer," Jack says.

"That's about the *only* thing I've been," Alec says.

"You don't mind gettin' your hands dirty."

"My hands've been dirty since I left home."

"And where's that?"

"Elmira, New York."

"East Coast boy," Jack says. "Never thought much of that part of the country. Seems to be plagued with corruption. The cities out there are disgustin'. The Big Rotten Apple. Washington, DC. Philadelphia's one of the filthiest cities we have. Rats skitterin' this way and that."

"In Elmira there weren't any rats," Alec says. "But there were plenty of Catholics."

Jack releases an unexpected laugh, four staccato reports in a surprisingly high, womanish falsetto. His eruption has him driving over the speed limit. There is the momentary sense that he could lose control and swerve into oncoming traffic. Alec can feel his hands digging into the upholstery.

Minutes later, after a long stretch of silence, they pull onto a quiet side street, and Jack says, "Welcome to Norwood."

As they get out of the car the snow continues to fall but the wind has died. The flakes are as big as acorns. Jack's modest, blond ranch house, situated between two similar homes, looks as if it is being slowly consumed by snowdrifts.

Jack reaches for Alec's gym bag and this time Alec doesn't decline. "Careful," Jack says during their approach up the sloping driveway. "My wife slipped on the walkway earlier and landed right on her can."

The winter cold is seeping through Alec's sneakers again. He removes the gum from his mouth, tosses it behind him. His big toes and anklebones and the arches of his feet are freezing. He should've taken a pair of socks from the laundry basket in Myra's living room.

Jack's front door opens directly into a wood-paneled living room. Dominating the space is a console television, on top of which sits a colorful ceramic figure of a clown lying on its side, perhaps an out-of-place cookie jar. A brown wool sofa has a matching armchair as partner, and the carpeting is gray, pilling here and there, as if a cat has had its way with it. To Alec's immense gratitude, the house is warm. His stomach twists toward the smell of cooking.

"Carole!" Jack calls out after closing the front door behind them. "Come meet my new friend!"

Moments later, his wife enters the living room. Carole is tall and pretty, dressed in a long Kelly green skirt with a matching cardigan over her blouse. Her synthetic-looking blond hair is either a wig or it's been so slathered with hairspray that it might as well be. That hairdo could stop a bullet, Alec thinks. When she steps toward him, she leads with her hips. She extends her hand and they shake. Her palm is warm from cooking.

"Carole, Alec," Jack says. "Alec, meet the big love of my little life."

"Lovely to meet you, Alec," Carole says and then quietly tells Jack that she just put the girls to bed.

"The rugrats," Jack says to Alec. "We gotta use our extra-indoor voices." He explains the situation to his wife—how he gave Alec a ride to his sister's place on the North Side but then she wasn't home. "I couldn't just leave him alone in this crazy cold," he says. "Poor kid don't even got socks on."

"Well, we got socks," Carole says. "I'll rustle up a clean pair for you." She turns to Jack. "Pork chops and lima beans, by the way. It's already on the table. And a tossed salad with thousand island. I'll go put out an extra place setting. And if you like pie, Alec, I got a great key lime from the Jewel, so you might wanna loosen your belt a notch." She heads back into the kitchen.

"What a gal," Jack says. He carries the gym bag down the hall to the guest room while pointing Alec in the direction of the bathroom.

Alec doesn't bother turning on the light but simply closes the door and sits on the toilet with the seat down. He feels the long day—all those many hours on the bus—settling in his neck and jaws. He removes his wet tennis shoes and swaddles his feet in a few layers of toilet paper, then puts the shoes back on. When he stands to get his bearings, the blood abandons his head. He recalls running out of his sister's apartment. This familiar cowardice is starting to be unbearable. In the morning he'll return to Myra's apartment and come clean to Denny. Knowing he can't endure seeing his reflection in the medicine-chest mirror, he leaves the bathroom without ever turning on the light.

In Jack's small dining room they eat rubbery pork chops and mushy lima beans. Milk has been poured into tall, amber glasses. Alec hasn't drunk milk since he left Elmira, more than a decade ago, and the smell and sight of it is almost nauseating. His mother made him and his sisters drink it, endlessly praising its health benefits. The calcium helped build up your bones and teeth. Without milk you'd never physically develop to your full potential. When he was little his sister Joan drank so much milk he imagined she would grow up to be seven feet tall with giant hippopotamus teeth.

"Not a dairy guy?" Jack says, obviously sensing his repulsion.

"I'm allergic," Alec lies.

"What happens to ya?"

"Trust me, you don't wanna know."

"Your plumbing goes ka-blooey," Jack says, as if he knows all too well about intestinal disasters.

"Hon," Carole says. "Come on now."

"Don't we got any pop?" Jack says.

"We ran outta the Fresca yesterday. I'm pretty sure we got pine-apple juice downstairs. Orange juice, too."

"But that's for my Mai Tais," Jack says, holding a spoonful of lima beans. He leans toward Alec conspiratorially. "Later I'll make you one."

"Oh, we got Ocean Spray!" Carole exclaims, sitting very erect. Her hair is like a golden swan perched on her head. She squares her body to Alec and speaks to him as if he's a child. "Would you care for some Ocean Spray Cranapple?"

"I'd love some," Alec says.

Carole rises and scoots to the refrigerator in her white heels. She's an attractive woman, not at all what Alec expected. Somehow Jack snagged a lady above his class. When he'd mentioned her in the car Alec imagined a female version of Jack: jowly and pudgy around the middle, a she-badger in ill-fitting polyester. Carole is more like an attractive, land-dwelling dolphin.

After she returns with a glass of the juice, she asks after Alec's sister. "When was the last time you seen her?"

"A few years ago," he lies.

"Are you two comrades?" Jack asks.

"In a way," Alec says. "We were never good friends, but there was always a certain closeness. We can go years without seeing each other and then when we do it's like no time's passed."

The three of them eat. The silence is scored by Jack's congested breathing. Alec is possessed by the thought that his new friend is not long for this world; he might be a few large pizzas away from a coronary.

"Be sure to save some room for the key lime," Carole says, when a little blond girl enters the dining room. She is wearing cotton footy pajamas patterned with tiny blue buttercups. "Sweetheart, what is it?" Carole says to the girl, setting her fork down and moving to her.

"Can't sleep," the girl says around the thumb in her mouth. Her eyes are puffy, as if she's suffered a spider bite. "The shadows look like monster hands," she mewls.

Carole turns to Alec. "She's talkin' about the neighbor's sycamore."

Another goddamn child, Alec thinks. Once you become aware of them they start popping up everywhere.

"Let's go close your curtains," Carole says. "Okay sweet pea?" The little girl nods and Carole says, "Be right back."

When they are gone, Jack says, "She was part of the package. Her and her sister. The stepkids."

The wind rattles the windows in the living room. There is something at once flimsy and permanent about this little house. Its low center of gravity gives it the air of indestructibility and yet it clatters like a cheap metal shed.

"Children make the world a brighter place, though, ain't it?" Jack says.

"Definitely," Alec hears himself reply unconvincingly.

For the first time he notices a painting of a hobo clown hanging on one of the dining room's paneled walls. The clown, whose face is made up garishly, is sitting on a milk crate and warming his hands by a small fire. It's a nighttime setting but in the far distance the sky glows orange, apocalyptically. There is something terribly sad about this clown.

Alec can feel Jack's gaze on him.

"I got a proposition," he says.

"You want me to eat the key lime," Alec says.

"No," Jack says, chuckling, "I want you to come work on my crew—whattaya say, huh? You could start Tuesday, use tomorrow to get your bearings. I'll start you off hangin' drywall. I pay my guys a real fair wage. I think you'd be a good fit."

"Drywall," Alec says.

"It's an honest day's work. It beats sittin' around, twiddlin' your thumbs. At least tell me you'll think about it."

"Okay," Alec says.

"Seriously," Jack says. "I get a good vibe from you."

Alec sees the past few months of his life unraveling before him like a spool of discarded thread. He'll be going from wrapping and taping and hauling furniture on one of Kerwood Flahive's moving trucks to hanging drywall in the middle of a Chicago winter. But a job's a job and he definitely needs one. He can't expect to freeload off Myra and Denny for more than a few weeks.

"You'll need good work boots and gloves, but I can front ya the money for that," Jack says.

"Yeah, I didn't come into town with much," Alec says.

Carole has now returned to the dining room, having changed into her nightgown, over which she wears a baby-blue terrycloth housecoat. On her feet are a pair of fluffy pink bunny-ear slippers. She's holding a pair of white athletic socks with blue and yellow rings.

"It looks like Alec here's gonna join my crew!" Jack says.

"Well, congratulations!" she says to Alec, handing him the socks and starting to clear the table. When Alec thanks her—for both the socks and the dinner—she says, "Oh, it's nothin'." She heads into the kitchen carrying the serving tray of leftover pork chops and lima beans, then calls back, "Oh, the key lime!"

"Let's save it for tomorrow," Jack says.

"But our guest!" she cries.

"You don't want no pie, do ya?" Jack says.

Alec shakes his head.

"He don't even want none," Jack calls to his wife. "You filled the kid up, he's fit to burst, ain't it, Alec."

"I'm fit to burst," Alec repeats. "Everything was great."

"Hon, I got the rest of this," Jack says of the remaining dishes and silverware. When Carole returns he takes her hand and kisses the back of it. "This one," he says. "I don't know what I'd do without her."

"You're the pot of gold," she says. "I'm the lucky one."

"You go to bed," he tells her. "Me and my new employee are gonna go down to the basement and celebrate."

"No music down there," Carole says.

"No music," he promises.

"This one and his hi-fi," she says to Alec. "How much REO Speedwagon can one man listen to, anyway?"

"We'll be as quiet as pillows," Jack assures her.

Carole kisses him on the top of his lubricated head and he squeezes her arm with his small, tense hand. Then Carole tells Alec that the guest room has been made up for him. "I put an extra tooth-brush out for you, too. It's still in the plastic so it's brand spankin'."

Alec thanks her again and they all say good night. Carole pivots and heads down the hall.

After the muffled sound of their bedroom door opening and closing, Jack turns the same hand that just squeezed his wife's shoulder into a jabbering, snouted puppet. *"It's still in the plastic so it's brand spankin',"* he ventriloquizes in a squeaky cartoon voice. *"Beep-bata-beep-beep-beep."* He rolls his eyes and juts his head toward their bedroom. "Sometimes I think I married a dang Chatty Cathy doll," he says under his breath. "Just pull the ring, you never know *what* she'll say next."

The two of them stifle laughter at his imitation of the famous commercial. When Jack laughs his face gathers in on itself, expos-ing a bluish row of short, crowded teeth.

DOWN IN THE BASEMENT, Jack uses a stainless-steel cocktail shaker to mix Mai Tais behind a makeshift tiki bar, which is framed by a faux grass ramada and strung with Christmas lights. A refrigerator flanks four shelves of alcohol and mixers and a rack that bears the aforementioned hi-fi system, whose rectangular speakers are set at opposite ends of the bar.

Hanging on the wall near the entrance is another painting of a clown. This one is done portrait-style, from the shoulders up. The clown looks hungover, beleaguered by the world, if not a tad angry.

"That's Pogo," Jack says, pouring the contents of the shaker into glass tumblers.

"You got a thing for clowns," Alec says.

"Hey, they get sad just like everyone else," Jack says, and carries their drinks to a small card table. "They gotta pay the fiddler, too." Alec joins him at the table and Jack passes him his Mai Tai. "Tastes just like Hawaii," he says. "Welcome to my little underground hideaway."

They clink tumblers and drink. The cold tangy beverage makes Alec's tongue go tight and small.

He notices an orange curtain drawn across a small entryway. "What's back there?" he asks.

"That's where I keep all the secrets to the universe," Jack says. He downs his drink in about two gulps and returns to the bar to make another batch. "I'll let you in on one such secret," he says as he's pouring all the ingredients into the shaker. "We are both here, right now. This is really happening. We are drinking Mai Tais and discussing the things that men discuss."

"No doubt," Alec asks.

"You got a middle name?" Jack asks.

"Joseph," Alec lies, for no reason he can tell.

"Like the father of Jesus."

"Don't remind me," Alec says, draining his Mai Tai.

"Catholic boy?"

"Not anymore," Alec says. "I'm done with all that."

"Joseph was a handyman, you know. Carpentry was his expertise. I believe he carried a hammer on his person. A hammer and a level." Jack returns to the table with the shaker and refreshes Alec's drink first, then refills his own tumbler. "Can I see your ring?" he asks, pointing at Alec's high school class ring.

Alec removes it and hands it to him.

"Notre Dame High School," Jack says, reading the engraving. "In Elmira. That's a nice one," he says, and hands it back.

Alec has never really understood why he keeps wearing the ring when everything else from his hometown feels like it's faded into the past.

Jack rises and heads toward the orange curtain. "Be right back," he says.

While he's gone, Alec takes a gulp of his second Mai Tai. Why is this strange man being so nice to him? he wonders. What the hell has he done to deserve this? For all of his disdain for his religious upbringing he finds himself considering the possibility of divine creatures. Human angels who appear and guide you during difficult moments. He remembers Father Bryce and the piece of paper in his pocket with the priest's phone number on it. Would he have arrived in Milwaukee by now? Over by the bar a rotary phone is affixed to the wall. Alec crosses to it, removes the piece of paper from the front pocket of his jeans, takes the receiver off the hook, and dials the number. Moments later, when a man's voice answers, Alec asks if Father Bryce is there.

"I believe he's turned in for the night. Would you like to leave him a message?"

"Maybe just tell him Alec called."

"I'll do that, Alec," the man says. "Can I take down your number?"

"No," he says. "Maybe I'll try him again tomorrow."

Alec hangs up and takes in the painting of the clown again. At closer proximity its head appears to have the same shape as Jack's. And there's something similar in the eyes, too.

Just then Jack comes through the orange curtain holding a small shoebox. "Pogo the Clown," he says.

"Who's the artist?" Alec asks.

"John is."

"Who's John?"

"John is the man who stands before you."

"Oh," Alec says, a little thrown. "I thought your name was Jack."

"Jack's sorta like my nickname. You can keep calling me Jack if that's your preference. Do you like the painting?"

"Yeah, it's colorful," Alec says.

"Color's maybe the most important thing in a work of art," Jack says. "Let me show you somethin'."

He nods toward the card table and they return to it. Then Jack opens the lid of the shoebox to reveal several class rings with various stones. "I collect 'em," he says.

"Where are they from?" Alec asks.

"Oh, here and there. Garage sales. Flea markets. Doodad shops. This one here's my favorite."

He hands a ring to Alec, who turns it between his thumb and forefinger.

"Glenwood High School, Class of Nineteen Seventy-three," Alec says.

"I found that one in the bathroom of the bus station. I just love the stone. The ruby redness."

"Where's Glenwood?"

"There's one here in Illinois, but I believe that Glenwood is Glenwood, Iowa."

"How do you know?" Alec says.

"Because when I hold it in my hand I get a feeling of the prairie."

Jack retrieves the ring, puts it into the shoebox, and secures the lid. Then he takes the box with him to the bar, where he mixes another batch of Mai Tais, and, leaving the box on the bar, returns to the card table to refill their tumblers.

"So according to your ring you were Class of Fifty-Nine," Jack says.

"I'm lucky to have this," Alec says, looking at his class ring. "I barely graduated."

"You know what's crazy, Alec?"

Alec drinks from his tumbler. "What," he says.

"You're older'n me!" Jack exclaims. His portly face has taken on a sheen. "When I seen you at the bus station I figured you for seventeen-eighteen! But you're friggin thirty!"

"Thirty-one, actually," Alec says. "I'll be thirty-two in March."

"That's just crazy!" Jack says.

"My whole family looks young," Alec says.

"Genes," Jack says. "Some people look just like their parents. Or they're bowlegged like their long-lost uncle Stubin. Or they're born into the world with spina bifida. Birthmarks shaped like the state of Texas, whathaveyou. Ain't genes the craziest thing?"

"Most of my family's tall like my mother," Alec says. "My dad's only about five-ten."

"How tall is Mom?" Jack asks.

"Six-three," Alec says.

"Your mother's six-three?!" Jack cries. "That's Amazonian!" He downs his Mai Tai, refills his tumbler yet again, and holds it up, offering a toast. "To all the little mysteries."

"To all the little mysteries," Alec echoes.

"And to Speedwagon."

"And to Speedwagon."

"Best band in North America," Jack says.

They clink glasses and drink.

"Can I show you a trick?" Jack says, setting his tumbler down.

"What kind of a trick?"

"It's a magic trick. A really good one." From seemingly out of nowhere, Jack produces a pair of handcuffs.

"Those are handcuffs," Alec says.

"You're dang right they're handcuffs," Jack says. "Genuine police-issued. Put 'em on and I'll show you how to get out of 'em."

"How?" Alec says.

"Just put the dang things on and I'll show you."

"Really?" Alec says.

"Really, really, really," Jack says.

Alec hesitates but takes the handcuffs and arranges one around his left wrist. It's as if he's watching someone else perform the action, as if some strangely detached part of him wants to watch the other Alec go all the way to the end of the trick.

"Do the other one, too," Jack says playfully, exposing those short blue teeth.

Alec starts to clasp the other one around his right wrist when Jack stops him.

"Behind your back," he says. "Or it won't count."

Jack gulps his drink and then moves to Alec and gently grabs his wrists and arranges them behind his back and secures the handcuffs. He then returns to his seat, cradling his soft fleshy chin with his hands. They sit there, simply looking at each other.

"Look at you," Jack says. "You're handcuffed."

After a brief silence, during which some subterranean heating system cycles on, Alec begins laughing hysterically. Jack laughs too — those odd, short reports again — and together they laugh so hard and loud that Jack has to bring his finger to his lips.

"*Sshshshsh!*" he says, still laughing. "We'll wake Carole!"

Alec swallows his laughter and forces it through his nose. "I got handcuffs on," he practically cries.

"Ain't this fun?" Jack says quietly.

"Best time I've had in a while!" Alec says. And it's true. He can't even remember the last time he's laughed this hard. His face feels gigantic.

Then from under the table Jack produces a short wooden dowel and a length of rope and sets the items before Alec. It's like he's conducting a game involving household objects for a group of children.

"What are those for?" Alec asks.

"These are the props for the rest of the trick," Jack says. "The essential props."

The rope, which has an eyelid loop at each end, looks like an expired, two-headed snake.

"How does it work?" Alec asks. He knows that he is somehow doomed, and still he doesn't want to change the course of whatever is going to happen.

"It's simple, really," Jack says. "I put the rope around your neck and slip this dowel through them two eyelids and start crankin' away until you disappear."

Alec laughs again, as does Jack.

"I'm gonna disappear?" Alec says, imagining a vast black void. Will he become part of it? Will he dissolve into a million tiny particles, like the finest black pollen, and float away in the void?

"Yes, sir," Jack replies. "Like I said, it's a magic trick. I start cranking on the dowel and then you disappear and those handcuffs you got on fall right to the floor."

"And then do I reappear?" Alec asks, his grin still making his face feel huge, rubbery.

"I've never seen that happen before," Jack says. "But when it comes to magic, you just never know! Let's give it a shot, huh?" Jack comes up behind Alec, loops the length of rope around his neck, and inserts the wooden dowel through the rope's two eyelids. "Can you see how it works?" he says, his breath—thickened by the Mai Tais—on Alec's neck.

"Sure, I see," Alec says, closing his eyes.

There is a brief pause during which Jack seems to withdraw into himself. Alec can no longer feel his presence behind him.

And then the rope and the dowel are removed from around Alec's neck, the handcuffs unlocked.

"I really thought you were eighteen," Jack says, confused. He returns to the little table and sets the dowel before him, staring at the implement as if seeking its counsel.

"Sometimes I wish I was," Alec says. "I'd get a do-over."

"They only give you do-overs on second-rate golf courses. I believe they call it a mulligan."

"I definitely could use one of those," Alec says.

"You're a nice kid," Jack tells him gently.

LATER IN THE CAR, they're quiet while Jack drives east through the freshly plowed streets of Chicago's North Side. After they came up from the basement he retrieved Alec's gym bag and then abruptly told him it was best to drive him back to his sister's tonight, citing something about the guest room having a mold problem.

During the silence Alec cycles through fragments of his life: his boyhood bed with its thin cotton blanket, blue as Easter; an old abandoned house back in Elmira, just beyond the banks of the Chemung River, half-charred by a fire, where he and his friend Sean Merlo would throw stones at its broken windows; an empty parking lot in Topeka where he found thirty-five dollars in a brown leather wallet; the walnut pews of St. John the Baptist that he polished as an acolyte, their cool smooth grains; a red fox with a dead gray squirrel in its mouth trotting through the backyard of a rooming house he lived in for a time in Sioux Center, Iowa, the fox's piercing amber eyes; the hummingbirds warring over the nectar contained in the trio of feeders that his mother hung from the eaves of the front porch, the setting sun backlighting the blur of their short, spastic wings...

Jack drops him off on Hoyne Avenue, and once Alec steps out of the car, despite the cold the two talk through the passenger's side window about Alec's start time the following morning.

"Eleven a.m.," Jack says. "Pack a lunch." On the back of a business card he writes the address of the house where his team is renovating a bathroom and hands it to Alec, telling him there's a westbound bus up on Montrose that will get him there in under an hour. "Try and be there fifteen minutes early so I can introduce you to the team."

"I will," Alec says. "Thanks for everything."

"Sure thing," Jack says, then produces his wallet and takes out a hundred dollars in twenties, folds the bills in half, and extends the knot of money toward Alec. "So you can get situated."

"I can't accept that," Alec says.

"Sure you can," Jack says. "Think of it as an advance. Welcome to the Windy City." Jack forces it into his hand. "See you tomorrow," he says, rolls the window up, and drives off.

Feeling oddly renewed, in the certainty that he has escaped some terrible ending, Alec stuffs the wad of money into the front pocket of his jeans and stares up at his sister's apartment building. And yet despite this extra chance, his self-loathing seems only to thicken. *You're a nobody*, he thinks. *You're a no-good, freeloading nobody. About to be thirty-two years old. Look at you.*

It's well past midnight and the Chicago cold has gotten downright absurd. Ogallala was nothing compared to this. He opens his gym bag and removes the Bible that Father Bryce gave him. He squeezes it for a moment. Just as the blood rushes to his hands he drops the Bible in a snowdrift, feeling the need to move. He closes his gym bag, shoulders it, and jogs east, to Damen Avenue, where he hails the first cab he sees.

"Where to?" the Negro cabbie asks him after his shuts the door.

The inside of the cab smells like menthol cigarettes.

"Take me to the train station," Alec says.

He imagines himself staring out the window of a speeding, cross-country train car, snowy fields in the distance. Silos and corncribs and tiny farmhouses besieged with icicles. He'll use the money Jack just gave him to go somewhere new. Maybe he'll head south this time instead. He'll go as far south as he can get, far away from this weather.

After a block, Alec asks if it's a big train station.

"One of the biggest in the country," the cabbie says. He turns down his soul music on the radio. "From Union Station you can get a train to just about anywhere."

Alec pulls out the Mickey Mantle collector card from the front pocket of his jeans. Using his thumb to prod one of the corners of its fiberglass casing he is seized by a pang of guilt, like a cold coin lodged in his bowels. But then he swallows a few times, imagines the warm Southern light on his face — the kind of light he's experienced only by gazing at cigarette ads and record albums by Elton John and the Allman Brothers Band — and the feeling passes.

PART TWO

7

JOLIET, ILLINOIS
MARCH 30, 1981

MYRA LEE

H E'S DEFINITELY IN CARBONDALE," Marna tells Myra on the way back from the nurses' lounge, holding two cans of orange Fanta and a large flat manila envelope.

Myra is putting a new Band-Aid over the blister that's formed just behind her left ankle. Her new nursing shoes have been tough to break in. Her old ones lasted four years at St. Francis up in Evanston, and four more here at St. Joseph in Joliet, but less than a week into her new position (she's just been promoted to Supervising Pediatrics Nurse) they'd worn through the soles. With the title bump and modest pay increase she figured the least she could do was splurge for a new pair of Annie Hi's.

"Dale saw him getting out of a white Datsun 200SX with Illinois plates," Marna continues as she sits down at the nurses' station, engaging in the usual struggle to get down to her chair. Her bad back makes her seem much older than her forty-four years. "And then he went into her house and they ate a spaghetti dinner and watched *WKRP in Cincinnati*."

"Did he ever come back out?" Myra asks.

"I'm afraid not, hon."

Myra never knew Denny to be a spaghetti eater. He rarely if ever ate any kind of pasta at all. He preferred meatloaf and potatoes or crockpot brisket with the special creamed-spinach recipe that she learned from her mother. The closest thing to spaghetti he ever ate was a lasagna that she made for his thirty-first birthday and he barely finished one helping.

Myra can feel all the blood rushing from her head. She hasn't heard a peep from Denny since he left her and Ronan some six years ago, when they were still living in the little white house with the flower boxes on the window ledges and the hickory tree in the front lawn. This was up in Wilmette, just north of Evanston, where they'd been enjoying a seemingly happy life for two years before Denny's abrupt, unexplained disappearance. The two-bedroom, single-story ranch house wasn't quite twelve hundred square feet but it was only twenty years old and featured a sunken living room and state-of-the-art kitchen appliances and an attached garage and zero damage to the foundation. After Myra's father helped with the down payment, her salary combined with Denny's could cover the mortgage and the bills and the monthly note for their red Volkswagen Beetle with a little to spare if she was frugal about the groceries. It was the kind of house in which you could raise a child, keep the refrigerator stocked, and still have a decent showing at Christmas. Even after Denny left, she wanted to remain in the house and raise Ronan on her own, but without her husband's salary she could no longer afford it and had to sell.

Marna is Myra's closest friend, and her husband, Dale, is a former Will County cop who got shot through the left femur during an East Side gang-related skirmish. Dale received an early retirement package, and now has his own carpet-cleaning business and does private detective work on the side. Dale was able to get a lead on Denny from his previous employer, Homewood-Flossmoor High School, where Denny had worked as a substitute teacher, and tracked him all over the western suburbs and into northeast Indiana, before finding him way the hell down in Carbondale, where Denny has purportedly been shacking up with a woman named Connie Fullmer, another nurse of all things. It turns out that Denny was under her care at a mental hospital in Harrisburg, where he had been admitted for over a year.

According to Dale, the incident that led to Denny's hospitalization occurred in Murphysboro, Illinois, where, in a quaint family neighborhood, he'd climbed a tree and begun screaming, "I only have the things that I was issued!" over and over again. By the time local police arrived, Denny had stripped off all his clothes and was violently shaking the branches of the tree as if to ward off attackers. The Veterans Association paid for his care at the Mulberry Center, in Harrisburg, where he improved steadily, month by month. His doctors got him on a psychoactive cocktail that regulated his behavior well enough that they felt he was fit to return to society and transition to outpatient status. Nurse Connie and Denny started dating immediately following his release.

Dale has typed up all of this in a five-page report that Myra has spent the past few days poring over at the kitchen table of her little two-bedroom unit in the Cedarwood Apartment Complex, over on Ingalls Avenue, where she lives with her son, Ronan, currently a sixth grader at Troy Junior High School.

The photos contained in the manila envelope, which Marna hands her now at the nurses' station, are the last bit of proof, and conclude Dale's services rendered.

Myra is afraid to open the envelope. She imagines Connie as a tall blond with long smooth legs, like Angie Dickinson from *Police Woman*. Deep down she's always thought herself to be too normal for her husband, and believed a prettier woman would eventually lure him away.

For the past four years, since their very first post-work drink at Earl's, Marna has encouraged Myra to forget about Denny. Even then it had already been a couple of years since he'd abandoned her and Ronan, who was just six when Denny never came home from work during an unlikely two-day, early-April blizzard that dumped a foot of snow on the Chicagoland area. It was a storm so powerful that it even shut down O'Hare Airport. There was no farewell note. Denny hadn't even bothered to pack his things. For weeks Myra had to stare at his clothes hanging in their closet before finally deciding to give them to Goodwill. It took her almost six months to remove his toothbrush from the plastic Chicago Cubs cup on the bathroom sink and drop it in the trash. Denny had just vanished like some horribly botched magician's trick. Of course Myra filed a missing person report. A few days after the snowstorm the police even sent a small search party through Wilmette's Centennial Park, thinking he might have tried walking home and got caught up in the snowstorm, but it yielded nothing, and meanwhile Denny never again showed up to his job at Homewood-Flossmoor, where he'd been substitute-teaching history. Since April 1, 1975 — that dreadful April Fool's Day smack dab in the middle of the decade — Myra hasn't heard a word from him.

For several months following his disappearance she was in contact with his half-siblings, Carl and Nora, but they knew nothing. For a long time Myra thought he was dead, but his body never turned up at the morgue. Deep down she's known he was alive all this time. She hasn't stopped dreaming about him — vivid, realistic dreams that leave her bereft, confused, and often in tears. Nights alone have been long, to say the least.

Ronan has been without a father since he was six. Every morning, still, Myra wakes to him sleeping on the floor beside her bed. Yes, even at twelve, Ronan crawls into her room in the middle of the night and curls into the fetal position next to her side table. Myra always leaves an extra blanket and a pillow for him. In the morning she simply shakes him awake and by the time she returns from the bathroom he's back in his own bed, in his room at the other end of the short apartment hallway, getting ready for school. When she finally brought the matter up to her mother, a few years ago, Ava Larkin simply said that Ronan was likely going through a phase.

"You all had sleeping issues," she told Myra. "Give it time. He'll eventually grow out of it."

But that hasn't happened. Myra has thought about seeking counseling for him, but the few times she made calls to a local child psychologist, she hung up the phone before the secretary could set an appointment. If there really is a problem with Ronan, she can't stand to face it. To make matters worse, when it comes to her own health, Myra's stomach has grown increasingly uneasy in the years since Denny's disappearance. It feels as if each year he's been away has caused various chambers inside her to slowly shut down. Her appetite has definitely shrunk. She can't remember the last time she finished a meal. In the nurses' lounge, Marna is always on her case about how she can barely eat half a sandwich.

Regarding Denny's mental problems, before they were married Myra was completely in the dark. The only thing he ever told her about was his honorable discharge from West Point, which he said was for "medical reasons." When pressed about it he would only acknowledge "a series of bad headaches" which were likely "stress-related."

What Myra came to learn later is what Denny told her one night after she found him sitting in their bedroom closet, fiercely clenching his knees to his chest and muttering to himself indecipherably. Even though it was the middle of August he had bundled himself in one of Ava Larkin's patchwork quilts. He was like a child hiding from the boogeyman. This occurred a little over two years into their marriage, when Ronan was a baby and they still lived on Hoyne Avenue, on the North Side of Chicago. After Myra was able to coax him out of their closet, Denny sat on their bedroom floor with his head in her lap and told her the story of his early days at West Point. He was only sixteen and by far the youngest cadet. After sustaining a knee injury during a track-and-field workout he had to be on crutches and was forced to join a company of fellow injured cadets—outcasts, really—called the "walking wounded." Myra already knew the story but the part she didn't know was that because of his youth Denny was constantly humiliated by his superiors for being "sweet," meaning "sweet sixteen." His platoon sergeant in the walking wounded was a giant football player from Colorado Springs named Aaron Wilde, who started calling him "Plebe Sweetie." The effeminate nickname caught fire, and no amount of push-ups he snapped off to prove his strength could reverse it.

Even his roommate, a mediocre blond kid from Louisville named Laird Plotke, jumped in on the fun. One night before Taps he said, "Hey, Sweetie, can I borrow your shoe polish? I'm running low."

And though Denny knew he could easily handle the guy, he simply acquiesced, telling him that his shoe polish was in the top compartment of his footlocker.

It didn't matter that Denny was both scholastically and athletically one of the elite members of his class. His knee injury—a badly torn meniscus that would take months to heal—saw him plummet down the Plebe food chain. Being relegated to a detail of cadets considered to be the lowest caste in the academy put him miles behind his fellow first-years. Toward the end of his second term things got so bad that he shut himself in his closet—likely in the same manner that Myra had discovered him that very night—and slashed his upper left arm with a serrated steak knife that he'd stolen from the mess hall. The self-inflicted wound accounted for the grisly scar on the inside of his upper left biceps.

"So it wasn't a series of headaches," Myra said, stroking his temples.

"No," he admitted. "I cracked up."

But what Denny could apparently never say out loud was that it was a suicide attempt. The self-mutilation occurred at a critical path of the branchial artery, thus providing the unfortunate distinction of his "Section 8 discharge," an official military classification judging a person mentally unfit for service. These details Myra only recently came to know through Dale's sleuthing.

Not yet ready to confront the photos, Myra slides the manila envelope into her purse and takes out her checkbook. She writes a check to Dale for $300 and hands it to Marna, who folds it in half and slips it into her pants pocket.

"If you want me with you when you look at those, just let me know," Marna says, squeezing Myra's shoulder. "We could go over to Earl's and sit at the bar, first round's on me."

Marna's been trying to set Myra up with Dale's friend, a Black man named Emile Wisdom. Emile, a Vietnam vet and social worker who lost his wife to cancer a few years ago, lives over in Lockport.

But at forty-two, despite not having a single gray hair on her head, Myra already feels like her days of love and sex and companionship are well behind her.

AFTER WORK, INSTEAD OF heading over to Earl's to meet Marna, Myra turns right on Oneida Street and heads for the interstate, where she takes the exit south toward Bloomington-Normal. For the first twenty miles or so she pays no attention to how much gas she has in her yellow Pacer hatchback coupe, which she got when she traded in the Volkswagen Bug last year. The Pacer is mostly glass and there are times when it feels as if she's driving a fishbowl, but its fuel efficiency has been a plus. She has to fill up the tank only a few times a month.

The radio seems hellbent on playing one sad love song after another. Chicago's "If You Leave Me Now," Bonnie Tyler's "It's a Heartache," Debby Boone's "You Light Up My Life," and on and on. By the time she reaches Pontiac, Myra turns the radio off, opting for silence.

The sun is starting to set, turning the sky a rich lilac over the wide western fields of Illinois. Myra stops to get gas at a Gulf station in Chenoa, where, after filling up her tank, the hard-of-hearing attendant insists on checking her oil even though she tells him not to bother. There is a payphone underneath the Gulf sign and Myra has a momentary impulse to call over to Earl's and apologize to Marna for not showing up, but the impulse is replaced immediately by a vision of Denny sitting beside beautiful long-legged Connie Fullmer on her sofa, watching television. She also thinks of her son, who, following track practice, is probably standing in front of the refrigerator, still in his running gear, staring at a package of cold cuts and trying to work out what kind of sandwich he'll make. The guilt of it thickens her tongue.

"Oil's fine," the attendant says, letting the hood slam.

With the sun down, Myra puts on the peach-colored cardigan that her mother gave her for Christmas. Including tip she winds up spending twenty-eight dollars, which is entirely too much money. She was going to use that money for tomorrow's groceries.

Before getting back on the highway, Myra retraces her map, which she marked with a red pen in the parking lot of St. Joe. She has about thirty more miles before she'll connect with Route 51, which she'll take for the remaining two hundred miles all the way down to Carbondale, which sits comfortably in the bottommost southwestern cleft of the state's chin. She promises herself that she'll call Ronan and check in on him as soon as she gets a chance.

FOUR AND A HALF hours later, Myra pulls up in front of a low, half-stone, half-clapboard single-family home at 703 South Dixon Avenue. The brown front lawn, not yet recovered from the fading winter, is treeless. The gutters on the left side of the roof appear to have been pried loose. The low evergreen shrubs along the front of the house are in need of a trim. Behind the living room window a faint glow illuminates the cream-colored drapes. It's just after 11:00 p.m. Myra parks across the street and kills the engine. It looks like the kind of home a small family lives in and she wonders if Connie Fullmer has children; if she and Denny have a child. Parked in the unevenly paved driveway is the white Datsun 200SX that Marna had mentioned. Beneath its hatchback is a bumper sticker supporting the recent Independent presidential nominee, John B. Anderson. This has to be Connie's car, as Denny was never politically inclined.

At the front door, when Myra's tentative knocks go unanswered, she rings the bell. A light brightens the living room drapes and a few seconds later the door opens. A short woman shaped like a fire hydrant stands barefoot before Myra in a beige terrycloth housecoat. She has big brown eyes, a dirty-blond Peter Pan haircut, and the jowly face of an English bulldog.

"Can I help you?" the woman says.

"Are you Connie?" Myra asks.

"I am," she replies.

Myra doesn't know what to say next. She is completely thrown by this stout, mannish woman. Connie Fullmer is a far cry from Angie Dickinson.

"I'm sorry to bother you so late," Myra finally says, "but is Denny here?"

"And you are?"

"I'm his wife," Myra says.

"Oh," Connie says, more surprised than defensive. "It's very late for him."

"Please," Myra says. "I just drove over five hours."

Connie simply looks at her for a moment. "Come in," she says.

She leads Myra into her eat-in kitchen and offers her a seat at her small table. The kitchen is very clean and smells faintly of bleach. Connie removes her housecoat, sets it over the back of one of the chairs, and asks Myra if she'd like anything to drink.

"Some caffeine would be great," she replies.

"I'm afraid I don't have coffee," Connie says, "but I have black tea."

"Tea is fine," Myra says.

As Connie fills the kettle, Myra realizes that they're both still wearing their white nursing pants. The back of Connie's long-sleeved baseball shirt lists all the cities for the Eagles' *Long Run* tour. Her bare feet are short and pale, almost childlike in their perfection.

While they wait for the water to boil Connie joins Myra at the table. "Where were you coming from?" she asks.

"I drove down from Joliet," Myra says. "That's where I live."

"You're a nurse, too," Connie says, pointing at Myra's shoes.

"Pediatrics," she says, reaching down and adjusting the Band-Aid on the back of her ankle. Until now, she all but forgot about the nagging blister. "At St. Joseph Hospital."

"I'm over at the Mulberry Center in Harrisburg," Connie says. "I'm a mental health nurse."

"I know," Myra says.

"Why would you know that?" Connie asks.

"Because I hired a private investigator to find my husband."

A tick-tock fills the silence. Myra scans the clean kitchen for the clock. There isn't a crumb on any counter. The only evidence of food is a box of Life cereal on top of the refrigerator. And then she finds it: a Felix the Cat clockface with whiskers to mark the time. Its eyes slide back and forth in unison with each faintly clacking second.

"Do you have kids?" Myra asks.

"I have a daughter," Connie says. "But not with Dennis. She's from my first marriage. She goes to SIU Edwardsville."

"He goes by Dennis now?" Myra asks.

"As far as I know," Connie says, "he's always been Dennis."

Myra nods and swallows. It feels as if her mouth is filling with wads of cotton. She doesn't have the energy to bring up the nine years of the man she knew only as Denny. He never once went by Dennis. Even his half-brother and half-sister called him Denny.

Suddenly the kettle sings. Connie rises and turns off the gas. She opens a cupboard and retrieves an earth-colored mug and sets it on the countertop.

"Is Lipton okay?" she says to Myra.

"Lipton's perfect."

"Milk?"

"Just a drop, please," Myra says.

While Connie prepares her tea Myra tries to summon the evening before Denny disappeared. It was a Tuesday night in 1975. He was late coming home for dinner. It was very cold for the first day of April, in the mid-thirties, and he'd walked all the way from the train station, over two miles. He wasn't wearing his green wool bucket hat—a hat he'd worn ever since their first fall together—and went straight into the bathroom without saying hello and didn't come out for several minutes.

During dinner he was quiet, distant. Myra couldn't get more than a few words out of him.

"How was work?" she'd asked him.

"Fine," he'd replied, hardly opening his mouth. He'd barely touched his meatloaf.

WOLF AT THE TABLE

When Ronan, who was in kindergarten, asked him if they were still planning on going to see the Cubs play the Expos at Wrigley Field on Saturday the 12th, which would be part of their opening home series of the season, Denny stared at his son as if he'd never seen him before.

"Oscar Zamora's pitching," Ronan said. At age six he'd already developed into a rabid Cubs fan. He was a Topps collector, and memorizing the backs of baseball cards was his favorite pastime. For his sixteenth birthday Myra had planned on giving Ronan her prized Mickey Mantle rookie card, but it mysteriously disappeared in 1973, oddly right around the time her brother Alec was supposed to come stay with her, back when they lived in the apartment on Hoyne Avenue, but Alec never showed. "According to the radio, José Cardenal's gonna be starting in left and batting second," he added.

Cardenal was Ronan's favorite Cub. He loved the veteran Cuban's outgoing style. He had a prolific Afro and was always making faces. In their small backyard Ronan would throw himself pop flies and try to imitate Cardenal's signature basket catches. He even wrote his uniform number all over his school supplies and notebooks: #1.

Denny didn't say anything but nodded twice.

Later in bed that night Myra tried to talk to him but he fell asleep before she turned the light off.

And the following day, April 2, 1975, the day the blizzard started, he never made it home. Myra had dropped him off at the commuter train for work and then taken Ronan to kindergarten. At the end of the day, after she completed her shift at the hospital, she picked up Ronan from school, prepared dinner, and headed to the train station with Ronan to retrieve Denny. But he failed to emerge from the Wilmette station doors. Myra waited for three hours, turning the car engine on occasionally to keep Ronan warm, always expecting Denny to be on the next incoming train, thinking he might have gotten held up at the high school because of the snow. Eventually she and Ronan headed home to a cold dinner.

Connie returns to the table with the mug of tea and sets it before Myra. "I'll go get him," she says, exiting the kitchen.

She returns less than a minute later with Denny, who is wearing gray cotton pajama bottoms, a white V-neck T-shirt, soft blue Chicago Cubs slippers, and a light blue terrycloth bathrobe similar in style to Connie's. He looks puffy, a little thick in the middle, and shuffles a bit when he walks. Connie guides him by his elbow and helps him sit at the kitchen table. He settles into his chair and places his palms on the surface as if he might reveal the results of a coin trick. After a long moment he finally makes eye contact with Myra.

"Hello, Denny," she says.

"Hello," he says.

He's clean-shaven and his hair, which is now slightly more gray than honey-brown, is worn in the exact fashion that Myra remembers, neatly parted on the side and trimmed over the ears. Despite the extra flesh he is still handsome. Myra can feel her heart contracting. She takes a sip of tea. She will not let the moment get the best of her. She will speak to him and get some answers. She composes herself, sits a little taller in her chair.

Connie sets a glass of water before Denny and squeezes his shoulder. "I'll leave you two alone," she says, and exits down the hall.

After a door closes in another part of the house, Myra and Denny simply sit across from each other. Myra does her best to not fidget. She can feel herself wringing her hands, which are in her lap, below the table. Despite her nerves her eyes have not left Denny, whose gaze is cast toward some inexplicable downward horizon of shame or fear or indifference. The Felix the Cat clock scores the charged silence.

"Do you know who I am?" Myra finally says.

"Yes," he replies.

The lone syllable pierces the soft tissue between her neck and collarbone.

"Who am I?" she asks him.

"Myra," he says.

"Well, that's a relief," she says.

Denny drinks from his water glass and places it down. Myra looks over at the Felix the Cat clock. It's already 11:25 p.m. The cat's eyes shift back and forth mechanically. She wishes she could take the clock off the wall or cover the damn thing. She searches Denny's face. He still won't meet her gaze. His breathing is very slow and easy. He definitely seems medicated.

"I'm not expecting anything," Myra hears herself begin. "I guess I just want a few answers."

Denny nods.

"It'll be six years, day after tomorrow," she continues, "since you disappeared. That's a long time, Denny." She drinks her tea, takes a breath. "For a while I thought you were dead. I had no idea what happened to you. You left behind a six-year-old boy."

He doesn't respond.

"Do you even remember us?" she asks.

"I do," he says.

Two syllables this time.

From her purse Myra produces a wallet-sized class photo of Ronan and slides it across the table. "He's a sixth grader now," she says. "He goes to Troy Junior High School. He's on the baseball team. Plays centerfield. He's fast and he's got a great arm. He hit leadoff this year. He's currently running track."

"Ronan," Denny says. His mouth twitches and then softens, hinting at the beginnings of a smile.

"He cares more about sports than his grades," Myra says. "He gets B's mostly but I'm hoping that he'll start to get serious about his studies because he's smart as a whip. He sees things in people that most others can't."

"I don't have any money," Denny says.

"I'm not asking for money," Myra says. "I didn't come here for that. We do fine by ourselves." She finds that she needs a breath. She inhales through her nose, exhales. She drinks her tea again, sets it down. "I just want to know why you left, Denny."

He nods several times, perhaps one nod per word? He takes another drink of water.

Myra goes on to tell him that she'll accept any answer. It might be that he simply got scared or that he met someone else or that he started gambling or that he started drinking or that he was no longer attracted to her. She promises him that she won't judge him. She just wants the truth.

He stares down at his water glass, transfixed.

"I've had this hole in me," she continues. "For six years I haven't stopped thinking about you. I spend every day hoping you're alive, that you're okay. And I'm glad you are..." She has to slow down. It feels like her thoughts are starting to tumble, that she'll say too much. She arranges her hands around the mug of tea. "It seems like you've met someone that you're happy with," she continues, "and I don't want to mess that up. But I have to know why you left us, Denny. You have to tell me."

"The light over the garage door," he says.

"The light over the garage door?"

"The big light."

"Over what garage door?"

"The garage door light," he says.

"Are you talking about our house in Wilmette?"

He nods, and for the moment says no more.

She can smell the Vitalis in his hair. It's the same tonic he used when they were married, ironically the same stuff her father used.

Then he tells her that the light started communicating with him.

"Oh," Myra says, thrown. Of course she knows, from his troubles, that Denny is a bit different, but she wasn't expecting a response this abstract. "What was it saying?" she asks.

"It was telling me to do things."

"What kinds of things?"

"Bad things."

"You can tell me, Denny. I can handle it."

"It was ordering me to hurt you."

"Oh," Myra says again. She can't quit fathom what this could mean. "To hurt me how? Badly?"

He nods.

"How long had this been going on?" she asks.

"It started when it would get dark."

"At night," she says.

"Yes, then."

"What about Ronan?"

"Him too," he says. "I had to follow orders."

"When did the light over the garage door start talking to you?"

"When it got dark," he says.

"But how soon after we moved to the house in Wilmette?"

"When it got dark," he repeats.

It dawns on Myra that he must not be able to comprehend a sense of chronology or personal history. It's as if he thinks in coloring-book images. There is a house. There is a light above the garage. There is the dark.

"How badly were you supposed to hurt us?" she asks.

"It was ordering me to use the hammer under the sink."

"So you were going to kill us with it?" she says.

He nods.

"And you felt you had to listen to the light over the garage door?"

"It was communicating orders from my superiors," he says. "Very strict orders."

"Which you had to obey," she says.

Another nod.

"Or else what?" she asks.

"Or else I would have to do it to all the other families."

Myra can feel tears streaming down her face. At least she's not wearing any mascara. All she put on today was lipstick, which she last applied in the bathroom on the fourth floor of St. Joseph, before leaving the hospital, when she still had every intention of meeting Marna at Earl's.

"To all the other families in our neighborhood?" she asks.

"In North America," he says.

"But you didn't do it."

He shakes his head.

"Because you didn't want to hurt us?" she says.

Denny nods twice and then reaches across the table and grabs a napkin from the little plastic rack decorated with sunflowers and hands it to Myra.

The last thing she wanted to do was cry in front of him. She blows her nose and dabs at her eyes and thanks him for the napkin.

The ticking clock again. That fucking cat's eyes darting this way and that.

Denny is now studying the picture of their son. His face is kind, swollen. This once virile, sharp-featured man is trapped inside the puffiness of medication, softened by seasons of forced lethargy.

"He's fast, huh?" Denny says, taking in Ronan.

"They have him doing all the sprints on the track team. His coach told me he's the fastest kid in the school. As a sixth grader he's already qualified for the state meet in two different events. He obviously got it from you."

"He looks like you," Denny says, bringing the photo a little closer to his face.

"But he has all of your expressions," she says. "Especially when he smiles."

Denny turns the photo over where Myra wrote on the back, in blue ink.

"Ronan Archibald Happ," he says, reading her handwriting. "Sixth grade. Nineteen Eighty. Troy Junior High School."

"He has your dimples," Myra says.

Denny turns the photo back around and says, "I'm sorry I don't have any money."

Myra shakes her head and reiterates that this isn't the reason she's come—despite what Sophia Toscas, the nice Greek family lawyer from Bolingbrook, told her, which was that she could sue him for six years of child support and have his Army benefits garnished.

Myra reaches across the table and takes his right hand in both of hers. Denny allows it. His hand is hairless and soft and cold. Boyish. His fingers are slightly curled as if he's hiding a stone.

"Are you happy here?" she asks him.

He nods again.

"Connie's good to you?"

"If it wasn't for Connie I would have never gotten out," he says.

"From the hospital?"

Another nod.

She's still holding his hand. It is tense, unyielding.

"They were gonna keep me there," he says.

"And she helped you," Myra says.

"She cuts my hair," he says.

"She does a good job," Myra says. "I like it."

"And we watch television," he adds.

She asks him what his favorite show is.

"*Mork and Mindy*," he says. "And *WKRP in Cincinnati*."

"Do you love her?" Myra asks.

"Mindy?" he says.

"No, Connie."

"Yes," he says.

It feels as if she's swallowed a mouthful of crushed glass. She takes a drink of tea and forces it down. "Would you ever be interested in seeing your son again?" she asks, setting her mug on the table.

"I worry about the light," he says.

"The light over the garage door."

He nods.

"From our old home in Wilmette."

He nods again.

"Does it still talk to you?" she asks.

"No," he says. "But I know it will."

"Well, if you ever start to feel more comfortable with the idea, I'm almost certain Ronan would be interested in getting to know you again. He's turning out to be a pretty great kid. I think you'd like him a lot."

Denny pries his hand away, lowers it below the table.

"We live up in Joliet but I'd be happy to drive him down here for an afternoon," she continues. "I'd give you some time alone with him and I wouldn't ask anything of you. Every boy deserves to know his father." She searches his face for some kind of acknowledgment of what she's just told him but his attention seems to have drifted toward a spot just beyond the threshold of the kitchen.

Myra has to wipe her face again with the now crumpled napkin. She can't believe how much pity she feels for this man who abandoned her, this man whom she's called a spineless coward to her mother and father and her three sisters and Marna and Dale and Sophia Toscas. Ronan is aware that his dad was this extraordinary all-city track athlete from Chicago who was the president of his senior class and won an appointment to the United States Military Academy at West Point when he was only sixteen. For some reason he doesn't remember his father. Even though Ronan was six when Denny left and they had spent so much time in the backyard playing catch, Ronan has somehow managed to block him out. Now his father is this mystery man who looks a lot like that actor from *The Electric Horseman*, Robert Redford. He knows him only from pictures in the photo albums.

Myra tells Denny that it's getting late, that she should go. "You can keep that," she says of Ronan's class photo, which he is still holding.

"I used to collect arrowheads," he says, the thought seemingly coming out of nowhere. "Starved Rock State Park."

"When you were a boy," she says.

"When I was his age," he says, pointing at the photo. "In Oglesby."

"You told me about your visits to that park when we were getting to know each other," Myra reminds him. "You have so many good memories from that place."

"The canyons," he says dreamily, and trails off.

"What about the canyons?"

But he doesn't answer. His thought seems to have expired like a moth flying into the dark.

Dale's report cited that the doctors at the Mulberry Center said when Denny was admitted into their care he was thought to be an unpredictably dangerous man who might harm himself or any third party. Myra found the phrasing oddly stilted, as if he were being described in legalese.

He puts the picture of Ronan in the pocket of his robe.

"Do you ever think about us?" Myra hears herself say.

"Yes," he says.

"What exactly do you think about?"

"Certain times," he replies. "Christmases. A drive we took to the mountains in New York."

"The Catskills," Myra says, encouraged. "We'd been to visit my parents in Elmira a few months after Ronan was born. And then we went up to Tannersville and stayed in that nice hotel for the rest of the week."

"I remember the goats," he says.

"The little goats on the wallpaper," Myra says.

"Their faces," he adds and stares into his water glass. "It was like they had thoughts."

That had been such a lovely week in Tannersville. Denny was so alive, so enamored of Ronan, and they were in love.

"Do you miss us?" Myra says.

He nods once, the movement so faint it is more like a flinch, as if he's dodging a mosquito. After his head comes to rest, his expression is one of profound confusion. He could be peering through the fog at something on fire.

And then a door closes and Connie is back.

"Time for bed, Dennis," she says, placing her hand on his shoulder. She's changed out of her nursing pants and into a pair of pajama bottoms that match his.

Denny's hand comes up to meet hers.

"Bedtime for Dennis," she says.

"Bedtime," he echoes.

And then with her hand still on his shoulder and his hand on hers, Connie asks Myra if they had a good talk, as if Denny is a young boy being visited after school by a classmate and now has to go wash up for dinner.

"I think we did," Myra says.

Denny pushes away from the table and rises. His movements are deliberate, slightly strained. Something has taken hold of his joints. It reminds Myra of her father, how slow his hands became once the arthritis set in, after thirty years of working levers and spindles and cast-iron crankshafts. Denny's face is still youthful, though, with very few lines. His eyes are surprisingly clear. She will have no problem remembering this version of him.

"Bye, Denny," Myra says.

"Bye," he says, facing the hallway.

She has the sense that his body's machinery has already started down an irreversible path.

"I'll put him to bed and then I'll see you out," Connie says.

Myra nods.

Denny doesn't look back as Connie guides him down the hall. This relationship somehow feels like livestock agriculture, Myra thinks. Animal husbandry. Denny is a bovine, Connie his dutiful farmhand. During the day she places him in a field. She sets a bale of hay before him and tells him when to eat, when to drink water, when to sleep. She gently leads him around with a rope. When it rains she brings him inside. Their arrangement seems so simple, almost absurd in its primitiveness, and yet a kind of love comes through. Between them there is a ritualized intimacy that Myra never really experienced with her husband.

AN HOUR LATER, IN a kind of trance, Myra crosses the Ohio River and pulls into an all-night diner in rural Kentucky, just outside Paducah. She has no idea why she decided to drive south on Interstate 24. At Marion she should have exited north, in the direction of Joliet. Instead she headed south, and now here she is. Before she goes inside she takes in the river, whose surface is oddly smooth, like obsidian, as if she could take her shoes off and walk out to the middle and wait for some strange being to appear and advise her about the next phase of her life.

The diner is sparsely populated. Moving back and forth behind a cutout framing the sizzling kitchen is a bald cook in a white T-shirt with the sleeves rolled up to the shoulders. A slow-moving waitress in a uniform the color of Pepto-Bismol greets Myra when she sits at the counter. Myra places her folded road map on the counter and arranges her purse between her feet. The last time she ate was her lunch break, some twelve hours earlier, and her stomach has been rumbling since she left Connie's house.

The waitress sets a menu before her and asks her if she'd like a cup of coffee.

"Please," Myra says.

Mounted over the jukebox and bolted to the ceiling is a color television, which is playing a rerun of the news with the sound turned down. At the other end of the counter a heavyset man dressed head to toe in faded denim is hunched over a plate of scrambled eggs and French toast. Outside it has started to rain.

Myra orders two eggs over easy with plain white toast and sausage patties. She dumps two plastic mini creamers into her coffee and downs half of it. Her hunger has made her jittery. Her hands tremble as she sets her coffee cup down.

"They shot the president," the man in denim says, nodding toward the television.

Dan Rather mutters silently to his viewers with a still-frame of President Reagan behind him.

"Who shot him?" Myra asks.

"Apparently some crazy kid," the man says. "He shot Reagan and three others."

"Is Reagan dead?" Myra asks.

"No," the man says. "Kid used a twenty-two caliber revolver. Shoulda used a forty-five. Or a nine mil. Either of those woulda done the trick. Guess he didn't like the election results."

Myra voted for Carter, thinking him to be a kinder man, and can hardly conjure Ronald Reagan. Instead the softened face of her husband—Denny's haunted eyes—takes hold of her mind.

A minute later a bell sounds from the kitchen and the waitress brings Myra her order, refills her coffee, and sets a large cup of ice water next to her coffee. Myra digs in, not even bothering with the salt and pepper. She wolfs down her eggs, then the toast, then the trio of sausage patties, immediately energized by the food. She downs her second cup of coffee. When the waitress comes back to top her off Myra asks her if they have a payphone and the waitress directs her to a paneled hallway at the back of the diner, opposite the bathrooms.

Myra heads toward the payphone with her purse and fishes out a few quarters. Her hands are shaking so bad she can't fit the quarters in the slot. She takes a breath and finally succeeds.

"It's so late," Ronan says, sleepily, when he answers. "Where are you?"

Myra looks at her watch. It's almost 1:30 a.m. She tells him that she went for a drive and lost track of time. An absurd lie, but she can't think of what else to say.

"You're coming home, right?"

"Of course," she says.

"You're never out this late," Ronan says.

"I'm sorry I didn't call until now. If you can't sleep you should heat up some milk in a pan. There's cinnamon next to the toaster."

"You missed my meet," he tells her.

"Oh, Ronan," she says, "I'm so sorry." In her singular focus on Denny she forgot about the meet, thinking today was only another practice. Her guilt surges again. "How'd it go?" she asks.

"I won the hundred and the two hundred."

"Congratulations," she says. "What about the relay?"

"We were way out in front but Dee Bynum got us disqualified for running out of his lane. We would've easily qualified for sectionals."

"You guys won't have any problem qualifying," she says. "Tell Dee to stay in his lane."

"I know," he says.

There is a pause. The sound of her son breathing on the other end soothes her.

"Where did you go?" he asks.

"Just for a drive."

"But where?"

"I went up to Starved Rock State Park," she lies.

"Why?"

"I just needed to clear my head. Things got a little intense at work."

"More kids died?"

"Yeah," she says. "This one little boy who'd been in a car accident didn't make it. He lost too much blood." She hates lying to Ronan. It makes her feel like her hair is falling out in clumps.

"Marna called earlier," he says. "She kept asking if I'd spoken to you. She seemed sorta worried."

"I was supposed to meet her at Earl's after work but I never showed up. My stomach's been bothering me."

"So take some Maalox," he says.

"I already did," she says. Another lie.

"That guy Emile called again, too."

"Did you write his number down this time?"

"He didn't leave one," Ronan says.

Back at the counter the waitress drops Myra's check and the women lock eyes and Myra smiles at her.

"Is that guy Black?" Ronan asks of Emile.

"He is," Myra replies. "I believe he's half-and-half."

"A mulatto."

"Yes," Myra says, "but you shouldn't use that word."

"Why not?" Ronan says.

"Because it isn't acceptable anymore. One of the nurses at work got chewed out for using it."

"So it's like the N-word now?"

"Sort of," Myra says.

"Why?" Ronan asks.

"I think it's because 'mule' is part of the word?"

"But mules are good animals," Ronan says. "There's nothing wrong with mules."

"But I think the point is that they're animals," Myra says. "And animals are below people."

"So what word should I use?"

"I'm not sure," Myra says. "Maybe 'mixed'… or 'blended'?"

"He's *blended*?" Ronan says.

"Sure."

"That makes him sound like a protein drink."

Myra laughs. Ronan can always make her laugh when she least expects it.

"Are you and Emile dating?" he asks.

"No," she says. "Marna's husband's been trying to set us up. Do you have a problem with him being Black?"

"No," Ronan says.

Sixteen rectangular four-story units make up the Cedarwood Apartment Complex. There might be a dozen white families in the entire subdivision. Despite her and Ronan being the only whites in their building Myra has always felt welcome. All the Black and Mexican kids treat Ronan as if he's one of them.

"I don't have a problem with Emile," Ronan says. "I was just curious. On the phone he seemed cool."

"How'd you get home from the track meet?" she asks.

"Coach Blazing gave me a ride."

"That was nice of him," she says. "I'll have to call and thank him."

"He wants me to start long-jumping. He thinks I could go eighteen feet. Seventeen-ten qualifies for State."

"Your father was a triple jumper," she says.

"I know," he says, "that's what I told Coach Blazing."

"That's how he hurt his knee when he was at West Point." Myra imagines Denny's face, his hand on top of Connie's, and her stomach gives way. "Did you eat anything for dinner?"

"I had that leftover Hamburger Helper."

"What about a vegetable?"

"I'll do double vegetable tomorrow."

"And your homework?"

"I finished it."

From her position at the payphone Myra can see the ongoing television coverage of the Reagan assassination attempt. The slow-motion footage of his security detail throwing bodies to the ground. The president felled like an elderly person on an icy street. "Did you watch the news?" she asks.

"No," he says. "Why, did something happen?"

"No," she lies again. "I was just wondering if they're saying anything about the Cubs yet."

"They're gonna be terrible again," he says. "Bill Buckner's the only good player they have."

"What about Iván DeJesús," she says.

"He sucks."

"I thought you loved DeJesús. You used to always imitate his batting stance."

"He's past his prime," Ronan says. "He still has a good arm but his range is crap...Are you crying or something?"

"No," Myra says.

"You just sniffled."

"It's raining here and it's making my nose run."

"You're outside?"

"No, I'm inside. I'm at a diner."

"Where?"

"I'm not telling you."

"Why not?"

"Because I don't have to."

"Are you at the Denny's on Jefferson?"

"No," she says.

"You *are* crying," he says.

"I'm not," she says, "I'm really not." Myra paws at her cheeks with her left hand, which makes her sniffle again.

"No self-pity," he says.

This is what she always tells him when he feels sorry for himself.

"You're tougher than you think," he adds.

She always says this, too.

"I am tough," she says. She sees her own hand on Denny's, sitting across from him there in that kittle kitchen, the sadness settling like pollen on their limbs.

"When will you be home?" Ronan says.

"Soon," she says. "Don't wait up for me."

"Okay," he says. "But you swear you're on your way?"

"I swear," she says. "And promise me you'll brush your teeth and go to bed."

"I will."

"Sorry I missed your meet," she says.

"As long as you come to Districts," he says.

"I will," she says.

"And Sectionals."

"And Sectionals."

"State, too."

"Of course," Myra says.

"I have to finish in the top two at sectionals to qualify for State."

"You will," she says.

"Don't get a speeding ticket."

"I won't," she says.

After hanging up, Myra goes into the women's bathroom and vomits her entire meal into the toilet. Lately it's been harder and harder to keep her food down. She's losing weight. And there's been more than one occasion when she's seen blood in her stool. It's probably an ulcer. Marna thinks it's all the stress of raising a twelve-year-old boy on her own. Working full-time with no break. Trying to make ends meet on a nurse's salary.

At the sink she rinses her mouth and goes out to the counter and pays the check and leaves a dollar tip. The older man in denim is gone. Myra collects her road map and thanks the waitress.

"Night, hon," she says to Myra. "Be safe out there."

It's still raining. For some reason, Myra finds herself turning onto Route 45 and continuing south. The rain turns the intermittent roadside lamps into smears on the windshield. On the radio it's only news about the assassination attempt on President Reagan.

The former Hollywood actor is only two months into his term. He was shot in the lung by John Hinckley, Jr. as he was leaving a speaking engagement in Washington DC. Several people were injured, including Jim Brady, the White House press secretary.

Myra turns the radio off. Nothing but love songs and terrible news. She didn't vote for Reagan but she pities him. She knows he was a former Democrat, that he was born in Tampico, Illinois, which is almost directly west of Joliet, not far from the Iowa border, some dozen miles east of the Rock River, and that he was the Governor of California for a time. She prefers Jimmy Carter's sense of decency and his stance on human rights, and believes he got unfairly criticized because of the gas crisis and the stagnant economy that he inherited, not to mention the horrible Iran hostage situation. Very few presidents could have survived those kinds of challenges.

When she reaches the outskirts of Oak Grove, Kentucky, Myra pulls the car onto the shoulder and looks at the map under the dome light of her Pacer. She could keep going south. The cities are staggered downward toward the Gulf of Mexico like a series of provocations. She could just keep driving and driving until dawn. She could take a quick nap in Memphis and still be in New Orleans before noon. She could watch the sun dapple the skin of Lake Pontchartrain. She could start her life over there. She could disappear, just as Denny did, six years ago. She could change her name and find a little carriage house and grow old and anonymous and unwitnessed. No more worries about Ronan or groceries or booster shots or parent-teacher conferences or showing up at that dingy hospital where children get abandoned and suffer and die all too often. She is briefly thrilled by this prospect, this possibility of shape-changing into something she's never known herself to be. She could start writing. Or take up watercolor painting. She could work in a used bookstore and speak with a strange accent. She could become promiscuous. She could paint the trim on her carriage house a vibrant, electric yellow. Her garden would be shaggy and strange. She would grow misshapen heirloom tomatoes and keep bees in the backyard. Inside her house she would walk around naked and seldom shower and let her armpit hair grow out and sleep on extravagant pillows. She would start smoking hashish and listen to Joni Mitchell and read John Cheever stories and the novels of Toni Morrison and Joyce Carol Oates.

But as the wipers clear away the rain, these thoughts start to disappear as if they were written with her finger on the windshield. She can only see her son. Ronan running around a cinder track. His long coppery hair lifting off his shoulders. His searching, hazel eyes, which he inherited from her. His boyish arms that will be marked with mosquito bites in a couple of months. His pale, oddly muscular calves. She shifts the car into drive, eases back onto the highway, gets off at the next exit, crosses over to the other side, and rejoins the road heading north.

From here it will take more than six hours to drive back to Joliet. After she re-crosses the Ohio River she will have to get gas and she'll most certainly need at least two more cups of coffee to help her stay awake, and she'll likely call in sick to work, but she's made a decision: she will not flee her life. She will return to her small unit on the third story of 2421 Ingalls Avenue, Building #6 of Cedarwood Apartments, where, on the floor beside her bed, her sleeping son will be curled anxiously into himself, awaiting her loving hand.

8

PADUCAH, KENTUCKY
APRIL 10, 1982

ALEC

THE BANKS OF THE Ohio smell especially rank today. Rank as a bag of warm trout left in the sun. Alec pushes the last cigarette through his pack of Pall Malls, lights it, and sits on his favorite thirty-inch cement rectangle, whose rebar shackle suggests that it used to be a hitching post of some sort, likely for smallish boats. Skiffs. Motorized rowboats. Canoes and kayaks.

According to the discarded *Courier-Journal* that he just used to wipe himself, it's a Saturday. Ronald Regan was on the front page again. Ronald fucking Reagan and his fake rubber hair. A former Hollywood actor leading the country. Go figure. It's just past noon and the sun feels good on Alec's face. He needs a shower and a shave and the sunlight will clarify him, purge him of all odors and bacteria. Twice a week he sneaks into the little halfway house over on Twelfth Street, where he lived for a few months after serving three weeks in jail for attempting to steal money out of the cash register at a bowling alley bar, and grabs a used razor out of the trash and whatever half-dissolved sliver of soap he can find. He'll shower and shave and use the toilet and even brush his teeth with his finger if there's any toothpaste on hand. If Ulysses, the ancient, half-blind Black man, is at the front desk, he can even sweet-talk him for a roll or two of toilet paper so he doesn't have to use the fucking newspaper every damn time he has to take a crap. But for now he is content to let the early April sun do its thing. Trust the power of ultraviolet rays. He throws the word around in his head: Ultraviolet…Ultraviolins…Ultraviolence…

Alec is about halfway through his cigarette when a boy comes out of the brush with a fishing pole and a small pink bucket that looks like a child's beach toy. The kid is wiry, blond, in jeans that are too large and an oversized University of Louisville men's basketball hoodie. His sneakers are caked with mud.

As the boy approaches, Alec takes one last drag from his cigarette and flicks it behind him toward the water. "Catch anything?" he asks.

"A little-ass blue gill but I threw that bitch back," the kid says.

"I wasn't aware that fish could be bitches," Alec says.

"Any living thing can be a bitch," the kid says.

"You might have more luck if you keep walking another quarter mile that way," Alec offers, nodding toward the small marina where he lives in his dilapidated houseboat. "There's a little dock where you can drop your line," he adds. "About four or five lopsided Blacks like to hang out there and fish and play dominoes but if you mind your own business they'll leave you be."

"I ain't afraida no Blacks," the kid says.

His hair has a tinge of rust, and up close Alec can see that the boy also has freckles, just like his sister Fiona, whom he hasn't seen since he left home, more than twenty years ago. Emma, the woman he was supposed to marry and raise a child with back in Nebraska, also had freckles. Alec briefly imagines the child he will never meet. Is it a boy? A girl? Is it some afflicted, half-formed creature in a wheelchair? Is it blind? Freckled like this boy who's just emerged out of the brush? He pushes the thought from his mind forever, like discarding a piece of litter.

But the years he's amassed and all their weight aren't as easily dismissed. When he thinks about his age, which is forty-one now, he can feel things slowly turning in his organs, like screws coming loose.

"What's in your pail—earthworms?"

"Nothin'," the boy says. "This is what I'm gonna carry my fish home in."

"What you aiming to catch?"

"A bass."

"With what bait?"

The kid reaches into the front pouch of his hoodie and produces a package of Oscar Meyer bologna.

"That's not gonna get you much more than a belligerent bullhead. And good luck wrestling that off your hook without getting stung."

"Ain't afraida no bullheads neither," the kid says. "I've caught plenty of 'em."

"You're not afraid of much, are you?" Alec says.

The boy just stands there with his rod on his shoulder, his blue eyes squinting in the bright sun.

"How old are you?" Alec asks.

"Thirteen," the boy says.

"You're small for your age."

"Says who?"

"I pegged you for about nine."

"Turned thirteen three weeks ago."

"So that makes you, what, an eighth grader?"

"Seventh."

"I was small for my age, too," Alec says. "Don't worry, you'll grow."

"As long as I get a big dick I don't care," the kid says.

"Well, I wish you luck," Alec says, laughing. "What's your name, anyway?"

"Grady."

"Hi, Grady," Alec says. "I'm Jack."

"Why you sittin' there like you ain't got nothin' to do?"

"Oh, I got plenty to do," Alec says. "I'm just tryin' to enjoy the sun a bit before I get to doing it."

Grady visors his eyes with his hands and studies Alec. "You from around here?"

"I'm sort of from all over the place," Alec says. "But Paducah is currently where I choose to make my residence. What about you?"

"I live in Brockport. Other side of the river."

"You don't like fishing in Illinois?"

"My mom's over here today," he says. "She lets me fish when she's got work on this side."

"What's your mom do?"

"She cleans people's houses."

"There's a lot of dirty houses out there," Alec says.

"She does offices, too. She's gonna start her own business soon. Her and her friend Nona."

"You get those freckles from your mom or your dad?"

"Prolly neither."

"Did your dad teach you how to fish?"

"No."

"Where's he today?"

"Hell if I know."

"Is he alive?"

"I think so."

"He skedaddled, huh?"

"Yeah."

"Sorry to hear that."

"My mom says he's a scumbucket with a capital S."

"Most men are."

"I think her and Nona are lesbos."

"Whatever floats your boat," Alec says.

"The other day I walked in on them sticking their fingers in each other."

"Like I said, whatever boats your float."

"Nona's got gorilla hands."

"You don't like her?"

"No, she's cool. We watch *Hill Street Blues* together. She used to be a power lifter. She can do like fifty push-ups."

"Sounds like an interesting lady."

"You got anymore cigarettes?" Grady asks.

Only then does Alec realize he's still holding his empty pack of Pall Malls. "Just smoked my last one."

"Lotta good you are."

"You shouldn't be smoking anyways," Alec says, scrunching the empty pack into a ball. "Especially at your age. Damn things'll stunt your growth. You'll never get that big pecker you're hoping for."

"If you had one left, you'd give it to me," Grady says.

"I would, huh?"

"I can tell."

Alec laughs and forces the crushed cigarette pack into the front pocket of his jeans. He wipes the film of sweat off his face with the red bandana he keeps in the pocket of his windbreaker, then folds the bandana into a square and returns it to his pocket. "Know anything about drumfish?" he says.

"Never heard of 'em," Grady says.

"They got a stone in their skull."

"Drumfish?"

"You can hear them vibrating when they come close. That's how they get their name. Each stone has a letter on it. If you catch one with the first letter of your first name on it, it'll bring you good luck for the rest of your life."

"Sounds like utter horse pucky."

"It's the God's honest," Alec says. From the back pocket of his jeans he removes an old leather wallet, opens the billfold, and takes out a folded piece of white paper. "Check it out," he says, and unfolds the paper to reveal a small gray stone, the size of a child's first tooth.

Grady steps close and peers down at it.

"See the *J* on there?" Alec says.

"That ain't no *J*."

"Sure it is."

"I seen dead bullfrogs that look more like a *J*."

"It's a goddamn lowercase *J*," Alec says. "Look closer."

Grady lowers his head. His hair has that feral musk that boys get when they don't bathe. The sour funk of his unlaundered hoodie rises sharply above him. His ears are probably filthy.

"You see it now?" Alec says. "How it curves at the bottom there?"

"I see it," the kid says, a tad mesmerized. "A little *J*."

Alec folds the stone back into the piece of paper, feeds it back into the billfold.

"So how'd you get lucky?" Grady asks.

"In many ways," Alec says. "I got my own houseboat for one."

"Like a boat you live on?"

"I sleep on it, eat on it, do any damn thing I please on it."

"Can you fish off it?" Grady asks.

"If I want to," Alec says. "But I don't like to fish where I sleep."

"What kinda bait do drumfish like?" Grady asks.

"Fiddler crabs is their favorite. You got a halfway decent bait shop in Brockport?"

"Yeah," Grady says. "The lady who runs the place's got a mustache but she brags about havin' everything."

"Then she'll definitely carry fiddler crabs. Here," Alec says, taking a ten-dollar bill out of his wallet, holding it out to the kid. "Go get yourself a dozen fiddler crabs and meet me tomorrow. I'll be right here at my spot. I might even have an extra cigarette for you, but I'll only let you have a puff or two. I'll help you find your special drumfish."

"I can't come tomorrow," Grady says. "It's Easter. I gotta go to church."

"Well, do me twice with a curling iron," Alec says. "Look at me forgettin' my high holidays. When's the next time your mom's got work on this side of the river?"

"I don't know," Grady says. "Prolly sometime next week. But I could come meet you on Monday."

"Don't you got school?"

"I'll come after. I get out around three. Bus drops me off around three-twenty."

"Can you do five o'clock?" Alec says.

"I can prolly be here earlier," Grady says.

"Let's make it five bells," Alec says. "Drumfish are easier to catch in the evening."

"Why, 'cause they get sleepy?"

"Somethin' like that," Alec says. "Their hormones and whatnot."

"Fish got hormones?"

"Fish are practically *people*," Alec says. "Hell, everyone thinks we come from monkeys, but we're definitely more like fish. We swim. Monkeys can't swim."

"Once I saw a monkey jerk off and fling his mess at a swimsuit model," Grady says. "Up at that fancy zoo in Chicago."

"I'm not sure I'll be able to get that image out of my head for quite some time," Alec says.

"Hit her, right in the hair," Grady says. "She was tall, too."

"I'll bet she was," Alec says, laughing. "Flying monkey spume."

Grady picks his nose and wipes it on his jeans. "What's your name again?" he says.

"Jack," Alec says. "You can call me Happy Jack."

"You think there's one of them drumfish stones with a G on it?"

"You're damn straight there is. And it's *your* G. And it's gonna bring you good luck, I swear to Elvis."

"I hear he died shittin' his brains out on the toilet," Grady says.

"That might be true," Alec says. "But that was his throne and Elvis was the king. Do yourself a favor, though. When you go home tonight, when you go to bed, before you say your prayers and fall asleep, imagine that drumfish swimming toward you."

"Like I'm in the river?"

"You're just on the dock with that fiddler crab bait on your hook and that drumfish with the letter G on the stone in its skull is miles away out in the Ohio, like way the hell over in western Pennsylvania or someplace, but it's swimming your way."

"Okay," Grady says.

"If you don't imagine it, it won't come," Alec warns.

They are quiet for a moment.

Grady starts moving his mouth around like he's chewing tobacco and then spits. "How come you didn't know it was Easter tomorrow," he says. "You don't got no calendar?"

"I s'pose I don't," Alec says.

"You're so lucky now that you don't need one?"

"The sun goes up, the sun goes down," Alec says. "That's all the calendar I need."

Grady finally accepts the ten-dollar bill, which Alec has been holding between his thumb and forefinger for some time now, and studies it hard. "Who is that s'posed to be?" he says of the face on the front.

"I believe it's Alexander Hamilton."

"Was he a president or somethin'?"

"I honestly don't know," Alec says. "Maybe. But he looks like my old aunt Frothingslosh."

Grady erupts in a fit of laughter. *"Frothingslosh!"* he shouts, still laughing.

"Now don't go spending that on cigarettes," Alec says after the boy's laughter finally dies down.

"I won't," Grady says.

Just then a small girl jogs out of the brush toward them. She's about half Grady's size, in yellow overalls with mud all over her knees and elbows. "I seen it!" she cries to Grady. "I seen the blobfish!"

"Shit," Grady says to Alec. And then to the girl: "Doris, look how dirty you are! Mom's gonna be straight-up pissed! Dirty-ass dummy!"

"But I seen the blobfish!" she cries. "I seen it, I swear! It was big as a dang dog!"

"Mom's gonna spank your stupid ass silly!"

"It had a face like a man's," she says. "Like it could talk words to you. Hey, mister."

"Hey, you," Alec says.

"This is my sister, Doris," Grady says.

"Nice to meet you, Doris. I'm Jack."

"Nice to meet you, Jake," Doris says.

"It's *Jack*," Grady corrects her. *"Happy* Jack, you fucking butter-head! And call him mister."

"Nice to meet you, Happy Jack," she says.

"Where the hell is Lisa?" Grady says to her.

"Oh, no," Doris says, covering her mouth.

"Better hope that blobfish didn't eat her."

Doris turns and runs back into the brush from where she emerged.

"She your only sibling?" Alec asks.

"Yeah," Grady says. "I don't think I could handle another little bitch like her."

"I have four sisters," Alec says. "Two of 'em are younger."

"Four sisters!" Grady says. "That must be hell. You like any of 'em?"

"Not really," Alec says. "Doris reminds me of my youngest one. Same color hair. Same blue eyes."

"Doris still shits her pants. I keep tellin' my mom to put her back in diapers. Shittin' her damn pants in the first grade like a complete idgit."

"She probably can't help it."

"She can, though," Grady says. "She does it for attention."

"She'll figure it out."

"She better," Grady says. "I'm tired of cleanin' up after her stanky ass."

"You're a good brother," Alec says. "I can tell. Better than I ever was."

The kid scratches at his neck, leaving streaks of pink.

"You meet me here Monday and I'll help you catch your drumfish," Alec says. "Get you that G stone."

"Five o'clock," Grady says. "I'll ride my bike."

"And don't tell nobody or that drumfish'll know and he won't show up. You can't tell your mom or Nona. Don't tell a soul, you hear me?"

"I won't say nothing."

Doris reemerges from the brush carrying her Cabbage Patch doll, whose stunned little granny face makes Alec think briefly of his sister, Joan, the retard. When he was in high school Alec used to sneak into Joan's room and plug her nose while she was sleeping just to see what it would do to her face.

"Was the blobfish still there?" Alec asks Doris.

"No," she says. "Lisa told him to go away." She turns her doll toward Alec, and it's as dirty as Doris herself, with splotches of mud marking her quilted arms and legs.

"Lisa's obviously got special powers," Alec says of the grubby little doll.

"Come on, skank, let's go," Grady says to his sister.

He grabs her hand and they head back toward the brush. As they are walking away, Grady turns back toward Alec, who is still sitting on his cement post. Alec salutes him like a general and Grady returns the salute.

LATER ALEC BUYS A fresh pack of Pall Malls from the 7-Eleven and on his way to the bathroom he steals a microwave burrito. After washing up in the sink he eats the burrito cold in about three bites. Walking the gravel road back to his houseboat, off North Water Street, he belches grotesquely.

He laid claim to the abandoned houseboat over a year ago, after he'd left the halfway house. When the marina officer, an old, arthritic, walrus-faced man known as the Colonel, came by to check on it, Alec had moved in. The Colonel wasn't up for haggling over it and simply told Alec he could have it. The former owner had purportedly "gone fishing and never come back." All Alec had to do was pay a minimal monthly lease for the marina plot and some marginal city taxes. The Colonel said he'd have to go fill out some official paperwork at the county courthouse building, and when, the next day, Alec did just that, the boat became his, as if it had been fated.

The houseboat is decrepit, riddled with fleas and bedbugs. Oftentimes after he's had too much to drink, Alec has considered setting fire to it to get rid of the pests. He even stole a fire extinguisher from a local bar where he's no longer welcome so he might execute a controlled burnout but he doesn't trust the possible downside, which is the entire thing going up in flames. Then he'd have nowhere to live and would find himself back at some fucking half-way house where you have to do group meetings with a bunch of other degenerates and talk about God and forgiveness and setting off on various paths of reconciliation.

There's no toilet on the houseboat and when no one's looking he'll often just piss over the edge. When he's drunk enough he'll even move his bowels in the same spot, plopping logs right into the Ohio.

There is a kerosene heating system that provides some warmth and a sleeping nook big enough for his long, aching limbs. His bedding is a nest of old Salvation Army blankets and a halfway decent sleeping bag that he found at a campsite just outside Lexington. For light, when he needs it, he uses a pair of hurricane lamps that burn slowly and efficiently on paraffin oil, which goes for about ten dollars a canister at the local hardware store. But after the sun goes down he prefers the dark anyway.

Except for his Mickey Mantle rookie card, which he keeps in its original lucite casing and stores in a three-inch slot that he carved into the moldering wood beside his bed, Alec has very little of value. Although he knows the card is worth a lot, he refuses to sell it, as it's the one piece of insurance he has in fending off complete destitution. He may need it down the line. At night, for safety, he padlocks the houseboat's front entrance from the inside. There is also an aft half-door, or his "midget door" as he likes to call it, which he's barricaded with an old woodstove that no longer works because the flue rotted out. He had to patch the exhaust portal with plywood.

For clean water, every other day he goes into town with a gallon jug, which he fills at the Paducah YMCA's reception area water fountain, where he's managed to charm the fat front desk receptionist, Ginny, into thinking that he likes her.

"When are you gonna let me take you out, Sweet Ginny," he'll say to her while filling up his jug.

"You stop that now, Jack," she'll say, blushing, her giant arms wobbling as she waves away his attention.

He sleeps with a bowie knife under his pillow and has his heart set on a snub-nosed revolver with a pearl handle that he regularly visits via bus at a pawnshop on Washington Avenue in Louisville. It's only $250 and he knows it will change his life in a meaningful way. He's already procured three boxes of bullets for it.

Alec sits at his makeshift table, which he's constructed from an old door that he found in the lane behind the poultry plant where he applied for a job and was swiftly rejected. He reaches for the bottle of Maker's Mark he keeps under the table, unscrews the top, then is reminded, cruelly, of its emptiness. Not even a drop remains. Tomorrow he'll have to go to the blood bank again. He's given more goddamn blood to that place than can be expected of one human. He's O negative and he knows this is his one true asset. His goddamn blood.

He sits there, in the exact same spot, feeling his houseboat swaying this way and that for what seems like several hours. His thoughts turn to cement pins in his head: money, bourbon, loneliness… money, bourbon, loneliness… money, bourbon, loneliness…

When it finally gets dark he cries, a sound from a boy, or a woman even, his voice high, unrecognizable, wheedling. He is so lonesome he has the thought to douse himself with kerosene and set himself on fire. He could walk out onto the back deck of his houseboat and dance a final, flaming fuck-you to the world, before plunging into the water, dead and charred, only his teeth spared the inferno.

He lights a match, considers the flame, and then joins it to the end of a cigarette, which he smokes while choking back his sobs, swallowing them whole like wads of dry bead. He will give the bastards another pint of his blood and use the money to buy a bottle of Maker's, groceries, insect repellent, athlete's foot spray, a canister of paraffin oil, and a new pack of underwear. He'll put forty of it in the little coffee can under his bed, which is dedicated to that pearl-handled snub-nosed .38 over in Louisville.

When he is halfway finished with his cigarette he strikes another match and lights the wick of one of his hurricane lamps and watches the season's first mosquito flit about the glowing nimbus, its sound like a tuning fork that someone has struck in some far-off nonexistent room.

"Please come see me on Monday," he says aloud to the walls of his moldering, floating cabin, thinking of his new friend, Grady, and fighting the urge to cry again. "Please, please, please come see me. I'll be waiting for you."

9

ELMIRA, NEW YORK
SEPTEMBER 7, 1985

AVA

THE INTERIOR OF THE confessional is downright rank. It smells as if someone's eaten half of a liverwurst sandwich and left its foul remains under the confessor's bench. Ava Larkin sits across from Father Gattas, who joined the parish after Father Oates, the longtime senior priest at St. John the Baptist, died in March. Father Gattas is young, perhaps only thirty, and came to Elmira from Santa Fe, New Mexico. Despite his youth, he delivers his sermons with the cool articulate calm of a man beyond his years, like some veteran movie actor playing a presidential candidate.

Father Gattas's pale profile, obscured by the perforated filament separating priest from confessor, is mostly in shadow. He possesses a round, open face and the same baby-blond hair as Ava's youngest, Lexy. Although there is a mahogany bench, Ava chooses to kneel on the padded tuffet. She is sixty-six years old and in the past few months the simple act of genuflecting has become a painful exercise. While working in her garden, she spends far less time on her knees than she did even three months ago, at the beginning of the summer. But kneeling is the least she can do, especially during the sacrament of confession. Jesus suffered so much more for our sins, after all. In recent weeks it's become difficult for her to extend her torso for more than a minute in this position without collapsing forward. Inserting a pair of tube socks into the hollows behind her knees helps alleviate the pressure—she can relax just slightly. The socks were her late husband's and she finds it comforting to carry something of Donald with her to church. Next Thursday will be the first anniversary of his death, and the ache behind both knees seems to have gotten worse with each passing month, as if her husband's ghost is starting to take hold of her joints.

It's quite muggy for September and Ava's brow is already damp. In one hand she clutches her white rosary and in the other a postcard she received in yesterday's mail. The rosary beads are made of seashells that were purportedly blessed in the nineteenth century by Pope Leo XII on the papal altar of the Basilica of St. Peter. Ava inherited the rosary from her mother toward the end of her life and, like her husband's tube socks, Ava carries it with her everywhere she goes. On the front of the postcard is a black-and-white photograph of a small clapboard church and on the back, in blue ballpoint ink, the name TIMOTHY DETTBARN is written in cursive, as well as a number she assumes to be his age, fourteen, and below that, in the same penmanship, the phrase SAYING HELLO AND GOODBYE. This is the twelfth such postcard she's received. Each one, which arrives in her mailbox toward the beginning of the month, features a church on the front, and a boy's name, a corresponding number, and the same mysterious, unpunctuated greeting/farewell on the back. The thing that has driven her into St. John the Baptist's confessional is that she knows the SAYING HELLO AND GOODBYE handwriting all too well: it belongs to her son, Alec. Ava realized this after she received the third postcard, all the back in December. She went up to the attic and unearthed his old school papers from a storage box. The H and the G were unmistakably the same: the posts of the capital H listing toward each other like a pair of foal's legs; the capital G bloated and sagging to the right, its curled bottom serif too small compared to the rest of the letter.

Following the confessional exchange, Ava has been kneeling for what feels like several minutes. She knows that it's her responsibility to begin the next part of the conversation. The silence is marked by the sounds of the old church: its creaking choir loft; the wind mewling through cracks in the large stained-glass window above the confessional; an echoey voice in the nave practicing a few phrases of the Latin Mass. Ava has attended this church since she was a little girl. She and Donald were married here. Her children were baptized and had their first communions here. All of them but Joan completed their confirmation here. It's truly been a second home, a place of refuge.

"You're awfully quiet today," Father Gattas finally says.

Ava apologizes. In the small confines her voice sounds weak and hollow. She is usually far more confident.

"What's on your mind, Mrs. Larkin?"

Ava stares at the postcard. The white church's humble square structure looks more suited to a roadside filling station or a small family bakery. The wooden sign driven into its narrow front lawn reads WOOLRIDGE BAPTIST CHURCH. The postmark is from Missouri.

"I guess I'm looking for guidance," she says, dabbing at her brow with the back of her hand holding the rosary.

"What kind of guidance?"

She turns the postcard over in her lap to reveal David Dettbarn's name and, below this, SAYING HELLO AND GOODBYE in her son's penmanship, the blue ballpoint ink weakly scrawled into the thick laminated stock. It's as if Alec wrote these four words on his knee. Ava pictures David Dettbarn as a thin farm boy with wheat-colored hair. Freckles across the bridge of his nose, skinned-up knees. But if he is indeed fourteen, then she's imagined him too young. Somehow she can't help but conjure innocence. Most fourteen-year-old boys are well into puberty, whereas she has summoned an eight-year-old.

"I'm afraid a member of my family has lost their way," she says.

"I'm sorry to hear that," the priest says. "Can you be more specific?"

She can see Alec so clearly. She's summoned him the night before she and Donald told him he had to leave. He was sitting across from them at the dining room table. His black hair was long and thick and starting to get curly in the back. In the past year his shoulders had noticeably broadened. Faint splotches of acne marked his chin and forehead. He was trying to grow a mustache, which looked like a collection of miniature spider legs above his lip. Compared to her daughters he appeared crazed, like some unshowered, feral drifter who'd broken into the house.

"Are you talking about one of your children?" Father Gattas asks.

He's young but smart. He can sense things in the pauses. He really does possess an impressive speaking voice, one that would be perfect for radio commercials. He could do an ad for a bank or a shoe store. He was probably captain of his high school debate team. She imagines him reciting Shakespearean sonnets in front of a mirror.

"...Mrs. Larkin?"

"It's my older boy," she says.

"Is he in some sort of trouble?"

"I'm almost certain that he is, yes."

"With the law?"

"I don't think it's like that," Ava says.

Again he asks her to be more specific. But she feels truly tongue-tied.

"Mrs. Larkin, in the short time that I've been acquainted with you I've never known you to be this unforthcoming at confession."

"It may be more about his soul," she says. "I think he's been adrift."

"Have you been *estranged* from...?"

"Alec," she replies. Saying his name—when was the last time?—causes her jaw to go slack. She has to bring her fingers to her lips and swallow. Again she can see her son's hair. Is it still dark? Has it turned gray? Is it salt-and-pepper? His eyes were always so brown, like those of a Spaniard or an Italian. He was the only one in the family whose skin immediately tanned in the summer. Everyone else burned so easily.

"So tell me about Alec," Father Gattas says.

"He's my only son," Ava says. "My only living son. He was an altar boy here."

"How old is Alec now?"

"He's in his mid-forties," she says. "He was always troubled."

She doesn't bother mentioning the offertory theft that took place at this very church—the incident that caused her and Donald to kick him out of the house. It was the one smirch in what has been an otherwise long and reliable family presence at St. John the Baptist.

"When was the last time you were in touch with him?" the priest asks.

"Oh, many years ago," she says, dabbing at her forehead again. "Twenty years, at least."

"And you're worried about him now because...?"

There's a rustling of paper and she envisions Father Gattas removing a stick of chewing gum from its foil, folding it into his mouth. Or maybe he's taking notes? She turns the postcard over, revealing the small church.

"I think he's wandered so far from what would be considered a good path," she says. "He could never find his place in the world. And now I fear that he's living in..."

"In what?"

"Well, in a very bad way," she says.

"In sin?" the priest asks.

The simple three-letter word carries a terrible implication. She sees Alec moving through a dark room, stealing things from the top of a bureau: a comb, a letter opener, a woman's hatpin. Is he still thin? Have his large veiny hands gotten thicker? He's carrying a small kitchen knife and his eyes are fixed upon the back of a young boy who is staring out a window.

"I'm afraid that whatever he's up to," Ava says, "might be something much worse than anything I can even conceive of."

Father Gattas tells her that it's okay if she's not ready to fully discuss the matter; she can come back in a few days when she's formed more specific thoughts and feelings. He adds that, if it would make it any easier, he'd be happy to speak more informally with her about the matter outside the confessional. "Do you know where Alec is?" he asks.

"I don't," she says. "He used to keep in touch with his oldest sister, but that stopped a while ago."

"And am I correct in assuming that you're feeling somehow responsible for his lack of direction?"

The word Ava's father would use for someone like Alec was *shiftless*.

"Yes," Ava says.

According to her father, anyone who wasn't ready either to work a forty-hour-a-week job or to answer the call of duty was *shiftless*. Stuart Farrell. Who'd grown up in Dublin, had moved to the United States when he was eight years old, had lived to be ninety-three, and could effortlessly quote the sermons and poetry of John Donne.

"All you can do is pray for your son," Father Gattas says.

Through the thin partition Ava glimpses the priest wiping his brow with a handkerchief. Part of her wonders if she should forgo the advice from this young priest and contact the authorities. Could the police help her find her son? Or would this postcard and the other eleven she's been keeping in the junk drawer below the phone in some way implicate him? The simple thought of somehow turning him in, of somehow alerting the authorities, is too much to bear. Besides, she doesn't even know where he is. What police station would she call?

"And you can also pray for forgiveness for the part you might've played in his wayward path," he adds. "But that's only for God to judge."

"I keep thinking something must have happened to him," Ava says. "Something I wasn't aware of."

"Why do you feel this way?"

"Because we raised our children to be good," she says. "Donald set such a fine example. And none of them are perfect, but Alec's sisters genuinely care about others." Ava squeezes her rosary. "We tried our very best with him, we really did."

"I'm sure you and your husband gave Alec every opportunity to have a good life. Sometimes there's nothing more we can do."

After Father offers her an act of penance, Ava quickly recites the Act of Contrition.

"Give thanks to the Lord for He is good," Father Gattas says.

"For His mercy endures forever," Ava says, and pauses on the notion of mercy. She can't help but think of Alec. Can she be as forgiving as the Holy Father? If her only living son is doing terrible things can she find it in her heart to be merciful? Even in the confessional this feels nearly impossible.

"The Lord has freed you from your sins," Father Gattas says through the partition. "Go in peace."

"Thanks be to God," Ava says.

After exiting the confessional booth, she sits in a pew near the back of the church and quietly thanks God for the Gift of His Mercy. She then recites her penance while continuing to clutch her rosary, which she still plans on bequeathing to Myra. She wishes Myra had had a girl to continue the tradition of the oldest daughter receiving the longstanding family heirloom. It's a shame that Fiona turned out to be an atheist, that Joan will never have children, and that Lexy married a Jew. Lexy and her husband, Barry, a vice president at a top-level Wall Street financial firm, have twin girls, Eve and Elizabeth. They live in a beautiful Tudor home in Rowayton, Connecticut. Barry looks like he could be the brother of Lexy's college sweetheart, Ed, who wound up breaking Lexy's heart after he graduated from Yale and moved to Switzerland. Why Lexy is so drawn to Jewish men is truly a mystery. Perhaps someday Myra's son, Ronan, will also have a daughter?

At the grocery store Ava buys a dozen eggs, a gallon of milk, a pound of lean ground beef, a pound each of ricotta and mozzarella cheese, two cans of tomato paste, and a package of lasagna noodles. While waiting in the checkout line she is confronted with a periodicals rack containing one of those awful tabloids whose front page features a picture of the movie star Rock Hudson. He is shirtless, lounging on the deck of a small yacht. The headline says that Mr.

Hudson has contracted the AIDS virus, that his health is in serious decline. The smaller print claims that he's had sex with over 20,000 men, that his entire career has been a lie. In the photo he looks thin, hollowed.

"It's true," the checkout girl says of the headline. "The homo plague got him."

Ava smiles and shakes her head. Who would pay sixty-five cents for such trash? she wonders. "Only fifty-nine years old," she offers. "God help him."

The Rock Hudson scandal makes Ava think of Fiona, who is currently living in a New York City railroad apartment with a homosexual who goes by the unfortunate name of Bobby John Krabbenhof. A hillbilly name. Ava has never met Bobby John but she imagines him to be tall and fey and exaggeratedly lissome, like a long switch of willow. High-voiced and lazy, a chirper of minor complaints, incessantly impersonating his favorite divas. Like Fiona, Bobby John is an aging actor, and from what Ava has gleaned from her second-oldest daughter, he mostly waits tables at a café near their West Village apartment. Has he been infected, too? Ava wonders. Despite his sexuality, has Fiona experimented with him? Is she going to contract this horrible virus by virtue of their close quarters? They do share a toilet, after all. As Ava carries her groceries out to her station wagon, she has to push from her mind images of Fiona and Bobby John engaging in unprotected sex, experimenting with sodomy, hosting orgies, welcoming the Devil himself into what she imagines to be their filthy apartment with a bathtub in the middle of the kitchen, a toilet mounted beside the stove, dead flies lining the windowsills.

At home, despite knowing it'll likely be a few weeks before she receives another postcard, Ava nervously checks the mail. Her hands are cold, even colder than the tin of the mailbox. After all this time, why is she suddenly having such a physical reaction to a potential postcard? Something has shifted. The very possibility of it appearing in the mailbox feels like a portent. For many months what seemed to be a cruel prank, an intentionally unsolvable riddle, now feels all too real. Alec could change the rules of this perverse game at any time. But there is no postcard; only an electric bill, an events calendar from church, and a few department-store flyers.

After she puts away the groceries and lays out everything she'll need to prepare dinner, she calls Myra. Since Donald died, nearly a year ago now, they've been talking on the phone once a week, sometimes twice.

"How are your knees?" Myra asks.

"Oh, they're fine," Ava lies. "Today's been surprisingly humid so they're acting up a tiny bit more than usual, but I can manage." She realizes to her surprise that she has twisted the phone cord around her left wrist. "How are things at the hospital?" she asks, unwinding the cord. She wants more than anything to bring up this postcard business. As she was carrying the groceries in from the car she promised herself that when she spoke with Myra she would immediately bring up the subject of Alec, but now she finds that she can't.

Myra tells her that she's been offered a job as the head nurse at a local boys' prison. They would elevate her title to the coveted "State Nurse" status, which would provide her with an improved salary and better medical benefits.

"How old are these boys?" Ava asks.

"Between ten and seventeen. Many of the older ones are already fully developed men but I'm told the guards there are very good. There are murderers and rapists," Myra adds. "But the really bad offenders are kept away from the general population."

Ten-year-olds raping and killing and committing arson, Ava thinks. Mere boys engaging in the atrocities of the Devil. She can't help but imagine Alec running rampant throughout this prison. She sees him at fourteen, the same age as Timothy Dettbarn, taunting his forty-seven-year-old sister in a juvenile prison, calling out her name from the dark of his cell. Alec, the troubled boy who never aged, damned by an eternal pubescence.

"Don't worry," Myra says, as if sensing Ava's unease. "I'll be taking a six-week self-defense class."

An hour later, in her garden, with her favorite basket hanging from the crook of her elbow, Ava picks a handful of tomatoes for her lasagna. The rabbits have chewed through the protective netting and decimated the season's final few heads of broccoli so she opts for a dozen or so knots of Brussels sprouts. Those damn rabbits. She loves watching them — they seem innocent enough with their large pretty eyes and velvety ears — but she doesn't appreciate the way they pillage her vegetables. Next year she'll have to use the metal meshing. She plucks a handful of basil leaves, adds them to her basket, and heads inside.

At around three-thirty Ava browns the ground beef and begins preparing a large casserole dish with all of her lasagna layers. When she's halfway done, realizing with annoyance that she's forgotten to add the lower layer of ricotta cheese, she scoops everything out and starts over. She usually doesn't lose focus like this. Normally she could make this lasagna with her eyes closed. Clearly she's distracted by the Dettbarn boy from Alec's postcard. It almost feels as if she's making the lasagna for *him*. She redoes the layers, careful to take her time with the ricotta, the ground beef, the diced tomatoes, the grated parmesan.

After placing the lasagna in the oven she grabs a pen and a notebook and, following a series of phone calls, with the aid of an information operator in the Woolridge, Missouri, area code, Ava manages to track down a phone number connected to the Dettbarn surname. Her breathing quickens. She attempts to slow it by exhaling through her nose a few times. This always worked during the early days of her marriage, when she wanted to calm her hands while sewing or while she would bring Donald his morning coffee.

After only a single ring a woman answers. "Hello?" says a high, tinny voice, a bit choked.

When Ava tries to speak she has cottonmouth. She gulps from

the glass of iced tea she was drinking while preparing the lasagna, then asks if Timothy Dettbarn lives there.

"Do you know something about my son?" the woman on the other end says. Her accent is a little Southern, her voice almost too gentle for this conversation.

Ava swallows hard and takes another drink.

"Do you have information about Timmy?" the woman asks again.

"I'm actually calling from the library," Ava lies.

"The library?"

"It appears that Timothy has some overdue books."

"But he never *goes* to the library," the woman says. "The only thing he reads are his comics."

"Well, according to our records —"

"Who is this?" the woman says, her voice leaping an octave.

"I'm calling from the library," Ava says.

"What branch?"

"The Woolridge branch," Ava says.

"There is no library in Woolridge," the woman says. "Whoever you are."

Ava can't speak. She stares at the boy's name on the postcard. She turns it over to reveal once again the humble white clapboard church, its small, unadorned steeple.

"My son has been missing for over four months and you have the gall to call about phony library books?"

And still Ava cannot speak.

"…Hello?" the woman says on the other end.

"I'm sorry," Ava says. "I obviously have the wrong Timothy Dettbarn."

"Well, how many Timothy Dettbarns can there possibly be in Woolridge, Missouri?!"

Beyond the kitchen window a large crow — practically a raven — hops around in the yard, picking through some early fallen leaves, no doubt searching for an apple core or a squirrel carcass or even a dead hummingbird. Greedy crows eating their own, Ava thinks, scavenging whatever they can get. Gluttons of carrion. The winter will likely have no effect on this creature. It will certainly outlast all the other birds, even the hardy blue jays.

"If you know something about my son please tell me," the woman ways, her voice cracking. "Please..."

Ava hangs up, her knuckles white as she continues to grip the receiver in its berth on the wall. A sharp pain seizes her left hip and shoots down her femur. She grabs at the back of her knee and the receiver slips off its cradle and falls to the floor. A fault line of arthritis surges in her hip.

"Okay, Donald," she says, smiling. "Now's not the time to flirt..."

After Ava resets the receiver on the phone cradle, she grabs at another brief throbbing behind her left knee. She refuses to take the Bufferin suggested by Doctor Trammell. It upsets her stomach and she doesn't like the taste. And she's certainly not interested in a prescription drug, which is very likely what caused Donald's abrupt decline, taxing his already weakened system. He lasted two months on dialysis and then his body just shut off in the middle of the afternoon. He was in his study, listening to his beloved Yankees. Donald had been disappointed in the team, third in their division, the entire season and although it would have been far too narcissistic a notion for him to admit, Ava suspected he felt that his deteriorating health had in some small way cursed them. When it came to the Yankees' fortunes Donald was boyishly superstitious. On game days he would always back his Chrysler into the driveway, believing that parking nose-in would all but guarantee a loss. When Ava found him in his chair, which had just been reupholstered in a forest-green moleskin, the game was in the seventh inning. Dave Winfield was batting and proceeded to ground into a double play. Donald's eyes were open, his mouth slightly ajar.

Ava thought her husband was simply stunned by yet another minor instance of bad luck and its accumulation throughout the disappointing '84 season. "Donald," she said. "Donald, honey."

But he was dead. It was as if a switch had been flipped, ceasing the functioning of his body's machinery.

Ava sits at the kitchen table and once again stares at the small church on the front of the black-and-white postcard...The white clapboards...the small sandwich board out front displaying the times of service...the overcast sky and empty parking lot. She again notes the lack of a cross on top of the roof. There is no holy statue signifying that it's a place of worship. It looks more like a malt shop that closed for the winter, like a place where you could order an egg salad sandwich. Why does each postcard feature a church on the front? What could this possibly mean?

Ava opens the small junk drawer under the phone and removes the other eleven postcards, secured with a rubber band, in the order she received them. At the top is the postcard from Pittsburgh, the first one she found in her mailbox nearly one year ago, in early October. It features a big Catholic church with a large green dome and two smaller green ones capping spires that flank both sides of the church's entryway. The text at the bottom of the image says IMMACULATE HEART OF MARY. On the back: JUSTIN HURLEY. 14. SAYING HELLO AND GOODBYE. The next one, which she received a few days after Halloween, highlights Our Lady of the Snows Catholic Church, in Climax Springs, Missouri. Printed on the back: THEODORE DRAKOS. 11. SAYING HELLO AND GOODBYE. The following one, not long after Thanksgiving, displays St. Raphael's Cathedral in Dubuque, Iowa, and on the back: WILLIAM RABE. 13. SAYING HELLO AND GOODBYE. Always a male name. Always the number. Always the strange greeting/farewell in Alec's faint hand. With regard to his penmanship, as a student he never used enough force. Ava was convinced it was a weakness of the will rather than any lack of wrist strength. Alec had the physical abilities of an athlete, after all. He could run faster and throw a ball farther than almost all of his classmates, yet there was something so frail and enfeebled, something almost cowardly, about the way he wrote.

When he was in grammar school Ava and Donald had even received a note from his seventh-grade English teacher, Sister Nolan. Three months ago Ava brought the note down from that box of Alec's school records in the attic. She removes it from the junk drawer and unfolds it.

> *Dear Mr. and Mrs. Larkin,*
>
> *Compared to his classmates, Alec's penmanship is grossly lacking, and I felt that it was necessary to bring the matter to your attention. Despite more than a few conversations with him, your son refuses to make any adjustments and I fear this will very likely hinder the prospects of his academic future. I think Alec is a smart boy with a lot of potential and I'd like to see him succeed. Please call me if you'd like to discuss.*
>
> *Sincerely,*
> *Sister Sheila Nolan*

Ava had a lengthy discussion with Alec about his handwriting problem. She stressed the importance of clear, readable penmanship and how it speaks to one's character, to one's sense of self, and to one's place in a society that relies on cultural fluency and readability. She even sat with him at the dining room table and made him write out the alphabet as well as several passages from the Bible. He eventually wrote with more force, but Ava concluded that it was only to appease her so he could go outside and join his buddies at the park, because only weeks later she would hear from Sister Nolan that the penmanship on his schoolwork was showing no improvement and, if anything, had become less discernible and more faded. Eventually Sister Nolan stopped trying to intervene.

AVA AND JOAN SIT down for dinner just after 7:00 p.m. Since Donald passed away, Joan has become Ava's sole companion. Ava still speaks to Myra and Lexy a few times a month, Myra sometimes twice a week. Flakey Fiona will even give her a call every so often to complain about her acting career, which, despite the occasional minor role in an off- or off-off-Broadway play, is practically nonexistent. Fiona will also cite her frustration with her slew of temporary day jobs, or the tribulations of another failed relationship with some man — usually married — whom she met at a museum, or among the scattered leaves of Central Park, or during happy hour at what Ava can only imagine to be a seedy bar with a filthy latrine and sawdust on the floor. During their last phone call Fiona bragged about having become adept at spotting a tan line around a man's ring finger. Though her daughter probably thinks her anecdotes are amusing, her shameful behavior still embarrasses Ava. And invariably, once she's offloaded one or two of these stories, the subject will veer, like a small boat damned by bad weather, toward a painful shoreline: Fiona's chronic insolvency. Which is always followed by a request for money. A few years back she did get cast in a life-insurance commercial that ran for a few months during the daytime soaps, but per usual she squandered that money on clothes and acting lessons and leftist books and pieces of half-broken antique furniture.

Almost forty-six years old and she still hasn't found a way to make a consistent living. Despite her intelligence and beauty — she still looks like she could be in her early thirties — she has no steady income and no man in her life. It's a crying shame, it really is. In high school boys would practically fall at Fiona's feet. But there was always something rebellious in her nature. It wasn't Alec's willful malevolence, nothing like that. It was that Fiona longed for another world. An adventure that assured freedom, no matter the cost.

After the years in New York there was the period when she lived with that outlandish fertility cult in an uninsulated barn in Massachusetts or New Hampshire or Vermont or wherever it was. Lesbians making their own clothes and defecating into holes in the ground, God help us. Scores of lost young women sleeping side by side in haylofts and empty corncribs, their menstrual cycles grotesquely in sync, bathing each other in streams and braiding each other's lice-riddled hair.

By Elmira standards Donald had left Myra, Lexy, and Fiona a respectable sum of money—almost twenty thousand dollars each—but Fiona burned through her inheritance paying off a catalog of debts. She had barely enough left to put a security deposit down on the West Village apartment she now shares with Bobby John. Since Donald's death Ava finds herself swallowing a lot of the maternal advice that she used to offer her most troubled daughter. She winds up listening to Fiona weep and sniffle and bemoan the unfairness of her profession and her tragic lack of luck. The histrionics eventually subside, of course, and they'll exchange a more composed goodbye. After Ava hangs up the phone, more often than not she'll take out her checkbook and send her daughter some rent money.

As much as Ava has loved her life in Elmira, there have been times when she's wondered what it would have been like to have seen more of the world. She's always wanted to go to Paris. She took three years of French in high school—she used to speak at the conversational level—and often imagined walking along the colorful, wide Parisian boulevards, but then she got married and immediately started having kids and now that all of them but Joan are gone, she feels content. Elmira *is* her Paris. For all of its simplicity there is beauty here, too. There is Pulaski Park and the Chemung River and the shops along West Water Street and all of the pretty homes in her neighborhood. She loves her house and her garden. She loves the way the leaves change in the fall. Sure, the past year has been hard—she misses Donald every day—but she's come to appreciate this new, more ascetic life.

Joan, who sits beside Ava as she always has, will never be the conversationalist her sisters are, but she's the one daughter who's been there through thick and thin. Not that she's had a choice. There was a period when Ava considered putting her in a home up in Waterford. Donald left ample money in a trust to cover this eventuality, and it would have been an easy two-hour drive north, but when Ava searched her soul about the matter she felt guilty imagining Joan being herded around the penitentiary-style grounds with scores of other mentally impaired adults. Joan wasn't used to being around others like her; she's always seen herself as normal. Ava had prayed and prayed and then simply let the notion fade away. And now they are companions. They rake leaves together and pull weeds in the garden together and Ava has even grown to trust Joan with the push mower, which saves her at least twenty dollars a month.

After Donald died Ava removed two table leaves, and now the claw-foot dining table is a perfect square of mahogany, just large enough for two people, or three if one of her church friends stops by for lunch. When the other children come to visit Ava can easily bring the other leaves up from the basement. She's hoping to have the girls home again this coming Thanksgiving. Myra says she and Ronan will drive all the way from Joliet. Lexy, Barry, Eve, and Elizabeth will come over from Connecticut. And hopefully Fiona will take the train up from New York City; Ava told her she could even invite Bobby John. She keeps pictures of her three grandchildren on the hood of the old upright piano and every time she plays it makes her so happy to look at their beautiful faces. It'll be good to have everyone — almost everyone — home. Ava is briefly reminded of the awful package Alec sent for Christmas all those years ago — that horrible Tupperware container of feces, which followed her and Donald's invitation to come home for the holidays. Such a vile, disgusting thing Alec had done, especially after they had extended an olive branch, just as the dove does to Noah in the Bible.

Joan says grace and after Ava pours the milk they eat for a while in their routine silence.

"Did you get more done on your puzzle?" Ava asks.

"I finished the edges," Joan says.

"Well, that's progress."

The puzzle is a still frame from Joan's favorite animated Disney movie, *The Lady and the Tramp*, in which a terrier mutt and a cocker spaniel romantically share a plate of spaghetti and meatballs at an Italian restaurant. The fact that Joan has completed the edges without any help is a sure sign of progress. At forty-one, despite her handicap, Joan still seems to be evolving mentally, which is a rare recent blessing.

* * *

AFTER AVA HAS DONE the dishes and laid them out to dry, she runs Joan's bath, and then goes into Donald's study to sit in his chair. She likes the new upholstery. The moleskin has a rich, almost velvety feel, and forest green was her husband's favorite color.

She turns on his radio and a hoarse, fast-talking deejay announces a song entitled "The Power of Love" by some rock-and-roll outfit called Huey Lewis and the News. Ava listens for twenty seconds or so and then turns the radio off and simply sits there, trying to conjure her husband. This is her nightly ritual: while Joan takes her bath, Ava sits in Donald's chair and remembers happier times. Tonight it's nothing special, just the image of him washing his Skylark in the driveway, the sun shining on his rippled shoulders. He submerges a large yellow sponge in a pail of sudsy water and drags it across the curved steel body of his prized car. Sometimes she gets the smallest details wrong. For instance, once she imagined him working at his shop table in the basement when the table has always been in the garage. He built it there and never moved it. But she forgives herself for these little mistakes. Recently she's finding that her memory has become as elusive as her dreams.

In the bedroom, Joan is already asleep. She occupies Donald's bed now, beside Ava's, because she's gotten too heavy for the stairs. At her last checkup she weighed more than 250 pounds and Dr. Kelly recommended that, in the interest of avoiding serious injury, Ava keep her downstairs. Joan's simple motor skills have never been great. Even when her weight was normal she usually required help making her way up to the second floor.

"Good night," Ava says to her daughter, even though Joan is sound asleep.

Her breathing is deep and congested, her snoring worse than Donald's, yet Ava loves her. She has spent many nights letting this horrible sound usher her to sleep.

Unable to settle her thoughts as she kneels in prayer, Ava pulls herself up by the bed knob and exits the bedroom. She intends to go into the kitchen to warm some milk in a saucepan—a warm glass of milk has always helped her relax—but she finds herself climbing the stairs. Some unknown force of will, seemingly belonging to the house itself, is pulling her toward the second floor. Each of the twelve steps bites into her failing knees. After a few deep breaths at the top of the stairs she enters Alec's bedroom.

These days Ava spends hardly any time on the second floor. Of the three bedrooms, Alec's is the one she's avoided most. It feels like some fabricated installation, as if a set designer from the local community theater took bits of evidence of Alec's early life and recreated the *idea* of his bedroom. The clothes he left behind are still neatly folded in the cherrywood Shaker-style dresser that once belonged to Ava's father. A pair of brown loafers he wore to church are neatly set on the floor of his closet. The truth is, aside from changing the sheets for the rare overnight guest, Ava hasn't moved a thing in this room since Alec left home, more than two decades ago.

In the drawer of his nightstand she finds a pack of unopened Viceroys. He always smoked, even as young boy, no matter how many times Donald would punish him. Did he leave the cigarettes behind just to spite them? Why else would he not take them with him? There is also a deck of playing cards, a Wrigley's spearmint gum wrapper, and two dirty nickels. Ava closes the drawer, as if leaving the items undisturbed will somehow help her solve the mystery of those postcards.

She then goes down to her aching knees (first left, then right) and reaches under the bed, where she discovers a shoebox, which has his full name—ALEC CHRISTOPHER LARKIN—printed on the edge of the lid. She opens the box. Inside she finds a rusty pocketknife, several fishing lures, and a shoehorn, which features a gold leaf engraving on the polished wooden handle that reads FATHER SHELBY OATES. What a strange thing to discover under her son's bed. Why on earth would Alec have Father Oates's shoehorn? Then again, if nothing else, her son was a thief. If he stole the collection money from his own parish, then who knows what he was truly capable of? It's a fine, tortoiseshell shoehorn, perhaps six inches in length. Is it a clue into her son's spiritual decline? How many more objects like this might she find hidden in this room? But maybe Alec didn't steal it. Perhaps Father Oates saw him admiring it one day and simply offered it to him? A gift to a once promising altar boy? Then again, Alec was always the black sheep. He was never beloved by anyone, especially at St. John the Baptist, where he was often chided for being late and warned multiple times that he would be relieved of his duties.

As she's about to replace the lid of the shoebox she notices something taped to its underside. She peels the tape away and removes a small black-and-white snapshot, a 3" x 3", with the date, AUG — 51, printed across the bottom of the white quarter-inch margin. In the photo is a naked adult male, sitting on a short stool, with an erection. His chest is covered with thick black hair and his flesh is very pale. Clenched between his teeth, like a pirate with a knife, is a shoehorn. His eyes are wild, theatrically so. His fists are planted at the knobs of his hips. His penis looks poisonous, like a curved creature that could strike you. Ava grabs the shoehorn again, turns it this way and that. Yes, it appears to be the same as the one in the photo, with the identical handle. At closer examination, Ava recognizes the man as Father Oates. The eyes are unmistakable. The snapshot is shocking, to say the least. Did Alec take this photograph? In August of 1951 he was only ten years old. Why did he have it? Why did he have the shoehorn, the photo's only prop? And had Alec left this shoebox here to be discovered someday as a spiteful piece of evidence? Like some sick little time capsule? It certainly seems that way. Ava's breath leaves her and something cold turns near her heart. The implications are too great to contend with. She puts the photograph in the front pocket of her housecoat.

Down in the kitchen she finally warms her milk in the saucepan. Just as it starts to simmer she kills the flame and pours the milk into a large coffee mug and adds cinnamon and a tiny bit of sugar. She sits at her small kitchen table, sets the damp teaspoon on a napkin.

As she waits for her milk to cool she reaches for the junk drawer and pulls out her collection of postcards. She removes the rubber band and deals them across the table, equidistant, one at a time, in a single long, clean row.

She peers down at the postcards. A dozen churches. A dozen boys.

SAYING HELLO AND GOODBYE.

The temperature outside has dropped, and somewhere in the bowels of the house the heat turns faintly on.

Below the row of postcards Ava places the snapshot of Father Oates.

The colder season will soon be upon them, she thinks. She and Joan will have to rake the fallen leaves. Soon after that it will snow. Somehow she knows it will be a long winter.

PART THREE

10

NEW YORK CITY, NEW YORK
JULY 8, 1991

RONAN

Not even twelve minutes into his walk from the East Village Ronan Happ is sweating through his clothes. At 9:45 it's already 80 degrees. The cool fountain mists of Washington Square Park are but a brief, cruel relief. It's the Monday following July Fourth weekend and the eighteen-dollar brown leather, size-thirteen wingtips that he bought on Saturday are just too fucking tight. Ronan usually wears fourteens, but when he tried these size thirteens on in the cramped, crowded vintage store on Seventh Street they felt pretty good. Now he's going to be late for work again. He should've just worn his Top-Siders. The Top-Siders are real quality leather, and the soles are still in good shape, but none of Ronan's co-workers at the publishing house wear "boat" shoes. As someone told him the other day at lunch, boat shoes are what you wear to a clambake, and on the fourth floor of the big prestigious publishing house in the Saatchi and Saatchi building, which takes up most of the southwest corner of Hudson and Houston Streets, the last thing you want to look like is someone who is about to attend a clambake.

Ronan works in sales. He reports directly to the National Hardcover Sales Director, Dan Van Asselt, a fellow Midwesterner from Chippewa Falls, Wisconsin. On Ronan's second day, Dan told him that he went against the grain and that he'd hired him because of his accent. Ronan's alma mater, Loras College in Dubuque, Iowa, a small, obscure Catholic school, is a fine enough institution of higher learning, but all the other assistants on the fourth floor are graduates of Yale and Columbia and Harvard and Cornell and smaller elite Northeastern colleges like Tufts, Williams, Hamilton, and Amherst.

At Loras, Ronan earned nearly straight A's and was also an All-American Division III track-and-field athlete, but despite these résumé gems, he is far from the realm of the Ivy League and his wardrobe is probably the first thing that gives this away. His three pairs of different-colored Dockers are in perpetual rotation, as are his four button-down shirts and six ties, two of which are phantasmagoric paisley numbers that he purchased from the sales bin of a men's store at the Dubuque mall. He could probably get away with the boat shoes if he worked in the editorial or art department, but in sales there is a different expectation.

Ronan lands at his cubicle almost ten minutes late and is greeted with a yellow Post-it note requesting his presence in Dan's office, ASAP. Ronan immediately begins sweating again, though this time it's triggered by pure, unadulterated anxiety. Because this can mean only one of three terrible things: (1) Dan has finally had it up to here with Ronan's constant three- to five-minute tardiness; (2) Due to the recession there's been a recent employee purge and he's getting laid off; or (3) He's been caught stealing Dan's wife's first edition of *The Catcher in the Rye*.

The third possibility causes Ronan's stomach to lurch and curdle. He almost throws up in his mouth.

Two weeks ago, knowing that his recently hired assistant would be stranded in the city during the Fourth of July weekend, Dan had invited Ronan to dinner at his Brooklyn Heights brownstone, on Remsen Street. Ronan enthusiastically accepted, of course. The dinner took place two nights ago, on Saturday evening.

Before the meal Dan and his wife, Elsa, a blond, willowy, deep-voiced Swede, gave Ronan a tour of their three-story brownstone. Elsa is from Stockholm but speaks English with excellent diction, deploying the hard *i* for *either* and the soft *a* for *tomato*. Her sharply pointed incisors are longer than her other teeth, giving her an air of savagery. During cocktails Ronan learned that Dan and Elsa had met five years earlier, at the annual American Booksellers Association's meeting in New Orleans. At the time, Elsa, who was only twenty-nine, owned and managed a small bookstore in Bath, Maine. Dan, who is nine years her senior (now forty-three), seems so normal, such a by-the-book, by-the-numbers kind of guy that Ronan almost expected his wife to be his college sweetheart. He imagined a former English major with muscular calves and anchor-woman hair. Maybe her name would be Kathy. How these two wound up together is anyone's guess.

During cocktails Ronan got the distinct sense that his boss had married above his station. Upper-level managers in book publishing do fine enough, but he can't imagine they earn the kinds of salaries that would allow for the purchasing of a three-story brownstone in one of Brooklyn's finest neighborhoods.

Elsa moved like an aristocrat. She poured the Rombauer red and held her wineglass as if it was soothing her fingertips.

The second floor of their brownstone showcased a beautiful, extensive, floor-to-ceiling, white oak library. Elsa, now a prominent children's book agent, is an avid book collector, and proudly directed Ronan to an entire shelf of first editions, which included, among other well-known titles, *Old Yeller*, *The Wind and the Willows*, and *The Catcher in the Rye*, which is his mother's favorite novel, and definitely on his own personal top five list.

After dinner, on his way upstairs to use the second-floor bathroom (Dan was occupying the first-floor facilities), Ronan found himself once again poised before that shelf of first editions. And then he felt his hand reaching toward the spine of Salinger's masterpiece. And then he was in the bathroom with it, standing under the charmingly distressed industrial sconce lamp, grazing the text with the pads of his fingers, marveling at the beauty of the design, the generous space left in the margins, drunk with the yeasty smell rising out of its binding. He was so besotted that he forgot to use the toilet and spent the rest of the evening with the book wedged into the small of his back, beneath his untucked shirt, really having to take a piss. He made sure to remain seated for the post-dinner bourbon that Dan insisted they drink.

"Did you have much Pappy Van Winkle in Iowa?" Dan asked, pouring two fingers over ice.

"This is definitely my first," Ronan replied, relieved that he'd chosen to wear an extra-large button-down shirt and a pair of pleated khakis that were downright roomy.

At twenty-two, Ronan seems to be cursed into always having to wear baggy clothes. He is 6'3" and inherited not only his grand-mother's height and long, rangy limbs but also his mother's thin-ness. He weighs 165 pounds after a big dinner. The combination of his orangutan arms and broad shoulders forces him to purchase extra-large shirts, which, if left untucked, billow about his waistline like an old-fashioned nightshirt. There is the constant need to mar-shal these blousy garments, meticulously folding them like origami into the sides of his waistline. On Saturday night he was thankful for the extra room.

After two more fingers of bourbon, he and the Van Asselts said their farewells without incident. Playing the role of the grateful assistant, Ronan thanked them profusely for inviting him over. It was his first July Fourth in New York City, after all.

"Well, I couldn't leave a fellow Midwesterner stranded in the East Village," Dan said, "especially with all those shenanigans going on in the park."

Ronan lives on Tenth Street, not even a full block west of Tomp-kins Square Park, where, since early May, police have been fighting with the homeless to extricate them from the park so that the city can embark on a major renovation. On Ronan's first day in New York hundreds of police in full riot gear manned the park's perim-eter, from Tenth to Seventh Street and between Avenue A and B. The longstanding homeless shantytown whose hub originated at the park's bandshell and sprawled in every direction was being destroyed and their occupants wrestled out by the NYPD, some-times in small groups, often one at a time. A week later the first Molotov cocktail was hurled from a Tenth Street rooftop between

Avenue A and B, the block directly east of Ronan's apartment. Fire took hold in the bushes next to the basketball courts. To Ronan it has all looked and felt like something that would happen in Beirut or Eastern Europe. It's a far cry from his undergraduate days in Dubuque, where the most intense campus protests involved students picketing for a beloved professor to be granted tenure.

"Dinner was delicious," Ronan said to Elsa on the Van Asselts' front stoop. It was the first time he'd ever eaten coq au vin and it really *was* delicious, as was the Rombauer. And then to cap it off were the assorted cheeses served on a restored seventeenth-century rowing oar that Elsa's Great-Great-Great-Great-Grandfather Aksel had used while boating on the River Pite. "I always thought Coco Van was a punk-rock fashion label out of Madison, Wisconsin," Ronan said, trying to be witty.

Elsa smiled — those sharp incisors gleaming — and kissed him on the cheek. "So fresh-faced," she said. "Do you even shave yet?"

"I do," he replied. "But only about twice a year."

Elsa laughed aristocratically.

"Don't worry," Dan said. "I didn't shave till I was around twenty-seven."

"And now he shaves *everywhere*," Elsa said, which left Ronan with the odd, disturbing image of his boss kneeling naked on the floor of his steamy second-floor bathroom, pawing aftershave lotion onto his freshly shorn ass cheeks.

After some good old-fashioned chuckles Ronan again thanked the Van Asselts for dinner and told Dan he'd see him at the office on Monday.

"Better beat me there," Dan joked.

WHEN RONAN ENTERS DAN'S office now, his boss is on the phone. Dan has a trio of succulents arranged in clay pots along his windowsill and a red-and-white Indiana Hoosiers pennant tacked horizontally to the wall over his bookcase — he is, improbably, a plant guy and a Big Ten guy.

Dan points to one of the two faux-leather Barcelona chairs on the other side of his desk. Ronan sits and after another minute or so Dan finally hangs up the phone.

Dan rocks back and forth in his white leather desk chair, his hands interlaced over his solar plexus. After several squeaky tilts he says, "So, you know why I called you in here, right?"

Ronan's mouth is dry. In his mind's eye he sees the copy of the stolen book. As soon as he got home on Saturday he wrapped it in one of his three towels and put it on the shelf of his closet so that Mrs. Dobroshtan, the old Ukrainian woman who rents him the room in her apartment, wouldn't see it. He swallows hard and says, "I'm honestly not sure."

"I just wanted to make it official," Dan says. "You're not going anywhere."

Is he referring to any plan Ronan might have hatched to escape down the back stairs? Has building security already been alerted? At this very moment are the police poised on the other side of Dan's office door?

"The purge," Dan continues. "Half the assistants in sales and marketing are getting the ax today. But you're safe."

Something inside Ronan, a soft, shapeless mass, shifts and drops. A gland releasing? An organ being freed from some crystalline web of anxiety? He exhales slowly through his nostrils.

"I didn't bring it up at dinner because I hadn't yet gotten word from on high that I could keep you. Be glad you didn't try and negotiate a bigger salary when I hired you."

"I am glad," Ronan says. "And grateful. Thank you, Dan."

"You're welcome. Keep up the good work. And if you can get me the call reports by the end of the day that would be great."

"Done," Ronan says, getting up.

"Oh, by the way, Elsa is crazy about you," Dan adds, just as Ronan is through the door. "She wanted you to have this." From under his desk he produces a gift-wrapped book and holds it out.

"Wow," Ronan says. He retraces his steps and taking the package from Dan. "How can I thank her?"

"Next time you're over just bring her a box of chocolates or something. She goes crazy for anything Godiva."

"Then Godiva it'll be."

Back at his cubicle, Ronan can't believe his reversal of fortune. He waits until Dan comes out of his office, re-knotting his tie, and heads to lunch. Once his boss is out of sight, Ronan peels the tape away from Elsa's gift and undoes the gift wrapping. It's a first edition of the English translation of Haruki Murakami's cult novel *A Wild Sheep Chase*, published two years earlier, by Kodansha International. Ronan has heard Stark Slovak, one of the reps who covers the Bay Area, gush to Dan over speakerphone about this novel. It's supposed to be some sort of mystical detective story. Slipped into the front jacket flap is a cream-colored bookmark, with a note on it, written in blue ink.

Ronan,

So lovely meeting you the other night. I thought you might like this novel. It's the story of a young man trying to find himself in a strange world. I think it glimmers, just like you. Enjoy.

x Elsa

Ronan imagines himself glimmering. He pictures a kind of translucent larval human, very small, the size of a gecko. He sees Elsa glimmering as well. She is full-sized, nude, walking toward him with her gleaming, feral incisors, brandishing Great-Great-Great-Great-Grandfather Aksel's boating oar. She has surprising full breasts and a dark thatch of pubic hair.

DURING LUNCH RONAN REMAINS at his cubicle and completes the hardcover call reports, a task that consists of transcribing and editing the sales reps' handwritten notes from their sales calls. The twenty-four-page printed report takes more than three hours to compile and proofread, and at 3:15 he walks into Dan's office and hands it to him while he's on the phone, then receives it back twenty minutes with Dan's red initials. Ronan spends the rest of the afternoon at the copy machine, suffering a series of paper jams and other tribulations that ultimately require him to power down and restart the rattling monstrosity.

When it's going well, for ten-minute snatches, the sound of the machine can be trance-inducing. During these lucky stretches Ronan often lets his mind wander to the play he's been writing, which has finally taken a definite shape. He embarked on it just after he arrived in the city. It's largely a memory monologue about a college-aged boy who accidentally kills his six-year-old sister while driving home from his summer job at a fast-food restaurant. As he nears the house, she scampers out into the road and he tries to swerve but runs her over. At this point, the story adds two other characters: the dead little sister (as a ghost), and the young man's mother, who, following the tragedy, goes mad and is institutionalized for the rest of her life.

Ronan discovered playwriting his junior year at Loras, while nursing an injury he'd sustained during track workouts. He had just undergone treatment for his strained calf and was limping back to his dorm room when he happened upon the Loras theater club rehearsing a play in a former machine shop near the sports complex. It was a surprisingly warm early-spring morning and the garage doors were open as they ran through the first act of Harold Pinter's masterwork *The Homecoming*. They had transformed a simple cement space into a '60s North London living room, complete with a staircase that improbably seemed to extend into infinity. Ronan was instantly mesmerized. It felt as if he had traveled in time across the Atlantic Ocean. The British accents and the odd, anxiety-filled pauses, executed perfectly by the actors, were bewitching. He eavesdropped for the rest of their run-through and couldn't stop thinking about the play the entire day and into the night. From that moment on, he feasted on contemporary drama.

Loras didn't teach a playwriting course, so he made it his business to read every modern play that was offered in the library and devoted that entire summer to trying to figure out how to write plays like Harold Pinter, Caryl Churchill, Sam Shepard, and John Guare. He turned out to be pretty good at it, with a knack for surprising actions and a good ear for dialogue. His subject matter managed to be both extremely dark and funny. Once Ronan started writing plays it became a compulsion, far more important than track-and-field or his other course work. It was all he wanted to do. New York was the only place for him after graduation, and he used a one-act to apply to Early Voices, a playwriting group hosted by a notable downtown theater company. To his surprise, he was invited to join.

Early Voices consists of five men and five women. Each writer receives a $1,500 stipend and a staged reading of whatever they develop during their year together. The group meets every Thursday, at 7:00 p.m., on the sixth floor of a building on Great Jones Street whose elevator sputters and pauses as if it's on life support. Ronan is the lone Midwesterner and one of only two straight men. He recently read aloud the first ten pages of his new monologue play to the group and was very encouraged by the responses of the other members. He has no idea where the monologue came from or where it is heading, but he often finds himself obsessed with it, almost as much as he is obsessed with another member of the group, Henny Woods.

Henny, twenty-five, whose full first name is Henrietta, is a recent graduate of Yale's playwriting MFA program (she also went to Yale for undergrad), and hails from a small town in rural northwest Connecticut. She is mixed-race (white father, Black mother), and possesses an astonishing globe of rich, curly hair the color of fallen maple leaves. In Ronan's opinion she is without question the best writer in Early Voices. She's also the bravest in that she's the only one who shares her thoughts about other people's work without worrying about hurt feelings or bending to the politics of wanting to be liked. She is equally blunt in her praise and criticism, and Ronan agrees with her more than anyone else.

Henny's father is a well-known abstract painter whose work is represented by a gallery on Greene Street. Her mother was a long-time member of the Paul Taylor Dance Company and now teaches modern at a private studio near their home in northwest Connecticut. Like Ronan, Henny is an only child. Unlike Ronan, she lives off the interest of a family trust that was established by her father when she was very young. The monthly dividend from this affords her a nice life. Upon graduating from Yale's playwriting program, she also received a monetary award for exhibiting extraordinary promise. Ronan learned of all this from another member of their writing group, Alexis, a recent Vassar grad who likes to wear striped train engineer caps and often audibly weeps when people read their stuff, regardless of its quality. Ronan has never been to Henny's apartment on Twelfth Street, just west of Fifth Avenue, but according to Alexis, it's a beautiful one-bedroom with high ceilings, herringbone wood floors, and a back terrace that overlooks a lush neighborhood garden.

After work Ronan will be attending a new adaptation of Chekhov's *Three Sisters* at the Atlantic Theater Company, in Chelsea. The theater is typically dark on Monday nights, but this is a press preview and Early Voices received a block of free tickets, which means Henny will very likely be there.

WHEN RONAN ENTERS THE foyer of the Atlantic Theater, a former church on West Twentieth Street, he is immediately confronted by a wall of photos featuring past productions as well as black-and-white headshots of the current ensemble, a handful of whom he recognizes from Hollywood and independent films. He takes his seat on the aisle with the rest of the group already in the back row.

The adaptation of *Three Sisters* has been written by the Atlantic's award-winning, iconoclastic playwright-in-residence. According to the program it will be performed in four acts, with two intermissions. Ronan knows very little about Chekhov other than his having been credited with some sacrosanct rule that if a gun is brought onstage it must be fired. And that his plays are long. It's just after 8:00 p.m. and he likely won't be home until midnight.

As the houselights dim, he makes eye contact with Henny, who is sitting several seats away. She nods to him as if they are rival detectives who've just arrived at a crime scene. His heart accelerates and he returns the nod. His head has never been so completely occupied by a woman. He will suffer through this evening with the scant pleasure of knowing they are watching the same play, which perhaps will provide something to talk about later.

The play is slow, with the ensemble executing a deliberate spoken cadence that seems almost clinical in its precision. Ronan is pleased that he recognizes the actress playing Masha from the John Hughes film *She's Having a Baby* and this awareness helps him get through the sluggish first act.

During the first intermission Ronan is getting some fresh air on the sidewalk in front of the theater when Henry approaches. She's wearing a light blue, man's button-down shirt with the sleeves rolled, loose-fitting linen pants, and brown leather sandals.

"Chekhov," she says.

"The master," Ronan says. Her sudden proximity makes him acutely aware of his hands. Not knowing where to put them, he clasps them behind his back.

"I don't hate it," Henny says.

"The guy playing Andrey is good," Ronan offers.

"Why are you all the way on the aisle?" she asks, poking him in the chest playfully. Her finger is stronger than he expected and he nearly loses his balance and has to unclasp his hands and find his feet.

"I was running late," he says, and can't help smiling, feeling a charge at her brief touch.

"The seat beside me is open," she says. "You should take it."

"Okay," Ronan says, embarrassed that he nearly fell over from her touch.

* * *

DURING ACT TWO RONAN can't focus on what's happening onstage because he is overwhelmed by Henny's scent, which somehow calls to mind freshly fallen Iowa snow as well as the oranges that his mother used to skewer with clove sticks and soak in simmering pots of cider during the holidays.

Henny watches the play with a keen severity. She leans forward with her elbows on her knees, seemingly uninterested in anything else. She rarely blinks, her gaze hard and forensic, with an air of being at once fascinated and repulsed, as if watching a dying animal on the roadside try to wrest itself to its feet. Her intensity makes Ronan feel ignorant to the turns of the play and its secret meanings, like a kid failing at an unwinnable carnival game. He imagines that she can simultaneously see the play's weaknesses and its strengths, that she feels burdened by her own intelligence, that she is sickened by the smallest dishonesty. And yet that she is witnessing it all with respect, with the commitment of her gaze.

Henny, it turns out, is the play Ronan is watching. He will do anything she asks.

During the second intermission, while waiting in line for the bathroom, he sees a woman he would swear looks like his aunt Fiona. He's never actually met his mother's oldest sister but he recognizes her from the photo albums. Since he was little he's been fascinated by the mystery of his beautiful aunt, with her fiery red hair, pale skin, and green eyes. According to his mother, in the face of her family's conservative Catholic upbringing, Fiona alone of the four Larkin sisters was the free spirit, the radical. Some years after a failed attempt at college, sick of helping care for her disabled sister, she left home in the middle of the night. Later there would be a prolonged stay at a lesbian fertility cult that was squatting in an abandoned farmhouse up in Massachusetts. But before that, in the mid-'60s, she lived for a time in the West Village and performed at Caffe Cino. Ronan has read about Caffe Cino, which is considered the birthplace of the off-off-Broadway theater movement and had a glorious ten-year run that started in the late '50s. The venue helped launch the careers of María Irene Fornés, Sam Shepard, and one of

Ronan's playwriting heroes, John Guare. When Ronan discovered his love for playwriting he would imagine himself hanging out in such places. On his way to work he's even walked past the legendary storefront on Cornelia Street that was once home to Caffe Cino. Now it houses a mediocre Italian bistro.

When Aunt Fiona's doppelgänger walks past him Ronan pivots and watches her return to her seat in the fifth row. She's wearing a long cream-colored linen skirt and a blue-and-white tie-dye T-shirt. Her red hair is gathered in a ponytail. His mother hasn't heard from Fiona in years. Ronan's always suspected that they had a falling-out. Aunt Fiona and Uncle Alec are the two of her siblings he's never met. Could that possibly be her?

There is no intermission between acts three and four, but instead a long blackout which is scored by a traditional folk song, sung a cappella and in Russian by a huge choir.

In the darkness Henny leans over to Ronan and whispers, "We're getting a drink after this."

"Definitely," he whispers back, doing his best to hide the thrill surging through his eyes. He forces himself to blink. "But not vodka," he adds.

Act four takes place in the unkempt field behind the house. There is a convincing scenic design featuring long yellowing grass, wilting wildflowers, and the petrified-looking trunk of a large tree. Leaves fall intermittently throughout. Sometimes the actors bat them away from their faces.

At one point there is a duel between the two men who are vying for the affections of one of the sisters. The stage pistols unleash a deafening crack, which pulls Ronan out of his stupor. At the play's end the three sisters hug a lot and cry and commiserate about working and growing old, and complain about how they'll never be able to return to their beloved Moscow. For the most part their collective sorrow feels false. Irina seems to be the only one shedding actual tears, which Masha and Olga use to lubricate their own faces, thus giving off the illusion that they're all authentically crying. Ronan finds himself rejecting the intended emotional denouement.

At the curtain call most of the audience leaps to their feet, executing, in Ronan's opinion, an insincere standing ovation. Aunt Fiona's look-alike is standing tall, practically on her tiptoes, and clapping with great fervor, the back of her tie-dye shirt oscillating intensely. But Ronan refuses to stand. He's sitting in the back row, after all, so he can get away with it. Henny remains seated as well, seemingly in her own world, a bit inscrutable, either totally baffled or still processing the final moments.

At the edge of the stage, the actors are exhausted, grateful, benevolent, humble, almost apologetic, not for the amount of time lost on this Monday night (going on four hours!), but for the gutting ride they just took the audience on, the aching grind of so much heart and soul and anguish they assume their fortunate witnesses have experienced. We know this was a difficult story, they seem to be saying. Thank you for taking it in with such courage, with such open hearts. Thank you for ingesting the virus of dashed dreams and unrequited love! Now we are all inoculated!

The cast applauds the audience. The fact that they are rewarding their own standing ovation makes Ronan a little sick to his stomach.

Afterwards Henny once more suggests a drink. "Just one," she says. "We need it."

It's almost midnight and Ronan has to work tomorrow, but he'd be crazy to turn Henny down. They head to an Irish pub a few blocks away, a regular Atlantic Theater Company post-show hangout. The smoke-filled bar features a lot of synthetic wood paneling and dying neon beer signs, but the jukebox is decent, and it isn't too crowded. From the bartender Ronan orders two house merlots, which he can barely afford, and he and Henny find an empty booth near the bathrooms.

"So, Chekhov," she says.

"Wasn't he a doctor, too?" Ronan says. "Busy guy."

On the jukebox, Van Morrison's "Moondance" plays.

At the bar a bunch of regulars are talking about the Yankees. An old guy in a bucket hat complains loudly about the new rookie centerfielder, Bernie Williams, who has been a huge disappointment thus far. "He'll never be Mickey Mantle!" he cries.

The jukebox changes to the Clash's "Train in Vain."

Henny drinks from her wine and sets it down.

Ronan loves her slim fingers, the knobs of her wrists, her face. He feels alive in her company, electric. He worries about his breath, about the fact that he hasn't showered since early that morning. In Henny's presence he can practically feel the pores of his pale skin dilating.

Then Ronan spots the woman who looks like his aunt Fiona, sitting a few booths away. "I know her," he tells Henny, nodding toward the woman. "Three booths down. The redhead."

Henny looks.

"I saw her at the theater when I was in line for the bathroom."

"Who is she?" Henny asks.

"I think she's my aunt."

"Jesus," Henny says. "Go say hi."

"I've never met her."

"Really?" she says, with a quizzical raise of her eyebrow. "All the more reason!"

Ronan rises with his wineglass and approaches the woman's booth. She is sitting with the actors who played Andrey and Irina. Like Ronan, she is drinking red wine, with a bottle of merlot set beside her on the table. In their regular clothes the two Atlantic actors seem smaller, less substantial, stripped of what little magic they possessed onstage.

"Excuse me," Ronan says to the woman, "I think I know you."

"Is that so?" she says with a bit mischief in her voice.

Up close Ronan recognizes the unmistakable green eyes, the dusting of freckles across the bridge of her nose. He knows her age to be around fifty, yet it appears that she hasn't a single strand of gray hair. "Is your name Fiona?" he asks.

"Uh-oh," the woman who played Irina says.

"And you are?" the redhead asks him.

"I think I might be your nephew," he says. "Ronan Happ."

The redhead sets her wineglass down, wipes her mouth with the back of her hand. "Ronan?" she says. "Myra Lee's son?"

"I have ID," he jokes.

She turns to her friends. "This is my older sister's kid. Holy fucking shit!" She stands and hugs him. Her hair smells like perfume and cigarettes. "Were you at the play?"

He tells her that he was. "Congratulations, by the way," he says to the two actors.

"Sit," the guy who played Andrey says. "Join us."

Ronan says that he'd love to but that he's with a friend, and points to Henny.

"There's plenty of room," the Irina actress says.

Ronan waves Henny over and she approaches with her almost empty wineglass and squeezes in beside him. He is now sitting between Fiona and Henny, with the two actors across from them. After introductions, the actor who played Andrey, whose real name is Niles, heads to the bar and orders a pitcher of beer for the table.

Fiona proffers the bottle of merlot to Henny. "May I?" she asks.

"Please," Henny says, and Fiona fills her glass.

"You were great in the play," Ronan tells the blonde, whose real name is Margot. It's a lie. He was mostly bored by her performance and found her to be brittle and whiny. In truth the actress who played Olga was his favorite sister. At the end, Margot was the one who seemed to be crying real tears, however, so he adds, "Your emotions during those final moments..."

"Well, at that point Irina is just absolutely devastated," Margot says. "You guys were a great audience, by the way. We heard through the grapevine that the *Times* was there tonight."

"It's still way too long," says Niles, who's returned with the pitcher of beer and five red plastic cups.

"It didn't feel long at all," Fiona says. "I could've easily watched you guys for another hour."

"There's always fat," Niles says, pouring beer for Margot and Ronan. "Think it and say it. That's the secret to doing Chekhov."

Fiona asks Ronan how long he's been living in the city.

"Since early May," he says, and tells her how he took a Greyhound bus east two days after graduation. How he walked all the way to the East Village from Port Authority because he was afraid to hail a cab. Luckily one of his literature professors at Loras had a connection to the Ukrainian woman he rents a small room from on East Tenth Street.

Fiona asks Ronan how her sister is.

He isn't sure what his mother's current attitude is toward Fiona, or hers toward his mother, and therefore doesn't know how much he should divulge. "She's good," he says, and leaves it at that.

Fiona tells the others how Ronan's mother, Myra Lee, is a pediatrics nurse in the Midwest, how she's the oldest Larkin child and was also always the most dependable, the most sober, the most level-headed in the face of any calamity, large or small. Toward the end something in her delivery turns airless, perhaps even a tad bitter. Is she jealous of his mother? Regretful? She peers into her empty wineglass and the table goes quiet.

Niles grabs the bottle of merlot. "May I?" he says to her.

Fiona nods and smiles and he refills her wineglass. "Are you in the theater?" she asks Henny.

"I'm trying to write plays," she says. "Actually we both are," she adds, nodding toward Ronan.

"Myra Lee's son is a writer," Fiona says. "How about that?"

Ronan asks his aunt if she lives in New York and she tells him about her apartment on Morton Street, a place she's had for over fifteen years.

"It's a one-bedroom with an alcove. The windows rattle when the garbage trucks go by and there's a bathtub in the middle of the kitchen but it has its charms."

"Are you still acting?" Ronan asks.

"I did a Tide commercial a few weeks ago."

"Hey," Margot says, "whatever pays the bills."

Something tugs at the corners of his aunt's mouth, like invisible mouse claws. Again, a bitterness creeping in, a momentary contraction within herself. Did she audition for the Chekhov play? Ronan wonders. Was she rejected? He imagines her on the outside looking in on her friends and their burgeoning stage careers. Fiona leans into a shadow of the booth, and Ronan is struck by the notion that she is fading right before his eyes, her pallor almost grotesque. He looks to Henny, so glad she's there beside him.

"If you ever need anyone to read your stuff, I'm around," Fiona says to Ronan, straightening up.

"Sure," he says.

"You, too," she says to Henny.

"Definitely," Henny says.

"I'm gonna go get another glass of this," she says, holding up her wineglass.

Henny and Ronan scoot out of the booth so she can squeeze by.

LATER, ON THE STREET, after filching a cigarette from Niles and saying goodbye to him and Margot, Fiona asks Ronan if she can borrow cab fare. "I left my bank card at home," she says. "I'd walk but I'm a little drunk."

Ronan winds up giving her ten dollars, which was going to be his lunch money for the next couple of days.

"I miss your mother," Fiona tells Ronan. "It's been way too long."

"I'm almost positive she'd be thrilled to hear from you," he says.

Fiona hugs him and kisses him on the cheek. Her breath is raw, soured by nicotine and alcohol. "It's really nice to finally meet you," she says. "I'm so glad I have a nephew." She says goodbye to Henny, who has been keeping a respectful distance. The women take a half-step toward each other and squeeze hands. "Two playwrights," Fiona says. "Good luck with that."

Henny laughs and tells her how nice it was to hang out.

Ronan then asks Fiona for her phone number. She digs into her large, colorfully embroidered tote, fishes out a pen, and writes down her answering service on the inside of a matchbook from the bar. Ronan pockets the matchbook.

Even though she lives south of the bar, she abruptly hails herself a cab heading north on Eight Avenue, as if desperate to get away. Ronan holds the door open for her as she slides into the backseat. As he closes it behind her he can hear her tell the driver her address on Morton Street. The expression on her face as the cab pulls away is that of a beautiful woman who has just been utterly ignored at a party.

HENNY PAYS FOR A cab to Ronan's place in the East Village. They stop at his corner deli, where Ronan buys a forty of malt liquor with his last five dollars. Now he'll have to finagle leftovers from the big editorial meeting scheduled tomorrow in the fourth-floor conference room.

When they arrive at his apartment, after trudging up four flights of stairs, Ronan is relieved to find that Mrs. Dobroshtan has gone to sleep. She usually turns in before 9:00 p.m. but sometimes she'll wait up to make sure he's made it home okay.

His room is just to the left of the entrance. Mrs. Dobroshtan's quarters are at the other end of the apartment. Their bedrooms are separated by an eat-in kitchen with its tidy breakfast nook, an old-fashioned parlor whose antique rosewood furniture makes it feel more like a room to be admired than sat in, and a long, tilting hallway where the bathroom is located. The "lavatory," as Mrs. Dobroshtan calls it, features a claw-foot bathtub but no shower, so Ronan has to sit in the tub like an oversized child and spray himself with a hose-and-nozzle contraption that he bought from the hardware store on First Avenue and Seventh Street.

Ronan's 10' x 10' Skinner box has a closet so small and narrow it looks more like a structure that was built to hide a water pipe. The dowel in it is at most sixteen inches long—not that Ronan needs much hanging space for the few belongings he brought with him from the Midwest. He has a navy blazer, the four button-down shirts, and, in addition to the three Dockers, a pair of nice wool trousers that will be good for the fall. His lone window, which has been painted shut, looks across Tenth Street and into another tenement window where he'll occasionally see an old man staring down at the street. The man is often shirtless and has a chest like two drooping spaniel ears. Ronan sleeps on a futon mattress whose frame he's jerry-rigged with a pair of wooden shipping pallets that Samir, the Yemeni owner of the corner deli, was kind enough to let him have. The futon is a remnant from Mrs. Dobroshtan's previous tenant, an NYU student who never paid his final month's rent.

His makeshift desk, a square of 30" x 30" street-found plywood set on four columns of cinderblocks, is up against one wall. On top of the desk is a spiral notebook and his most valuable possession: an Apple Macintosh Classic personal computer. Beside the computer rests a small stack of floppy disks. The top one contains the file for his new monologue play, which he is calling *Pieces of the Night*. There is also a takeout coffee cup filled with pens, loose change, and a few subway tokens.

On the floor next to the desk, climbing up the wall, are all the books he's either bought, found, or taken from the sales department's free-and-review kiosk. Opposite the desk and pushed up against the wall is a beautiful walnut highboy dresser, one of Mrs. Dobroshtan's antiques, which, along with the futon, came with the room. Currently only three of the eight drawers are filled. On top of the dresser is a cheap, oscillating fan that Ronan bought for three dollars from a homeless veteran selling his wares off a sheet on Second Avenue.

The only thing on the walls is a framed track-and-field photo from the NCAA Division III National Championships at Baldwin Wallace University in Berea, Ohio. The photo features the six Loras College athletes—four men and two women—who qualified for Nationals. Ronan finished second in the hundred meters and third in the two hundred meters. His four-by-one-hundred-meter relay team took first—Ronan ran anchor and caught the guy from the University of Wisconsin–La Crosse in the final twenty meters—and in the photo there are gold medals hanging around his neck and those of his three relay mates: Eric Fullilove, Demetrious Gord, and Ed "Scooter" Silas. The four of them, along with the other two athletes, stand together on the infield near the long-jumping pit, joyously smiling, arms slung around one another, their gold medals reflecting squibs of late-afternoon Ohio sunshine. This meet was only three months ago, but it already feels as if years have passed.

Ronan levels the picture and sits at his desk chair, a wobbly wooden relic he found in front of the Pyramid Bar, on Avenue A. His aunt's matchbook pokes his thigh in his pocket and he sets it on the desk. When he finally pries off his wingtips, he has to resist audibly sighing. His toes are in knots. Blood rushes to his aching arches. He offers Henny the futon, which is neatly made.

"Spartan," she says, dropping her bag and sitting cross-legged.

"I don't have much of a choice," he says. "I arrived with a suitcase, a backpack, and this computer."

"Which you hauled all the way here from Port Authority," she says. "A true modern pilgrim."

Ronan opens the forty by slamming the edge of the metal cap down on the corner of one of the cinderblocks supporting his desktop—a stupid college trick—but before he can offer the bottle to Henny she rises off the futon, stands before him, and starts unbuttoning her shirt.

"So we're doing this, right?" she says.

Ronan nods, dumbly, takes a drink from the forty, and watches her undress. Her clothes fall from her like a stage trick.

He didn't have any serious girlfriends in college. He dated here and there and slept with one girl, Pam Bindner, who was his first sexual partner. Pam, from a nearby farm town called Lost Nation, turned out to be very Catholic, not on the pill, and extremely interested in not only marriage but also, and more important, having at least three children. One night in her dorm room, after a few beers, she confessed that this was the sole reason she had enrolled at Loras: to begin the dream of her Catholic, natural-family-planning journey through life. The admission freaked Ronan out and he stopped seeing her shortly thereafter.

But while he's not completely inexperienced, he's certainly never had a woman—much less a woman like Henny, whose beauty is even more profound than he could have anticipated—stand before him and disrobe so unselfconsciously.

"You like?" she says.

He nods again and she turns away from him and bends at the waist, letting her hands slowly slide down her thighs, her knees, the backs of her calves. It's a kind of performance. Her head is upside down now, her left cheek grazing her right knee. Her incredible head of hair—that magnificent orb—seems to pulse below her. Her eyes peer back at him, almost daringly.

"What are you waiting for?" she says.

Ronan finally stands, sheds the clothes he's been wearing since 8:00 a.m., and moves to her. "We have to be quiet," he tells her. "My roommate."

Henny brings her finger coquettishly to her lips and nods.

AN HOUR LATER THEY lie on his futon. From atop the highboy the oscillating fan blows over their damp bodies.

"Sorry about the heat," he says. "Someday I'll be able to afford AC."

"After your first Broadway hit?"

"After my first bank robbery," he jokes.

They have sex again, and this time it's less like a dream, far more earthbound—if anything, a little clumsy. While kissing they knock their teeth together. They laugh so loud that Ronan forces one hand over his mouth and the other over hers. He winds up snorting and has to blow his nose into his discarded T-shirt.

"*Quiet!*" she whispers through his hand.

He loves the fragrant, peppery smell of her head and neck. Her ears are a paradise. Her skin, a drug. Everything about her makes him feel drunk and slow.

When they are finished he reaches into his small closet, grabs his old Loras College sweatshirt, wraps it around his waist, palms Fiona's matchbook, and excuses himself down the hallway to the bathroom, where, after a long piss, he rinses his mouth in the sink. He can smell Henny's sex on his hand. It makes him deliciously weak.

In the front parlor, he sits on one of Mrs. Dobroshtan's pair of identical antique loveseats, grabs the touchtone phone, inspects the number on the matchbook, and calls his aunt's answering service. Part of him simply wants confirmation that it's really her number. Another part of him wants her to answer, though he's not entirely sure why. After four rings an automated voice comes on the line and says that the number has been disconnected.

When he returns to his room Henny is sitting at his desk, still naked, studying the track-and-field photo, which she's removed from the wall. Ronan is once again stunned by her beauty. She is so free, so relaxed in her nudity.

"That was at Nationals," he says, standing near her, taking in her lean, slender shoulders.

"You're one of two Caucasians," she says. "Your pallor is sort of amazing. Especially next to those other guys."

"My nickname was Milk," he says.

"Is milk supposed to be fast?"

"No, but it's really, really white."

"What was your event?"

"I ran the hundred, the two hundred, and the four-by-one-hundred-meter relay."

"So you're fast," Henny says.

"At Nationals I finished second in the hundred and third in the two hundred. Those three guys to my left and I were National champs in the relay. I ran the anchor."

"So you're like *fast* fast," she says.

"My dad was Chicago city champion in both the long jump and triple jump."

"It's in the genes," she says.

"I inherited his speed and his bowlegs."

"I like those bowlegs," Henny says. "Where's your dad now?"

"I don't know," Ronan says. "He left when I was pretty young."

"Where'd he go?"

"No one knows," Ronan says. "He's never really resurfaced."

"So you were raised by your mother."

"Yeah."

"The nurse."

"The nurse," he echoes.

"Brothers and sisters?"

"I'm an only child," he says. "Like you."

"How did you know that?"

"Alexis told me."

"She just offered that up?"

"A few weeks ago after the writers' group we had drinks."

"You know she has a crush on you, right?"

"Well, I basically spent the whole night asking her about you."

"Seriously?"

"The first time I saw you, Henny, I said to myself, 'I have to know everything about this person. Date of birth, height, weight, hometown, shoe size. Is she right-handed? Left-handed?'"

"You're serious."

"I grew up collecting baseball cards," he explains. "I'd obsessively memorize them, all the stats, every detail, but I was especially into the personal information, which usually included some little trivia tidbit."

"Like what?"

"Like: *While at Napa High School, Bill Buckner was twice named an All-State wide receiver.* It would help me fall asleep at night. I'm a really good guesser of people's personal stats."

"So how tall am I?" she asks.

"I would say five-eight."

"Not bad. Five-seven-and-a-half."

"Your posture is sort of elite," he says. "That gives you the extra half-inch."

"And my weight?"

"One-twelve, one-thirteen?"

"One sixteen," she says, shifting a bit in his chair, "but that's at the end of the day, before I go to bed. And I think my scale is a few pounds heavy."

"So then I'm right," he says.

"And my shoe size?"

"Eight in women's."

"Oooh," she says, "you're legit."

"I could have a booth at the carnival."

"What else would you put on the back of my baseball card?"

He asks her middle name.

"Elizabeth," she says.

"Henrietta Elizabeth Woods hails from northwest Connecticut—"

"Cornwall," she says.

"*Cornwall*, Connecticut," he says. "She is left-handed. High school?"

"Groton. A prep school in Massachusetts."

"For high school she attended Groton Academy—"

"It's the Groton *School*."

"For grades nine through twelve she attended the Groton *School* and then Yale University for like nineteen years after that, where she graduated with honors."

"No 'the.' Just Groton School. And grades eight through twelve. And it's *was* graduated."

"*Was* graduated with honors," he parrots.

"And I was at Yale for undergrad and grad," she says, "which was six years, not nineteen. More please."

"When the striking Ivy Leaguer watches a play she leans forward with her chin cradled in her hands and her elbows driven into the tops of her thighs like she's taking in a slow, distant car crash."

"I like that," she says, smiling, tugging a little at the sweatshirt still wrapped around his waist. "What else?"

"She prefers wearing men's shirts that are too large. So she can hide her beautiful body in them."

"Keep going."

"She has a constellation of moles spanning the small of her back that looks almost artistically arranged. Her eyes change color depending on what she wears. If she wears a blue shirt they look gray. If she wears a green shirt they take on a yellow, almost wolfish quality. At the writers' group that she attends on a weekly basis she sort of clucks when she doesn't like someone else's work. It's like a hollow wooden sound. Like maybe a child's toy falling off the countertop. She also makes this clucking noise when she's embarrassed."

"I'd like corroborated testimony of this clucking."

"One of her teeth on the top left row is slightly discolored but you can only see it when she uncorks a big smile, which is rare. The veins in the tops of her hands make the onlooker think that she studied piano as a child."

"It was the clarinet. But my veiny hands are probably from mixing my dad's paints. He's a painter."

"I'm well aware," Ronan says. "Thanks to Alexis."

"I mixed enough damn paint to last a lifetime. And I danced, by the way. My mom was with the Paul Taylor Company for almost twenty years."

"My detective work had already uncovered that fact as well."

"I'm just telling you, I danced. Running fast is in your blood, dance is in mine. I did ballet from age three to fourteen." She flexes her left foot, showing off a pronounced arch.

Ronan kneels before her and takes her foot in his hands. It's strong, coiled, heavier than it looks. "Were you good?"

"To prima *Swan Lake* you have to be able to do sixty fouettés on each leg, and by the time I was twelve I could do thirty-two. So I was definitely on my way to playing Odette. But they don't let you dance six hours a day at Groton."

"Do you miss it?"

"The ritual but not the pain. Until a few years ago I had troll feet. Calluses, missing toenails—and the ones that managed to stay on looked like rotting oyster shells. My blisters had blisters." She wiggles her toes and flexes her feet a few more times.

"They look pretty good now," Ronan says.

She gets out of the chair and steps toward the futon, where she turns to him. She leans back against the corner, holding the pillow to her breasts now. "So your mother the nurse," she says.

Ronan sits in the chair, adjusts the sweatshirt around his waist, retying the arms, and tells her how she moved steadily up the Pediatrics ladder at St. Joseph hospital in Joliet, Illinois, until she was offered a job at the local juvenile prison. "Last month she was promoted to Stateville," he says. "The big-boy house. So now she's handing out meds to *adult* rapists and killers."

"Do you worry about her?"

"There's always a guard present, but she's only five-four and like a hundred and ten pounds soaking wet. So yeah, I worry."

"Is that what you would write on the back of her baseball card?"

"I would write, 'Myra Lee Larkin Happ. Date of birth: June fifteenth, nineteen thirty-eight. Hometown: Elmira, New York. Height: five feet four. Weight: a hundred and ten pounds—'"

"Soaking wet."

"Soaking wet is such a cliché," Ronan teases.

"A hundred and ten pounds walking out of a swamp," she offers as an alternative. "Who'd you get your height from?" Henny asks.

"My grandma Ava is six-three."

"Jesus. And Myra Lee Larkin's foot?"

"Size seven."

"Eyes?"

"Hazel verging on gray."

"What else?"

"An alum of the University of Chicago's prestigious nursing program, Myra Lee Larkin is a shy beauty with dark brown hair who's never really known how pretty she is. The oldest of six children—"

"One of whom I met tonight."

"Yes, one of whom Henrietta Elizabeth Woods from Cornwall, Connecticut, met tonight."

"Aunt Fiona."

"Fiona Larkin, the freewheeling, second-oldest Larkin sister who purportedly joined a lesbian fertility cult in Massachusetts sometime in her twenties."

"No shit?"

"I'm not clear on the details but that's the family folklore, I shit you not. I think she's always been pretty troubled. It seems like she still is."

"Because she's an out-of-work actress?"

"Because she shamelessly borrowed ten bucks from me after I told her I worked a poverty-level job in book publishing."

"I'm not sure that's adequate evidence. But back to your mother's baseball card."

"Myra Lee's youngest brother, Archie, died of rheumatic fever when he was an infant. Alec, the third-oldest, disappeared sometime in the mid-sixties and was never seen again. In addition to Fiona, she has two other sisters: Joan, who is mentally handicapped and still lives with my very tall grandmother, and Lexy, who went to Vassar, married the head of a successful hedge fund, has twin daughters, and lives in Rowayton, Connecticut, in what one might describe as a sprawling estate mansion. Myra Lee's husband, Denny Happ, left her and her young son, Ronan, on the day of an unlikely blizzard on April second, nineteen seventy-five. She has few friends and relishes her solitude. At fifty-three she has less than ten gray hairs and swears that she's never dyed it and never will. And she makes an excellent meatloaf, which is a slight variation of her mother's legendary recipe."

"That's a helluva baseball card."

"The print would have to be really small."

Henny grabs the forty, which they've all but ignored, drinks, grimaces because of its obvious warmth, swallows, and asks his middle name.

"Archibald," he says.

"So Mom named you after her dead baby brother."

"Should I be worried about rheumatic fever?"

"Ronan Archibald Happ," she says.

He loves the way she says his name, how it makes her smile in a sly, secretive way, as if she's written it on a piece of paper and slipped it into a beloved book.

She takes another sip from the forty, passes it back. "What about Denny?" she asks.

Something goes loose in his chest.

"Oof," she says. "That bad, huh?"

"What?"

"Your face just did something."

"He's sort of a mystery," Ronan says.

"Is he still alive?"

"Apparently, yes," he says. "I don't think my mom's ever gotten over him."

"She never remarried?"

"She's barely dated anyone else."

The fan oscillates a few times, blows the warm air around.

"And what about you?" Henny asks.

"I date," he says. "No one at the moment, but I'm almost positive that there's some keen interest from a slightly older woman in my playwriting group."

"I was asking about your father," she says. "Have *you* gotten over him?"

"There's really nothing to get over," he hears himself say.

"How do you mean?"

"I don't even remember him."

"Nothing at all?" she says.

"There are fragments. Like he wore this hat in the winter, one of those Irish tweed bucket hats, something Michael Caine would wear in a seventies film. It was forest green with little bits of red and gray."

He drinks from the warm forty, passes it to her. She drinks and passes it back.

"All I know about him besides his high school track glory is that he went to West Point for a little over a year and was discharged for being deemed mentally unfit for duty." He drinks from the forty again, swallows, and sets it on the floor. "He's schizophrenic," he adds, and as he says it, he realizes it's the first time he's told anyone this about his father. It feels as if he's cleared a bunch of debris out of a coat pocket. "Like the kind of schizophrenic who has serious breaks with reality," he continues. "I think he might have been hospitalized for a time. But that's all I know."

"What does your mom say?"

"She never talks about him. I assume it's just too painful for her. Like I said, I don't think she's ever gotten over the guy."

"For some reason I thought you grew up in this big Midwestern Catholic family," Henny says. "In a house with an endless staircase. Old upright piano in the living room. Family photos all over the walls. Station wagon. The front yard overrun with leaves in the fall. A fort in the woods behind the house."

"That was my mom's family," he says. "Except in upstate New York. I grew up in a two-bedroom apartment in a sketchy part of Joliet, Illinois."

"'Sketchy' meaning...?"

"Gangs. Drugs. Lots of single moms on welfare. Eight-year-olds smoking menthol cigarettes. The shells of pillaged cars half-sunk in the manmade pond."

"I guess we all make assumptions," she says.

She tells him about Cornwall, Connecticut: its vast rolling hills; the dairy farms; the endless fields of wildflowers; its famous covered bridge. As a child she'd danced the Maypole at the spring festival. "It was basically like growing up in a Norman Rockwell painting," she says.

"Thank God you're freakishly talented, or I'd hate your guts."

"Fucking classist," she says, then lets the pillow fall, crawls over to him in the chair, and kisses him again. Her mouth is warm and full, sweet from the malt liquor. "That thing's louder than a speedboat," she says, pointing to the fan.

"I don't picture many speedboats up in northwest Connecticut."

"Oh, yeah?" she says playfully. "What do you see there?"

"A smattering of roadside vegetable stands. Teenagers walking into beautifully lit woods, smoking the joints that they found in their parents' twelve-thousand-dollar mohair ponchos that they will take with them to Amherst or Williams or Wesleyan—"

"Or Yale," she says.

"Or Yale," he says.

"So what happens to all those ponchos?"

"They get left at various dive bars in all the economically depressed college towns scattered along the Northeast seaboard, to be discovered and taken home by the lucky townies who happened to be throwing darts until last call that night."

"Not bad," she says with a laugh. "You probably won't be surprised my parents have a place on Cape Cod. One of our neighbors, the Leddingtons, own a bowrider. It's white with a red racing stripe. They call it *Cookie*. They actually painted that on the hull."

Ronan imagines Henny sunning herself on the beach in Cape Cod. He is beside her, pale as a sail. "*Cookie* the speedboat," he says. "Sounds like a children's book."

He lowers himself off his wobbly street chair, kneels, and embraces her. He can't help himself. Entwined, they move back to the futon, scooting on their knees.

After they land on the mattress he mentions that Alexis also told him about her amazing apartment; how she lives off the interest of her father's trust.

"Are you paying her a fucking retainer fee?" Henny says.

"I could see you two were friends. I just wanted to know more about you."

"Alexis makes it sound like my life is a series of annoying tableaux: Henrietta Woods, in her Chanel bathrobe, lounges on her immaculate Victorian furniture; Henrietta Woods insouciantly flips through one of her many high-end coffee-table books; Henrietta Woods takes her morning tea at her Bill Willis occasional table."

"Or on her rear terrace overlooking a lush neighborhood garden."

"What the fucking fuck, Alexis?"

"Your place sounds really cool," he says. "You should invite me over."

"That's a big step for me," she says.

"You feel weird about your wealth."

"Playwrights are supposed to be broke, right?"

They are sitting shoulder to shoulder on the futon now, with their backs against the wall.

"I work, too, you know," Henny says. "I sit for an art school. A few times a week."

"You pose?"

"It's called sitting," she says. "I'm not doing *Playboy* pictorials."

"Are you naked?"

"For the most part, yes," she says. "Sometimes there's a scarf or a piece of muslin to break things up. But it's the human figure they're studying."

"Life Drawing," he says.

"I'm good at it because of my dance background. I can hold positions for a long time."

"Does it pay well?"

"No," she says, "but I don't do it for the money. I like the feeling of becoming someone else."

"Like another character?"

"Yes," she says. "Under that level of scrutiny, that intensity, I get to transform. Change my spots. I like the control of that."

Somehow this hidden life of hers spooks him. This person who shape-shifts under the gaze of others. Is she an exhibitionist?

Henny takes the forty from the floor, moves back to the futon, and drinks, then holds the bottle between her arches, her feet curling around it like hands. After a silence she says, "What about you? What secret are you prepared to share, Ronan Archibald Happ?"

Still wrapped in his sweatshirt, he rises from the futon and moves to his closet. From the small overhead shelf he removes a bundle swaddled in one of his three towels and unwraps it, then turns back and hands her the book.

She looks at the spine, opens it slowly, and pages through the front matter. "This is a fucking first edition," she says, tracing the text on the copyright page with her fingers. "Where'd you get it?"

He tells her the story—how his boss had him over to his

brownstone for dinner on Saturday; how his wife collects first editions; how following the meal he excused himself to the bathroom and went up to their second-floor library and removed the book from its shelf and spent the rest of the evening with it wedged in the small of his back.

"Are you borrowing it?" she asks.

"I think I'm a thief, Henny."

"Holden Caulfield would be proud," she says, returning the book to him.

"Holden Caulfield wasn't a thief," he says. "He was just really confused."

"But didn't he steal that record he gives to his sister? The one that breaks into pieces?"

"He buys the 'Little Shirley Beans' forty-five from a record store on Broadway," he says. "It's one of the only record stores that's open on Sundays. He says he spends about five bucks but he's probably exaggerating."

"You really know your *Catcher in the Rye*," she says.

"*The Catcher in the Rye*," he says.

Henny is still holding the bottle with her feet, and Ronan is still facing his closet, his back to her.

"So what do you think of my secret?" he says.

He half-expects her to get dressed, grab her bag, and leave. Instead, she tells him that it turns her on a little.

"So you're not about to leave?" he asks

"I'm not going anywhere," she says.

As he clutches the book with both hands, a rush of warmth surges through him, and he feels another swelling in his groin.

"I want to sit for you," she says.

"I'm not artistic in that way," he says, re-swaddling the book. "I wouldn't do you justice."

"Then you could just watch me," she says.

"And you would just sit there?"

"Like I am now," she says.

But he can't see her because he's still facing the closet.

"I won't even look at you," she says. "You can ask me to hold any position. Your wildest dream…"

He places the book back on the closet shelf and finally turns to her.

"I want to feel your gaze on me," she adds.

"And who would you become?" he asks, fully erect.

"I don't know yet."

He steps toward her on the futon, where she takes the length of him in her hand and pulls him closer. This time they assume a classic missionary position, Henny's miraculous head of hair settling into the corner of the room. They are just below the lone, inoperable window, streetlights weakly silvering its smudged glass. With her left hand Henny clutches the narrow sill. Ronan gives most of his weight to his elbows and eases into her. This time it's tender, careful, as if they're both recovering from injury.

"Yes, like that," Henny says quietly. "Slow, like that…"

He tries to go even slower than she's asking, to lower his heartbeats, to extend time. He fixes his gaze on her. She will transform into something magical. A sorceress, a mermaid, a half-deer, a ghost in a forest. Her eyes are greenish, silver, burnished, their pupils wide and deep. He fantasized about this scene so many times but never in a million years did he believe it would come true.

Make this last, he is telling himself. Make it last…

Later, Henny falls asleep with her face turned into him. Her faint beery breath warms the hollows of his chest.

Ronan has the distinct thought that his life is turning into a story: an epic novel that spans nearly a century. The book is a foot thick, heavy as a slab of oak, and filled with the promise of a heroic life but also the tragedy of innumerable, unresolvable sorrows. One part of the novel is ending as another begins. All the words, one by one, will fill him up, make him whole. He is only twenty-two, but he is ready. He is a thief, after all…and an artist…and now, a lover. His body is so pale beside this beautiful woman. His breath is almost blue.

11

JOLIET, ILLINOIS
MAY 9, 1994

MYRA LEE

THE CORRIDOR LEADING TO the condemned man's holding cell smells of inmates and bleach. Even after nearly three years Myra still hasn't gotten used to it. There is something distinctly, oppressively masculine that cuts through the sterility of the hallways at Stateville Correctional. It's the sharp animal funk of many combined smells: scalp sebum, rancid armpits, foot fungus, unclean mouths, and morbidly dirty, unwashed groins. Outside it's a cool, overcast, early-May afternoon and when Myra arrived for work this morning there was a light rain dappling the windshield of her car. Inside the prison, especially in the Death Row sector, there is no sense of the weather or seasons or even hours passing. In the nurses' quarters, unless she's looking directly at the cafeteria-style clock on the wall, Myra can't ever tell you what time it is. She had to stop wearing her watch because it only made her shifts seem to drag on. Somehow the mystery of time at Stateville is preferable to knowing how many more hours remain.

This will be only the second execution of an Illinois convict since 1962, when the state did away with the electric chair. Charles Walker, who shot and killed a couple while they were fishing in a southern Illinois creek, was the first, having been executed at Stateville four years earlier. It's very likely that Myra is being taken to the same holding cell where Mr. Walker spent part of the last day of his life.

Myra has seen the little chamber where the executions take place. It features a simple flat examination table outfitted with many straps to hold the condemned man still. The brick walls have been painted cornflower blue, and a large window provides the small observation theater a direct view of the grim proceedings. Inside the chamber the window is mirrored, such that the condemned man is granted a final view of himself. Myra has often wondered if this was done on purpose, as an attempt to force the subject to have some sort of ultimate personal reckoning.

Myra saw the execution chamber for the first time during orientation. She was immediately struck by the color of those walls, the same color she and Denny had painted Ronan's baby room during the last trimester of her pregnancy. She wonders if it was chosen in an effort to be humane. Is it meant to evoke a feeling of childhood? Of a bright, beautiful sky? Of heaven? Or, conversely, is it meant to be a cruel joke? An irony of extreme proportions? After all, the condemned subject, who was transported up from Menard Correctional by helicopter at around 4:30 this morning, is surely going to hell. From what Myra has heard, he raped and murdered thirty-three boys and buried many of them in cement in the crawl space of his home up in Norwood.

When Myra arrived for work, at 6:45, news trucks were already parked just outside the prison walls. A group of religious protesters was disembarking from a large yellow school bus with sandwich board placards containing scripture. Outside, a woman with frizzy hair—their leader—was barking anti–death penalty rhetoric through a bullhorn. Gathering at the opposite end of the parking lot were those on hand to cheer the execution. There was also an unaffiliated third group which comprised newspaper journalists, nuns, and a tearful bunch clutching enlarged color Xeroxes of the killer's victims affixed to giant rectangles of cardboard. There was even a trio of men dressed up like clowns. One of the clowns had set up a coffee station with oversized thermoses and Styrofoam cups arranged on a folding table and was charging twenty-five cents a cup. Another clown was handing out free umbrellas. Police barriers had been set up to keep the throngs well back of the main gate. Myra had never before seen such activity.

Sion, a slow-gaited, long-striding enormous Black guard who recently transferred in from Centralia Correctional, is accompanying her to the condemned man's holding cell.

"He's been here since early this morning," Sion says. "He's in there with Londell right now."

Londell is the biggest, scariest Death Row guard at Stateville. At 6'8" and 275 pounds he's even larger than Sion. Londell was an honorable mention All-American tight end at Illinois State University in the mid-'80s and was drafted by the Detroit Lions but sustained a career-ending shoulder injury during his first preseason camp. Suffice it to say that Londell fears very few mortals and Myra always feels extremely safe whenever he brings an inmate to the nurses' quarters.

"You know they got him a desk in there?" Sion says. "With a doggone telephone? Killed all them boys and he gets a *phone*?"

"Well, it is his last day on earth," Myra says.

"I don't care if it's his last day on *Jupiter*," Sion says. "In my book, you kill that many people, you get zero phones."

Sion knocks on the door and moments later it buzzes. He holds it open for Myra. After they both pass through the threshold the heavy steel door closes and clicks.

Sion was correct—there's a metal, military-looking desk and, yes, there's also a touch-tone phone. The setup gives the condemned man sitting behind the desk the air of a small-town entrepreneur who works out of a shed. On the other side of the desk is a chair for visitors. Is this chair for her? Myra wonders. A priest? His lawyer? Next to the phone is a Dixie cup of water. The condemned man is white, portly, with a pale, clean-shaven face and silver hair, a little on the long side but neatly combed and shiny with some sort of lubricant. His cleft chin is fleshy, prominent. Londell stands behind him like an edifice of brown flesh, his titanic arms folded in front of him. He seems to take up half the room, which is warmed by bodies, fragrant with the same hair tonic—no doubt the condemned man's—that Myra's father wore until his dying day. The familiar odor throws her. At this moment the last thing she wants to feel is anything familiar. The man is portly and mischievous-looking, like some neighborhood ice-cream vendor who teases the babysitter. But Myra knows looks can be deceiving. As she learned during her mandatory self-defense training, when in the presence of an inmate one must be ready for anything, regardless of how physically unimpressive he might be or how many guards are present.

"On your feet, Mr. Gacy," Londell tells the condemned man, who stands slowly, as if hobbled by a strained hamstring. "Nurse Happ is here to take your vitals."

"Hello," he says to Myra, who returns the greeting and says nothing more.

She has been instructed by Head Nurse McGee not to engage in conversation with the subject; her simple assignment is to administer and record the condemned man's vitals and then return to her post.

Myra places her medical bag carefully on the ground. Is she supposed to sit in the chair? Should she remain standing like Sion and Londell?

The condemned man's wrists are shackled in front of him, as are his ankles. He wears the standard, light blue, Stateville-issued collared shirt, matching pants, white sweat socks, and slippers. They obviously gave him a new set of clothes when they processed him earlier this morning. Myra wonders if it's because the warden is proud of having such a high-profile criminal wearing the Stateville uniform or if the condemned man somehow ruined his Menard Correctional clothes on the way up from Chester. It is widely known that an inmate will sometimes soil himself as an obnoxious act of defiance.

From her bag Myra removes an old-fashioned mercury thermometer. "May I?" she says. She would not normally ask this question, but the odd circumstances have stoked her manners.

"As long as it ain't goin' in my pie hole," the man says with a wry grin. His teeth are short and bluish.

"Just open your damn mouth," Sion tells him.

The condemned man complies and Myra inserts the thermometer under his tongue. He closes his mouth and begins humming—either "Yankee Doodle Dandy" or "Good King Wenceslas," she's not sure which.

Next will be his blood pressure. Myra removes the somewhat unwieldy black monitor, undoes the velcro, and drops it in her lap.

"Who sees him next?" Sion asks Londell.

"Either the chaplain or his lawyer, I forget."

Myra removes the thermometer. The silver segment of mercury stops a hair before 99 degrees. Myra notes it on the form attached to her clipboard and returns the thermometer to her nurse's bag. Later she'll drop it in a dish of antiseptic. It is now a thermometer that has been inside the mouth of a serial killer. She could have it frozen in amber.

"You figure out what you wanna eat yet?" Sion asks the condemned man.

Sion will often tease the Death Row inmates, and the question comes as no surprise to Myra.

"At first I was gonna just ask for a box of donuts," the man says. "But then I told the warden's lackey that I wanted a dozen fried shrimp, a bucket of Kentucky Fried Chicken original recipe, an order of french fries, and a pound of strawberries."

Myra's stomach turns painfully at the recitation of this final menu.

"And to drink?" Sion asks.

"Diet Coke," Gacy says.

"You gonna eat all that garbage," Londell says, "and then finish it off with a Diet Coke?"

"Ironical, ain't it?" the condemned man says. "They're gonna let me have a picnic right on the grounds, too. I got family comin' and everything."

The condemned man laughs emphysemically. His breath is foul, fecal. Myra covers her nose. His short blue teeth, like those of a sullen child who's trying to conceal stolen candy in his mouth, look gluey when he laughs.

ADAM RAPP

"Donuts have names that sound like prostitutes," he continues.
"I heard that in a song. Pretty slick lyric. The guy who sings it ain't
on the same level as Speedwagon but you gotta hand it to him, it's
slick as a Butterball turkey." He drinks from the Dixie cup, easily
negotiating his manacled wrists, and adds, "You can tune a piano,
but you can't tuna fish."

"Fool's talkin' nonsense," Londell says.

"Sex, drugs, rock-and-roll, disco sucks and so does soul," the
condemned man says.

"That shit was about fifteen years ago," Sion says.

"Homeboy's out of touch," Londell says.

In Illinois, execution by lethal injection involves the administration of three different drugs through intravenous tubes. The
first, sodium thiopental, is a surgical anesthetic that causes the loss
of consciousness. When the condemned subject is asleep, a combination of potassium chloride and Pavulon are pumped through the
tubes. Pavulon paralyzes the diaphragm. Potassium chloride stops
the heart. If the drugs are properly administered, death comes pain-
lessly in about seven minutes, while the condemned subject is asleep.

Myra fits the velcro sleeve around the condemned man's left
arm, repeatedly squeezes the rubber ball until the sleeve's bladder
inflates, then turns the release valve, allowing the hissing air to
escape. The condemned man's skin is lifeless, rubbery. He disgusts
her but she has only two more vitals to record—his pulse and his
breathing rate—and then she can go back to the nurses' quarters.

After she removes the blood pressure unit from his arm, she
records his results on her clipboard. 125 over 80. Not as high as
she would've guessed considering his physical condition and the
stress he must be enduring. The rate is actually normal for his age,
which, according to his chart, is fifty-two. He was born on March
17, 1942. He will be executed this evening. It's May 9th and he will
be brought to the bright blue death chamber around midnight.
According to the schedule he won't live more than an hour or two
into May 10, 1994, a Tuesday.

Myra is nearly fifty-six. To think of her own life being cut short before she could enter her seventh decade sends a chill down the backs of her legs. She can feel it traveling over her calves, settling in her ankles. Her mother is seventy-five. Despite her knee problems she's as healthy as a horse and will likely live to be a hundred. Myra has always had the strong sense that the Larkins will outlast most people. She sees herself growing old in a little farmhouse somewhere in the northeast. New Hampshire or Maine or the rolling hills of Vermont. A simple house with a woodstove and good insulation and a garden in the back. She'll live out her days reading books and taking long walks in the woods. She thinks of her sisters: Fiona, Lexy, and Joan, all firmly in their middle years, all healthy. And her brother, Alec, wherever he is, whatever he's up to. No one's heard from him in years. A sadness tugs at her insides when she tries to imagine his face as an older man.

"The way I see it is this," the condemned man continues as Myra takes his left wrist. "We all lie side by side in the silence of the night. The good and the bad. The living and the dead. There are wolves and there is a prairie."

Myra finds the man's pulse with the pads of her fingers.

"Which category are you in?" Londell asks him.

"Oh, I'm in the *Good* category," he says. "And the *I'm Still Alive* category. I definitely ain't no prairie."

"But soon you'll be dead," Sion says.

"Maybe," the condemned man says.

"Maybe what?" Londell says. "You think Governor Edgar's gonna come pardon you or some shit?"

"You think President Clinton gonna swoop in on Air Force One?" Sion adds.

"Sometimes the machine don't work," the condemned man answers. "Last time the lines was all kinked up."

Myra knows this to be true. According to Nurse McGee, who's been the head nurse since the early '80s, Charles Walker's lethal injection was botched because the lines were tangled and it wound up being a painful, grueling death. She is suddenly distracted, loses count of the condemned man's pulse, and has to start over.

"Oh, it's gonna work this time," Londell says. "I can promise you that. They got a brand-new machine. Made this one special, just for you."

"Then I might have to disappear before they turn it on," the condemned man says.

"And how you plan on doing that?" Sion asks.

"Magic," he says. "Abracadabra, bibbidi-bobbidi-boo. I'll turn myself into a termite and slip right through the cracks."

"I see you more like a fat-ass roach," Sion says.

"Funny you should say that," the condemned man says. "You wanna know why?"

"Why?" Sion answers, taking the bait.

"Because some roaches live an awful long time. Even longer than them giant tortoises in the Galápagos."

Try as she might to avoid looking directly at the condemned man—this odd Gacy character—Myra can't help herself. He has razor burn about his jowls. He missed a few spots shaving, and four tiny hairs, like white, half-grown insect legs, sprout along the soft, fleshy ridge of his jaw. And there is a faint fuzz in his large left ear, whose canal is rich with brown wax. The Vitalis in his hair is now in concert with his natural odor, which is something like congealed bacon grease left in a frying pan.

"And what if your magic words don't work?" Londell says to him.

"Yeah, what if you don't disappear?" Sion adds. "Then what?"

"Then I die," the condemned man says. "And I want my funeral service to be a ten a.m. white mass at St. Francis Borgia. Up by Schiller Woods. In my opinion, the absolute best Catholic church in Chicago. I'm gonna wear a blue houndstooth double-breasted suit, a white shirt, and a red tie with royal blue stripes. The stripes'll match the stained glass they got goin' on behind the altar." With his manacled hands he drinks from the Dixie cup again. "I want my hands to be folded over my chest, in a steepled fashion. Like I'm prayin' the 'Our Father.' I'd show you but I got these dang cuffs on."

"We can imagine it just fine," Londell says.

"And I'm gonna have 'em wrap a black rosary around my thumbs," he adds. "Just to complete the picture. The smallest details make it authentic, you know?"

Finally there is a long silence. Myra counts his pulse for only thirty seconds. It yields forty-five heartbeats. This man has a pulse of ninety. She would've guessed much higher, easily over a hundred. based on his body type, his fleshiness. She releases his wrist, records his pulse on her clipboard, and removes the stethoscope from her bag.

"Oh, and the congregation's gonna sing my three favorite hymns," he starts in again. "'Amazing Grace,' 'How Great Thou Art,' and 'Holy God, We Praise Thy Name.'"

"You gonna be cremated?" Sion asks.

"Heck no," the condemned man says, "that's not my style. The plan is for me to be buried at Maryhill Cemetery up in Niles, in the plot at the head of my father's grave. The coffin's gonna be silver-gray with a white interior. I'd prefer calfskin, but that can get pricey. I'd settle for bonded hide, but not no pleather. That's for you jigaboos," he says to Sion, "for your imitation sofas and your car interiors and your nigger pimp faggot slacks."

Sion shakes his head slowly. "Listen to this fool," he says.

"You talkin' about faggot slacks," Londell says, "but you had your way with all them boys you killed."

"Oh, that wasn't me," the condemned man says.

"Who was it, then?" Sion asks.

"This other guy. Looked like me, moved like me, even sounded like me, but the fact of the matter is that it was a totally different person."

"That what you tell yourself?" Londell says.

The condemned man smiles—to himself, it seems—and shakes his head as if in some rueful, private knowledge of his innocence, the grand indignity of being a doomed martyr egregiously wronged by the universe.

"My understandin' is that there was this one kid that got away. Dark-haired kid. Tall. Real good-lookin'."

"Oh yeah?" Londell says. "Why'd your friend let that one go?"

"Cause he was too long in the tooth. My sources tell me he's prolly still out there roamin' around, tryin' to figure things out."

Myra inserts the tips of the stethoscope into her ears and sets the drum in the center of the man's chest. She listens to his breathing, the rhythm of his heart. His heartbeat is large, strong, once again not what she expected from his unfit appearance. She imagines him building up his hidden strength by dragging bodies across the floor of his house in suburban Norwood. He probably couldn't lift the Chicago phone book over his head more than a few times, but he can manipulate a young man's body, thick with rigor mortis, into any shape he desires. She has the keen sense that his heart will continue beating long after he's dead, that in the middle of the night it will thump maddeningly in the heads of all the grieving mothers of his victims. Those poor women who have been cursed to outlive their boys.

"Hey, I just hope the dang Cubbies get their act together," the condemned man says, seemingly out of nowhere. "They've only won eight games! Eight goddamn games!" He shakes his head.

Myra can't help but think of Ronan, a true die-hard Cubs fan, and how he used to watch every game on WGN. He'd sit too close to the television and she'd often have to beg him to move his chair back.

"My lawyer's got all the details about the funeral service," the condemned man then says to Sion. "We confabbed about it yesterday. You boys should come. I'd be happy to make sure you get put on the invitation list. And you, too, Myra."

It shocks Myra to hear her name coming out of the condemned man's foul-smelling mouth. How could he possibly know it? He smiles again and her stomach twists into a fist. Her insides have been giving her trouble for months now. Her bowel movements are wildly inconsistent, at times very painful, and her appetite has been half of what it used to be, as if she has reverted to those excruciating years after Denny left.

She is somewhat relieved when she realizes that she failed to remove her ID laminate, which is clipped to the shirt pocket of her nursing uniform. Normally after she clocks in in the morning she leaves it on her desk, just like her watch. Thank God he didn't conjure her name through some dark act of sorcery.

"There's gonna be some good grub at the afterparty," the condemned man says, almost gloating, as if he'll be there in disguise, having risen from the dead.

Myra imagines him skulking around in the background of some cheap restaurant in Norwood. A place with old carpeting and a secondhand buffet. He's wearing dark sunglasses and a long beige raincoat, overloading his plate, belching aloud without covering his mouth, mocking those who've come to pay their respects, whoever they might be.

"Baby back ribs," he adds to Londell, twisting his torso, peering at him over his shoulder. "Chitlins. They might even have some black-eyed peas for you two giant porch monkeys."

WHEN MYRA LEAVES WORK the crowds outside the prison have doubled, maybe even tripled. Several squad cars from the Joliet Police Department are on hand, as is a fleet of state police cruisers. The news trucks have assembled their satellites, and cameramen are lining up shots with reporters. It's still somewhat bright out, twilight really, calm, not quite summery. It's the kind of night that Myra would have watched a Cubs game with Ronan, before he went off to college, the kind of night they might eat together on the sofa with plates in their laps.

She gets in her car and elects to keep the windows rolled up. As she grips the steering wheel a sharp pain, like a piece of metal twisting, stabs deep in her abdomen, as if she swallowed an earring in her sleep—or her engagement ring, which she still keeps in the little porcelain box beside her bed. The pain is so intense that she has to hold her breath until it passes. She counts to fifty. The numbers are like scarecrows erected at the edge of a vast cornfield. She must touch one and run to the next, touch that one, run to the next...

* * *

ON HER WAY HOME, almost in a trance, Myra stops at the Kentucky Fried Chicken on Jefferson Street and orders a three-piece original recipe dinner, which consists of a breast, a wing, and a drumstick. For her two sides she chooses small Styrofoam containers of mashed potatoes and corn.

Back at her apartment she arranges her food on a plate and sits at her small kitchen table with the seven o'clock news playing on the TV in the living room. The anchors are talking about the condemned man she just visited in that strange little holding cell with the desk and the telephone. In a matter of hours—just after midnight—he will be executed by lethal injection. According to the anchors, he enjoyed a picnic dinner with members of his family on one of the lawns of the prison grounds. After that he had a conversation with a Catholic priest, who chose to remain anonymous. The anchors repeat the news that Myra already knows: that the condemned man murdered and raped thirty-three young men from the Chicago area and buried many of them in cement in the crawl space of his Norwood home.

At Stateville the onsite reporter, a woman with a low, soulful voice, likens the proceedings to a sporting event. There are superfans. There are religious groups. Nuns and priests and a party of Chicago-area rabbis. There are families of the victims holding lit candles and displaying large pictures of their murdered sons. There is a small band of men dressed up as circus clowns who are dancing to the condemned man's favorite band, REO Speedwagon, whose hit album *You Can Tune a Piano, but You Can't Tuna Fish* is being broadcast from a boom box. Drums can be heard beating in the background.

"Are these the drums of justice, or the drums of evil?" the onsite reporter asks rhetorically.

Myra recalls the condemned man's sickly breath, his short, dim teeth, his restless, pale, manacled hands, the four white hairs along his shapeless jawline, the cleft in his fleshy chin. She wonders if the unfortunate undertaker who will have to prepare him for his wake will shave those random whiskers or if they will be left alone; if Gacy will be cocooned in his leather-clad fantasy casket in the same hygienic state in which he was executed. Then again, maybe all of that talk of his funeral and his double-breasted suit and the afterparty was just a lot of hot air. Myra has always been under the impression that after his execution a condemned inmate is cremated.

She eats half her chicken breast and a forkful of corn, but quickly loses her appetite. She doesn't even bother opening the side of mashed potatoes. There's another twisting in her stomach. The fried food probably wasn't the best idea. And suddenly she remembers, with a wave of nausea, that Kentucky Fried Chicken was part of what Gacy intended to order for his last meal, right down to the original recipe option. The notion must have somehow gotten into her subconscious. She forces her hand over her mouth to keep herself from vomiting. Quickly she swallows three mouthfuls from her water glass, then a fourth.

After she scrapes her plate into the garbage and places her dirty dishes in the sink, she returns to the living room and changes the TV to WGN Channel 9. The Cubs are playing the Cardinals in St. Louis. It's in the top of the third inning and they're up 3-1. It's a good start for a change but she decides to turn the television off and take a shower.

The hot water—thank God there's hot water!—is the best thing she's felt all day. It makes her weak, sleepy. She releases an audible sigh. She doesn't even bother shampooing her hair. She doesn't have the energy. Lifting her arms over her head would take too much effort. She can't recall the last time she's felt this tired. Afterwards she can barely towel herself off. She has to sit down on the toilet to put on her nightgown. It's only just after 8:00 p.m. but Myra decides she will go to bed early. She'll need all the rest she can get for work in the morning.

Before she turns in she goes out to the kitchen and calls Ronan. "Hey," she says to his answering machine, "I just wanted to hear your voice." She has to swallow again, to keep from getting sick, and sits down at the kitchen table. All this swallowing. All this needing to sit. "The Cubs are playing the Cardinals tonight," she continues, "they're up early, but I'm sure you know that. I think Mark Grace is their only decent player this season…" She's so sleepy she has to resist letting her head rest on the table. "Everyone at work likes the White Sox," she says. "I constantly get teased about being a Cubs fan. They keep saying Joliet is on the South Side of Chicago and that I need to wake up and join the party."

Unbidden, she imagines Ronan being beckoned into the condemned man's house up in Norwood. Gacy sees him walking by on the street and waves him over. He coaxes Ronan down to his basement with his oddball charm, deploying his knowledge of giant tortoises and Cubs trivia and quirky song lyrics. He offers Ronan something to drink, slips a powdered barbiturate into the mixture, invites him to join him on an overstuffed loveseat. She forces the image from her head.

"I miss you, Ronan," she adds. "I love you…"

She hangs up the phone. She could fall asleep right there. But a woman who wakes up at her kitchen table is not right for this world. This is either a drunk or a pathetic woman and Myra is neither of these people. She forces herself to her feet, turns off the kitchen light, and shuffles to her bedroom.

Before she falls asleep she turns to happier thoughts, imagining Ronan walking along the streets of New York City with his beautiful girlfriend, Henny, whom he's been dating for three years. Myra still hasn't met her, but she's planning a weeklong trip to New York in July. She keeps a Polaroid of the couple on her refrigerator. Ronan sent it two months ago. In the Polaroid they are standing in front of Leshko's Diner on Avenue A. It's the winter and they're bundled in many layers. Ronan is operating the camera and his right arm is extended. They look like they're in love. According to Ronan they're still crazy about each other and they've been talking about moving in together. Two playwrights falling in love in the greatest city in the world—how romantic. Myra sees them holding hands on the subway, getting dinner at a pizza parlor in the Village. Then they go see a movie and share a big bucket of popcorn.

Myra falls asleep envisioning Ronan and Henny watching a movie and holding hands with their giant bucket of popcorn wedged between them.

JUST AFTER MIDNIGHT, MYRA wakes to a searing pain in her lower abdomen. The kind of pain that causes the brain to flash white. The kind one feels in one's molars. When she tries to get out of bed it feels as if she's been impaled by hot glass, bitten by a wolf, stabbed in her sleep by a thief with a dagger. The flash of white leaves lightning in her head, a surging through her spine.

She hears her own voice cry out in a strange register that she doesn't recognize. It echoes in some torn canyon of flesh deep within her.

She manages to hurl herself to the floor and writhe her way to the kitchen, where, by some sheer force of will, she yanks on the phone cord hard enough to dislodge the handset. By the time she gives the emergency operator her details, blood is beginning to pool underneath her. She can't fathom its source. It's as if a valve has been released, and the corona of blood expands around her on the linoleum, purplish, slow, thick as syrup, its smell both metallic and fungal, like old silverware left in the mud.

The feeling is of a great emptying, a hollowing out...Her nightgown is sopping with blood, her hair is taking it on...

Her last conscious thought is how fiercely her hands are clinging to the aluminum leg of the kitchen table.

12

TUNICA, MISSISSIPPI
APRIL 19, 1995

ALEC

THE BOY, HAVING STAYED up all night, is sitting on the floor in front of Alec's thirty-inch flatscreen, his hands cradling the Nintendo Super NES control module. It's after 7:00 a.m. and he's been playing *Super Mario World* since around 4:30, which is when they stopped drinking Mai Tais and finished smoking what little bit of weed Alec still had on hand. The boy said the weed would help get him into the zone and Alec was happy to oblige him. He would have continued to make drinks but he'd run out of both the Bacardi and the triple sec, and besides a case of Coors Light the only other alcohol on the premises happened to be a bottle of isopropyl, which he uses for cleaning the endless cuts he gets on his hands and wrists from fishing and rowboating. The bottom line is that this kid must have a hollow leg. Or he has one of those systems that alcohol simply doesn't affect. He obviously has the metabolism of a six-year-old. The agreement Alec made with the boy was that if he could beat his high score then he would give him his very special collectible baseball card. The weed certainly put him an extremely focused mind state.

He met the boy at the local casino, where Alec spends his afternoons. For seven days a week he can be found in the slots or "fruiters" room, invariably outfitted in one of his many short-sleeved Hawaiian shirts, a pair of multi-pocketed water-resistant cargo shorts, and his trusty sport sandals with memory-foam soles. From his spot in front of his favorite third-row slot machine, he'd been clocking the boy for several minutes. The boy had certainly stood out in his red St. Louis Cardinals baseball hat, matching oversized T-shirt, big baggy basketball shorts, ultra-white tennis shoes, equally white socks pulled high, and dark braids creeping down the back of his neck like so many charred and rubber-banded lizard tails. The boy was chewing a coffee straw (also red) and affecting a bit of a limp. There was a lot going on. In Alec's quick assessment, this kid was all pomp and swagger, with nowhere to go and zero money to spend.

Alec's slot machine had already taken $80 of his $200 investment without so much as a single triple bar. It was turning out to be a gusher. But when the boy stopped to watch him — at that precise moment in fact — Alec pressed the play button and hit double centerline cherries and won himself a cool $657.42 ... *Kablooey!*

"You must be good luck," he said to the boy, who might've been sixteen at the most.

Alec printed his winnings slip and headed to the box office. And of course the boy tailed him.

"It looks like you're following me," Alec said as he stepped up to the bulletproof plexiglas.

"How long was you on that slot machine?" the boy asked, chewing his straw.

"Maybe twenty minutes."

"Don't the music drive you crazy?"

Alec listened for a moment, cocking his head to the left a bit, really taking in the tinny din of the slot machines. Today the wheedling fruiters were particularly merciless.

"It's like Santa's elves mad losing they minds," the boy said.

"After an hour or two you don't even hear it," Alec offered.

"You win like that a lot?"

"Every time," Alec answered, a flat-out lie, though it was true he fared better at the fruiters than the table games. There had been a period maybe four months earlier when he'd had a groove going with three-card poker, but he'd gotten tired of having to contend with the various personalities. Sunburnt fat women. Asian drifters in their stupid fucking sunglasses. Old arthritic widowers with their dentures and lopsided flea-market wigs. He eventually came to prefer the companionship of a machine.

"What's your secret?" the boy asked.

"Two hundred dollars," Alec said. "Load her up all at once and keep pressing that play button. If you haven't won anything decent by the time it gets down to a hundred, you cash out, go home, turn on the boob tube, and consider it worth it for the free drinks."

The boy stood by, chewing his coffee straw, while Alec collected his money. When Alec glanced over at him he was adjusting the brim of his Cardinals cap, whose silver sticker was still affixed to the back. He was maybe six feet tall, very little body fat. His calf muscles looked like a pair of sculptures that had been installed above the top of his long white socks. He was dark-skinned but not in that *National Geographic*, African-subcontinent way.

Alec requested all twenties, and Nikki, the female cashier with the blond frizzy hair and rodeo-clown makeup that Alec has come to really appreciate, processed his money down to the exact coinage in less than thirty seconds.

"Not a bad day, huh?" Nikki said.

"Better than yesterday," Alec replied, tipping her the loose $17.42.

She thanked him by blowing him a kiss. "Spend that wisely now, John."

Ten minutes later they were tooling down Highway 61 in Alec's gray '78 Chevy Malibu to the Sonic, where Alec and the boy both ordered SuperSONIC bacon double-cheeseburgers with cheese tots and blue coconut slushes. After the little skinny redhead with the freckles delivered their food in her roller skates they ate in silence for a while.

"What's your name, anyway?" Alec asked the boy.

"Jermaine," he said.

Cars sluiced by on Highway 61. The weather was outstanding.

Jermaine ate quickly, almost inhaling his burger, attacking his cheese tots like they deserved to be bullied.

Alec rolled his window down and unleashed a hellacious burp that tore through his chest's softer tissues. "So do me a favor," he said.

"What's up?" the boy said.

"Explain to me what harebrained process leads a kid from Mississippi to the horrors of becoming a Cardinals fan?"

"I'm not from Mississippi," the boy answered.

It turned out that he hailed from East St. Louis.

"What's the difference between St. Louis and East St. Louis?" Alec asked.

"East St. Louis is on the other side of the river," the boy explained. "The Illinois side."

"Land of Stinkin' Lincoln," Alec said. "You here with your parents?"

"With my moms," the boy replied.

"Isn't she gonna be wondering where you are by now?"

"Nah," he said, sipping his slush. "She's busy playing blackjack. She was up when I skated."

"What if she goes looking for you?"

"She'll prolly just think I met a girl. Like at the swimming pool. Or in their bumb-ass workout room."

"That happens a lot, I'll bet," Alec said. "You meeting a girl."

"Definitely enough," Jermaine said.

"Your mom's okay with that?" Alec asked, offering the boy the rest of his cheese tots.

"She knows I handle my business," Jermaine said, accepting Alec's tots without hesitation. "Long as I use my jimmies."

"Jimmies?"

"Jimhats," the boy said. "Condoms," he added, when Alec's face was still blank.

"*Aaah.*"

"She trusts me."

"Trust is an important thing," Alec said sagely.

"I'm hip," Jermaine said. "Mad important." And then he stared out the window as if working through a difficult thought. He loved gnawing on that straw. "She's not really my moms if you wanna know the truth," he said.

"Who is she?" Alec asked.

"She's more like my auntie."

Alec tossed their trash into the outdoor bin, and they swung back out onto Highway 61. The early-evening air was heavy with humidity. There was an inevitable feeling lacing the coming night. A velvety assurance that soothed the fine hairs on Alec's forearms. His new punch-pink Hawaiian shirt had been a good purchase. One hundred precent rayon. Only forty bucks at the casino gift shop. Super soft to the touch and patterned with marigolds. He liked the way it made him feel.

Alec turned on the radio. Seal's "Kiss from a Rose" was playing. Alec immediately tuned it off.

"Thank you," Jermaine said. "Can't stand that song."

Alec was enjoying his new friend's company. They were definitely becoming buddies. The mosquitoes would be feasting soon, he thought. They always started hunting around sundown.

"Your name's John, right?" Jermaine said.

"Indeed it is," Alec said.

"So where we goin', John?"

"Anywhere you want," Alec answered. "But there's not a lot to see here in Tunica. You need me to take you back to the casino?"

"Nah," the boy assured him. "I like the change of scenery. The environmentals and whatnot."

"I got weed back at my place," Alec said.

"Bet?" the boy replied. "Let's do that."

On their way to his place, Alec asked Jermaine if he was an actual baseball player or if he was just a fan wearing the costume.

"I'm legit, John," he said proudly, at work on a fresh coffee straw. "I *play*, yo." And Jermaine went on to say he was the starting shortstop on his varsity team as a freshman, batting leadoff.

"What school?" Alec asked.

"East St. Louis Lincoln," he said. "The Tigers."

"What are your school colors?"

"Orange and Black."

"Makes sense for tigers. So you're starting as a freshman?"

"Word is bond," Jermaine said.

"Wow," Alec said. "So you're what, fourteen?"

"I'll be fifteen in August."

"Fourteen is a perfect age," Alec said. "So much ahead of you. I thought you were older."

Whether it was true, Alec didn't know, but someone had once told him that American Blacks develop quicker than their white contemporaries because of all the fast-food hormones. It's why they go through puberty sooner. And why they have bigger dicks and get diabetes. Alec, himself a late bloomer, was cruelly denied his first pubic hair until he was fifteen.

"You probably don't even shave yet," Alec said.

The boy definitely had a baby face.

"I know *you* do," Jermaine countered. "At least you need to."

Alec laughed. It was true. He hadn't shaved in days. His salt-and-pepper scruff was starting to look a little wolfish.

"You prolly don't got a wife," Jermaine said. "Or a girlfriend."

"What makes you say that?"

"Cause you can't eat no pussy with all that mess on your face."

"I stopped eating pussy about three thousand years ago," Alec said.

"You musta hit a nasty one."

"Or an entire school," Alec said. "As in fish." He popped a square of Nicorette into his mouth. "You *like* doing that?" Alec said.

"I love the shit, yo," Jermaine replied. "I don't care what they say. Gimme a coupla Bacardi-and-Cokes and a proper spliff and I'll lick a pussy all night."

Alec laughed for a solid minute and let the image linger for the next few miles. They drove past a car that had been abandoned on the shoulder. Someone had already smashed up the windows and taken the wheels.

"Can I let you in on a little secret?" Alec said after turning onto the exit ramp. And this is where he revealed his prized possession: his 1952 Mickey Mantle rookie card.

"For real?" Jermaine said.

"Maybe the best center fielder in baseball history," Alec said. "Hall of Fame. Bona fide Yankee legend. Card is in mint condition."

"*Mickey Mantle?*" Jermaine said. "*Word?*"

"I shit you not," Alec said. And then he asked if the boy liked to play video games.

"Hell yes," the boy had said. "I got a Nintendo back at my auntie's place."

"I have the Nintendo Super NES," Alec said. Which was truer than the blue in a Southern blue sky. And then Alec made his offer: "You any good at *Super Mario World?*" he said.

"Hell yeah I'm good at that shit," Jermaine boasted.

"Beat my high score and I'll give you the Mantle card."

"For real?" the boy said.

"For real," Alec confirmed.

"What's it worth?" the boy asked.

"At least a hundred grand," Alec said. "Maybe more." Which, according to the recent blue book citation, was also true.

"And what if I *don't* beat it?" Jermaine asked.

"Then you don't get the card."

"But what do I gotta do for you?"

"Nothing," Alec said. "The pleasure of your company is plenty good for me."

"How much time do I get?"

"Let's say until the sun comes up."

"Then fuck it," Jermaine said. "I'm down."

AND NOW HERE THEY are, in Alec's living room, just after 7:00 a.m. *Super Mario World* is definitely a game Jermaine has played before; he's better at it than Alec speculated. It only took him about two tries to get within a reasonable range of Alec's high score. He is clearly fluent in the ways of this particular control module. Alec also has *Donkey Kong Country, Earthworm Jim,* and *Magic Carpet,* but in his estimation this kid was likely already good at those.

"How many of those coffee straws do you go through in a day?" Alec asks him.

"Like skeighty-eight," Jermaine says. "Red straw's my thing."

"Well, you've chewed the absolute bejesus out of that one."

Jermaine's eyes are fixed on the screen. He's hardly blinked the entire time Alec's been standing there. "Can I get another Red Bull?" he asks.

Alec turns and heads into the kitchen. He opens the fridge, which is loaded with Red Bulls and Coors Lights. He grabs a Red Bull, returns to the living room, opens it, and sets it down beside the boy on the half-inch fire-retardant carpeting.

Jermaine completes a round of the game and exhales, frustrated.

"You're definitely getting closer," Alec says. "I just might have to go dig out that old rookie card after all."

"I'm definitely gonna wax your score," Jermaine says.

Alec's house, a double-wide with baby-blue vinyl siding, sits on fifteen-foot-high reinforced timber stilts. In the front a cedar staircase zigzags up to the entrance and a matching one in the back serves as a fire escape. He bought the house two years ago for $18,000 cash. It has two bedrooms, a full bathroom, a kitchen, a living room, and surprisingly good central air. Built in the early '70s, it used to function as a kind of weekend hunting, fishing, and drinking lodge for a man named Carl Ulis and a coterie of his buddies. Ulis, who'd purportedly smoked filterless Pall Malls since he was nine, lived to be 106, and willed the house to no one, which made it an easy grab when it went up for probate. The smell of Pall Malls and Zippo fuel had been so thoroughly absorbed into the sheetrock that Alec was driven to start smoking Pall Malls himself, a habit he was able to kick only with the Nicorette gum that he is now addicted to.

Alec hasn't done much to improve the place, but he did add a satellite dish, a microwave oven with a lazy Susan interior platter, a stacked washer-dryer unit, a halfway decent chocolate-brown leather sectional, a drip coffee maker, and the Samsung television that Jermaine is currently planted before, all of which were paid for by his beloved slot machine in the third row of the casino's fruiters room.

Jermaine comes to the end of another snowboarding run, fails to get within even three seconds of Alec's high score, and frustratingly discards the control module. "I gotta take a piss," he says. He jogs down the hall, toward the back of the house, his braids bouncing, and closes the bathroom door.

While the boy is in the bathroom, Alec heads over to the fridge and opens the freezer. He contemplates putting a pepperoni pizza in the oven, smothering it with a can of black olives, but thinks better of it and shuts the freezer. A pizza will only make him sleepy, after all.

From the fridge he removes a Coors Light, pops the top, drinks half of it in one swig, and belches epically.

"Hey, man," Jermaine says, having returned from the bathroom, "something don't smell right back there. It's like shrimp gone bad. Like something straight up died."

"It's my septic," Alec says. "The tank leaks when the water table's high. We happen to be in a flood zone here at the lovely Tunica Cutoff."

"Why do they call it the Cutoff?" Jermaine asks, chewing on yet another red straw.

"Because round these here parts is where things tend to get *cut off*," Alec says with an exaggerated redneck accent.

"Like what?" Jermaine says.

"Electricity," Alec answers, shedding the accent. "Phones... heads. I'm kidding." Alec drinks, burps again. "Back in nineteen thirty-something," he continues, "the Army Corps of Engineers cut off the flow of the Mississippi in advantageous spots to help commercial ships avoid a bunch of lengthy, pain-in-the-ass, U-shaped, contortionist bends. They did cutoffs in over a dozen places."

"Were you in the Army?" Jermaine asks.

"Me?" Alec says. "No way. No even close."

Then Jermaine asks him what he does for a living.

"I'm an independent contractor," Alec says.

"So you like work for yourself?"

"That's right," Alec says. "I'm my own boss."

"Word," Jermaine says.

Alec opens the cupboard above the sink. He thought there might be some Lysol spray in there. Something to cover up that shrimp smell. No luck. He closes the cupboard. "Hey," he says. "I know one thing we have in common."

"What?" Jermaine says.

"The Mississippi," Alec says. "That endless, legendary, godforsaken river."

They toast to the Mississippi. A Coors Light and a Red Bull.

"To the Mississippi," Alec says.

"To the Mississippi," Jermaine echoes.

From his pocket Alec produces his package of Nicorette, pushes two squares though the foil, pops them into his mouth.

"What are them bags of cement for?" Jermaine asks, pointing toward the end of the hallway, where five orange bags of Quikrete are stacked, one on top of the other, with a shovel propped against them.

"A home-improvement project," Alec says. "I need to reinforce the stilts that support this house. Every few years you have to re-cement their bases, or things can start to get wobbly."

"But why'd you bring 'em inside?" Jermaine says. "Ain't they heavy?"

"Yeah, those bastards are eighty pounds each," Alec says. "It wasn't no cakewalk hauling 'em up here, let me tell you. I about wrecked my back, but you can't leave 'em outside. They get wet and it's all over. I'd throw a tarp over 'em but someone could still take 'em. Around here damn near every nimrod and their ugly sister has a pickup truck. They'll grease the hinges right out of your front door if you're not careful. Trust me, it was worth the haul. All five bags, all four hundred godforsaken pounds." Alec shakes his head, take a breath. "I'm fifty-four years old but I still got some gas left in the tank. Tearing up my back a little wasn't nothin' a few hours of icing couldn't help. You're an athlete, you know about that kind of stuff. Inflammation and whatnot."

"John, yo, you fifty-four?" Jermaine says. "I thought you was, like, forty at the most."

"Well, I'm flattered," Alec says. "You'll have to tell that to my knees."

"Arthritis?"

Alec nods. "It'll flatten your ass faster than a frying pan," he says, and takes another drink. "I bet you're fast," he adds. "You a base stealer?"

"Yeah," Jermaine answers, "I steal bases. I stole home once."

"You got those young, fast-twitch muscles," Alec says, and finishes his beer. He crunches it in his hand, tosses it behind him. It clatters in the empty sink.

Jermaine seems agitated. Something has shifted in him.

"Everything okay?" Alec says.

Jermaine just sands there chewing his straw. Fatigue is finally starting to soften his face. His braids look dumb. Alec suppresses the urge to pull off each of the little pink rubber bands and watch the boy's braids unfurl themselves and bloom into some intergalactic soul brother's Afro from the '70s.

"You want me to drive you back to the casino?" Alec says.

"Not till I beat your high score and take that rookie card," Jermaine says.

He doesn't want to return the boy, of course—no, not in the least—but sometimes it pays to reverse the psychology. He figured this out long ago, with the first boy he took in. It had happened in Versailles, Missouri, during the summer of 1982, when he brought a Greek boy back to the basement of a derelict home he'd been squatting in. The basement had been furnished with a half-collapsed, bucket-seated corduroy sofa and a ping-pong table. The ping-pong table came complete with a pair of paddles and a dusty, unopened box of balls. Versailles, pronounced "Versayles" by the locals, was a shitty little town with a halfway decent lake, hardly a police station, and its share of abandoned houses. It was just after July Fourth weekend and you could still smell the fireworks hanging in the humid, mosquito-infested air. Alec was riding a cheap ten-speed bike he'd purchased for twelve dollars at a yard sale. Held together with duct tape, the bike was workable as long as he used only the first three gears. Alec came across the boy on the outskirts of town, walking alone on a frontage road. He appeared to be in a daze, as if the dragonflies darting about the dirt shoulder had hypnotized him. With his dark hair and large eyes the color of charcoal, the boy reminded Alec of himself at that age. He was a little fleshier in the middle than Alec had been but he liked him nonetheless.

He hopped off his bike and befriended the boy by offering him a stick of Wrigley's spearmint chewing gum, a gesture he followed by telling the boy about the prized ping-pong table. It turned out he loved ping-pong, almost as much as Rock 'Em Sock 'Em Robots—but not quite as much. The boy said his name was Teddy. He was eleven.

Just as they were about to enter through the cellar door of his house, Alec used a similar reverse-psychology tactic on Teddy, insisting that he probably shouldn't play ping-pong with a stranger, especially without his parents' permission.

"I don't need permission," Teddy insisted. He had a foreign accent that Alec couldn't quite place but liked.

At first things couldn't have gone better. They played a best-out-of-three tournament. Alec let Teddy win, of course—he played with his left hand—and it was the most fun he'd had in as long as he could remember. To celebrate Teddy's decisive victory, Alec took the paddle out of his hand and led him to the sofa, where he opened a bottle of Boone's Farm Strawberry Hill, which he poured into two Dixie cups. Teddy drank two mouthfuls but didn't want any more after that because he said it tasted like medicine.

At first Alec was gentle with the boy—he didn't want to be like the priests had been with him—but then Teddy got scared, and just as Alec's blood went heavy with desire, the boy started fighting with him, grabbing at Alec's wrists and whining and whimpering. Alec was overwhelmed by a feeling of shame so profound that he felt his only choice was to make it disappear, to somehow reverse its hold on him, to clear out the gunk thickening his blood. And he finally did something about it—something he'd wanted to do for a very long time. He thought of it as simply putting the boy to sleep. The act gave him so much peace.

Later, while going through the boy's clothes, Alec would see the name THEODORE DRAKOS scrawled in permanent marker on the inside of his light blue, short-sleeved, Sunday school shirt. It was the first name of what would come to be many. Theodore "Teddy" Drakos. A name he would never forget.

"I wish I could make us another batch of Mai Tais," Alec says to Jermaine now. "Sorry my supplies were low. I wasn't expecting company."

"More weed would be better," Jermaine says. "Help me focus." He sits back down.

"Hey, before you start," Alec says, and reaches into one of the many pockets of his cargo shorts. He produces a postcard and hands it to Jermaine.

Jermaine studies it for a moment. "Isn't that your house?" he says, pointing at the color image on the front of the postcard.

It's true. It's Alec's house, with the baby-blue vinyl siding, the stilts, the satellite dish on the roof, and the address, in black pig-iron numerals, just above the mailbox.

"I had a bunch of these made at this little office-supplies store up in Robinsonville," Alec says of the postcard. "Would you do me the honor and sign it for me?"

"Like, you want like my autograph?"

"If you wouldn't mind," Alec says. "I have a feeling it's gonna be worth something someday."

"But you've never even seen me play."

"Sometimes you look at a person and see something," Alec says. "You just know."

"Shit, I'll sign it," Jermaine says. "Whatever's clever."

Alec hands him a black felt-tip pen. "Print your name first," he says, "then sign below it. It's more valuable that way."

"Cool," Jermaine says, and in childlike block letters, he prints his name on the blank side of the postcard. He then writes his signature directly below it. "You want me to put my uniform number on there, too?" he asks.

"No," Alec says. "But what is it?"

"One," Jermaine says. "For obvious reasons."

"Who wore number one?" Alec says.

"Ozzie Smith, homie."

"He played shortstop, right?"

"*Plays*," Jermaine says. "Don't retire my man just yet. The Wizard of Oz is the best defensive shortstop of all time. Some people want to put Cal Ripken up there, or like Barry Larkin, but I'm not havin' it."

"Ozzie's the one who does all those backflips," Alec says.

"He does backflips, has won some crazy amount of gold gloves, played in mad All-Star games, stole mad bases. One of the greatest Cardinals of all time."

"Then by all means," Alec says, "add your uni number."

Jermaine nods and adds a large #1 beside his signature, then hands Alec the felt-tip pen, the postcard.

Alec takes a moment to read it. "Thanks for this," he says. "Seriously."

Then Jermaine asks Alec if he can finally see his fancy baseball card. "You haven't even shown it to me," he says.

Alec reaches into one of the other pockets of his shorts—the special pocket that zips—and produces Mickey Mantle's rookie card, which is preserved in a thin magnetized lucite frame. He flashes the front, the back.

"Damn," the boy says. "That's like *for real* for real."

He reaches for it but Alec pulls it away.

"Tsk-tsk, not yet," Alec says. "You still have to beat my score."

Jermaine hits the reset button on the handset, starting the game over. As the game's intro music plays, Alec crosses to the living room window and lowers the blinds. According to his green Rolex Submariner Hulk watch, which he won in a late-night poker game down in Boca Raton two months ago, it's almost 7:45 a.m. The sun is weak today, hardly lighting the skin of the lake. A loon dives for a fish but comes up empty.

"To help you focus," Alec says of closing the blinds. "I want to give you every opportunity to succeed."

For the next hour, the boy plays the *Super Mario World* with newfound determination, his brow furrowed, his bottom lip tucked under his top row of teeth, giving his face a goofy, rabbit-like appearance. He fails four times, then takes a break and drinks another Red Bull, which Alec had set beside him on the carpet.

Alec can't stop laughing. Lying back on the sectional he puts away another three Coors Lights, then a fourth. He's starting to feel a little drunk, a little sleepy. He decides to make a pot of coffee, but abandons that project when he realizes he's run out of filters.

"You want music?" he asks.

"Nah," the boy says. "Lemme focus."

After another two failures, Jermaine stands and starts doing jumping jacks, then push-ups. He runs in place, counting out a hundred, his thighs firing like pistons, his knees ramming into his outstretched palms. Then he sits and begins again.

By 8:00 a.m. he comes within six-tenths of a second of Alec's record. And then three-tenths of the record twenty minutes later. And then, finally, at 9:10 a.m, he beats it by two-tenths of a second.

Alec is half-awake on the sectional with his legs outstretched, having kicked off his sandals.

"Yo, John!" Jermaine cries. "I did it! I beat your score!"

Alec sits upright, then unfolds himself to standing, fighting the chronic ache in his ankles and knees. He takes a step toward the flatscreen.

Jermaine is in the process of entering his initials, "JAH," at the top of the leaderboard, sending Alec's "JCL," down to the number-two slot.

Alec offers his sincere congratulations.

"I had the will," the boy says, completely wired still. "You gotta have mad will."

"What's the 'A' stand for?" Alec asks of the boy's initials.

"Anthony," Jermaine says. "Jermaine Anthony Holloway." He turns to Alec. "What's the 'C'?"

"Christopher," Alec says. "John Christopher."

"Anthony and Christopher," Jermaine says. "Ain't they both saints? I know St. Anthony is the patron saint of lost things."

"Then maybe he can help me find my old Zippo," Alec jokes. "Or the last thirty years of my life."

"I can't remember what St. Christopher does," the boy says.

"He's probably the patron saint of toothaches and bad knees," Alec offers.

"I think it might be travelers," Jermaine says. "Like tourism and whatnot."

"Why do you know so much about the saints?" Alec says. "You religious?"

"My auntie collects 'em," Jermaine says. "Those little figurines that are like yay tall. She's got a whole glass cabinet filled with 'em."

"Is that what she does with her blackjack money?"

Then a stillness passes over Jermaine and he simply says, "Fuck." He bolts upright, still clutching the control module. When he reaches his full height he accidentally yanks the gaming port out of the side of flatscreen, which causes the television to switch to the morning news.

The onscreen image features a federal building in Oklahoma City, Oklahoma billowing with smoke. A famous news anchor is describing the events. He is beside himself with confusion, grasping for common sense, for facts.

"A massive car bomb exploded outside a large federal building in downtown Oklahoma City," he says, "shattering that building, killing children, killing federal employees, and civilians. The chaos in downtown Oklahoma City resembled Beirut after what police believed to be a twelve-hundred-pound car bomb ripped through the nine-story federal building only minutes ago. More than five hundred people were already in their offices, and over fifty children were in a daycare center on the second floor . . . "

It looks like something out of a Hollywood movie. Alec and Jermaine both watch, utterly mesmerized.

"Is this real?" Jermaine says.

"I think it is," Alec says.

The smoke just keeps billowing out of the building. It's almost too real to be true. The boy's bottom lip has drawn up under his teeth again. They continue watching the news, riveted by that endless apocalyptic smoke.

By the time the news story has shifted to another reporter at the scene, Alec has produced a pair of police handcuffs. Slowly, quietly, he cuffs first Jermaine's left wrist, then his right.

"Yo, John, what the fuck are you doin'?" Jermaine says.

But the rag doused with chloroform is already over the boy's face, and not even a minute later, after a brief struggle, the boy is rendered silent and his body goes limp.

Out on the lake the engine of a motorboat has scared off the loon and two men are fishing for white sturgeon and crappie and drumfish. The bait shops, which opened at dawn, have likely sold half their haul of night crawlers and crickets and maggots; they always do on mornings such as this. It's probably not even 70 degrees yet, cool out there on the lake.

Alec imagines the morning sun finally streaming through the clouds, dappling the skin of the water. The two-headed rope and wooden dowel have been taped under his leather sectional all this time, for easy access.

It's going to be a beautiful day.

13

EUREKA SPRINGS, ARKANSAS
JUNE 14, 1997

MYRA LEE

THE THIRTEEN-HOUR TRAIN RIDE from Chicago to Little Rock felt interminable. Myra's small sleeper cabin made things a little more comfortable, but by the eighth hour the boredom was like a giant featureless mass that only reminded her of her own acute loneliness. She finished Anne Tyler's *The Accidental Tourist* in under eight hours, and while she'd enjoyed it, she didn't much feel like starting it over. Every few pages she had to take a break, as her eyes, along with everything else, were tired. Despite her fatigue and the recent pervasive weakness she's been experiencing, as long as there was something to grab on to every few feet, she felt confident moving about the train. She even enjoyed a conversation she had with an old Black man in the dining car. His name was Udonis Bunch and he was on his way to visit his son's family in Midlothian, Texas. Mr. Bunch had a voice like some rich, mysterious sap that bleeds from an ancient tree. He told her all about his five decades managing concessions at Chicago's old Comiskey Park, right up until the stadium was demolished after the 1990 season. When he asked her what she did for a living and she told him she'd been a nurse at Stateville Correctional in Joliet, he lit up, as his youngest brother, Fennis, happened to be there, serving a lifetime sentence for murder. Mr. Bunch didn't go into any details about his brother and Myra didn't press him about it. During her tenure at Stateville she'd never come across Fennis Bunch, which meant that he was probably living a well-adjusted, peaceful existence there, and she told Udonis Bunch as much.

"What a small, small, itty-bitty world this really is," he said.

Despite Mr. Bunch's pleasant company, Myra regretted the decision not to fly, which she'd avoided on the fervent advice of Dr. Baron, her original, Chicago-based oncologist, who'd warned that the cabin pressure would not be good for her recovery and that long-distance driving wasn't a good idea either because of the demands of concentration, not to mention the fact that she might need her pain medication. Despite being in some state of serious discomfort almost every hour of every day for the past year or so, Myra is still conservative with the pain meds. She doesn't like how loopy they make her feel.

Myra completed her most recent chemotherapy program only three weeks ago and she's still getting her strength back. Two years ago, after Myra recovered from her first round of chemotherapy, it looked like her cancer would go into remission. The scans were promising. Dr. Baron, normally a staunch realist, seemed genuinely hopeful. To celebrate Myra's near-clean bill of health, Lexy and her husband, Barry, helped Myra secure a mortgage for a modest house in Waitsfield, Vermont, a small town in the northwest part of the state. Unfortunately, the remission was short-lived, and Myra has endured two cycles of chemotherapy treatments since then. The one she just finished happened at a clinic in nearby Montpelier, and Lexy came to stay with her in Vermont while she battled the intense fatigue and nausea.

Tucked into the hills, the fully winterized house sits on an acre of land, with its own private dock on the Mad River. A little over 2,000 square feet, the 1921 Sears & Roebuck bungalow is light green with white trim, and features a second-floor dormer window. There is a screened-in front porch and an additional four-seasons porch, which has been built onto the back of the house. It is surrounded by evergreen trees and Myra has ample space for gardening. After a couple of decades in a cramped, two-bedroom apartment with music blaring from all corners of their building at any given hour, the house has felt like paradise to her. There is the river, as well as hiking trails and so many birds. Waitsfield is so small it barely appears on the Vermont state map, but Myra loves the seclusion. She finally has a peaceful place to live out her days.

Always thin, Myra has lost more weight this time than she did during her previous two chemotherapy cycles. Back in Joliet, after the first cancer re-emergence she had to start another cycle. Toward the end of that second treatment she weighed in at ninety-four pounds and Dr. Baron decided to keep her overnight so they could feed her intravenously. This is now the second re-emergence of the cancer. Her new oncologist in Montpelier, Dr. Anthony, was hopeful that the cancer would go into remission—but her most recent scans proved otherwise. Myra has gained some of the weight back but not nearly enough. Her hands look huge to her, the knobs of her wrists monstrous. The trouble is that her appetite just hasn't fully returned. She eats like a toddler, all soft foods: applesauce and light broths and Jello recipes. Even the protein shake she's been prescribed doesn't seem ever to settle right. Often an odd metallic odor—something like pennies in the bottom of a rusty coffee can—leaks from her mouth, and everything tastes like metal.

Her general exhaustion, meanwhile, is still intense and with the slightest bit of comfort she can fall asleep in less than a minute—in chairs, on park benches, in the cabin of a rattling train car. She's even fallen asleep on the toilet a few times. She sticks to showers, not allowing herself the luxury of a bath out of fear of drowning.

From Little Rock, where she stayed last night, the drive up to Eureka Springs in her rental car, a Ford Escort, took another three and a half hours. She had to stop three times: first to refuel; next, to take a short nap in a rest area; and finally, to gather her thoughts in the parking lot atop Magnetic Mountain, where, as she'd promised her mother she would, she went to see a giant sculpture of Jesus known as *Christ of the Ozarks*. The sculpture is over sixty feet tall and looks as if it has been made out of white marzipan. Christ's arms are stretched wide in a benevolent fashion, suggesting the crucifixion. Ava Larkin would not be pleased that there is no actual cross and would likely dismiss it as blasphemous pagan folk art, or, even worse, as something altogether "Lutheran." Myra parked the car and crossed the manicured lawn that leads to the sculpture. It was slow-going, as her legs have gotten weaker and weaker lately. She owns an aluminum walking cane and although she travels with it—she promised Dr. Anthony—she refuses to actually use it. It's currently resting on the bed in her motel room like some terrible, inevitable prop, waiting for her to be lame, once and for all.

There were five or six other people milling about the *Christ of the Ozarks* grounds and taking photos. The statue bears very little resemblance to the portrait of Christ that Myra grew up with in the Larkin dining room. That version of Jesus—a realistic oil painting that hangs in the dining room to this day—depicts him as a thoughtful, somewhat troubled man with prominent shoulder blades, suffering, kind hazel eyes, and a crown of bloody thorns. This statue, on the other hand, is like something out of a Claymation Christmas special. Her mother might actually find it amusing. At least Myra can tell her she kept her promise and paid the visit.

Back in the car, in addition to applying lipstick and rouge, she removed her head scarf and reapplied tea tree oil to her scalp. Myra's third cycle of chemotherapy in three years has started to make her head itch. This is the third time she's lost all of her hair, which is only starting to bear the smallest hint of fuzzy regrowth. She's gotten somewhat used to going bald by now but she didn't experience this kind of scalp irritation the first two times. Clearly those mysterious poisons have done something to her skin. Her friend Marna suggested the tea tree oil—she uses it for the eczema that plagues the backs of her arms—and it definitely helps. Her silk scarf is white and features several colorful birds: Eurasian bullfinches and orange-breasted robins and a pair of red cardinals. It was a gift from Ronan after she'd completed her first round of chemo. Over the scarf, she often sports a blue Chicago Cubs baseball cap, which she is currently wearing as she pulls into Myrtie Mae's Cafe, on Van Buren Street.

At 2:30 p.m. it's already over 80 degrees—hot for mid-June in this part of the country—and after she rolls up the driver's side window of her rental car she takes a moment to gather her things and adjust her headscarf in the rearview mirror. Twenty minutes earlier she spoke to a man with a prolific, nicotine-stained platinum beard who was manning the front desk of a residential motel where she'd been directed by a priest. Father Joseph, who happened to be the only person present at St. Elizabeth of Hungary Catholic Church, wouldn't reveal much about her brother, Alec, beyond his employment at the church as the groundskeeper. The priest was busy setting hymnals in the pews and humming to himself when Myra entered the small church. With a little pressing he disclosed that Alec, who now goes by Jerry, was very likely enjoying his typical Saturday off. Myra then took another tack and told Father Joseph how St. John the Baptist, her family's church back in Elmira, was an important cornerstone in the community and especially important to their family. She showed the priest her ID and he somewhat reluctantly agreed to give her Alec's address at the Statue Road Inn, where the man with the long platinum beard told her he was likely at his favorite lunch spot, Myrtie Mae's.

Myra decided on making this trip to Eureka Springs in the wake of her mother receiving another of Alec's disturbing postcards, which Myra learned about only the previous Christmas, when she and Ronan spent the holidays in Elmira. After Joan had gone to bed and while Ronan was upstairs, on the phone with Henny, Ava opened the drawer below the phone and removed the postcards. On the front of the one that Myra is currently carrying in her purse is a four-color photograph of the very church she just visited: St. Elizabeth of Hungary of Eureka Springs. In blue ballpoint pen ink, scrawled across the church's small bell tower in Alec's strange, faint handwriting, is the line THIS IS WHERE I WORK. Ava took Myra through every single postcard—there are twenty-one in total—and this was the first time Alec had added anything more than the name of a boy, the number presumably referring to the boy's age, and the oblique phrase SAYING HELLO AND GOODBYE. Her mother told her she had received a dozen of them in the space of a single year, back in the mid-'80s, and that they had become more intermittent since then.

Seventy-seven at the time, with ailing knees and the constant care of Joan to worry about, she said it was nearly impossible for her to travel. Despite still recovering from her recent treatment, Myra offered that she would go. It would break the monotony of waking, sleeping, napping, and managing her nausea. It would force her to be in the world and engage with other people, which Myra knows is always a good thing while on the mend. After all, over the years she's been the one person Alec has been in touch with, though not at all during the past decade or so. The truth is that the last time she heard from her brother was on Thanksgiving in 1988, when she and Ronan stayed in Joliet and hosted dinner at the apartment. Marna and her husband, Dale, who'd tracked Denny down all those years ago, and two guards from the prison came over for dinner. With Ronan home from college, Myra was so happy. Then she answered the phone just as the pumpkin pie was being served, and it was Alec telling her that he needed money. He was drunk and slurring his words. It was just five hundred dollars to pay his rent, he said. He was calling from Phoenix, where he claimed to have a job lined up at a company that installed septic systems. He would pay her back, he swore on his life—this despite the fact that he never had, not one single time. How many dozens of similar calls had Myra fielded before that one, and she always wound up wiring Alec something, even if it was a third of the amount he requested. That Thanksgiving was the first time she denied him the money and it turned out to be the last time she would hear from him.

Despite this nearly decade-long gulf between them, Myra still sees herself as Alec's last connection to the family. And despite her fatigue, she's managed to convince herself that this trip is going to be worth it. She had to go back to Joliet anyway to ship some boxes to Vermont that were in storage. Lexy was kind enough to drive her the fifteen hours from Vermont and help her with the boxes. And then Lexy dropped her at Chicago's LaSalle Street Station before heading back to Connecticut.

During her illness, Lexy has been the one sibling who's really been there for Myra. Like Alec, Fiona has also receded from Myra's life. There was occasional contact for a few years back in the '70s, following her affiliation with that women's cult in Massachusetts, but it was a random five-minute call here and there, not even during the holidays, and when Myra would ask her anything regarding the details of her life—did she have a job, how was her health, was she dating anyone—Fiona would become vague and quiet and end the call shortly thereafter. All she knows is that she still lives in New York City and continues to pursue acting, which seems tragic, a woman her age still trying to make it in that industry. Lexy also shared with Myra the story of Fiona asking to her to lunch last year. Fiona took the train up to Rowayton, Connecticut, where Lexy agreed to meet her at her favorite café. It turned out that Fiona had broken her wrist and wound up asking Fiona for five thousand dollars to cover the medical bills as well as a month's rent. Because of her lack of work, she explained, she'd lost her medical benefits. She even conjured some tears as she wolfed down her tuna sandwich and salad. Going against her better judgment, Lexy agreed to help her, and wrote her a check right there at their table. Fiona, of course, swore that she would pay Lexy back, wiping her tears away. Lexy hasn't heard from Fiona since. She told Myra that she had a vague hunch that Fiona's cast wasn't even real, that it looked like a stage prop. So Myra does have hope that this trip will bear some kind of re-connection between her and one of her lost siblings—her only living brother, for that matter.

And now here she is, 600 miles from Chicago, 1,400 miles from her home in Vermont. It's been a long few days, to say the least.

As she approaches the café she passes a copy of a newspaper left on a bench. The front-page headline reads "McVeigh Jury Decides on Sentence of Death in Oklahoma Bombing." She heard the story reported earlier on the radio on her way to Magnetic Mountain and was relieved to hear that some of the families of the deceased might find some peace in the wake of this tragedy. She almost picks up the stray paper but is distracted by a man sitting in a booth by the window. His face is hardened, beset by a kind of bitterness that

Myra recognizes from many of the haunted, alcoholic men she knew in prison. It's Alec. His dark eyes are ringed with fatigue, perhaps sleeplessness. Yes, it's Alec, she's sure of it. She is shocked by how much her brother has aged. He would have turned fifty-six in March. The last time she saw him — almost forty years ago, during a trip home from nursing school — his hair was as black as their father's shoe polish. Now it's thinning and gray, iron-colored really, and his face has taken on weight. Even from the parking lot Myra can see that Alec is still handsome, despite the swollen eyes and obvious hard living. His short-sleeved red Hawaiian shirt features a pattern of white palm trees. He is alone, eating methodically and drinking from a coffee mug.

When Myra enters the café she is greeted by a young woman with a distinctly Southern accent. Myra points to Alec's booth and the hostess follows her there with a menu. When Myra slides in across from Alec he is in the process of shoving at least two pieces of bacon into his mouth. On his plate are scrambled eggs, hash browns, and buttered toast. He looks up. Myra grasps that he has no idea who she is, and why would he? She's bald. She's been through three rounds of chemotherapy. She probably looks nothing like the girl he knew some forty years ago.

"Hi, Alec," she says.

He stops chewing and simply looks at her.

"It's me," she says, "Myra."

He has the teeth of a tobacco chewer. Each of his elbows is swollen, probably bursitis. "Myra?" he says.

"Your sister," she adds. "Myra Lee."

"Wow," he says. "Really?" He swallows his bacon and drinks from his coffee mug. He then sets the flats of his large hands on the table. They are misshapen and twisted like their father's. Dark hairs sprout along the segments between his knuckles.

"You're surprised," she says. "I don't blame you."

Already an ache of sadness is forming in her chest, like an indissoluble cherry stone. Myra swallows, trying to force it down, but her mouth is dry. She asks if she can have some of his water and he nods exactly once, but warily, as if she's a medical professional performing an examination. She takes his glass and gulps a mouthful. The chemo always makes her feel parched, no matter how much water she drinks.

"What are you doing here?" Alec asks. His voice is dehydrated, torn in places, as if belonging to a man who has survived heart attacks and fires.

"I just felt like I needed to see you," she says.

"Oh," he says. "Why?"

"Well, for one thing, I've been sick."

"Okay," he says.

"I have cancer." She explains that she was diagnosed three years ago, that it's gone into remission twice but returned each time. Then she removes her Cubs hat, her head scarf. "I'm bald as a melon," she adds. "From the chemo."

The look on Alec's face is one of mild disgust, as if he's just happened upon a goat shitting on the sidewalk.

"And it's my birthday tomorrow."

"So you came looking for your long-lost brother as a birthday present to yourself," he says. "Now there's a real doozy. You want me to jump out of a fucking cake?"

The remark, his blatant lack of regard for her, stings. Myra puts her scarf back on, leaves the Cubs hat on the seat beside her.

Alec drinks from his mug and says, "There are like ten thousand birds on your do-rag."

"My son gave it to me after I completed my first round of treatments."

"Ronny," he says.

"Ronan," she says.

"Ronan, right. How old is he now?" Alec asks.

"He's twenty-eight," Myra says.

Suddenly a middle-aged waitress appears and asks Myra if she'd like to order.

Myra has to clear her throat to ask if they have any cottage cheese.

"With or without pineapple bits," the waitress says.

"Without, please. I'd love a ginger ale, too."

"Sprite okay?"

"That's fine," Myra says.

After the waitress moves off, Alec asks Myra how she tracked him down, in a tone that feels addressed to a private detective or a bail bondsman.

She explains about stopping by the little stone church with the bell tower and being directed by Father Joseph to the motel on Passion Play Road, where the man with the platinum beard told her that this is where Alec came for his lunches.

"But how the hell did you know I had anything to do with St. Elizabeth's?"

Myra reaches into her purse and produces the postcard. She points to the phrase THIS IS WHERE I WORK. And then she takes out the rest of the postcards and sets them on the table.

"Those were for Mom," Alec says. "Not you."

"Mom wanted to come," Myra says, "but she's not getting around so well these days."

"What's wrong with her?" Alec asks.

"It's her knees," Myra says. "They've gotten pretty bad. And she refuses the surgery that would help to repair her cartilage. She can barely work in her garden anymore. She walks with a cane now." Myra doesn't even bother bringing up their father or Alec's conspicuous absence at the funeral.

Alec stares at his food for a moment and then makes an X with his fork and knife over it, as if the image of their mother walking with a cane somehow poisoned his food.

"What about church?" he says. "What does she do, stand?"

"She mostly sings in the choir now," Myra says. "So, yes, she stands. That's easier." She searches his face for some clue of who he's become: a scar or a discoloration. A tremor. But it's the same face he had as a boy. Just older and fleshier and cut with wrinkles here and there.

Alec won't meet her eyes.

"So here I am," Myra says.

"You're like a regular Magnum PI. You took a real shot in the dark."

"I figured it was worth the gamble. I only have one living brother, after all."

He picks something out of his coffee mug, flicks it onto the floor.

"So why Jerry?" she says.

"Why *not* Jerry?" he replies, and sips, turns the mug one slow revolution between his hands, then stares into it as if it will provide the clue for getting through this awkward encounter.

Myra decides not to press him on the matter.

"So what kind of cancer is it?" he says, setting the mug down finally.

"Stomach," she says. "And it's in my colon, too."

"Are you in a lot of pain?"

"It comes and goes," she says.

"Do they give you anything for it?"

"Yeah, but I don't like taking it," she says. "The meds just toxify my liver and give my body one more reason to be angry with me."

"Well, I am currently accepting donations," Alec says. "If you're just chucking your pills in the river, that is."

Is this an attempt at irony? Humor? Myra tries to smile. Her face feels slow, rubbery.

"How long do you have left?" he asks, with no more emotion than if he's asking whether the warranty on a toaster oven has expired.

"There's no telling," she says. "If I respond well to this most recent round of treatment things could turn around."

"And if not?"

"Then I'll probably be lucky to see a grandchild."

"Ronny's married?"

"Ronan. No, but he's with someone and they've been together quite a while."

Alec goes silent. His dark pupils are vacant. He clearly has no interest in his nephew, much less his actual name.

Myra points to his plate. "I'm sorry if I caused you to lose your appetite."

His face, which used to have that rich olive complexion, has turned ashen, bloodless. A rime of salt-and-pepper stubble marks his cheeks and chin and neck, while thistles sprout from his ears. His hair is long and unwashed, unhealthy. He looks like a divorcé who plays in a mediocre cover band.

"What are you really doing here, Myra?" Alec finally says. "It's been like seven thousand years. Why track me down now?"

"You're my brother," is all she can offer. "I've been worried about you. We all have." She realizes that she's been flicking the rubber bands that are securing the collection of postcards. She stops, brings her hands to her lap. "Can I ask you some questions?" she says.

"As long as they're not math-related," he says.

His old stock phrase. Myra smiles, then self-consciously covers her mouth, a habit since the chemo dimmed her teeth. "Are you with anyone?" she says, removing her hand from her mouth. "Do you have a family?"

"No and no," he says. "Not even a dog. Not even a goldfish."

It pains her that he has so little regard for his own loneliness. She knows hers all too well, after all. "Father Joseph told me you're the groundskeeper at the church," she says.

"I am a mower of lawns. A trimmer of a variety of bushes. A handler of the occasional wasp nest. Sometimes I have to deal with the deer who come around to snack on the roses."

"How do you keep the deer away?"

"I have a pellet gun. Pop 'em in the ass a few times. They learn quickly. Unlike humans."

Myra tells him about the concoction that their mother uses. "Cayenne pepper and olive oil and all this other stuff. Douses her garden with it."

"Sounds like a lot of shopping."

"It's more humane. And it really does keep them away."

"I have bacon," he says. "Want any?"

"No thanks," she says.

He tells her she looks thin, like concentration-camp thin.

"I still don't have much of an appetite," she says.

"Chemo's just poison, right?"

"Technically, yes," she says. "But carefully created to attack the bad stuff and help the body heal."

"I wouldn't do chemo in a million years," he says.

"What would you do?" she asks.

"Let the worms have at me," he says. "The world is designed to destroy you, anyway. Some of us go quicker than others. It's all a game and it's not that complicated. I'd rather wrestle an alligator."

Myra hears a slight twang in his voice. Is this an affectation? Or just the natural way we take on the music of our surroundings? She asks him what he does for fun.

"*Fun*?" he says, his voice jumping an octave. It's as if she's uttered a foreign word.

"For pleasure," she says, "for recreation."

"I like to fish," he says. "There's a good lake around here, an unbelievable coastline, with caves and whatnot. It makes the Chemung look like an end-of-the-world urinal. Has a ton of large-mouth bass, bream, crappie, every kind of catfish known to man." He looks at the back of his wrist as if there's a watch there. "I just quit smoking," he adds. "That used to be fun."

"I'm glad you quit," she says.

"I miss it," he says. "It gave me something to do."

"Do you attend church?"

"I spend half my life there, mowing the fucking grass, if that counts."

His curse word is like a knife thrown into a wall. But why should she expect politeness? Alec never was polite about anything.

"It's a living," Myra offers.

"I guess you could call it that," he says.

"What other kinds of jobs have you had?"

"Not the kind to write home about," he says. "The same ones I used to have back when we were in touch. I've hung drywall, shoveled gravel into the backs of trucks, painted about umpteen thousand houses. Cash jobs mostly. And I've done other things, too. Things I'm not necessarily proud of. I've become a halfway decent gambler."

Myra doesn't even want to begin with it. He certainly looks like a criminal, like so many of the men who wound up at Stateville Correctional when she was there. Con men and arsonists and rapists. Cold-blooded murderers. There was always something missing in their eyes, something lost in the center of the pupil, a feral absence. Coyotes have the same look. Sharks and hyenas, too. Poisonous snakes.

"How long have you been here in Arkansas?" she asks.

"Long," he says. "Not long. Semi-long. What does it matter?"

"I'm just curious," she says.

"I got sort of a home base down in Mississippi. Right on the water. I call it 'The Place Where Dreams Run Wild.' My own little piece of paradise."

"So you go down there when it gets cold?" she asks.

"Somethin' like that," he says.

The waitress appears with Myra's order. The blob of cottage cheese has been scooped onto a wedge of iceberg lettuce. Myra has no appetite but she needs the fat and protein.

"Do you ever think about us?" she asks Alec and steers a forkful of cottage cheese into her mouth. She feels immediately nauseated but makes herself swallow.

"*Us?*" he says.

"Your family," she says. "Your sisters."

"The *Larkins?*" he says. He pronounces his surname as if it's a comical country Western band. "Not really. I wonder about *you* sometimes."

"About what exactly?"

"Just the general stuff. Is Myra fat? Is Myra skinny? Did Myra join a gang of traveling minstrels?"

"Where does Myra live?" she says, offering him a question of substance.

"Aren't you in Shit-cago?" he says.

"No, I'm not. And speaking of Chicago, I've always wondered why you never showed up at our place, all those years ago. You said you were coming from Nebraska to live with us. And then nothing. You didn't show up—and not even a phone call. What happened there?"

"What happened is life happened," he says. "Trees fall in the forest. Bridges collapse. Sinkholes appear out of nowhere."

"Anyway," Myra says, not wanting to entertain his obnoxious explanation, "I just moved to Vermont. Got a little house right on the Mad River. Lexy and her husband, Barry, helped me out."

"Why Vermont?" he asks.

"I love the rolling hills. And the birds. I have a little garden. I can see the Green Mountains from my front porch. I figured if this was getting close to the end it would be nice to be in nature."

"'This' meaning your life," he says.

Myra feels herself nodding slowly. Her brother has still hardly looked at her.

"I'm sorry you're sick," he says.

"Thanks," she says, knowing it pained him to say this. Exhibiting sympathy always only made him feel uneasy at best. "And how's your health?" she asks.

"Who knows?" he says. "Who cares?"

"I do," she says. "When was your last checkup?"

"Sometime during the dissolving sixties," he snarks. "Why, did you come all this way to give me a physical?"

Myra lets the remark pass.

"I probably drink too much," Alec says. "I've definitely shredded my lungs. I'm sure I've broken bones that I had no idea were broken. I'm like one of those old cars that miraculously still starts."

"Are you getting enough sleep?"

"What are you doing here, Myra?" he says curtly, tossing his napkin onto his plate.

She gathers herself. "I want to know what's going on with all those postcards," she says.

"They're just postcards," he says. "Haven't you ever sent a post-card before? Are you not a sender of postcards?"

"With boys' names on them? Their age? 'Saying Hello and Goodbye'? What is that?"

"It's a riddle wrapped inside a booby trap," he says. "Or maybe it's a bad joke stuffed inside a jack-in-the-box."

"What kind of a bad joke?"

Alec drains the rest of his iced tea, then shakes his glass, causing the ice cubes to rattle.

"Are these boys made-up? Are they real?"

"What do you think?"

"I honestly have no idea," she says.

"Maybe you should use your imagination," he says. "Or has the chemo ruined that part of your brain?"

His cruelty comes so easily; it always has. Nothing was ever too low for Alec. He terrorized Joan without the slightest bit of remorse. He delighted in his sisters' humiliations. Myra notices for the first time that he's missing an upper molar on the right side and wonders when he last saw a dentist. Five years ago? Ten? Twenty?

"Alec, if you're doing something to these boys..." She fills her spoon with a lump of cottage cheese but doesn't raise it to her mouth.

"Like what?" he says.

"Like hurting them in some way."

Something tugs at the corner of his left eye. He lifts his glass, takes an ice cube in his mouth, holds it between his teeth as if he will crunch down on it, then spits it directly into Myra's face. It strikes her squarely between the eyes, then ricochets off the chrome napkin dispenser, and skitters across the table.

"Alec, have you thought about getting help?" is all she can say, stunned.

He finally looks at her directly and says, "You think because you used to send me pity money that you have the right to come down here and lecture me? You're turning into our self-righteous bitch of a mother."

Myra grabs her napkin and dabs at the spot where the ice cube struck her.

And then, as if on cue, a boy enters the café. He is maybe thirteen or fourteen, mid-pubescent, brown-skinned, with shoulder-length black hair. He looks like he could be Hispanic or Native American. He wears a yellow T-shirt with Woody Woodpecker on the front, swimming trucks that are too big, and off-brand sneakers with no socks. He walks right up to the table.

"Hey," he says to Alec.

"Hey," Alec says back to him. "This is my sister Myra."

"Hey," the kid says.

"This is Lake," Alec says to Myra.

"Nice to meet you, Lake."

The boy is filthy, as if he's just run through a barren cornfield. He smells like sour laundry and unwashed hair. Mosquito bites riddle his soft brown shins. A scab on his left arm, just at his biceps, is inflamed, ringed in pink, probably infected.

"Sit," Alec tells the boy.

Lake slouches down beside him. His arms are thin, hairless. His dark eyes are large and alert, wondrous. He's still at that age where everything is elastic. His body brims with exuberance and young muscle. He could grow three inches in a month. But the boy won't look at Myra. She knows that sometimes her baldness scares people, especially children. They know she's trying to hide her affliction under the scarf.

"You hungry?" Alec asks the boy.

"I ate," Lake says.

"What?" Alec says. "Another candy bar?"

"I had a peanut butter and jelly sandwich."

"And what else?"

"Some Pringles."

"You need to eat better than that. You'll end up looking like me. Eat a vegetable or three."

"I'll eat more later," Lake says, and then he leans his head on Alec's shoulder.

At first Myra is touched by their familiarity, this father-son gesture. Alec simply stares back at her. He doesn't blink. Then Myra feels a chill take hold. The chemo has hollowed her out, thinned her skin. Sometimes it's like a cold dinner fork is slowly turning inside her.

Lake looks off obliquely. It's as if his physical contact with Alec has caused him to go soft-focus, as if he's beset by daydreams.

"Lake," Myra says to the boy, "how do you and Jerry know each other?"

Lake opens his eyes.

"We met over by the Little League diamond," Alec answers for him. "We're both baseball fans, ain't it, Lake?"

"Jerry takes after our dad," Myra says.

"No, he doesn't," Alec says.

"Our father was a huge Yankees fan," Myra explains to the boy.

"I could care less about adult baseball," Alec says.

"I prefer the Cubs," Myra says, holding up her baseball cap to show Lake.

"I like the Cardinals," Lake says. "They got Royce Clayton."

"Well, then you and I are bitter rivals," Myra offers gently.

"The Cubs are like the bumbiest team in baseball," Lake says. His head is still on Alec's shoulder.

"Do you play on a team?" Myra asks.

"He should be," Alec says. "He's better than just about every kid in Eureka Springs. He can hit, he catches anything thrown to him, and he runs like a panther."

"Why don't you play?" Myra asks.

"Cause it costs mad money," he says. "You got two hundred bones?"

"I'm afraid I don't," Myra says.

The boy claws at his chest, causing Woody Woodpecker to sneer. "Who's older?" he asks.

"I am," Myra says. "By a few years."

"Why you got that do-rag on your head?" he says.

"Because I don't have any hair and I think the birds on this scarf are prettier to look at than my funny-shaped head."

"She's sick," Alec tells Lake.

"You got AIDS or somethin'?" the boy asks.

"I have cancer," she tells him. "But I'm hopefully in the process of recovering."

"Your breath smells like a car," Lake tells her, smiling cruelly, obviously proud of his little nasty barb, no doubt trying to impress his mentor.

While Alec laughs, Myra covers her mouth with her napkin and then takes a sip from her Sprite. With his mouth open, she notices her brother's missing molar again. Maybe he swallowed it in his sleep? Or did he drink half a bottle of cheap whiskey and pull it out with pliers?

"What happened to your arm?" Myra asks Lake, who is picking at his scab.

"He scraped it on the side of the rowboat," Alec says. "When we were fishing the other day. Right, Lake?"

"Yeah, I scraped it," the boy says. "But don't worry. My body's got superpowers."

He lifts his head off Alec's shoulder and stares out the window.

Who is this boy? Myra wonders. What the hell is going on here?

After a moment Lake returns his head to Alec's shoulder and closes his eyes.

Alec grins at her. From deep in the reaches of her brain comes a memory of the time when he was twelve and she walked in on him in Fiona and Lexy's room as he was dousing the crotches of all of Fiona's underwear with ketchup. When Myra asked him what he was doing he said he was teaching her about her period. His face was plagued that day by this same wolfish grin.

"So did you get all the information you need?" Alec says.

"I guess I did," Myra says.

"Then maybe it's time for you to go," he says.

And just like that Alec's nose is bleeding. Rich blood slowly descends from both nostrils. Lake looks up at him and then takes the napkin off Alec's plate and holds it to his nose. Alec simply allows the aid. The napkin turns pink, then red.

Heat fills Myra's cheeks. She goes into her purse and produces a ten-dollar bill, which she leaves next to the postcards, then exits the booth. Her ankles ache and the short path out of the café takes longer than she hoped it would. The last thing she wanted was to seem enfeebled in front of Alec.

Outside, the heat engulfs her like a cloak. She knows she should've drunk more of her Sprite. If nothing else, the sugar would've given her some energy. On slightly wobbly legs she makes it to her Escort. She keys into it, starts the engine and the air-conditioning, and sits there in the driver's seat. She has a direct view into the booth where Lake is still beside Alec, who has taken over holding the napkin to his nose. He makes Lake eat a piece of bacon, then a piece of toast. Lake chews with his mouth open. Defiantly. Ava Larkin would laugh at the boy and call him a hellion. After several mastications, Lake swallows and opens his mouth, as if to show Alec that he isn't hiding any of it. His tongue is surprisingly large, pale as an oyster. Alec sets the blood-soaked napkin down, reaches into his back pocket, produces his wallet, and gives Lake some money. Lake stands and stuffs the bills into the front of his swim trunks. Then he hugs Alec and jogs out of the café, across the parking lot, and down the street.

Without thinking Myra drives after him. At the stop light, as he's jogging across the intersection, she leans over and rolls down the passenger's side window. "Lake!" she calls out. "Get in, I'll give you a ride."

He stops in the middle of the street and turns to her. When the traffic light changes to green she pulls over and he gets in the car.

"Where you going?" she asks.

"To the mall," he says.

"I'll drop you off," she says.

"That way," he says, pointing directly ahead of them.

Myra pulls back onto the street. In the small, hot car the combined odor of his unwashed body and dirty clothes is sharp, fungal.

Myra asks him to please put on his seatbelt and he does so. "Do you live around here?" she says.

"I live with my moms," he says. "Over in Victoria Woods Apartments."

"Do you have brothers and sisters?"

"An older sister. But she's over in Kuwait."

"Is she in the Army?"

"Marines," he says.

"What's her name?"

"Missy. But everyone calls her Sticks 'cause she's so skinny." He picks his nose and wipes it on his swim trunks. "Keep going straight," he says.

At the next stop light she looks over at him. He's staring out the window and gently tapping the scab on his arm.

"It seems like you and my brother are pretty close," she says.

"Jerry's cool," he says.

"Do you spend a lot of time together?"

"He takes me fishing and stuff," he says. "Sometimes I stay over at his place."

"At the motel?"

Lake nods.

"I imagine his room is pretty small," she says.

"He's got cable and a microwave."

"How many beds are in the room?"

"Just one," he says.

The light turns green and she keeps driving. She can't help imagining this boy in the bed with Alec. She can't bring herself to envision the rest of it.

"They got a pool, too," Lake says. "Jerry's teaching me to swim."

"That's nice," she says. "What does your mother do?"

"She was workin' at the Pizza Hut but they let her go. I don't know what she's doin' now."

"And your dad?"

"He lives in Texas," Lake says. "The mall's at the next light." After Myra pulls into the mall's entrance and puts the Escort in park Lake asks her for some money.

"What do you need it for?" she says.

"Video games," he says.

"What's your favorite game?"

"I like this old game called *Scramble*. You fly a spaceship and bomb a bunch of civilizations. I'm about to solve that bitch."

Myra reaches into her purse and pulls out her wallet. She gives the boy a ten-dollar bill. He takes it from her agitatedly, as if she's settling a long awaited IOU.

"Can I ask you one more question?" she says.

"What," he says.

"Does my brother do anything inappropriate with you?"

The question is phrased as if she were a social worker. It's too formal and she knows it. When she worked at the juvenile prison the counselors would speak to the boys this way and Myra always felt that it only pushed them away. This rhetoric of the noble adult.

"I don't know what that means," Lake says.

"When you sleep in the bed with him," she says. "Does he make you do things that you aren't comfortable doing?"

"All he does is teach me how to sleep better," the boy says.

"And how does he do that?"

"He just talks to me."

"About what?"

"About how maybe we'll live in a house someday. And about how maybe he'll marry my moms."

"Does he date your mom?"

"No, but I've shown him pitchers of her."

"Do you think they would like each other?"

"She's pretty fat," he says, "but she can sing like Whitney. Jerry says he likes fat bitches, so..."

Myra swallows. Her mouth is utterly dry. "Does anything else happen when he's teaching you how to sleep better?"

"Sometimes we drink this purple cough syrup stuff."

"Because you have a cough?" she asks.

But Lake doesn't answer because he's out of the car, closing the passenger's side door behind him. He's one of those boys who appears and disappears, like a cat on a rooftop, the bough of a maple tree, a window ledge. He exists as part of the world's sleight of hand.

The rush of heat from the slamming door strikes Myra in the face like a warm rag.

WHILE SHE IS REFUELING her rental car at a Shell station on the outskirts of town, a female police officer pulls up to the neighboring pump. The officer is white, young, broad-shouldered, impressively built. Her navy-blue uniform is clean and well-creased. Her sandy-blond hair is pulled back into a ponytail. She wears mirrored sunglasses. The brass name plate above her right pocket reads N. HUDOCK.

Myra, feeling too weak to squeeze the nozzle, asks the woman for help. "Would you mind?" she says. "My hands just aren't strong enough today."

"Of course," the officer says and takes the nozzle from her.

Myra can see her reflection in the chrome of the gas pump. Standing beside this impressive, sturdy woman, she looks like a stuffed doll.

"Going through treatments?" Officer Hudock says.

"I just completed chemo," Myra says. "My third cycle. Hopefully the final one."

"My dad went through it," the policewoman says, removing her sunglasses. "Pancreatic. Fortunately they caught it early. Still, some days he was so weak he could barely sit upright. But he's strong as a bull again."

"Glad to hear it," Myra says.

"I'm Noel," the officer says.

"Nice to meet you. I'm Myra."

Noel finishes filling up Myra's rental, then sets the nozzle on the pump's cradle. "Is there anything else I can help you with today?" she asks.

Myra tries to swallow. Through her cottonmouth she says, "There is, actually." And she begins telling Noel about the young boy who just robbed her, not even twenty minutes ago. She'd given him a ride to the mall, trying to be nice, because he'd looked so desperate and alone walking along the road, and then he asked her for money. As she was going into her purse to give him some change, he snatched a ten-dollar bill out of her wallet. It was only ten dollars, she acknowledged, but because of her condition she hasn't been able to work these past few months. "Right now every dollar counts," she finishes.

"Did the boy give you his name?" Noel says.

"Lake," Myra says.

"That's gotta be Lake Lakota," Noel says. "We've had similar problems with him in the past."

"We were parked in front of the mall when he took my money," Myra says. "During the drive over he told me he was going to go there to play video games."

"I'm sure he's still there," Noel says. "Would you like to press charges?"

"I don't want to ruin the kid's life."

"You'd be doing him a favor, trust me," Noel says. "We've given him more breaks than you can count. Just last month he broke into this old lady's home. She caught him red-handed stealing her DVD player."

"Why didn't she press charges?"

"Beats me," Noel says. "Maybe she felt sorry for him because he's a Native boy. His mother is a complete mess and he has no father. His home life isn't good. But maybe consequences would do him some good."

"If you were to go arrest him what would happen?"

"Technically, he mugged you, which is a serious crime," Noel says. "I don't think the DA has much sympathy left for this kid. He'd probably get sent to juvie over in Bentonville until his arraignment."

"Is it a good place?" Myra asks.

"From my experience it's one of the best facilities in the state," Noel assures her.

* * *

AFTER NOEL FILLS UP her police cruiser, Myra gets in her Escort and follows her back to the mall.

Ten minutes later, Noel, along with two male security guards wearing yellow windbreakers, is walking Lake Lakota out of the mall's main entrance and toward Myra's car. His hands have been zip-tied behind his back.

Myra gets out of her car, and Noel and the two security guards walk the boy over to her. There's an abrasion on his right cheek, suggesting a struggle. Myra imagines his face being driven into the carpeting of the video game arcade, adult knees boring into the flesh between his shoulder blades.

"Is this him?" Noel asks.

The boy won't look at her.

"Look at her," one of the security guards orders him.

He does so.

"That's definitely him," Myra says.

The boy spits harshly onto the pavement.

"Hey!" one of the security guards barks, then jerks the boy's wrists to make him stand up straight.

"Lying bitch," the boy hisses at Myra.

The two security guards jerk him sharply upward again and then Noel begins reading him his Miranda rights as she signals to the other two to walk him over to her police cruiser. After she secures him in the caged backseat, she locks the door and returns to Myra.

"You're doing the right thing," she says. "That kid might finally get his life together."

"I hope so," Myra says.

"Good luck with your recovery," Noel says, offering her a ten-dollar bill.

Myra never saw the money materialize. Is it the same bill she gave Lake? No, he would've spent it on the arcade game. Is it Noel's money? Myra accepts it without comment, crumpling it in her right hand.

Noel heads back to her car, where she thanks the two security guards and gets in on the driver's side. Moments later her siren squawks once, her revolving lights flash on, and she pulls out of the parking lot with the boy's figure silhouetted in the caged backseat of her cruiser.

LATER, AS MYRA DRIVES along a winding, rural stretch of road in search of a motel, a deer runs out in front of her car. She is driving well below the speed limit, but she can't stop in time and rams through the animal. Given the compact size of her rental car, she would have expected the impact to be more substantial, but it felt as though she had struck merely a half-empty suitcase or a bag of groceries. In her rearview mirror she can see the animal oddly contorted in the center of the road.

She pulls the car over and gets out. The front of the Escort is badly dented, with bits of fur clinging to a corner of the Arkansas license plate. One of her headlights is broken. She walks back fifty yards or so to the deer, whose neck is broken. In fact, half of it is severed, Myra sees, and blood is pooling around it on the pavement. Only now does she realize the deer is just a fawn, its coat still dappled with white spots. She looks around for the mother. There are woods on both sides of the road but no sign of the doe. Myra feels a terrible sadness, the purest absence of joy, as if someone has reached inside her chest and wrung all the blood from her heart. At least the young deer didn't suffer.

Is this some sort of punishment for lying about Lake? she wonders. Was that infraction worth this level of retribution? After all, she was trying to protect the boy. But her God has always been a retaliatory one. He has taken her husband's mind, her health, and so much of her happiness. He even took her baby brother in his infancy. He's always been ruthless. Why would anything change now?

She grabs the fawn by its rear hooves and pulls it over to the shoulder. Her legs feel feeble, as if all the chemotherapy has cooked the muscle away. The little deer seems impossibly heavy for its size but she's determined to get the animal off the road. It feels like the animal has been stuffed with lead. She is lucky that no other cars are approaching. As she drags it toward the shoulder, its blood marks their path. The heat rising from the young animal's body is unfathomable. Myra wishes she had something to cover it with. She always keeps blankets in the rear of her car up in Vermont, but the rental won't have anything in the trunk. The crows will no doubt have their way with the poor thing.

After she finally gets the fawn off the road, she has to go to a knee and nearly collapses on top of the animal. It takes almost all her strength to stand. She feels cored out. Her car, just across the road, might as well be a mile away.

Later, when she gets to her motel room, she'll take a cool shower and call her mother back in Elmira and tell her that Alec has a job as a groundskeeper at a nice Catholic church, that he lives in an upstanding residential motel. She will say that they had a pleasant lunch—that he even offered to pay for it, but that they wound up splitting the bill.

She will tell her mother that he's missing a tooth and has gone mostly gray but is still handsome and his health is good. The postcards, he claims, are just a mean joke. She will not tell Ava Larkin about the boy. There is no sense in breaking her mother's heart.

14

LONDON, ENGLAND
JULY 27, 1998

RONAN

HIS AGENT WARNED HIM about the dreary weather but Ronan had no idea that it would rain so much in London. It's the final Saturday of July and it feels as if it hasn't stopped the entire month. This has been Ronan's first trip abroad and it's a far cry from Hemingway's colorful Pamplona or what he imagined from James Salter's Autun, France, in *A Sport and a Pastime*. He's already bought and lost three different umbrellas this month, and as he jogs along the storefronts of Goldhawk Road toward the Bush, the theater company producing the world premiere of his new play, *Near*, he determines to invest in a decent raincoat with a hood. He would never lose a raincoat—it's too cumbersome—whereas if he could account for all the umbrellas he's lost since he moved to New York City seven years ago it would probably equal a month's rent.

He's just come from a liquor store, where he purchased two bottles of Jack Daniel's for Anton and Reese, the two American actors starring in his play. Conveniently, the store is only a block away from the apartment that the Bush is renting for him, on the corner of Goldhawk and Hammersmith Grove. The tidy studio has a Murphy bed, a portable washer-dryer machine which he has yet to figure out, and a cockpit-style bathroom so small that his knees are practically in his mouth every time he sits on the toilet.

At the liquor store he'd asked for Maker's Mark, but the hard-of-hearing proprietor could only offer him Jack Daniel's, a Tennessee whiskey rather than the classic Kentucky bourbon that is drunk in his play. The proprietor didn't see the difference between them. "As long as it gets you pissed," he told Ronan.

Opening night—or "press night," as it's known in London—is tomorrow, Sunday. Ronan's already gotten a gift for the director, Harold Hull, the brilliant, beloved, Falstaffian leader of the Bush, of whom Ronan has grown incredibly fond. In addition to witnessing Harold expertly guide *Near* through the rehearsal process, Ronan has also drunk many glasses of red wine and pints of stout with him at O'Neill's, the street-level pub one story below the Bush, where, following each rehearsal and preview performance, Harold holds court in his favorite corner booth, presiding over the cast and crew. The conversation, always conducted by Harold, swerves entertainingly from American politics to punk rock to what constitutes a good English "trifle" to what minor London celebrity might have been spotted in the eighty-seat theater that night.

Harold, fifty-six, a former carnival barker (and Eaton alum), is a beast of a man. He is 6'4", weighs over 300 pounds (22 stones), and possesses the largest hands Ronan's ever seen. A survivor of two minor heart attacks, he had a pacemaker installed in his chest three weeks before his fiftieth birthday. In addition to his heart condition he suffers from gout and is currently enduring a tenacious flare-up (big toe), thus the walking cane, which looks like a conductor's baton impossibly supporting the listing, limping form of a giant. And then there's the psoriasis riddling his hands, cheeks, neck, and forehead. And yet with all of these afflictions there is still the sense that Harold Hull will outlive half of England.

Whenever he drinks, which is every night, things often turn ugly, usually after his third merlot, at which point his speech begins to break down and he winds up unleashing a random but extremely nasty remark aimed at one undeserving member of the party. The other night he told Anton that although he was a pretty solid actor he was mostly a lazy twat who relied on his poor man's Hollywood charm, blond Beach Boys look, and rarely made his scenes about anyone but himself. Two nights before that he'd told Reese, a petite but feisty girl with long curly auburn hair and intense green eyes, that she was too worried about her perfect drama school diction to ever really live in the actual circumstances of her character, and that she might be better off focusing her career on shilling commercials for cashmere holiday jumpers on American telly. (She cried.) That same evening, to Muriel, his assistant director, who clearly loves him like a father, he slurred bitterly that she was too posh to ever make anything of any consequence. (She also cried.) And then he called his longtime stage manager, Ian, a kind bald man in his early forties, "a humongous cucumber with ears" and said he was so sexually undefinable that he might as well belong to a giant species of useless gourd, suggesting he drop his trousers to prove to the table that he'd been assigned a proper pair of testicles.

These cruel attacks seem to come out of nowhere, at which point Ian will nod at Dawn, a recent drama school graduate and intern, who will produce the company petty-cash envelope, remove a ten-pound note, and hand it to Ian, who will pass it to Harold under the table for taxi fare, a gentle cue to wrap things up. The night often ends shortly thereafter, and Harold always shows up the following day apoplectic at himself, bearing a sincere apology to the entire company and a bottle of expensive French wine for whomever he can remember abusing.

So far the only person who's been spared one his drunken attacks is Ronan.

Harold is married to Katja, a Dutch writer and former actress who is as beautiful as she is deeply in love with her troubled giant of a husband. Ronan first met her when he and Anton accompanied Harold in the taxi to their home in Notting Hill. Harold was so shit-faced that they feared he wouldn't make it from the taxi to his front door. Katja greeted them at the gate as Ronan and Anton helped her staggering husband across their bluestone path, up the three steps, through the front door, and into his three-story, Portland Road home. As they negotiated Harold through the foyer and deposited him onto his living room sofa, he garbled various declarations, one of which was his intention to somehow contract an incurable virus, moonwalk into Parliament, and "gob" on Prime Minister John Major. Once on the sofa he quickly passed out and broke into a long, comical symphony of snoring.

Katja, who had already prepared a pot of tea, implored Ronan and Anton to stay, exiting to the kitchen and returning with an entire tray of cheeses and salamis. At first Ronan couldn't tell if she was starved for attention or simply desperate to have a buffer around in case Harold woke up angry, but he and Anton parked themselves in armchairs and kept her company, touched by the late-night generosity and impressed by the patience she exhibited in the face of her gruesomely drunk husband, who was now unconscious on the sofa, his barrel chest rising and falling like some volcanic island on the verge of an eruption. Katja laughed at each of his inebriated snorts and grunts, and it seemed this must be the crux of their love story: Harold was the brilliant artist who fell tragically into nightly alcoholic stupors, and Katja was the dutiful wife who was always there to clean up his messes and help him get sober and back on his gout-riddled feet.

But that night Ronan learned that Katja was a successful, award-winning playwright and translator whose celebrated adaptation of Strindberg's *Miss Julie* had recently been produced at the Donmar Warehouse (a bigger theater than the Bush). In the early phase of her career she'd worked solely as an actor, often at the Royal Shakespeare Company, which is where she met Harold, who directed her in a production of *Midsummer*. They would soon fall in love ("Harold looked like a young Terence Stamp back then," Katja told them) and form their own theater company, Midnight Corpus, whose mission was leaving Shakespeare and the classics behind in favor of new plays concerned with the modern world. Working out of a small theater in the back of a pub in Islington, they collaborated on over twenty original projects. Katja wrote and Harold directed, often to great critical acclaim, and they even switched roles a few times. Eventually, through the help of public funding and robust ticket sales, they were able to employ a small company of actors—eight in total—who were incredibly dedicated to what became known as "MC." Several Midnight Corpus members went on to have impressive film and television careers.

As first impressions go, Harold and Katja seem to be enacting the kind of creative and romantic relationship—aside from Harold's drunken stupors—that Ronan wishes he could have with Henny. Theirs has been increasingly maligned by an unspoken competitiveness, especially recently. Early on, Henny was well ahead of Ronan when it came to productions logged and awards won. He learned so much watching her navigate the exciting turns in her career that for a while their disparity in success was a comfort to him. But as he found his own footing, and experienced a handful of successful world premieres, things grew more even. During the past year they have found themselves in uncharted waters, as their productions have pulled them to different cities for months at a time. The last time they were together—six days at the beginning of June—was troubled. Something between them seemed to have atrophied. Their smallest rituals felt mechanical. Conversations during meals were halting, if not chilly. There was a lunch at their favorite East Village spot, Cafe Mogador, during which they said hardly a word to each other.

During those six days they slept together only one time and on the morning Ronan left for London, he woke to a note on Henny's kitchen table:

> *I went for a walk.*
> *Have a good trip.*

She didn't even sign her name.

They've only spoken twice since he's been in London. International phone cards are expensive and the handful of booths in the little Internet café near his apartment are almost always full.

Henny is currently at the National Playwrights Conference at the Eugene O'Neill Theater Center, in Waterford, Connecticut, where she is workshopping her new play. Over drinks last week, Harold cautioned Ronan about dating another writer. Two playwrights dating each other, Harold said, was the equivalent of two infected creatures fighting for the sole available dose of a vaccine. According to Harold, the one time he and Katja tried writing plays simultaneously it almost ruined their relationship. Things always went much more smoothly when she was the playwright and he was the director. He warned Ronan that he was better off falling in love with a ficus tree than a fellow playwright.

"But you can't have sex with a ficus tree," Ronan countered.

"Cut a fucking hole in it and stuff it full of oysters!" Harold cried.

Ronan appreciates Harold's bawdy humor, his stark honesty, his disdain for anything remotely fashionable. But most of all he appreciates Harold's deep feelings for his play that's about to open. At its heart, *Near* is the simplest of love stories: two lost souls—a Gulf War veteran, Briggs, and a young Midwestern runaway, Birdie, find each other on the mean streets of New York. They wind up squatting together in a condemned building on the Lower East Side. They tolerate each other for a while. At the brink of their splitting up, Birdie finds out that she is very sick, and Briggs, who has his own medical and psychological problems, nevertheless winds up caring for her until the final blackout. The play is really just two people stuck in a room and one of them having a hard time leaving. Ronan took the title from a Tom Waits lyric, "But I'd trade off everything just to have you near," from a song called "Saving All My Love for You," the third track on his album *Heart Attack and Vine*.

Seeing Harold bring his play to life and coax Anton and Reese toward their brave, touching performances has been an incredibly inspiring experience for Ronan. Because there are so few available seats at the Bush, Harold makes a habit of viewing the play from the hollowed space underneath the audience risers. On more than one occasion Ronan has spied him weeping as the stage lights were fading to black.

For press night Ronan has bought Harold a hat. He purchased the whiskey-colored Brisbane fedora two days ago from Bates, a hatters shop on Jermyn Street, near Piccadilly Circus. It's an exact

replica of the one Harold currently wears, which is stained and losing its form. The hat cost nearly two hundred pounds, the most money Ronan has ever spent on anyone besides Henny, but he truly loves this man and believes that the hat is worth every penny. Muriel, the assistant director, joined him on his quest to find it; the hat had been her idea, after all. It was day one of tech rehearsals and Harold had given everyone the morning off so that the crew could get the set installed. Ronan and Muriel took the tube to Piccadilly Circus and spent the afternoon dodging the rain and dipping in and out of the various shops. After finding Harold's gift they grabbed lunch at an Indian restaurant on Regent Street.

Muriel, twenty-four, is wickedly funny and speaks with a "highborn" accent that Ronan is familiar with from watching videos of Noel Coward plays at Lincoln Center's theater performance library. Muriel studied acting at the Royal Academy of Dramatic Art, but is now determined only to direct plays, not to act in them, as she finds the life of an actor to be a series of demeaning misadventures. She told him all of this over lunch at the Indian restaurant where Ronan enjoyed his first chicken korma. Muriel also happens to very pretty, with dirty-blond hair, deep brown eyes, and slightly imperfect, perfectly crooked teeth. According to Harold, she is the daughter of an English lord. In the rehearsal room Ronan keeps finding himself inching his chair closer and closer to hers.

Now, arriving at last at the Bush, Ronan hands off the bottles of Jack Daniel's to Ian, the stage manager, with instructions to set them in the actors' dressing rooms before tomorrow's half-hour, and asks Ian to print out an e-mail from his aunt Lexy that he received this morning. Then he heads down to O'Neill's. Per usual, the late-afternoon crowd is sparse, with the spot at the end of the bar occupied as it is every day by an old man, easily an octogenarian, sitting in what appears to be a thin golf cart. Ronan has seen him drive this cart in through the French doors at the back of the pub and park at the end of the bar, where he'll order two double scotches and sip them at such a slow pace it's always a surprise when he finally orders another round.

From his pocket Ronan removes the printed email from his aunt Lexy and spreads it on the bar. It reads:

> *Ronan, Your mom is back in the hospital. There was a rupture in her colon. She's in stable condition after surgery and your Grandmother and Uncle Barry and I are with her in Montpelier. No need to come home. Dr. Anthony assures us that the surgery was successful. Just wanted to let you know. Hope all is going well in London.*
>
> *Love,*
> *Aunt Lexy*

The bartender sets his pint of Guinness before him. Ronan takes a long drink. And then another.

The thought of his mother going through yet another health scare while he's across the Atlantic makes him feel helpless, guilty, like a useless son. Was the rupture in the middle of the night, like the last time? Was she gardening? Walking up the steps of her front porch? Refilling one of the hummingbird feeders? He considers getting on a plane, but with his play about to open, he consoles himself that Aunt Lexy, Uncle Barry, and Grandma Ava are there. Other than emotional support, he reasons, there's probably not much more he could contribute.

The truth is, Ronan still hasn't told anyone in London about his mother's illness; he figures it would just be a distraction, and he'd felt confident about coming to London. His mother had been doing well since her last round of treatments, a year ago, and he'd been checking in with her at least twice a week. She insisted that he go to London and take part in the rehearsal process leading up to the world premiere of his play. Nevertheless, the dread of her illness has eaten away at him. He hasn't been sleeping much. At first he chalked it up to jetlag, but since that period has passed, he's still only been able to manage a few hours of sleep a night and has developed dark circles under his eyes.

From the bartender he orders another pint. At barely past 4:00 p.m., it's a little early to be drinking consecutive Guinesses, but he needs it. After a long pour the bartender slides a fresh pint in front of Ronan.

Behind him he hears, "Save some for the punters."

He turns to find Muriel at his right shoulder. Her hair is wet from the rain. She wears a jean jacket over a white Joy Division T-shirt with faded black lettering. Her brown eyes, kind and round, belie her cutting wit.

"Knockin' back the Guinness already," she says.

"Apparently there's more fortified vitamins and minerals in this stout," Ronan says, "than in most breakfast cereals." He takes a gulp for good measure and licks the froth from his upper lip.

Muriel continues to stand at his shoulder, strands of wet hair plastered to the sides of her face. "You okay?" she says. "You look like your favorite team just bungled the cup."

"I'm fine," he says. "But I think the rain has finally affected my mood."

"It does keep pissing down, doesn't it?"

"Are you watching the play?"

"Of course," she says, seizing his Guinness and helping herself to a gulp. "Taking notes for Harold. He's actually sitting in the audience tonight. Last chance to fix anything before the real bastards come."

"The real bastards meaning the critics."

"The realest bastards of them all," she says, setting the glass down. "That fat fuck from the *Evening Standard*'s sure to be there. Plath de Jong. Sits right up front, always takes his shirt off, makes it all about him."

"He really takes his shirt off?"

"It's his not-so-subtle way of protesting about the temperature. Harold turns the air off as the houselights are fading so the audience can hear the actors. The chap is a decent writer but he hates everything. But don't worry, others will gush. They'll see your doomed characters as victims of the American class system and applaud your blistering critique of a government that forgets its veterans and lost daughters."

"Harold told me the reviews don't matter so much here."

"Oh, they matter," she says. "It isn't like New York, where it's the fucking *Times* or fuck all. Does Ronan read his notices?"

"He does."

"And if they're bad he can't get out of bed, he starts thinking about shoving his head in the oven?"

"They've never been *that* bad," he says.

"And if they're good?"

"Pizza parties and primal screams."

"That sounds like the title of a bad rock-'n'-roll memoir."

Ronan laughs and drinks. "In New York good reviews mean more life for the play, which means more money for the playwright."

"And more pints of Guinness for *friends* of the playwright," she says, again seizing his pint and quaffing. "As far as fat fuck de Jong goes, you must wear his hateful notice like a badge of honor." She sets the pint glass back on the bar.

"I'll rip it out of the paper and shape it into a perfect bowtie," he says.

"By the way," she says, "I wrapped Harold's gift. He's going to love the hat." And with that she heads for the staircase, promising to see him afterward and buy the first pint.

RONAN SPENDS THE FIRST act of the play in the green room. His dialogue transmits over the tinny, archaic PA speaker as if the play is being broadcast from a distant planet.

Anton and Reese sound like they're in the pocket, digging into the moments without indulging in pauses, which is one of Harold's pet peeves. He can't stand actors who want you to see their work, who mug for the audience. He can't tolerate actors who are unwilling to keep secrets.

One of Ronan's favorite things about the Bush is that, whether before the play or during the intermission, you can take your drink from the bar up to your seat in the theater. He also loves their over-stuffed plaid loveseat in the green room. If he folds his long legs just so he can get pretty comfortable. He fades while staring at the foamy dregs at the bottom of his third pint.

"It went well, it really did," Harold says as Ronan brings him a glass of the house red.

Harold is wedged into the corner of his usual booth, next to Muriel, already holding court. Ronan is clutching a pair of lagers, one for himself and one for Muriel, beside whom he slides in, handing her her Grolsch. Opposite Harold sit Ian and Dawn, each with a pint of Guinness. Anton and Reese have begged off, perhaps with a desire to preserve themselves for press night.

"Cheers everyone," Harold declares, holding up his wine. "To tomorrow."

"To press night," the others say.

"Fuck 'em all in their miserable hearts!" Harold adds.

And they all say "Cheers," clink their glasses, and drink.

"It sounded good from the green room," Ronan says, and asks Harold if he was pleased with the performances.

"He wept again," Muriel says. "Admit it, you wept like a baby."

"Well, they *moved* me," Harold says. "And our playwright's gob-smacking *play* moves me." He turns to Ronan. "And this is my last wine, by the way, so don't you dare bring me another. Whatever they're pouring tonight is shite anyway."

The pub is nearly full, as it usually is after the play. Following the curtain call most of the audience comes straight down and orders a drink. Ronan likes to eavesdrop on their conversations. Unlike New York, there are no photographs of the playwright anywhere on the premises, and they have no idea he's the author. He loves how the anonymity allows him to spy. While he was waiting for Harold's glass of wine he overheard an older woman at the bar say that the play was "quite good for American fare."

Ronan drinks his Grolsch, so close to Muriel that he can smell her sweat mingling with her deodorant. He's on his fourth beer since the intermission and hasn't eaten anything in hours. He should order food from the bar. One of their hamburgers, with its strange, Spam-like consistency. Or the blood pudding and whipped potatoes. There's also a fish-'n'-chips shop on the other side of the Shepherd's Bush Green.

Harold begins cataloging some of the VIPs who are expected tomorrow night, a list that in addition to some thirty critics (Plath de Jong among them) includes several members of his old theater company and a well-known Australian rock star. And just like that, he's finished his glass of wine. Ian nods to Dawn and she starts to get up, no doubt to head to the bar for a replenishment.

"Don't you dare," Harold tells her, and she freezes. "As I said earlier, this is my only one tonight. Tomorrow I'll be so drunk I won't even need my cane. Ian, help me into a taxi."

Dawn and Ian rise and Harold budges his girth across the booth and uses his cane to straighten himself. His gout flare-up is obviously getting the better of him, and as he makes his way toward the exit he appears too preoccupied with his throbbing toe to offer a proper farewell. Dawn passes a ten-pound note from her petty-cash envelope to Ian, who follows in the director's wake.

Twenty minutes later Ronan and Muriel are about to enter her apartment in Notting Hill. During the cab ride he found himself staring at her pale, open, pretty face when she leaned in for a kiss, which was deep, perfect. It was the first time in five years that Ronan had tasted another woman's lips and he felt an immediate pang of guilt that almost kept him rooted in the taxi when Muriel emerged. He even asked the driver to keep the meter running. But Muriel paid the fare and tugged at his wrist and he was dislodged without fanfare.

"Hot as Morocco in here," Muriel says, leading Ronan through the dark of her warm apartment, which smells of black tea and oranges. She opens a window. The air brings the scent of ozone into the room, a trace of car exhaust.

Moments later they are standing before each other in what he assumes to be her bedroom, where she sheds her jean jacket, her Joy Division T-shirt, and then her bra. Her breasts are fuller than he expected, her nipples pale and erect. They kiss again and her hand goes to his groin. He is already hard. Shame hasn't had the slightest effect whatsoever. Even in the dark, Ronan notices the soft well of her collarbone, two small moles along length of her neck. As he moves to kiss her again, Muriel untucks his shirt—a white, slightly threadbare Oxford, unbuttons it, and lifts it over his head. The cool air from the window grazes the warmth of their conjoined torsos. The rest of their clothes come off as they head for her large four-poster bed. Ronan hangs his jeans from one of the bed knobs. There is no discussion about what they might do, how they might protect themselves. It happens smoothly, effortlessly. Muriel begins with her hand and then uses her mouth and then pushes Ronan back onto the mattress, mounts him, and guides him inside her. She feels so different from Henny, somehow more lush, and she's freer with her body. As he starts to tense she tells him that it's okay if he wants to come inside her, that she's on the pill. When he comes it feels like lightning surging through his calves and hamstrings, as if he's being delicately electrocuted. It feels so primal, so certain. He stays hard, continuing on, and when Muriel orgasms, her hands swim out in front of her like a blind woman who's walked into a cloud of bees. Her voice is high and she loses control of her body and falls on top of Ronan as if she's been knifed. They hold each other, panting, sweaty.

Muriel is fuller than Henny. Ronan loves the softness of her middle, the warmth of her face on his neck. He is most surprised by the lack of guilt he feels—how easy it was, like hopping over a puddle.

"Was that okay?" Muriel asks.

Ronan nods. He finds that he can't speak.

Rain simmers on the window.

"If you need the loo, it's down the hall on your left."

He nods again and gets out of bed, slips into his underwear and jeans.

Muriel's bathroom is clean and spare. Seafoam-green tiles. A little basket of sculpted soaps: lavender and baby-blue turtles and geese. This seems odd for Muriel. Post-punk concert T-shirts and old-lady soaps. But the English are a strange sect; you never can quite pin any of them down. Who would've ever guessed Harold's house to be so beautifully furnished with its antiques and colorful rugs? When Ronan drops his pants to piss he is suddenly so light-headed he has to lower the toilet seat and sit. He is drunk, dehy-drated. Their sex is fragrant, rising up from between his legs. He hasn't pissed sitting down since he was a child and it makes him feel enfeebled, cowardly.

After washing his hands he stands in front of the mirror with his fists on the cold porcelain basin. For the briefest moment, like some beleaguered, shaggy, sleep-deprived detective in a '70s film, he believes himself to be doomed by some wrongness deep within him. It is microscopic, almost untraceable. An invisible protein eating away at the filament of goodness that binds his heart to his groin. His pale body, less muscular than it was only a few years ago, has been softened by moral weakness. He just had sex with the assistant director of his new play when he's supposedly in a commit-ted relationship with a woman he loves.

There is a knock on the door.

"Everything okay in there?"

"I'll be out in a second," he tells her.

"I'm just making some tea," she says.

After retrieving his shirt from the bedroom Ronan heads out to the kitchen, where Muriel is heating a kettle. She's wearing a silk robe now, pale blue, patterned with blackbirds, open in the front, revealing her soft brown thatch. How quickly she's shed her tom-boy persona.

"You're fully dressed," she says, removing biscuits from a box of Walkers shortbreads and setting them on a small wooden tray. "Was it that bad?"

"It wasn't bad at all," he says, buttoning his shirt. "In fact it was just the opposite."

Ronan sits at her small white circular kitchen table, whose resin surface is smooth, unblemished. Muriel sits on the counter, the kettle warming beside her on the stovetop.

"But your shame and guilt drove you back into your jeans," she says.

The kettle whistles and Muriel reaches over, kills the flame, and hops down from the counter. She pours the boiling water into mugs of PG Tips, sets them on the tray, and brings it over to the table. Her calves are muscular, powerful. She really is lovely. She turns and opens a cupboard, retrieves a bottle of honey; from her refrigerator, a small carton of milk.

"Is this the first time you've cheated?" she asks.

"Yes," Ronan replies.

"How does it feel?"

"Part of me feels terrible."

"And what about the other parts?"

"The other parts want to go back to bed with you as soon as we finish this tea."

"Henny, right?" Muriel says.

"Yeah, Henny," he says, and just saying her name makes him feel like something is wedged between his molars.

"Are you still in love with her?"

"Lately there's been this drift," he says. "This sense that…" But he trails off, can't finish the thought.

"That what?" she says.

"That we might not last or make it or however you want to put it."

"How long have you been together?" she asks.

"Five years."

"Anton told me she's quite the playwright."

"She is," he says. "And she's directing her own work now, too."

"I s'pose she also hangs her own lights. Does a crack sound design."

"She probably could," he says.

"Does it get competitive between you two?"

"Not really," he says. "But success is more recent for me. I've been lagging behind her for most of our relationship."

"All of that's about to change," she says.

"You think?"

"This play of yours is going to absolutely floor people."

Ronan spoons honey into his tea, adds a splash of milk as he's witnessed Harold do during rehearsal breaks. "She has more courage," he says, stirring. "With her writing."

"I happen to think *Near* is pretty fucking courageous," Muriel says, biting into a shortbread biscuit. When she chews she reveals the slightest overbite. He loves her mouth, its childishness, its surprising fullness.

"In New York," he says, "there's this word that the critics like to use when they're impressed with a playwright: *Unflinching*. Henny is the epitome of unflinching."

"Cool as a cucumber," Muriel says.

"She doesn't give a shit what anyone thinks about her work."

"And you do?"

"I sometimes feel that I'm desperate to succeed. That I'm too concerned with being liked."

"Henny sounds very impressive."

"She comes from money," Ronan says, surprising himself.

Since he and Henny have been together he's kept this to himself. A provocative mixed-race playwright whose work deals with social-justice issues has no right to be rich, after all, at least in the eyes of the world. Very few people know about Henny's trust fund, her famous painter father and fancy apartment, or the fact that she grew up in an insulated, affluent part of northwest Connecticut. It's the major reason why she refuses to do interviews. Ronan is convinced that her agent tells others in the industry that Henny is from Harlem or the Bronx.

"Her father is a successful painter," Ronan continues. "She makes money on commissions and productions but she lives off the interest from a trust fund and she lives well. We eat at nice restaurants. I get fancy Christmas presents."

"So she can *afford* to care less," Muriel says. "I have to admit I can relate."

He tells her what Harold had shared with him—about her being the daughter of an English lord. "It's true," she says. "My family owns a bunch of land near Devonshire. In many ways my life is set."

"So why do theater?"

"Because it scares the shit out of me," she says. "Because I get to hang out with people like Harold Hull, who, like your girlfriend, doesn't give a crap about what people think."

"I'm pretty sure Harold is my hero," Ronan says.

"Just being around him has taught me so much. Not just about blocking and tablework and how to get through tech, but about how to take a risk, how to be more fearless about failure, how to create the kind of work that makes the audience forget what tube stop they came out of."

"Is your father okay with you working in theater?"

"I think he'd prefer that I marry a suitable man with a good parcel of land and a proper inheritance. Start a family and all that fairytale stuff, but that's not going to happen. At least not for a while, anyway."

They drink their tea. Muriel twists in her chair and opens the kitchen window wider. The clean smell of rain slips across the table. Ronan loves how effortlessly she arranges herself in flattering positions. The former actress still knows how to hold an audience.

Muriel catches him staring at her. "Don't worry," she says, "I'm not expecting anything." She drinks, sets her mug down.

"Are you in a relationship?" he asks.

"I am. In fact he should be coming through the door with his cricket bat at any moment," she says with a smile. "No, I'm currently unattached," she adds.

"If I wasn't with Henny…"

"You'd what, smuggle me back to New York in your suitcase? Profess your love for me on the Staten Island Ferry? Take me up to the top of the Chrysler Building for a mug of hot cocoa?"

Ronan doesn't respond.

"When you say her name it makes you more handsome," she says. "You must stop that. Shall we go back to bed?"

Ronan can feel his hands starting to shake. The spoon he's been holding clatters on the tabletop.

Muriel takes his left hand in both of hers. "You're trembling," she says.

"I haven't had much to eat. It's probably my blood sugar." He tells her about his track-and-field days, how the workouts were so intense that he'd lose his appetite and later his blood sugar would plummet and he'd break into a cold sweat and wind up shoving fingerfuls of peanut butter into his mouth.

Muriel sets the box of Walkers shortbreads before him. Ronan ravenously eats the remaining four biscuits. He hasn't felt this hungry in as long as he can remember. So much for the concept of Guinness as meal replacement.

After Ronan polishes off the Walkers they go back to bed. Once again Ronan sheds his clothes and they are fucking in what seems like less than a minute. She feels so good, so soft and silky, like rich, warmed velvet. He comes inside her again. They both spasm and Muriel cries out, clutching a bed knob. She asks him to stay inside her. He does so until he goes limp. They fall asleep folded into each other, the rainy air sliding over their damp bodies.

Ronan's sleep is fitful and brief, as if he's fallen asleep standing in the entryway of a building. He wakes to the various shapes in her room, which he didn't even notice before. There are clusters of laundry, a marble-topped cluttered vanity with a round mirror, stacks of books and playscripts forming a skyline along one wall, above which hangs a framed show poster of Pinter's *The Homecoming* that features an elderly man in a white smock sharpening a long knife over a butcher's counter. On her chest of drawers: withered orange peels, a constellation of English coins whose various thicknesses seem somehow counterfeit, a canvas tote from Rough Trade Records, and, beside it, Harold's gift, the hat box wrapped in decorative red paper.

Muriel continues sleeping deeply, calmly, so serenely it's as if she isn't even breathing. She really is beautiful. And smart. And funny. But what the fuck is he doing here? He's always been judgmental of undisciplined men. All those narcissistic male actors who cheat on their girlfriends. Fellow male playwrights who get hammered with their cast after the show and wind up going home with the ambitious young actress or the quirky assistant costume designer.

Cars pass by on the street below. A drunk belts some English Premier League team's victory anthem—is it Arsenal's?—the words sloshing around his mouth.

Ronan feels far away from himself, as if there is a canyon in the room. He is on one side of the rim and another version of him is on the other, turned away, in shadow. He is like a child who has woken up in an unknown house after falling asleep during a long car ride. Muriel's clothes are strewn everywhere: jeans and T-shirts and skirts, bras and panties, hoodies and mismatched tennis shoes. With great clarity, Ronan suddenly understands that the attrition of life, with the slow erosion of all of its tiny connective tissues (love, comfort, sex), eventually leads to a place where the simple arrangement of garments loses its importance and one's bedroom becomes a chamber of chaos. Eventually these piles of things will block the entrance, take over the bed. The very room itself will be digested by all the things that should be placed in drawers and hung in closets.

His heart feels like it's spinning in his chest. And now his hands are shaking again. He dresses quietly, slides into his underwear and jeans, his running shoes. He doesn't want to wake Muriel. She sleeps like a sunbather, like she's spent half the day floating on the warm sea. Her back is so lovely, the knobs of her spine gently shaping her flesh. He grabs his shirt.

From the street, the odd two-note arrangement of an English police car dopplers by, fades.

Ronan counts to one hundred, hoping the numbers will calm him.

What the fuck is happening? Why are things racing in my head?

When he reaches one hundred he grants himself permission to

exit the room, shuts the door behind him. He puts his shirt on and heads down the hall.

When he enters Muriel's kitchen, Harold is there, seated at the round table. The psoriasis on his cheeks and neck seems to radiate through the darkness.

"Ronan," he says. He's not wearing shoes or socks and his gout-riddled feet look disfigured, troll-like.

"Harold," Ronan says. "What are you doing here?"

"I could ask you the same thing," he says. "Havin' a shag with my assistant?"

Ronan realizes that he isn't blinking. His eyes feel huge, dry, wooden. He has the keen sense that he might start falling back-wards through thousands of feet of ink-black space.

"You should grab on to the counter there," Harold says. "It'll help you stay in one spot."

Ronan does so, clutching the edge of the counter. "What time is it?" he asks.

"What time would you like it to be?" Harold says. "It doesn't really matter, does it? The bloody earth gyrates on its old rusty axis. The Thames still gurgles and thrashes about." He produces a silver flask. "Fancy a snort?" he says.

"I thought you weren't drinking any more tonight."

"Oh, come on, mate," Harold says. "Let's have a drink and a chin-wag."

"What are you doing here?" Ronan asks him again.

"I've come to deliver your instructions."

"Instructions?" Ronan says. "What instructions?"

Harold takes a swig form the flask, sets it on the table.

"Does Muriel know you're here?" Ronan asks.

"What do you think?" he says.

Is Harold cheating on Katja with Muriel? Is Muriel seducing every man in the company, crossing them off a list, one by one? Has she also fucked Anton? Ian? What about Dawn, or Reese? Is Muriel into women, too—just some indiscriminate nymphomaniac? Then again, what right does Ronan have to her? He's the one who's cheating.

Harold draws his hand over his beard and says, "So let's just get to those instructions, shall we?"

Ronan grips the counter even harder. And now there's a ringing in his ears, faint as a tuning fork, and a pressure forming in his chest.

"You need to take a knife out of that block over there," Harold says. "Choose carefully. I might suggest the serrated one, as it will give you more options."

"More options for what?" Ronan says.

"Well, you could easily stab her with that one, but you could also cut her throat. Scrambling her vocal cords will assure an optimal level of silence."

"You're saying I should do this to Muriel?"

"Those are your instructions, yes," Harold says.

"Instructions from who?" he asks.

Harold doesn't answer. The psoriatic whorls on his neck and cheeks have turned darker, bloody, scabrous. They are beginning to spiral. His toenails are like talons.

The pressure in Ronan's chest has intensified. It's like two heavy hands compressing his sternum. His breathing turns rapid, shallow. He can't quite get enough air. He swallows hard and asks what will happen if he follows the instructions.

"You shall find endless relief," Harold says.

"And if I don't?"

"Then there will be endless consequences."

The ringing in Ronan's ears has doubled. Two shrill tones now, like screws boring into his temples. Just breathe, he tells himself. Just breathe.

"Henny will be extremely pleased," Harold adds.

Ronan feels himself nodding. He crosses to the countertop, reaches for the block of knives, removes the serrated one, gripping the handle.

"Who are you talking to?"

Ronan turns. Muriel is standing there, in her silk robe, which is closed in the front this time.

Ronan looks to the table. Harold is no longer there.

What the fuck is going on?

"You were just talking to someone," Muriel says.

"But nobody's there," Ronan says.

"No, not that I can see."

"I guess I was talking to myself," he says.

Muriel's arms are crossed now. She looks suspicious, defensive. "Why are you holding that knife?" she says.

Ronan sets the knife on the counter. He knows he should slide it back into its designated slot in the butcher block but he fears that if he touches it again he might actually carry out Harold's instructions. It feels as if he is made of sand. He rubs his fingers together. Granules of his flesh crumble to the floor.

"Ronan," Muriel says.

He closes his eyes, opens them, thinking Harold will be at the table again. He's not. "I have to go," Ronan says. "I'm sorry."

He exits, leaving her front door open, and doesn't look back. He can hear his own footfalls echoing down the stairs. They sound incredibly heavy, monstrous.

On the street it's still raining. He jogs over to Portobello Road, where all the market stalls are closed, their gates pulled shut. He hails the first taxi he sees.

"Would you like the radio?" the driver asks.

Ronan can see the man looking at him in the rearview mirror, his eyes hard, vacant, reptilian. He shakes his head. He can't stop thinking about his right hand clutching that knife, the feeling of his fingertips crumbling to the floor.

Fifteen minutes later the taxi stops in front of his apartment building on the corner of Goldhawk Road and Hammersmith Grove. He pays the driver and exits the cab.

Standing in the cool air again is good. The spray of the rain helps him feel a little closer to the realm of what he knows to be normal. He crosses the street and enters his building. Once inside the foyer, he checks his mailbox. Inside is a flyer from the Bush advertising his play and an envelope whose return address bears the logo of the Eugene O'Neill Theater Center, in Waterford, Connecticut.

He opens the envelope. Inside is a letter. The familiar penmanship causes him to lose his balance and he reaches for the wall.

The letter reads:

Dear Ronan,

>*I'm pregnant.*
>*Sorry that this news had to come to you in the form of a letter but I didn't know how else to tell you. Somehow I couldn't do it in a phone call and I didn't want to wait.*
>*Waterford is lovely. I've been spending a lot of time at the beach, reading and thinking...My play isn't working. The rewriting process has been horrendous. My dramaturg is an eighty-year-old man who was a script doctor in Hollywood. We just don't click. I wish you were here. I think you could help me fix it.*
>*The food is terrible—it's worse than the cafeteria fare at Yale. But there is something about the foggy evenings that feels magical for a few hours every night. This is the part of the world that influenced so many of O'Neill's plays. Speaking of O'Neill, tomorrow we're supposed to go visit his family home, which is in New London. Apparently it's the house that's described in meticulous detail in Long Day's Journey, right down to the titles on the spines of books. It's supposed to be haunted. I hope I run into a ghost.*
>*I'm not sure I want to be a mother, Ronan. But I'm not sure I don't want to be one, either.*
>*Do you want to be a father?*
>*There's talk of a hurricane heading this way. It'll be my first tropical storm so wish me luck.*

By the time you receive this it's very likely that the crazy weather will have come and gone and your play will have opened. I hope it's a huge success. It's a beautiful play. The Bush is lucky to have it and you.

Break a leg.

Sending you all my love.
H

To Ronan's surprise, Reese enters the building, damp from the rain, pulling an umbrella behind her. "Fancy meeting you here," she says.

"Hey," Ronan says to her. He's still a bit stunned by the letter and at first can offer nothing more. "You're wearing normal clothes," he adds, after an awkward silence.

"I know," she says. "Hard to believe, right? All you ever see me in is Birdie's weird sweatpants."

"Don't forget her hoodies."

"And her excellent, extra-large hoodies," Reese allows. She tells him that she and Anton ended up coming by O'Neill's, after all, and that Ian and Dawn said that he and Harold and Muriel had left early.

"Sorry," Ronan says, "we thought you guys were skipping drinks. We all figured it was wise to make it an early night. Harold was the first to leave, believe it or not."

"He's clearly resting up for tomorrow," she says. "It's what I would be doing, too, if I could relax and fall asleep."

Ronan closes his eyes and sees Harold sitting at Muriel's kitchen table. His wounded face. His grotesque bare feet. He opens his eyes and asks Reese what time it is.

She looks at her watch and tells him that it's just after 2:00 a.m. "What are you doing up at this hour, anyway?" she says.

He tells her that he was out taking a walk. "Couldn't sleep, either," he adds, only a half-lie. "Nerves, I guess." For the slightest moment Ronan finds himself questioning whether or not Reese is really there.

"Tomorrow's a big day," she says, finally collapsing her umbrella, snapping it skinny above its curved handle. "Or I guess that would technically be today now."

"Press night," Ronan says.

Somehow the action with the umbrella has confirmed her presence. She can't be a figment.

"Press night," she echoes. "Everyone's really excited."

Ronan then proffers the letter from Henny and asks her to read it aloud to him. "My eyes have been bothering me," he lies, "and I can't quite make out the writing."

Reese takes the letter from him. "Would you prefer a mid-Atlantic accent?" she jokes. "It's rare that I get to show off my rigorous Carnegie Mellon conservatory training."

She begins reading the front of the envelope—the address and return address—with a crisp, mid-Atlantic accent, hitting all the consonants, her tongue playfully curving and extending the vowels, continuing on with the date and the salutation at the top of the actual letter, but the accent abruptly disappears when she gets to the first line, citing Henny's pregnancy.

Reese stops reading. "Jesus, Ronan," she says.

"Please keep going," he says.

"Are you sure?"

"Yes," he says. "I just want to make sure I'm not crazy."

Reese clears her throat, continues reading in her normal voice this time, recounting the part about Waterford's foggy evenings, the terrible food, the planned visit to Eugene O'Neill's family home, and the rest of it. When she's finished she hands him the letter.

He thanks her. He says that he really does have trouble making out Henny's handwriting. "She's left-handed," he adds, absurdly. "It has a funny slant."

"Are you okay?" she asks.

"I think so," he says. "It's just a lot to take in."

They stand there in silence.

"I should probably get some sleep," he eventually says.

"Well, if you need anything, don't hesitate to knock on my door," she says. "Seriously."

He nods and Reese says good night and heads up the stairwell with her umbrella.

Ronan remains in front of the mailboxes. He can feel his hand pressing into the wall. The fluorescent overhead light buzzes above him. The letter from Henny, with its incredible news, is in his other hand. Its actual weight is insubstantial but it might as well be an anvil.

Do you want to be a father?

After a while he pulls his hand off the wall, carefully refolds the letter, puts it back into its envelope, and ascends the stairs to the fourth floor, where he keys into his sparsely furnished apartment, unlatches the Murphy bed from the wall, lowers it to the floor, lies down, and falls into a deep, dreamless sleep.

15

WAITSFIELD, VERMONT
JANUARY 23, 2001

MYRA LEE

Fʀᴏᴍ ʜᴇʀ ꜰɪʀsᴛ-ꜰʟᴏᴏʀ ʙᴀᴛʜʀᴏᴏᴍ window, Myra adjusts the tube connected to her IV stand and looks out at her driveway, where Bogdan, the local Serbian man with a beard so prolific it's like something out of Melville, has just finished plowing. Three-foot drifts—ramparts, really—frame both sides of the thin strip of asphalt with a precision that verges on artistic intention. In the heaped snow Bogdan's enormous silver pickup truck with its candy-yellow plow looks like some intergalactic craft that could forge a path to the top of one of the nearby mountains and launch itself into the heavens. Bogdan really is an artist, angling his plow to spray pristine arcs of snow in whatever direction he so chooses. It's the final week of January. After all the brouhaha, George W. Bush is officially the new president. Myra's telephone is of the archaic, analog push-button variety. She still doesn't have Internet. Here in her house in northwestern Vermont it might as well be the '80s and she likes it this way.

When it snows this much—nearly a foot has fallen over the past three days—Myra knows to park her Toyota on the street in front of the house, which gives Bogdan access to the driveway. She was feeling too weak even to navigate the steps of the front porch, though, and so she had to ask Keith, her full-time live-in hospice nurse, to move the car to the street for her.

But two days ago, when her son pulled up to the house in his rental car, despite her acute fatigue Myra was sure to greet him from the front porch, not only to properly welcome him but also to warn him against parking in the driveway. Ronan duly beached his car on the other side of the street. When he emerged, shouldering his weekend bag, and crossed the street, Myra was a bit shocked at his general appearance. He had visited just before Christmas, but something had obviously taken hold in him even since then. At first she thought it was merely the long drive from New York that was affecting his usually pleasant temperament and spirit, but there was something in his eyes that suggested otherwise. He hadn't shaved. He needed a haircut. When they hugged he felt hollowed out, full of ache, like the world has started to get the better of him. And he didn't smell very nice.

"You're thin," she said as they entered the house.

"I weigh the same," was his curt reply.

In addition to his slightly haggard look, he also seemed more remote than usual, a little guarded and lost within himself, which hadn't been the case during any of their recent phone calls. Since the birth of her grandson, Bruce, Myra knows that things have been difficult for Ronan. He never had the example of a father to draw on—Denny had left when he was still so young—and he has confessed to her that he often feels a bit out of his depth. But he is trying and she has faith in him. After all, she did raise him well.

Bruce will be two in March. The mingling of Ronan and Henny's blood has produced a beautiful, copper-skinned boy with curly, peach-colored hair, and unusual, inquisitive eyes that preternaturally shift between the color of green tea and something altogether silver. Myra is thrilled to be a grandmother. After Bruce was born, despite her declining health, she took the train down to New York City for the christening and she's been able to see them a handful of times since. She's grateful that Henny and Ronan have twice made the trip up to Waitsfield, but since Henny accepted a two-year professorship at Northwestern University, visits haven't been possible. For the past year Ronan has been splitting his time between Chicago, New York, and Vermont. And now here he is after having driven for nearly six hours from the city. No wonder he seemed hollowed out.

Although Ronan hasn't spoken much about it, Myra has a hunch that there is more to his current semi-separation from Henny than the simple fact of geography. She knows that for most of their relationship Henny has been the primary breadwinner. Her salary at Northwestern is very good and the university also provides health insurance as well as extra financial assistance for childcare. Ronan's career has been on a steady climb for the past few years, and he's reached the point where he no longer has to work a day job. During the early days, after he quit the world of book publishing, he would take whatever odd job he could find. He moved office furniture. He did part-time paralegal work. He temped for a financial magazine. Twice a week, for over a year, he tutored a boy from a wealthy Upper East Side family, for which he was paid handsomely. But then the boy's parents sent him away to a boarding school in Bern, Switzerland, so that job ended. However, while that part of the struggle is over, according to Ronan his playwriting advances and commissions are modest compared to the salaries of other young New York City professionals. Money is still unpredictable, and even when it comes, after agent and lawyer fees, the checks are always much less than he thought they would be.

For the past few hours he's been encamped at her dining room table with his laptop, working on a TV pilot. His agent has been encouraging him to take a crack at writing for television, as it pays much better than the theater. It doesn't seem like he's enjoying it much and when she asked him what the pilot was about he said something about pretty, well-dressed people saying pithy, ironic things to each other for two or three pages at a time.

During last night's dinner Ronan explained that in order to get Writers Guild insurance, which has excellent medical and dental coverage, he has to sell something to Hollywood, be it a television pilot or a screenplay. He also revealed that Henny's been pressuring him to pull more weight financially. Then, after a long silence during which he drank a great deal of wine, he told her he's been struggling with his meds. Since his first psychotic episode, which happened in London a couple of years ago, he's been seeing a psychiatrist once a week, who prescribed him Clozapine. Dr. Cantor is a British woman in her sixties. When Ronan first told Myra about the doctor, she felt the slightest pang of jealousy, knowing that he tells Dr. Cantor things he can't bring himself to share with her. That's how therapy works, after all.

Dr. Cantor is expensive, as is the cost of Ronan's meds, and Henny has been paying for all of it. Ronan admitted to Myra that in recent weeks there have been a few mild episodes, which are more likely to occur when he forgets to take his medication. There was a three-day period during which he just stopped taking the pills to see what would happen. He confessed that he saw some things that weren't actually there: a car, a bird, a ten-speed bike. Nothing serious.

Seeing *people* who aren't actually there is the truly scary part of his condition, he said. He shared with her the handful of characters he'd hallucinated prior to his meds program: the director from London; a strange, very thin naked woman with large white wings—a kind of human swan—who was perched on the arm of the sofa in Henny's apartment; a child sitting on top of a government mailbox in their neighborhood, holding a giant turtle.

"So I really need to sell this pilot," he added. "Being crazy is expensive."

Myra wishes she could give him some money to lessen the burden, but everything she had in savings went toward buying the house. At the time, if she had known anything about Ronan's impending mental illness she would have thought twice about it.

Nevertheless, she is so happy that he made the trip north, and she's almost giddy that their plan is still intact. Soon it will be time.

IT'S JUST AFTER THREE o'clock. Bogdan has finished plowing the driveway and the light outside is already starting to wane. The river has frozen over and as she peers out at its thick mother-of-pearl surface she wonders when the ice skaters will return. It's already the final week of January. Last year they started showing up the week of Christmas. Even in the Vermont winter air, which can sometimes feel like a vast, solid, freezing rectangle that gets colder with each passing minute, she enjoyed watching them from her dock all the way into early March, when the Mad River finally thawed. As the darkness would roll down over the hills from the east, they would skate with lighted hurricane lamps and flashlights, so that from a distance it looked like the fireflies of her youth pulsing over the Chemung River. Maybe it's just been too cold for the skaters this year?

As Myra shuffles from the bathroom into the hallway she can see Keith sitting with Ronan at the head of the dining room table, their backs facing her. In addition to being an excellent hospice nurse, Keith is a former semiprofessional hockey player, which must be one of the most unlikely backgrounds in the history of the caregiving profession. She feels a special bond with him. Perhaps it's as simple as being cared for by another nurse. Keith has long blond hair, an enormous, leonine forehead, and deep brown sunken eyes. His shoulders are as wide as a bookcase, and his hands are large and somewhat disfigured, as his fingers have been repeatedly broken from hockey. At first glance he's downright scary-looking; he could easily be cast as a ruthless Viking warlord. But he's actually one of the kindest, gentlest people Myra's ever known. He moved into one of the two upstairs bedrooms three weeks ago—not long after Ronan's previous visit—and since then he's been nothing less than a godsend. There are evenings when, after reading by the woodstove in the living room, she is too weak to stand and he will carry her to bed here on the first floor, where she moved before Christmas. She knew the stairs would be more and more difficult as her condition worsened and it has made things easier for her to stay on the first floor. She has lost quite a bit of weight in the past few months—she's under a hundred pounds again—so it can't be that difficult for Keith to carry her, and she prefers this to her dreaded wheelchair, which rests in the corner of her bedroom.

She has come to view the wheelchair as an abdication. Even as her body slowly dissolves, she refuses to give in to the will of that damn chair. Perhaps there's something in the act of being carried that brings on the possibility of being transformed into a child? An improbable reversal of her fate. She could be the subject of a fable: the woman who drew so near to death that her life started over. But if she ever gets in the wheelchair the magic will end. The spell will be broken and she will shatter like a cheap dinner plate thrown against the wall. So the wheelchair remains wedged into the corner of her bedroom, untouched.

She knows the substance of what Keith and Ronan are discussing and elects to give them space. They've talked on the phone a number of times in recent weeks but this is the first time they've met in person. Keith is Myra's third at-home nurse. The other two, each of whom fulfilled their respective two-month stints and moved on to other assignments, were fine, but Keith is Myra's favorite by a long shot.

Remarkably, Myra's hospice care is into its seventh month, which is far longer than anyone could have anticipated. Fortunately for her, her benefits she earned from her tenure at Stateville Correctional cover the costs. She makes seldom use of the morphine plunger to manage her pain, which is constant and considerable. What started out as an intestinal ache accompanied by occasional sharp cramps, at the beginning of her hospice program, has become an all-consuming state of agony, at times almost abstract in its paralyzing power. Yet she hardly ever turns to the morphine, as she knows it will overtax her liver and further toxify her already compromised system. And despite not having much of an appetite, pairing this strategy with the consumption of lots of fatty foods, like McDonald's cheeseburgers, which Keith fetches for her during his daily trip into nearby Montpelier, seems to satisfy the tumors and keep them from feasting on whatever healthy tissue might remain in her stomach and colon. Myra has become her own biochemistry experiment. She knew it would get to this point—that she simply wouldn't give in to the cancer—so after learning she could trust Keith, she hatched the plan with him.

Keith is in his third month of service. Toward the end of his initial assignment with Myra he requested to stay on with her and the agency agreed. Myra couldn't be more grateful. Tonight Keith will be staying in a hotel in Montpelier so Myra can be alone with her son.

"She's up!" Keith says, rising from the table and coming to meet her in the hallway.

Myra has given nearly all of her weight to her IV stand, which is outfitted with a small oxygen tank. Sometimes she feels as if she competes with the small, iron vessel, whose density is hard to fathom. She has to stop for a moment and fix her respirator mask, which has slipped off. She is suddenly lightheaded, short of breath. Her right palm finds the wall as Keith takes over fixing her mask. She stares at her hand on the wall. It looks somehow prehistoric, reptilian.

"Thank you," she says to Keith. Under the mask, her voice sounds far away, girlish.

Keith simply smiles and tends to her oxygen line, which has worked its way under one of the wheels of the IV stand. She lets her body lean into him. He smells like woodsmoke. She's tempted to drape herself over his back, which has formed a perfect, welcoming tabletop, but she resists. Although she would never admit it, there are times when she secretly enjoys this rag-doll existence, Keith as her dominant dance partner, the effortless strongman. She doesn't indulge in this pleasure here in the hallway, though, as she wants to appear as able-bodied as possible in front of Ronan.

Lately she's been able to make only one of these trips away from her bed per day. She usually aims for around 4:00 p.m., so she can sit at the dining room table, warm her hands around a mug of chamomile tea (at this point she can stomach only a sip or two), and catch the sun setting over the Mad River. After all, she moved up to northwestern Vermont for these very reasons: the humming-birds and the rolling green hills and the magnificent sunsets over the river. It's a far cry from the iron sky of Joliet, where she'd spent more than two decades of her life.

Keith helps her to the table and before he eases her into her chair that faces the dining room window she gives him a long, wordless hug. When they break from the embrace there are tears in his eyes.

"It might snow," she tells him. "Please be careful driving."

"My Subaru won't let me down," he says, wiping his eyes and putting on his puffy winter coat. "I'll check in with you tomorrow," he tells Ronan.

Ronan nods and thanks him and then Keith leaves through the front door. Myra remains very still as she listens to Keith cross the deck of the screened-in front porch and descend the steps. His boots crunch in the snow toward his car, parked across the street, behind Myra's Toyota.

"He's a good man," she says after his car pulls away.

"He cares about you a lot," Ronan says.

Her tea has already been set on the little square denim coaster. Keith always makes everything so easy. She's caught her breath and feels comfortable removing the respirator, which she lowers to her chin.

"You didn't want any tea?" she says, forming her hands around the mug.

"Not right now," he says.

"Are you hungry?"

"I had a sandwich earlier."

"Keith might have already told you this but the fridge is stocked with things you like. There are a few different frozen pizzas in the freezer too."

"Thanks," he says.

He's having a difficult time taking her in, and she says, "I know I'm not so easy on the eyes these days."

"Mom," he says. "Don't."

"Well, it's true," she says. "You can hardly look at me."

"I'm sorry," he says. "It has nothing to do with your appearance. You're still pretty."

"You're ashamed of something," she says.

He can't respond. It's as if he's been forced to hold a sharp stone in his mouth.

"If you don't want to go through with this—"

"We're doing this," he says, his eyes finally meeting hers. "It's just not easy."

"I know," she says, "but you've always been brave. You're one of the bravest people I know." She drinks from the tea. Her wrists are so weak she can barely bring the mug to her lips. She manages to take a sip and lower the mug back to the coaster.

"Do you need a straw?" he asks.

She shakes her head. Her skull feels too large, as if her brain is sliding around inside of it.

"How are you feeling?" he asks.

"Everything tastes awful," she says. "Like ground-up pencil lead. Cheeseburgers, chicken soup, ice cream—doesn't matter, it's all pencil lead. I can smell the chemicals coming out of my pores. We chose a good night."

"Let's talk about other things," he says.

She looks to the woodstove in the living room and sees that Keith was sure to bring in plenty of wood from the shed. At least two or three days' worth.

"Did you talk to Henny?" she says.

"We spoke earlier," he says. "She said Bruce got excited when he heard my voice coming through the phone, so that's something."

"It sounds like you guys had a nice Christmas."

"Evanston was a tundra," he says. "New York City has spoiled me. I don't know how you and I managed all those winters in Joliet. New York City winters are mild compared to what we went through in the Midwest. The windchill alone."

"But things between you and Henny were better."

"It was a start," he says. "We're definitely trying again. After we got through the first night..." He can't complete the sentence.

Myra knows that Ronan and Henny separated for nearly the entire pregnancy. The incident in London had caused him to have a breakdown. He flew back to New York the day after his play opened and had to be hospitalized. Ronan spent nearly a month in the psych ward at Beth Israel (a stay that Henny paid for), where he was heavily medicated and under constant psychiatric supervision. Then he moved back to the Ukrainian woman's apartment in the East Village for most of the pregnancy. Henny let him come home, for the final two weeks and he was beside her during the birth. The photos make it seem as if they are the happiest couple in the world, with baby Bruce between them, his little turtle arms swimming out, but things never seemed to quite get back on track for them. There was Ronan's second hospitalization a few months later. Henny found him in the kitchen, in a kind of fugue state, stabbing himself in the thigh with a fork repeatedly. The stress of becoming a father had obviously triggered something in his brain. He had to return to in-patient care for a few weeks, until his medication was correctly adjusted. And later, after Henny went to Northwestern, apparently she started seeing a woman—a Directing fellow from her department—though that didn't last long. Ronan has never mentioned anything, but Myra suspects he Ronan has also strayed from the relationship. If they would only forget their progressive ways and get married once and for all it would probably solve most of their problems. Since he started the Clozapine he's been doing much better. She's glad that he and Henny just spent Christmas together.

Ronan swallows and starts again: "When everything's wrapped up here I'll go to Chicago and spend another few weeks with Henny and Bruce. That's what we agreed upon." He adds that there's a little storefront theater on West Belmont that wants to do a reading of one of his plays, and that should keep him occupied for a few days. When he speaks it's only after a deep breath, as though the words themselves are exhausting him.

"Bruce will be thrilled to see his daddy again," Myra says.

"I miss him a lot," Ronan says. "I miss her too."

"She loves you," Myra says. "There's never been any doubt about that."

She can feel the sadness hanging on her son. It presses down on his left shoulder as if a sandbag has been set there.

She brings the oxygen mask to her face for a few breaths, luxuriating in its cool easy current. "You know the Toyota is yours," she says, lowering the mask. "You're already on the insurance and it's all paid off. You just have to take it in to get the oil changed now and then. It still gets around thirty-five miles per gallon."

"I'll definitely come back for it," he says.

The light through the living room window is fading even more. With all the cloud cover there's not going to be much of a sunset tonight. The icy surface of the river is silver, like burnished sheet metal. The other day a group of teenagers were out there drinking and sliding around. They left their beer cans, which clattered about for a while, as well as a red scarf, which is still clinging to the skin of the ice. The wind, having picked up, rattles the dining room window.

"I know I've mentioned it before," Myra says, "but I have to thank you again for sending the book. I was very moved."

Months ago, at the start of her hospice care, she received a UPS package containing a first edition of *The Catcher in the Rye*. On the title page was a simple note in blue ballpoint ink:

> *To Mom*
> *With Love*
> *—Ronan*

It's a book they both adore; she'd given him a copy for his fourteenth birthday and he was instantly smitten. When he turned fifteen they started the ritual of reading it aloud to each other during the Christmas holiday, which is when Holden Caulfield is wandering through the streets of New York City. Until this past Christmas, the last time they were able to complete a full reading was during his final year of college. They stayed in Joliet that year and wound up reciting chapters aloud to each other on the sofa. It took them only a few days to finish it. Though Myra was quite tired and Ronan had to do a lot more of the reading, they were able to reprise the ritual the previous month, before he went to Chicago to be with

Henny and Bruce. Aunt Lexy and Uncle Barry were able to come stay with Myra for the holiday.

"I read some more of it again after you left," she says. "It only gets better with age." Her mug of tea has cooled completely but she keeps her hands around it. After a long silence she asks Ronan to go shave. "Please," she says. "I want to see your face."

He tells her that he didn't bring a razor.

"Keith has one," she says. "He uses the upstairs bathroom."

Ronan pushes away from the table and heads upstairs, lumbering on each step. How did this exceptional former sprinter come to be so slow-moving? So withdrawn? Her son will grow out of this depression. He will not become Denny. The drugs will heal him; she's convinced herself of this.

While he's gone she plants her elbows on the table, using them to push herself up from her chair, and manages to work her way upright. She then grabs her rolling IV stand and heads toward the living room, inching along at a glacial pace. It takes her nearly three minutes to go fewer than ten steps. Each smooth, wide pine floorboard is like a mile marker, a series of telephone poles along a country road.

Once in the living room she heads toward the cherrywood rolltop desk, a gift from Lexy, who found it a few years ago at an antiques store in northern New Hampshire when she and Barry were on their way up to help move Myra in. She sits on the wicker chair, raises the desk's curved, slatted front, and removes a large stuffed manila envelope. Mustering her strength, she stands with the envelope, slow and steady, using every available muscle in her feet, her legs, her aching hips, and starts the journey back to the dining room. After three steps, she drops the envelope and it cartwheels in the opposite direction. Turning around and bending over to retrieve it would be an impossibility. She leaves the envelope where it landed and continues shuffling toward the dining room table.

With this illness time has become a ghoul that changes shape. It thickens, grows solid, transforms into a litter of cats that crowd her feet and claw at her shins. And then, just like that, they disappear and there goes another day with so few moments of relief. Seconds become thumbtacks of pain. Minutes, railroad spikes. An hour is an old iron cookstove hanging from the ceiling by a horsehair. She should've taken something for the agony. One depression of the morphine plunger's little red button—a toy, really—would do the trick. Keith all but insisted on it earlier this morning, yet Myra, to use one of her mother's favored terms, is bullheaded. It would be so easy to press that button but she wants her mind clear during this important time with her son.

She finally makes it back to the dining room table, and using her wrists, forearms, and elbows, lowers herself onto her chair. Nothing in the middle of her body seems to be connected to anything above or below it. She's like a wooden puppet that got flung into the street. She brings her hands to her mug of tea, which is utterly cold now. Myra checks her reflection in the spoon resting on the table and is glad she put on a bit of makeup when she was in the bathroom. Not too much, nothing garish. Just some lipstick and a touch of rouge. Since December her cheeks have become so sunken and sallow. Her hair has grown back from her last round of chemo, but it is thin, oddly curly, almost colorless, not the rich brown it once was. She started going gray only a few years ago, and if she hadn't done the aggressive treatments she might still have her thick head of brown hair, even into the beginning of her seventh decade. No gray hairs but all this cancer. God might give you one good thing but seems hellbent on blighting the rest of you. Sometimes she regrets the choice to have gone through all the chemotherapy, to have absorbed all that poison.

Ronan returns to the dining room. His flesh is pink from the shower. His hair is damp and he's parted it on the side. This is how he wore it in high school. With the clean shave he looks like a boy again. Her boy. There are times, she can't help notice, when he really resembles Denny. It's an expression he takes on when he can't answer a question, when he's confused. It's in the prominent brow, the way the eyes seem to deepen and fall prey to dark thoughts, to the wolves in his head. Or perhaps, though she doesn't want to think so, it's a cravenness, an unwillingness to face something. Ronan has also finally changed his clothes. He arrived in pair of blue jeans and a loose gray sweatshirt, which he's been wearing for two days, and now he's in a thick, cream-colored fisherman's sweater and a pair of butterscotch-colored corduroys.

"What a difference," she says as he enters the dining room. "Was the water hot enough?"

"The water was perfect," he says.

She asks him to retrieve the manila envelope that she dropped on her way back to the dining room. He does so, his movements so fluid and easy it's almost obscene. The shower has loosened him up, eased his mood. He hands her the envelope. Myra unclasps the top, removes seven white envelopes, and deals them onto the table. Each one bears a name:

> MOM
> FIONA
> JOAN
> LEXY
> ALEC
> RONAN
> DENNY

She lets Ronan take them in for a moment, then says, "You'll need to deliver these in person," she says. "We can't risk a postal date on the envelopes."

He asks if anyone knows where his uncle Alec is.

"Grandma Ava knows," she says. "You'll have to check with her." She returns the envelopes to the manila mailer, pushes it toward him, then hides her monstrous hands in her lap. "Please don't read yours yet," she says.

"I won't," he says.

"Promise me."

"I promise," he says, meeting her eyes. He takes the envelopes out again, looks through them, one by one. "And where's my dad?" he asks.

She swallows. Her mouth is dry, raw, as if she was forced to swallow a spoonful of sand. This incessant dehydration. No matter how much water she drinks she's always parched. "He's at a VA hospital in southern Illinois," she says.

She knows that the mystery of Ronan's father has always been difficult for him. There is an emptiness there. A dark, endless cave. Early on Myra made a choice not to tell him the story of his father. If for no other reason, it was to protect herself. She was so in love with Denny Happ. She would've done anything for him, suffered any humiliation, given a limb, a kidney, her life. Conjuring him was—and still is—just too painful. His unexplained departure, the years of silence, the discovery of him in Carbondale, his shocking explanation of his illness—taken together it's easily the greatest sadness she's known.

"He's been an in-patient there for three years now," she adds.

"I didn't even know he was alive," Ronan says.

"He is," Myra says. "I'm sorry I haven't told you until now. You know the subject of your father has always been a struggle for me." Even talking about Denny now makes it feel as if she's losing precious oxygen.

"How did you find him?" Ronan asks.

"Last year someone from the VA hospital contacted me because he had listed us on his will," she says, gently bending the truth. The fact is that she was the one who tracked him down through the Veterans Health Administration in DC as she was writing her own will. She plans to send him three photo albums chronicling their early days living in Chicago and Wilmette.

"Is he ill?" Ronan asks.

"Not terminally, no," she says. "At least not that I'm aware of." She brings the oxygen mask to her face, takes a hit, and continues: "But he has schizophrenia, Ronan. Apparently he's on a lot of medication." She exhales, takes more oxygen. "The things that you struggle with—your condition—I think it's inherited."

Ronan's face is beset by an expression he used to make when he was a little boy, after he'd wake up from a nap and was confused. She knows she could tell him so much more: about her visit years ago to Connie's house; how Denny sat with her at her little kitchen table; how he confessed to being instructed by other forces to murder her and Ronan. But it's just too excruciating. She doesn't want to spoil these final moments with her son. It will have to be enough for him to know that his father is alive.

"What VA hospital?" Ronna says.

"The one in Marion," she says. "It's near Carbondale."

There is a silence. Only embers popping in the wood-burning stove, which Keith made sure to light before he left.

"I'll take him his letter," Ronan finally says. Tears glaze his eyes and he tries to hide them but his face is so cleanly shaven that his cheeks glisten in the firelight.

She asks him to help her into the living room. He comes around the table and offers his arm, which she clutches with both hands and pulls herself up. After she gets her balance he slowly leads her and her IV stand into the living room, one step at a time, and eases her into her calico wool recliner, the same one she's had since her earliest days in Chicago, her beloved reading chair. It used to be catty-corner to the sofa but a few weeks ago Keith set it beside the wood-burning stove so she could be warm while she read.

Beside the chair sits an old crate of vinyl records. As Myra settles in, Ronan crouches and flips through them: John Denver, Patsy Cline, Simon and Garfunkel, John Prine, Fleetwood Mac...

The fire hisses. A piece of kindling cracks. Ronan opens the metal door, feeds some wood into the stove, closes it. Then, from the wall over the crate of records, he removes a framed 8" x 10", autographed, black-and-white picture of baseball great Mickey Mantle.

"Grandma Ava brought that with her the last time she and your aunt Joan visited," Myra says. "My dad gave it to me for my fourteenth birthday."

"I had no idea you liked Mickey Mantle," Ronan says.

"I met him once," she says.

"Oh really? Where?"

"In Elmira. At this old diner where your extremely strict grandmother would let me go by myself after church. It was my first bit of independence. A few precious free hours following Sunday mass. It was the summer after seventh grade." She fits the mask over her face yet again, takes some oxygen, then lowers it. "He came over to my booth and sat down across from me. He ate half my sandwich and I shared my milkshake with him. I had no idea who he was. He'd just been sent back down to the minors to work on his swing and he was passing through town."

"He just plopped right down across from you?" Ronan says. "Didn't you think that was a little weird?"

"It was a little weird," she agrees. "But there was something about him. Something I was drawn to. When I was walking home it started pouring rain and he gave me a ride."

"Wow," Ronan says. "You were, what, like, thirteen? He was an adult."

"Believe it or not, it wasn't creepy," Myra says, though she knew even back then that she was too young for what she was feeling when she was parked with him in his yellow Chevy Bel Air with the whitewall tires. She wanted him to kiss her on the lips. She longed to taste the fullness of his perfect mouth. It would've been her first real kiss. He looked like a movie star. He was so handsome, with such a winning smile. "I used to have his rookie card," she continues. "Another birthday gift from my dad. He gave me that when I turned sixteen. I'm not sure what happened to it. It disappeared when we lived in Chicago. The card would definitely be worth quite a lot now... The truth is, I don't know if it was really Mickey Mantle. I suppose he could've been anybody."

Ronan places the autographed portrait of Mantle back on its nail and runs his hand along the spines of the books in the bookcase, which spans an entire wall. Hundreds of books. From the mahogany credenza opposite the sofa, beside the record player, Ronan picks up another picture frame: a small, 3"x3" black-and-white snapshot of his father. Denny Happ is sitting on a park bench, under a canopy of trees. He's wearing a dark sport coat over a white button-down Oxford with the collar open. His hair is neatly combed, parted on the side, almost identical to Ronan's now. Denny is looking directly at the camera, smiling. He couldn't have been happier, Myra remembers.

"I've never seen this one," Ronan says.

"That was after we got back from our honeymoon," she says. "The day we moved in together. He's twenty-six there. After he carried his things up to my apartment we walked over to Humboldt Park and had a picnic lunch. I made tuna fish sandwiches and we drank warm Cokes. It was so hot that day."

"They look alike," Ronan says, holding the framed picture of his father beside the Mickey Mantle portrait.

"Your father was a very handsome man," Myra says. "You get your looks from him."

"That's not the only thing I got from him," Ronan says and taps on his head a few times, a reference to their shared madness.

"You're going to live a great life," Myra says. Her voice has gone even fainter. It's as if she gets an allotment of words each day, and now she's starting to run out. She takes another hit of oxygen and continues: "You got help when it mattered. Your father wasn't able to."

"Do you still love him?" Ronan asks.

"Some version of him, yes. But it's been a long time since that person existed. I don't know who he is anymore."

Ronan looks out the window. His attention has drifted off, as if his eyes are following something blowing in the wind.

"You have your writing," Myra says, "your beautiful son...and Henny. You have so much. You have an opportunity to be the father that yours never was."

"I want that," Ronan says, returning his gaze to her. "I really do."

"Then it will happen," Myra says.

He sets the framed picture of his father back on the credenza and then goes into the dining room and returns with a chair. He places it a few feet in front of her, sits. Only the hissing of the woodstove now. More crackling.

After a silence Myra says, "So Keith walked you through every-thing?"

Ronan nods.

"And you're still up for this?"

He nods again. It's as though each nod is marking time, signal-ing the inevitable.

Myra takes another hit of oxygen and begins going through all the basic household things that need to be fixed: the pendant lights above the kitchen island keep shorting out; better gutters are needed for the garage; new windows are a must for the living room; the upstairs toilet runs—the flap probably has to be replaced; one of the screen panels on the back porch is torn and could use a patch or two. The water heater is over twenty years old and he'll eventu-ally have to get a new one; Lexy and Barry agreed to take care of that. And they said they wanted to repaint the exterior. He and his cousins can work out the main color and the trim. The humming-bird feeders are in a box in the basement.

She tells him about the bookstore in town. "They have a great contemporary fiction section," she says. "They even have few shelves dedicated to modern drama. Last time I was there I told them about you and Henny, how they should be ordering your plays."

She loves his smile. She knows he's doing his best for her.

Her words continue tumbling out. She loses her wind again and has to speak through the respirator.

She's prepared lists, put all the bills in order. Keith has cleaned the place top to bottom. He even hired a couple of housecleaners to help him. They spent an entire weekend scrubbing the floors and washing the windows inside and out and organizing the kitchen.

She reminds Ronan that she wants to be cremated. Despite knowing it will upset her mother, she doesn't want a religious ser-vice. She wants him to put together a memorial back in Joliet, in Pilcher Park, in the spring. He should invite Lexy and Barry and the twins. And Fiona. And her mother and Joan, of course. She also mentions Marna, and her husband, Dale.

"It's all written down," she tells him. "It's all in your letter."

He nods yet again. She is sixty-two years old. She would be sixty-three in June.

Ronan lowers her oxygen mask. He produces the orange pre-scription bottle that Keith gave him before he left. He undoes the top, shakes out two pills, then a third.

His soft, smooth face. This boy. This man. Her son.

"Are you absolutely sure about this?" he says to her.

She just stares at him. Her face is so tired. All of these final words have really exhausted her.

"Mom," she hears him say. "Blink twice if you're sure."

She blinks. And then she blinks again.

He hands her the pills, one at a time. This orange pill, Darvocet-N 100, is similar in shape to the white fuel tank at the side of the house. Ronan holds the cup of orange juice before her. She doesn't even recall him going into the kitchen for it, but there it is. He is steadying the metal straw in the cup. Myra places the first pill on her tongue, draws the sugary liquid into her mouth, swallows. She places the second pill on her tongue, drinks again, swallows again, and then the third. She can feel the shape of each pill forging its path down the muscles of her throat, three soft descending rect-angles. She has the clear thought that the smallest manmade things can bring us pleasure, relief, peace. The poetry of medicine. These precisely engineered compounds that ferry us to other realms. She is grateful to science, in awe of this world of miniatures, the child-like shapes, their dollhouse colors, the ease with which medicine mingles with the bloodstream. This is magic.

The mask is back on now.

"Did you swallow them all?" she hears her son ask.

She opens her mouth, lifts her tongue.

"Good," he says.

He is her father, her father's father. There is something ancient in his poise. He could've been a doctor. He's a natural.

He crosses to the sofa and returns with a patchwork quilt, one of her mother's. He sets it on her lap and then brings the corners up to cover her shoulders.

Now he's holding the book, which was on the coffee table.

Suddenly a warmth begins to fill the space behind Myra's eyes and she closes them. The warmth soothes the length of each arm, the hollows in the undersides of her knees, the knobs of her wrists, the arches of her feet...her jaw. It feels like love, this warmth blooming throughout her body. A final, enduring affection.

"Now?" Ronan says.

She nods. "Afterwards you'll stay here with me, right?" Seven more words. Cottony. The vowels and consonants coalescing. She had seven remaining.

"Just relax," he says. "I'll be right here."

Myra briefly opens one eye, the right. It takes everything she has. Her lid is like weighted velvet, impossibly heavy. In the living room window, through the faint glow of the light mounted to the side of the front porch, she can see that it has started to snow again. It falls straight down, perfectly so...Her lid falls with it.

Ronan opens the book and starts to read: *If you really want to hear about it, the first thing you'll probably want to know is where I was born, and what my lousy childhood was like, and how my parents were occupied and all before they had me, and all that David Copperfield kind of crap, but I don't feel like going into it, if you want to know the truth...*

Myra's mind is flooded with strange, disconnected images: the tiny green tomatoes of her mother's garden, summer bees somersaulting over the rhubarb patch, their purplish sturdy stalks...the slowly undulating catkins of a willow tree...her sister Fiona as a child, barefoot, walking backwards through the front lawn while blindfolded with one of their father's neckties, her pale hands reaching behind her, Alec hiding in the lilac bushes, grinning...holding her son's pulsing figure for the first time, the miracle of his tiny fingers, his body bathed in amniotic fluid, the cruelty of his blindness...a winter deer at the edge of the woods, its thick gray hide riddled with black ticks...the old tire swing hanging from the sycamore tree in front of her family home, turning gently in the breeze...

Her eyes are too heavy to open.

Ronan stops reading. She can hear only the sound of her slowing breath, disembodied...slow as the sea...slow as a hemlock tree.

She can feel Ronan removing her oxygen mask, a sudden coolness around her mouth. She can feel the squeeze of his strong warm hand on hers as he resumes reading: *Where I want to start telling is the day I left Pencey Prep. Pencey Prep is this school that's in Agerstown, Pennsylvania. You probably heard of it. You've probably seen the ads, anyway...*

Myra can feel herself grinning.

Her son's voice is like a piece of thread being slowly pulled away from this room, out of this house that she loves, this house filled with books and firewood and simple comforts. She follows his voice over the hide of the nearby mountains, into snowy forests stripped of their leaves, along the rugged shores of ancient lakes, across vast, unending plains of wheat and corn and lentil, through rocky mountains, deserts, canyons, and on into blue oceans of infinity.

PART FOUR

16

MARION, ILLINOIS
AUGUST 13, 2002

RONAN

IT'S LATE AFTERNOON AND Ronan has been driving for almost two whole days. Although the air-conditioning doesn't work, which is a drag in the muggy Southern heat, his mother's fuel-efficient Toyota has otherwise been nothing less than dependable. He spent last night at a Motel 6 just outside Knoxville, Tennessee, where the room smelled like a breakfast burrito and the bed was about as comfortable as sleeping on a folded raincoat. It's the second full week of August. Ronan's plan is to take care of two pieces of family business—one in northwest Mississippi and the other in southern Illinois—before driving across the country to Los Angeles, where he's been hired to write for a new television show. He'll be in LA for ten weeks. It'll be his first official writers' room.

The new show is about a former-tennis-pro-slash-breast-cancer-survivor who starts a lesbian detective agency. Ronan was hired by the show runner, a Peter Pan–looking woman named Brenda Ball, who was the creator of one of the most successful primetime soaps of the '90s. Brenda had read a few of Ronan's plays and, as she explained to him over lunch at Balthazar in Soho, she needed a heterosexual man on the team to serve as a kind of "hate police" for the straight male characters. One of these characters is a rival private investigator, unfortunately named Pete Stonebridge, who may or may not be in love with the former-tennis-pro-slash-breast-cancer-survivor.

At the end of lunch, Brenda Ball offered him the job, right there at the table, while she was in the process of paying the check. Beyond her ultra-fit, slightly New Age, West Coast vibe (she requested a side of bee pollen with her tea), Ronan found her to be wickedly funny and disarmingly honest. There is a pilot script and a second episode, and the plan for the writers' room is to help Brenda crack an entire season of television, one that is so compelling the cable network will have no option but to shoot it.

After a few days of negotiations between the cable network's business-affairs office and Ronan's agent, he accepted the job. The money is good, certainly much better than anything he's made in the theater, and after a long conversation with Henny, he decided he was ready to give the other coast a shot for ten weeks.

Ronan's son, Bruce, now three, is currently obsessed with the idea of small plastic construction vehicles being operated by dogs and flown into space. His son is the main reason he took the television job. It will be the first time he is able to financially contribute to the boy's future in any meaningful fashion. In a way Ronan could not have expected, not having had a father he can remember, he is deeply in love with his son. Being apart from Bruce these past few days has already been almost physically painful. The next ten weeks are going to be tough.

Moments ago, just after Ronan merged onto Interstate 55 north, the rain, which had been a steady drizzle, turned apocalyptic. Even with the windshield wipers on max Ronan can't see a thing now. He pulls over to the shoulder, flips on the hazards, and decides to wait it out. Another car ahead of him has also pulled over to the shoulder. He's never seen rain like this. A man could run faster than the cars are currently driving.

He checks his cell phone, which miraculously still has reception. He dials a number, lets it ring a few times, and is relieved when Henny answers.

"Are you in Marion?" she asks.

"I still have a few more hours," he says. "I just drove directly into the craziest rainstorm that I've ever seen. I had to pull over."

"I'm glad you caught me," she says. "I was about to head up to my office."

Henny is now chairing the graduate playwriting program at Columbia. At thirty-six she's the youngest person ever to hold the post. Shortly after Myra died, Henny left her post at Northwestern and accepted the offer at Columbia. They still live in her apartment on the Upper West Side, where, after an added wall to create Bruce's room, quarters are pretty tight.

"The sitter should be here any moment," she adds.

"How's the play coming?" Ronan asks.

"I never thought in a million years I would write a ghost story, but here I am writing a ghost story."

"It's so much more than a ghost story," Ronan encourages her. "It's about loss and an old Victorian plantation home and generations of family secrets."

"*And* there are songs in it," she says.

"And there are *songs* in it," he echoes. "Sung a cappella, I might add. Which is weird, but why would anyone expect anything less from Henrietta Woods?"

"I love you," she says.

"I love you more," he says.

"Is the rain freaking you out?"

"Not really," he says. "It's just impossible to see the road."

"You took your meds, right?"

"I did," he says. "Don't worry, I'm fine."

A few more cars creep past on the highway. The rain is pummeling the hood of the Toyota. Ronan finds himself reflexively palming the ceiling, as if to support it.

"Okay," she says, "I should go. Good luck in Marion."

"I might actually get there if this rain lets up."

"Only two weeks, right?" she adds.

"I already bought the plane ticket," he says. "It'll be just for the weekend—they'll want me back on Monday—but it'll be nice."

Since Ronan's second hospitalization and their separation, Bruce has brought them closer together. Ronan was present for the birth of his son, but soon afterward he had to complete another month-long, in-patient treatment at Beth Israel. It was when Henny and infant Bruce came to visit him there that the vulnerability they shared cut through all of their competitive career angst and mutual infidelities. His son's hands—the delicate skin of his palms and the tiny pads of his fingers. Something about touching them, holding them, feeling them clutch his index finger, and Henny's tearful joy at witnessing it, forged a connection between the three of them. The look in Bruce's eyes, as well as their beautiful color, were unmistakably Henny's. But the shape of his mouth—its tough little corners—came from his father. Even with the pharmaceutical cotton in Ronan's brain, it was the most emotion he'd ever experienced. The feeling of possibility that came with the arrival of his son and Henny's willingness to stay committed gave him all the hope he needed to get well. Something incredibly powerful was bared in that little Beth Israel visitation room. Henny and Bruce came to visit him every day after that, until he was released, and together they've been on a good path ever since.

"I already miss you," Henny says.

"I miss you too," he says. "Give Bruce a hug and a kiss for me."

As the rain continues to pulverize the Toyota, Ronan removes a postcard from his back pocket, then reaches into his backpack on the passenger's seat and joins it with the other half dozen that have been secured with a paper clip. The image on the front of each is identical: a photograph of a blue house on stilts. On the back is a single male name, a number likely pertaining to the age of the subject, which was his grandma Ava's presumption, and below the number, the odd phrase SAYING HELLO AND GOODBYE. Ronan shuffles through several of them...BLAKE CARDINAL...DREW EADES...ALBERT PAGAN...JERMAINE ANTHONY HOLLOWAY.

Ronan received the postcards from his grandma Ava, when he visited her in Elmira. He'd driven up from the city to hand-deliver a letter from his mother, written just before she died. He stayed in Elmira for the entire weekend, helping his grandmother, now in her eighties, clear a bunch of things out of the basement. He inherited his height from her. She was also once 6'3" but has shrunk with age so that they no longer stand eye to eye.

That first night during dinner he asked her if she knew where his uncle Alec was, as he had a letter intended for him as well.

Grandma Ava excused herself from the dining room table, went into the kitchen with her walking cane, and returned with the seven postcards. "That's where he is," she said, pointing to the little blue house on stilts.

"He's hiding in the Mississippi River," Aunt Joan blurted from the other end of the table.

"Your brother lives in *Mississippi*," Grandma Ava corrected her. "The *state*, Joan, not the *river*."

It's taken him more than a year to find the courage to make this trip, but since he was already driving out West for his new job, Ronan figured he could head south first and deliver Uncle Alec's letter, and then head up to Marion, Illinois, for the final delivery.

Not even an hour ago, in a steady rain, he made his way through the strange, blighted town of Tunica, Mississippi. The lush farmland he passed, including a field of brown cows huddling in the rain like conspirators, seemed at odds with the abandoned shantytown of makeshift houses so haphazardly constructed with plywood, scavenged lumber, and corrugated tin that they looked like a stiff wind could have blown them all to smithereens. There were entire lots of mud, abandoned cars stripped of their parts, an old ice cream truck jutting halfway out of a meadow of wildflowers as if the earth itself had imagined it.

After a number of turns on half-finished streets, Ronan pulled up to the house featured in the postcards, one of many homes in the area erected on stilts. When Ronan got out of the car, the rain ceased, as if on cue, and he could suddenly hear birds. A good omen, hopefully.

The place to the left of his uncle's, a dirty white cabin barely bigger that a tollbooth, featured an American flag draped over the roof and at least three No Trespassing signs. The one to the right, a mint-green rectangular bungalow whose stilts were riddled with enormous blobs of birdshit, looked to be unoccupied, its windows broken, the front door torn from the hinges.

Uncle Alec's house perfectly matched the image on the post-cards: the baby-blue siding; the dark stilts; the cedar steps zigzag-ging up to the front door, some twenty feet above Ronan's head. Parked in a rectangle of uneven asphalt directly under the house was a dinged-up gray Chevy Malibu from the late '70s. It had a Mississippi license plate below the rear bumper.

Ronan climbed the wobbly cedar steps and knocked on the front door. There was no answer. He couldn't see anything in the window because the blinds were pulled. Setting his ear to the door, he heard nothing. He descended the stairs and walked around to the back of the house, where he was met with an almost identical, equally wobbly cedar staircase, which he climbed carefully, feeling it might collapse at any moment, as if it was booby-trapped.

On the top landing, parked before the rear entrance, sat a wheel-barrow holding a shallow pool of mixed concrete. A four-foot shovel was propped against it. Ronan touched the mixture, still damp and clumpy. He tried to peer through the small window framed in the back door, but it had been dressed with a piece of dark fabric.

He grabbed the doorknob. There are irrevocable moments in a person's life and he understood that this was one of them. A malev-olent force, heavy and dank, seemed to pervade the air. Whatever was on the other side of that door was almost certainly something he didn't want to know about, especially if it turned out to require an action on his part beyond the delivery of this letter. He didn't turn the knob. He let go and headed back down the wobbly stairs, praying they wouldn't collapse.

After he came around to the front of the house, from his back pocket he produced his mother's letter. The mailbox had been crudely attached to the front right stilt with baling wire. The only thing inside the mailbox was an ad circular featuring bargain prices for Rico rice, Wesson corn oil, and a Perdue whole chicken. Ronan put the ad circular back in the mailbox, set his mother's letter on top of it, and lowered the lid.

He then went over to the Chevy Malibu and looked in through the front passenger's side window. Fast-food bags littered the floor. A lottery ticket, already scratched off, lay on the passenger's seat. Cocked in one of the two circular drink containers between the seats was a blue Nintendo Game Boy Advance.

Does Uncle Alec have a son? he wondered. Or a daughter? Is there an unknown cousin in the family? As if involuntarily, Ronan's mind walled off other, darker implications.

Scattered in the backseat of the Malibu were a few aluminum Coors Light empties, one of them half-crushed, a handful of discarded receipts, and a pair of cheap sunglasses.

Ronan tried to open the passenger's side door but it was locked. Then he tried all the other doors. No luck. This might be all he would ever come to know of his uncle Alec: an old Chevy Malibu containing a Game Boy, a scratched-off lottery ticket, and a collection of fast-food trash. Even though he'd factored in an extra hour for a possible visit with him, he was running behind schedule. He'd had a hard time finding Tunica and had spent nearly an hour asking for directions at two different gas stations and later from a security guard in a casino parking lot. He had an important appointment in Marion, Illinois, for which he couldn't be late.

That's when the rain started again. He was dry under the shelter of Uncle Alec's strange, lofted house. For a moment he just stood there watching the rain pelt the windshield of his mother's Toyota. What would she make of this? he wondered.

Along the half-mud-half-gravel street, a wild dog jogged by, weaving its way through a slew of dirty potholes. The dog was scrawny, rangy, wolflike, with lunatic eyes. Even from a distance Ronan could see that its coat was riddled with mange. The animal continued zigzagging amid the potholes and sickly puddles of filth and disappeared around a corner.

Now, as Ronan waits out the rain on the interstate shoulder, he can't seem to get the image of that wild dog out of his head. At least he was able to deliver his mother's letter. He upheld his promise to her. He unlatches the glove compartment, drop's his uncle's strange postcards inside, and returns his attention to the apocalyptic storm.

Some fifteen minutes later, with sheets of water sluicing across the pavement, the rain at last slows to a steady patter. Ronan kills the hazards, adjusts the wipers to a slower speed, and pulls back onto the highway.

He arrives at the VA hospital in Marion, Illinois, around 8:00 p.m. His appointment was for 7:30, and once he has apologized profusely he's able to convince the receptionist—an older veteran in military greens—to try to reschedule the meeting with his father.

"You'll have to speak to Dr. Petrides," the receptionist says.

Minutes later, after an armed security guard checks Ronan's backpack, Dr. Petrides, a kind bald man in civilian clothes, comes to meet him in the reception area. They shake hands and Ronan apologizes again for his tardiness, citing the crazy rainstorm around Memphis, and how he was forced to pull over on the shoulder and wait it out.

Dr. Petrides explains that his father is in the activities center but that he will set up a room for them. "He's already eaten and taken his meds," the doctor says. He adds that because of his father's daily regimen, only twenty to thirty minutes can be allowed for the visit. His father will be skipping a good portion of his hobby hour, the doctor tells him, and then there will be two other blocks of activities that he'll have to complete before settling down for the evening. "It's difficult for him when his routine is disrupted," Dr. Petrides says.

"What's his hobby?" Ronan asks.

"Currently he's been making potholders," the doctor says. "He's getting quite good at them."

Ronan agrees to the guidelines and Dr. Petrides escorts him past reception and down a white hallway. After a few turns down two other identical hallways, they arrive at a series of visitation rooms. Dr. Petrides opens a door and leads Ronan to a round wooden table.

A pair of folding chairs flank the table, with a few additional chairs along the wall. The room smells of floral carpet cleaner. Aside from an instructional poster charting an evacuation path in case of a fire, the walls are bare.

"As I told you over the phone," Dr. Petrides says, "your father will seem relatively normal but his memory is pretty fragmented."

"I understand," Ronan says.

After Dr. Petrides leaves the room there is only the faint buzz from the overhead fluorescent lights. With his backpack in his lap Ronan feels like a kid in grade school sitting outside the principal's office. He sets the backpack on the floor, which is covered with institutional, spleen-colored carpeting. The four windows, all undressed, are clean as new. All this neutrality. There isn't a speck of dust to be found. He is surrounded by seemingly endless, antiseptic blankness.

If Henny hadn't helped him find proper treatment, four years ago now, he might've landed in a similar situation. During his two stints at Beth Israel there was a similar cleanliness, a similar institutional smell. Perhaps sanitary blankness is the key to keeping the madness at bay? White walls. Science-lab lighting. Dreary carpeting. Thank God for Dr. Cantor. Her prescribed cocktail has proven to be very effective. The ritual of his medication is simple, consistent. It's like taking two multivitamins every morning. He is boundlessly grateful to be living a normal life.

Ronan checks his cell phone. No messages. No text from Henny. He can feel his stomach tighten, his breath go a bit shallow. He's a little sleep-deprived, owing to the restless night at the Motel 6, but he is up for this. He's going to be fine, he tells himself. Although he knows, from his mother, that he was six years old when Denny Happ disappeared, he has no memory of the last time he saw his father, who is now his only living parent. No matter what might come from this encounter, he's still going to get in back in the Toyota and head west to start a new chapter in his life.

The door opens and Dr. Petrides leads his father into the room. Denny Happ is taller than Ronan thought he'd be, a solid six feet, though his posture is a bit hunched. His shoulders are turned inward in a protective manner, perhaps to shield his heart. Ronan stands immediately, as if he is greeting an emperor. His father has bowlegs, the same legs Ronan inherited: jumper's legs; the legs of a sprinter. He is wearing light-blue, pinstriped pajama bottoms; a plain white T-shirt; a cream-colored housecoat; and, on his feet, brown corduroy slippers. When he walks, each step is carefully considered, equidistant, as if he is walking over broken glass.

Dr. Petrides leads him over to the table. "Denny," he says, "This is your son, Ronan."

His father nods, not quite meeting Ronan's eyes. He's a little heavier than Ronan anticipated. A slight potbelly protrudes over the waistline of his pajama bottoms. He possesses a soft face, and clear, clean-shaven skin. There is a slight tremor at the corner of his mouth. His eyes are the same rich, cerulean blue of the Chagall print that hangs over Ronan and Henny's dining room table back in New York. (It's a painting called *The Bay of Angels*—a mermaid suspended above the Bay of Nice—mentioned in the first chapter of one of their favorite novels.) Denny Happ still has a full head of dark blond hair, which goes platinum and a bit silver at the temples. He wears it parted on the side, as in all of his pictures. Despite his slow, deliberate movements, he looks a good deal younger than sixty-one.

"I'll let you two get acquainted," Dr. Petrides says, helping his father sit.

Ronan thanks him and the doctor exits.

His father watches the door close and seems to fix his gaze at some spot between Ronan and the exit.

For a minute or so they just sit in silence. Nothing about his father spurs Ronan's memory. He simply doesn't remember him. This broken man with the slight tremor in the corner of his mouth. This shuffling creature in corduroy slippers. Yes, this is his father. A once-exceptional athlete who was awarded an appointment to the United States Military Academy at West Point. There are photos proving their early connection: Ronan and his father taking a bath together, building a snowman with Mom, gathering piles of fall leaves behind their small house in Wilmette, visiting the Shedd Aquarium. His mother told him that before his father left them he was pretty good to Ronan. He taught him how to catch and throw a baseball. His mother reminded him more than once that he probably wouldn't have discovered the Cubs if not for his father's love for them. Ronan is hoping that some small action, some tiny movement of his father's face, will dislodge one of these anecdotes in his memory.

To embark on what he hopes will be a fruitful exchange, Ronan presents his father with a photo of his son. In the wallet-sized studio photo Bruce is wearing a striped T-shirt of many colors. That day Henny picked out his hair into a soft golden Afro. His skin is like butterscotch. His smile, huge. He has dimples: one in each cheek and one in the center of his chin.

"That's your grandson," Ronan says. "Bruce."

His father takes the photo and looks at it for a long moment.

"Bruce Nehemiah Happ," Ronan says. "Nehemiah is my partner's father's name. I wrote it on the back."

His father continues studying the photo, the tremor at the corner of his mouth still fluttering, almost infinitesimal.

"He's three now," Ronan says.

His father smiles. His grin is sweet. Sad but sweet. And he has dimples. Ronan can now see where all the dimples in the family come from. His father turns the photo over, stares at the handwriting on the back. He nods and, in a janitorial manner, slips the photo into the right pocket of his housecoat. He still can't quite look Ronan in the eye.

There is a long silence. Each second feels like a lost breath, a stone to be cleared from a path. The lights buzz overhead.

"Dr. Petrides told you about my mom, right?"

His father nods again.

"Before she died she wrote you a letter," Ronan says, pulling the envelope out of his backpack.

He sets the letter on the table. It's a simple white envelope with

DENNY written in his mother's hand. Even during her decline her penmanship was strong. Until this trip Ronan has been keeping Denny's letter in the copy of *The Catcher in the Rye* that he'd given his mother at the onset of her hospice care, which she, in turn, willed back to him. He plans to someday give it to Bruce. A long journey from a brownstone in Brooklyn more than a decade ago—and who knows where it was in its first forty years.

His father takes the envelope in both hands, which are hairless and pale. He turns the envelope this way and that, as if to check it for a hidden prize, and then, as with Bruce's photo, he places it in the right pocket of his housecoat. Perhaps this pocket is filled with other items he might discover throughout his day: guitar picks; nine-volt batteries; a dim nickel; a plastic spork from the commissary. From the other pocket of his housecoat, his father then produces a chocolate-brown potholder and offers it across the table.

Ronan takes it in his hands. Its simplicity is remarkable. The woven cotton cross hatchings are perfectly spaced. It's a meticulous design.

"I use a loom and a crochet hook," his father says. He speaks with the slightest Chicago accent. The words are as evenly spaced as his steps. "The last part is tricky," he continues. "I double-hooked the corner there. You can finish it without a crochet hook but it's a lot slower. That's a good one. You can throw it in the wash—it won't come undone."

Ronan thanks him, genuinely moved by the unexpected gift. He holds it for a moment, switching it from hand to hand a few times, and puts it in his backpack.

Then his father finally looks at him directly, finding his eyes. Ronan is struck by his face, its surprising lack of wrinkles, its boyish softness. He recalls that final evening with his mother in Vermont, how she asked him to shave, and he wonders if his father shaved knowing that he'd be meeting his only child, if he was careful not to miss any spot. Does his father require a nurse to help him with these simple hygienic tasks? His pupils are large, likely dilated from whatever psychoactive cocktail they have him on.

His father tells him that he can ask him whatever he wants, that he probably has a lot of questions. The statement is cogent, responsible. It feels unscripted, like the thought authentically formed in his head the very moment it was uttered.

"Really?" Ronan says.

His father nods. Strangely, his eyes are no longer that piercing blue of the Chagall print, but gray now. How did that happen? Ronan wonders. The roof of his mouth goes suddenly cold.

"Ask me anything," his father says.

Ronan takes a breath and then asks his father the thing that has haunted him for most of his life. It's the same question that would render his mother silent, whether they were eating dinner or driving home from one of his junior high track meets. No matter what kind of mood they were in, no matter the circumstances, she could never answer it. Her mouth would gather into itself as if it had been sewn shut. Only in the final conversation of her life did she at last approach an answer with him.

"Why did you leave?" Ronan hears himself say.

The question hangs in the air for a moment. Only the faintly buzzing fluorescents overhead.

"All I know is that you never came home the night of a blizzard. I guess the question has been on my mind a lot lately because of Bruce." Ronan pauses, making sure to explain carefully. "Being a father now, I want to understand how these things happen. I'll try my best not to judge you. I just want to know the story."

Denny Happ nods. His chin settles in the space between his collarbones.

"Because there's always been this blankness," Ronan adds.

"There was this light over the garage," his father starts, raising his chin.

"What garage?" Ronan says. "The one in Wilmette?"

"Yes, a floodlight. Above the garage." His father goes quiet but starts muttering to himself almost soundlessly.

"What about it?" Ronan says.

"It was issuing instructions," his father says.

"It was talking to you?"

"The instructions were being communicated from an important superior," his father says, his eyes unblinking, his gaze fixed to some other realm. "An all-important superior."

"What were the instructions?" Ronan asks.

" . . . To hurt you," his father says. "And your mother."

Ronan's stomach goes cold. A chill rises up his throat like heavy liquid metal. He forces himself to swallow. "Hurt us how?" he says.

"With the hammer under the sink."

Ronan imagines a simple hammer: its flat iron nose, its sharp rear claw; the dense concentrated weight of its head; the amount of damage it could do to someone's head. "Hurt us bad?" he says.

"Yes," his father says.

Ronan can't ask the next question because he knows the answer. "The hammer under the sink in the house in Wilmette?" he hears himself say, the easier alternative. His voice, very flat now, has lost its recognizable timbre.

A confused look passes across his father's face, his brow gathering. It's as if he can't connect the concept of Wilmette to the hammer. "The instructions were very official," he says.

"And this was all coming from the light over the garage," Ronan says.

"Yes," his father says. "And if I didn't carry them out..." But then, just like that, he trails off. The thought seems to have lost connection to anything else, like a floating ember dying just beyond the perimeter of a campfire.

"What would have happened if you didn't carry out the instructions?" Ronan says. He can't help but imagine some atrocity beyond his own father murdering his child and wife with the family hammer. Would he have run rampant through the entire neighborhood? Would he have turned the hammer on himself? He is reminded of that horrible night in London when he experienced his first full-blown psychotic hallucination: Harold Hull appearing out of thin air and issuing his murderous directive to use a kitchen knife on the woman Ronan had just slept with. His hands clench into fists.

His father's eyes are suddenly blue again, oddly lifeless, doll-like, unblinking, as if he's an automaton and there's been a malfunction. And now he's on his feet—his chair goes tumbling—and he's moving in the direction of the door, shuffling toward it in his slippers, his steps quicker than when he entered the room.

When his father arrives at the door Ronan has the distinct impression that he doesn't have any understanding of what it is. He regards the door as if it's not a physical structure through which to exit, but rather a mysterious portal with its own shimmering intelligence. His right hand is poised in front of him as if he's perplexed by an unconsummated handshake.

"Dad," Ronan calls from the table.

The word sounds so foreign coming out of this mouth. Like a piece of clumsy dialogue issued by an inexperienced actor... *Dad*...For the first time he sees what a weak, insubstantial word it is. Three letters, one syllable, with a lone vowel barely held up by two bookending consonants... *Dad*...Like a wad of soaked cotton landing on the floor.

Just as Ronan rises to go help him, his father grabs the door handle, shifts it downward, and exits.

IN THE PARKING LOT, Ronan starts the Toyota and simply sits in it, letting the car idle a bit with the window down. He yearns for some kind of emotional apocalypse. After all, that was how he'd always imagined an encounter with his father: one filled with intense emotion, tears and yelling and sorrowful groans. Not the emptiness of what just transpired. All he can conjure now is a vague, almost indeterminate ache. It's more like a dull throbbing that he feels in his ankles, of all places, as if he's recovering from a mild sprain.

It's dusk and the heavy, slate-colored clouds are unnaturally low. His immediate plan is to drive as far as he can into the night. But he feels hollowed out, as if he's skipped too many meals. Should he stop somewhere and eat first? Even some fast food would do the trick.

A pulse of heat lightning brightens the horizon. It's a rich pink color, oddly structured, like a colony of giant, upside-down peonies.

In the adjacent parking spot a woman is getting out of her car. She's Black and wears a Veterans Hospital laminate on a lanyard around her neck.

"Did you see that?" Ronan asks her.

"See what?" the woman says, shutting her door.

"That crazy heat lightning."

"I didn't see any heat lightning."

"Really?" Ronan says.

"Was there heat lightning?" she says.

"Must have been something else," Ronan says.

The woman uses her key fob to power-lock her door and heads toward the hospital.

And then Ronan sees it again. The flowers are purple this time and appear to be melting. He definitely took his medication. He shouldn't be seeing things. He closes his eyes and inhales through his nose, exhales through his mouth.

With his eyes still closed he reaches into his backpack and finds his cell phone. He calls Henny, simply pressing the upper-right button for an easy redial, but it goes straight to her voicemail. He elects not to leave her a message; he doesn't want to worry her. He considers calling Dr. Cantor, but decides to ride it out, still breathing through his nose. He executes thirty breaths, inhaling on a three-count through his nostrils and exhaling through his mouth as if blowing through a plastic straw. Each breath helps to calm his mind, to settle the gnawing in his stomach. This is the exercise that he and Dr. Cantor developed together. She felt it would have a positive association with his track-and-field days and be a good way to lower his heart rate. Ronan tries not to think of his father: how his chair went tumbling; how confused he was standing before the door. He pushes these thoughts from his head by focusing on Henny and Bruce. He imagines the two of them at the playground at Tompkins Square Park, Henny pushing Bruce on a swing, Bruce's tennis shoes arcing up toward the trees...

After the thirtieth breath Ronan opens his eyes. The sky is normal again. The breeze slipping through his window carries the smell of cut grass. He is also aware of the resiny, plasticine odor of the vinyl dashboard, the faint scent of gasoline, the musk of his deodorant.

Normal smells. A normal sky.

Minutes later Ronan makes his way through the town of Marion, Illinois, passing the quaint square, which boasts a surprisingly tall, whitewashed bell tower, a trio of empty park benches, and a Minor League baseball stadium in mid-construction, whose celebratory bunting reads: FUTURE HOME OF THE SOUTHERN ILLINOIS MINERS!

After refueling at a gas station on the outskirts of town, seized by the terrible image of that hammer under the sink in his short-lived, boyhood home in Wilmette, he checks the glove compartment. He is relieved to find only an owner's manual, the car registration, and his uncle's postcards. Why would anyone, especially his mother, keep a hammer in their glove compartment? It's an absurd notion. Hoping this isn't the beginning of compulsive hammer checks, he shuts the glove compartment and snuffs out the thought.

Ronan exits the gas station and heads back toward the interstate. In the coming hours he will pass through Missouri and then Oklahoma. There will be rest stops. There will be many, many road signs and billboards to comfort him along the way, to give his mind ballast.

He returns to the image of Henny and Bruce at the playground. His son has moved away from the swing and is scampering toward two other children lining up at the slide. Henny jogs after him, laughing at his inconsistent gait. Bruce is still finding his legs, after all. He runs like an exuberant older drunk, a beloved uncle scuttling across the dance floor at a wedding. They arrive at the base of the slide and Bruce is next to go. He couldn't be more excited. Henny boosts him up onto the ladder, and now he's on his way.

17

ELMIRA, NEW YORK
APRIL 21, 2003

ALEC

THE FIRST THING HE did was drop his teeth off in the family mail-box. Two days earlier he'd had them all pulled by a veterinarian down in Aiken, South Carolina. The vet, a bowlegged old man with the face of a stunned mackerel, called himself Dr. Dewey. He specialized in horses, mules, and Huacaya alpacas. He performed the job for five hundred dollars cash. He worked out of a renovated horse stable that smelled overwhelmingly of cedar mulch and cat piss. It was simple, really. Dr. Dewey shot Alec's mouth full of Novocain, and, with a pair of dental pliers that he proudly claimed to have used on himself back in the "Reagan Eighties," spent three hours extracting Alec's teeth, one by one. Alec was amazed by the old man's brute strength. Upon extraction, more than a few of his teeth released a stench so awful that Alec nearly choked on his own vomit. Dr. Dewey, who was clearly used to the foul odors of beasts, didn't bat an eye. When it's all said and done, Alec was bitterly reminded, the body turns into little more than a revolting, inflamed sack of rot. That afternoon, with his stitched gums thawing, he wandered through a disorderly flea market in Aiken's quaint town square, where he happened upon a pair of used dentures, purchased them for twelve dollars, glued them into his mouth with a tube of Fixodent Ultra, and continued his journey north in his gray Chevy Malibu.

As soon as he arrived in Elmira, the previous night, Alec checked into his downtown, thirty-dollar-a-night SRO, and slept fitfully on the lumpy twin bed that smelled like Easter egg vinegar and buffalo wings dipping sauce. This morning he drove to a used-car dealership and offloaded the Malibu for eight hundred bucks. He could've gotten more for it, he damn well knew it (the undercarriage had almost zero rust, a rare resale asset), but he didn't have time to waste. He walked from the dealership directly to the house he'd grown up in.

It was more than two miles from there to Maple Avenue, and although, at sixty-four, Alec still looks better than most men his age, his joints are riddled with a migrating, haphazard scourge of endless inflammation that made it slow-going. He walked past the Chemung River, where he'd fished as a boy, without giving it more than a sniff, and then the old diner, still called Kylie's, with its original fading signage, where his sister used to slink after Sunday mass to read books.

Weeks earlier, as he was hatching his plan, Alec came to the decision that on this important day he would not give in to the luxury of cars or bikes or public transportation. He wanted these final hours to feel primitive, as if he were some doomed Bible character dragging himself through the desert, a primordial beast-man cursed with the wrath of all living things, vultures circling overhead, jackals in the foothills awaiting his flesh. Recently his arthritis had been especially tenacious in the backs of his knees, but the pain meds—the bottle of Oxy that Dr. Dewey threw in as a bonus—were putting a surprising spring in his step and a gassy goofiness in his brain. In the coming hours he intended on ingesting each one of the ten remaining pills. Why a horse doctor was stockpiling opiates intended for humans was anyone's guess.

Alec had also known he wanted this whole thing to go down in the spring, after the thaw and the softening of the earth. And what better spring month is there than April—the month of daisies and sweet peas. His mother used to sing about such things while working in her garden. She always loved to hear herself sing, whether the songs were church hymns or ballads about fucking vegetables. She couldn't ever get enough of the sound of her own voice. And as fate would have it, it was the day after Easter Sunday. You could still see the idiotic decorations marking the porches and doorways of his old neighborhood. Bunnies and crosses. Cardboard cutouts of Jesus looking more like a New Age sandwich maker with Wella Balsam hair than the Son of God. So much fake grass clogging the curbside, enough discarded Easter baskets to sod an infield. Everything seemed to be lining up. Resurrection was in the air!

As Alec approached the house he'd grown up in, the old sycamore was the first thing that caught his eye. It looked thinner, a bit blighted, incapable of producing leaves. It wasn't dead, but it wasn't entirely alive either. The other trees along Maple Avenue were in bloom. Probably too many neighborhood dogs had pissed on the sycamore. Too many of the Larkin cats had screwed under it, releasing their evil spume. The sound of cats copulating might as well be the sound of babies getting murdered. Alec used to watch a stray tom have his way with female strays along the docks near his old houseboat down in Kentucky. The thing was long and black like a lynx. It raped Molly after Molly. It was like witnessing a great criminal, a warlord. Clearly too much meanness had soaked into the roots of the Larkins' sycamore and made it sick. After all, trees can get cancer, too. Certain ones bleed just like humans.

The house itself was the same unmistakable fecal brown, but the trim, which had been painted pea-green, was new. The front porch still sagged a bit, with the same warped floorboards. There was birdshit along the outer windowsills. Alec recalled how during the early spring the local male robins would fly wildly at their own reflections, mistaking them for other male competitors. In late March and early April, as the sun rose, they could always be heard thumping into the windows, fighting themselves, and they'd wind up shitting all over the porch. As a boy Alec had been tasked with policing all the birdshit. Those stupid-ass fucking birds! Whose white gluey mess was as impossible to clean as spilled paint. Nothing really changes, Alec thought. Not people, not trees, not houses. No matter how much praying or chanting or chamomile tea. We're all just doomed to be what we are. You're a post, God says. You're a fucking one-eyed crow. Good luck!

Alec ran his fingers along the ledge of the porch where his mother had set out a series of empty flowerpots. He had to quell an impulse to knock them into the bushes. Instead he approached the front door and dropped the small burlap pouch containing his teeth into the old tin mailbox. On the pouch, with a black Sharpie, he'd scrawled MOTHER. Between the front door's mullions—the glass was still shockingly clear—he could see Ava Larkin, whose long, insectile figure was folded into a wheelchair that had been parked at the threshold of the foyer. She wore gray sweatpants and men's slippers—probably his dead father's—and a tattered brown crew neck sweater. Framed perfectly in the rectangular window she looked thin and very old. Hell, she *was* old! In her mid-eighties now. Her flesh sagged from the bones of her face. Her once jet-black hair had gone as fine and fair as the guts from a pod of milkweed. The peaks of her knees protruded absurdly above the wheels of her chair. This woman will never die, he thought. She's like some colorless, immortal praying mantis. She's all exoskeleton. Try driving a knife into her and it would bounce right off. That long-limbed, self-righteous bitch is going to outlive all the rats and termites. The hyenas in Africa will perish before she does.

A fat Black female nurse wearing fuchsia medical scrubs appeared at his mother's side and began tending to her mouth with a washcloth. The nurse's straightened hair was so shellacked it looked somehow fireproof. She started speaking in a childlike manner to his mother, who simply nodded her head. Her eyes looked about as full of life as those of a taxidermied porcupine.

Alec descended the front porch steps and walked around to the side of the house. Through the living room window he could see his sister Joan sitting on the sofa. She looked as big as a sea cow, dressed in what appeared to be a giant baby-blue terrycloth onesie with footies. Joan Larkin, the fucking blank-faced manatee with her Three Stooges hairdo. She's almost sixty now and still wearing baby clothes. A giant teddy bear filled with pancake batter.

Alec was tempted to go around the back and trample whatever was growing in his mother's garden—no doubt as robust as ever. He could practically see the rhubarb and tomatoes and black-eyed Susans bursting through the soil. He would've delighted in stomping it all to hell but decided against it when he saw the postal lady pushing her delivery caddy down the Larkins' driveway.

Alec reached into his cargo shorts and fingered out another Oxy from the pill bottle. He popped it into his mouth and swallowed it dry. Keep the golden river flowing, he thought. Let it flow, let it flow...

He waited for the postal lady to deliver the Larkins' mail and then circled back around but elected not to reclimb the four steps to the front porch. There was still so much to accomplish on this important day. What would he have said, anyway? *Hey, dummies, guess who?* Would they have even known who he was? Maybe his mother's brain is too fried with dementia or Alzheimer's or whatever old-people disease it is that makes you imbecilic and repetitive. And Joan probably would've thought he was the fucking ice-cream man.

It was two miles to St. John the Baptist. Even though it was a cool spring morning, probably in the low sixties, he was breaking a pretty good sweat. The last time he'd walked this much was some twenty years ago, when one of his shitty cars—one of those supposedly invincible Volkswagen bugs with the engine in its rear end—broke down in French Lick, Indiana, and he had to hoof it along a two-lane road for what seemed like half the day. The Oxy was making his brain feel warm and slippery, like anything could turn into a laugh at any moment, like he was some fat, lovable uncle liquored up during the holidays.

The church was empty. Everything looked the same. The pews. The stained glass windows. The statue of the Virgin Mary in her blue robe, her downcast, humble eyes. God won't crush you like an ant if you cast your gaze dirtward. Alec giggled. The Almighty's army of priests are the same way: they never look you in the eye when they're pawing at you or making you touch them. They turn you into God—the child giver of such brief and pathetic salvation.

God and shame are like two sharp knives in a box: reach inside, take your pick.

Alec couldn't help recalling the various St. John the Baptist priests and their weak, high-pitched mewls of pleasure in the vestry. Father Oates and Father Nickel and Father Farrell, who made him swallow. The thought curdled his stomach, yanked the laugh right off his face. It was as if God—or one of his halfwit angels, or some ass-kissing saint—was hiding behind him and keeping score in a cheap spiral notebook. He gulped hard and his flea-market teeth lurched in his mouth. If all went according to plan he would have to put up with the rubbery, fake-fruity taste of the denture glue for only a few more hours.

Alec walked right up the center aisle and sat his flat ass down in the third row and tried just to take things in. The pews, their familiar, cool wooden surfaces, the leather-bound hymnals stacked perfectly in the corners. There was very little evidence of Easter Sunday. Maybe the wreaths hanging from the altar? Maybe the yellow roses set at the base of the crucifix? As if Jesus could dip his feet and have himself a giggle. The Oxy was making all the order of this place seem a little dumb and funny. Dopey. Everything was in its right place. Dustless. What was the point of it all?

The unmistakable odor of St. John the Baptist was stronger than ever. Over the years Alec has suffered innumerable broken noses and he figured his sense of smell had been greatly diminished, but the stink of his boyhood church had only gotten more intense. Frankincense and wood polish and that ancient, yeasty funk of the vestments. All those fucking unwashed heavy cloaks reeking of cheap deodorant and hair tonic and liver and onions. And then there was the metallic, stale, mysterious aroma of holy water. Why does holy water have a smell? he wondered. It's fucking glorified *tap water*. All they do is mix in a teaspoon of *table salt*. It's not even *distilled*. He should've burned this place to the ground fifty years ago. He imagined it going up in flames that reached to the clouds.

He felt his face grinning again, when a priest with a patchy brown beard quietly appeared over his right shoulder and asked him if he was there for confession.

"Nothing to confess," Alec said.

He got the distinct impression that the priest thought he was homeless. The truth was, despite taking the SRO down on Lake Street, he was homeless, at least technically speaking, as he'd sold his house in Tunica before leaving on this trip. He most certainly looked the part. He was unshaved, unshowered. There was a film of sweat or some other survival lather migrating across his face and neck. His stringy gray hair was almost down to his shoulders. And the decade-old Hawaiian shirt, ratty cargo shorts, and velcro flip-flops, combined with egregiously fungal toenails, didn't exactly smack of a person meaningfully engaged with society. He was also pretty rank. The last time he'd properly bathed himself was in a hurricane-damaged motel room in Mexico Beach, Florida, which was four days ago…or was it five? For a week he's been driving aimlessly, from town to town, in any direction, avoiding the inevitable. His mission seemed to come into sharper focus after he had his teeth removed.

"Do you need a place to rest?" the priest asked, polite as a Girl Scout.

"Oh no, I'm fully rested," Alec replied.

"I'm Father Carroll," the priest said.

Alec told him it was nice to meet him and left it at that.

The priest then informed Alec about the local shelter they worked with. "I'd be happy to make a call," he said.

"I'm just sittin' here, thinkin'," Alec said.

"Anything you'd like to free from your conscience?"

Alec did momentarily consider the absurdity of the notion: the great unburdening of confession. Kneeling across from this bearded dolt in the rickety confessional, reciting the prayers of his youth, that skanky old Act of Contrition, which he still probably knew by heart, despite having potted a good portion of his brain with drugs, alcohol, and everything in between.

"The truth of the matter," he said, "is that I actually stopped by to make a donation." From a pocket of his cargo shorts he produced a quarter. "Heads or tails?"

The priest chuckled in that good-natured, effeminate way of men of the clergy. "Tails," he said.

Alec flipped the quarter in the air, caught it, and revealed the result on the back of his left hand. "Your lucky day," he said. Then he fished an envelope out of another pocket and from it removed a cashier's check for $14,825.00, the exact amount he'd gotten for his house-on-stilts in Tunica, Mississippi, a week earlier. Immediately after depositing the money into his account he had the teller make the cashier's check out to St. John the Baptist Catholic Church in Elmira, New York. Despite the minor improvements Alec had made to the house, he got less for it than he'd paid, but he didn't have time to haggle with the buyer, a recent divorcé from Saginaw, Michigan, whom he'd met at the Caribbean stud table back at the casino.

Before handing over the check, he had to separate it from a letter he'd received from his sister, Myra, the previous summer. This important letter, executed in blue ballpoint, featured his sister's pristine cursive handwriting, its curves and flourishes as perfect as the asses of ducklings. Although it was dated Tuesday, November 14, 2000, for some reason he hadn't discovered it until almost two years after that, placed mysteriously in his mailbox with no postage or return address. In the body of the letter he'd discovered six words containing the code which had led him to today's mission. He'd circled each word with a red felt-tip pen:

    you
    ache
    sadness
    shifted
    life
    stop

After passing the check to the priest, Alec stuffed Myra's letter into the envelope and returned it to his pocket.

The priest stared at the check in disbelief. "Are you serious?" he said.

"Deeply serious."

"Are you a friend of the church?"

"Old friend, yeah."

"Are you from Elmira?"

"I lived here many years ago," Alec told him, as if he were from another time altogether, like some sword-carrying medieval dragon slayer. He didn't bother adding that for most of his youth he'd served as an acolyte, then the head altar boy, and that he'd been caught stealing a sizable haul of offertory money when he was nineteen.

"So you used to attend St. John the Baptist?" the priest asked.

"I did in fact frequent this holy establishment," Alec said, the Oxy lubricating his oral abilities. "In my misspent youth. And since then I have been traveling the land mostly by foot." He raised his decrepit sandals, showcasing his toenails, most of which were the color of root beer. "And now that I find myself back in the place of my birth I wanted to swing by and get a whiff of St. John the Baptist's old truculent crotch." He had no idea what "truculent" meant, but he'd heard someone use the word at the casino once and he liked the way it sounded.

"Can I ask your name?" the priest said, smiling, his beard framing his benevolent little mouth. He was clearly as charmed as he was confused. "I can't quite make out the signature."

"Maximillian Mud," Alec answered and rose, his fleshy heart-attack stomach and upper torso waggling a bit. Then he pivoted in the direction opposite the altar and flip-flopped down the aisle toward the exit, grinning with bitterness.

"Well, thank you, Mr. Mud," the priest called after him. "Or whoever you are."

Part two of his duties were done.

Now, ACCORDING TO THE cheap mariner's clock affixed to the wall above the lopsided card table in his Lake Street SRO, it's just after

9:30 p.m. When he checked in the previous night the room had smelled like an old roast beef sandwich and aerosol deodorant spray, and now you could add beer breath to the mix. The college kid he befriended earlier at the bar—Nash LaMore is his name—sits across from him. LaMore, who is tall, white, blond, and absurdly tan across the pronounced flange of his forehead and the bridge of his nose, is a freshman currently playing centerfield for the Corning Community College Red Barons.

Alec first encountered the kid that afternoon, following his church visit, as he sat encamped in the bleachers of Elmira College's tidy, well-kept baseball field, with its manicured outfield grass and purple-and-gold dugouts. The Corning program was apparently borrowing the local college's facilities. Alec watched LaMore shag deep, towering fungoes, one after the next, with the soft-handed, thoughtless ease of an expert baker catching loaves of freshly baked rolls with a quilted basket. LaMore later ran the bases, exhibiting the kind of stride more often associated with antelope. It was efficient, effortless, an optical illusion in which he was going much, much faster than he appeared to be. Then he took batting practice, and holy shit could this kid rake. He was clearly the best player on the team. There wasn't anyone else even close. He stands as tall as Alec used to be—a lean, broad-shouldered 6'2"—and to Alec's mind was a different species of athlete out there on the field.

After the coaches broke up the post-workout group circle, Alec waved Nash over and introduced himself as a scout for the Florida Marlins and asked him if he'd like to get a cup of coffee. Nash said yes, of course he would, and after he'd showered and changed into his civilian clothes, he met Alec at a tavern just beyond campus, where Alec used some of the money he'd gotten for his Malibu—his "Marlins petty cash," as he thought of it—to buy Nash LaMore a meal and beverages while he got the kid to tell him his life story.

Nash, who hails from Manteno, Illinois, had set a bunch of school records at Manteno High and had made the All-State first team for small public schools, which resulted in him being recruited by many minor Division I baseball programs throughout the Midwest.

But even as a senior he was extremely thin, barely 155 pounds, so programs from the Big Ten who had sent their lower-level coaches to scout him weren't that impressed when they sized him up and shook his large but meatless hand. Rather than go to a smaller D-I, Nash opted to take the community-college route and be a bigger fish in a smaller pond, where he'd have a better chance of standing out and, who knows, maybe even getting drafted or invited to a Big League camp. Crazier things had happened.

"Based on what I saw today, I think that's definitely in your cards," Alec assured him during their second round of beers.

Since the spring of his senior year Nash has grown two inches, put on twenty pounds of muscle—whey is a wonder protein—and cut two-tenths of a second off his sprint time down to first base. He's a centerfielder but the coaches at Corning are trying to convert him into starting pitcher because of his freakishly great arm. There have been scouts from big Division I programs stopping by spring practices almost every day. Yes, word has gotten out about Nash LaMore, the late bloomer, the best-kept secret this side of the Mississippi. The assistant coach from Syracuse was here yesterday, for instance, and another one from Lehigh University was on hand the day before that. But Alec, whose business card says his name is Jerry Karlin, is the first pro scout to shine his light on him.

Before he left Mississippi, Alec had ordered a box of four-color business cards from a storefront Xerox shop in Crenshaw. He even managed to get the official Marlins logo on there. The cards are damn impressive, on high-quality stock. That meant they weren't cheap and he got the smallest possible batch—250—figuring he'd need to hand out only four or five before getting some poor sucker to bite. And wouldn't you know it, the first one he used worked like a charm. Talk about inevitable!

JERRY KARLIN
SENIOR SCOUT
THE FLORIDA MARLINS

When he handed the card to Nash LaMore, the kid's face lit up like a jukebox in the backroom of a last-resort dive bar.

Over a free meal of chicken fried steak and mashed potatoes and consecutive pints of Coors Lights, Nash LaMore opened up about his small-town-Illinois life. His father, Jimmy Jack, a truck driver and former AA player (a first baseman who could really hit), had died of cancer just last year. He'd taught Nash to bat left-handed when he was five, thus the beautiful, effortless swing. Nash was raised by his mother, who still teaches history at his high school alma mater. Manteno is in the northeast part of Illinois, not far from the Indiana border, and is famous for its insane asylum.

Nash told Alec of his mother's youth, when she and her high school girlfriends would go find escaped asylum men standing motionless in the cornfields like confused scarecrows, unable to make sense of their whereabouts. "They'd bring them sandwiches," Nash said, as his eyes emitted a magical light, the kind of special light found only in the eyes of a cornfed golden boy from a good mother.

Alec nodded appreciatively and shook his head throughout, marveling at the kid's resilience and dedication. "Wow," he kept saying. "Just fucking wow…"

After the life story, Alec got down to business.

"You got all five tools," he told the kid. "As the cliché goes, if he can run and he rakes, he's got what it takes." Alec went on to gush about Nash's speed, the ease with which he ran down fly balls in the outfield, his explosive first step out of the batter's box, and, most important, his beautiful swing. "You actually remind me a lot of Mickey Mantle," he offered.

And that's how he hooked him—good old Mickey Mantle.

Though Mantle had been dead and gone for the better part of a decade, the kid was crazy about him. He'd even gotten compared to him on a few occasions by some old-timers, he said. He had the same blond hair, and like Mantle he's a switch hitter and better from the left side, and he threw right-handed. He also had Mantle's speed.

"You're taller," Alec said. "And you probably have a better arm."

He added that, in his humble opinion, it would be a shame for his coaches to stick him on the pitcher's mound and waste all those other tools — the hitting, the fielding, that effortless speed.

Of course, this was when Alec flashed his trusty Mantle rookie card, the bait of all bait when it came to kids like Nash LaMore. He practically produced it out of thin air like a fucking magic trick, telling Nash that he carried the card around the same way some people carry around bits of Scripture or pictures of their wives and offspring.

"Mantle's my Messiah," Alec said. "The gold standard."

Nash, who was on his fourth beer, couldn't believe his eyes. His father, the late Jimmy Jack LaMore, was Mantle's greatest fan, he said, and when the old man was teaching his son to hit left-handed he tried to model his swing after the Yankee legend.

How crazy is this? Alec thought. It was like watching a toddler walk toward a birthday cake.

When he told the kid he owned the bat that Mickey Mantle had used to hit his first homer in the majors — the actual bat featured on his rookie card (*the famous yellow bat!*) — Nash was so overwhelmed he just about turned into a tuft of baby powder, and Alec doubled-down by flashing the rookie card again. Then he took another Oxy and bought the kid another beer. And another one after that.

Alec really does have the bat. It's a counterfeit, of course. He found the early-'50s, thirty-four-inch, Louisville Slugger at a garage sale in Asheville, North Carolina, on his way north from Mississippi, Alec had spray-painted the garage-sale find yellow, just as it appears on the Mantle card.

After they drained their fourth round of beers — or maybe it was the fifth — Alec told the kid that he would give him the card and the bat if he did him a personal favor.

"Really?" the kid said. "You'd give it to me?"

"The thing might be worth a million by now," Alec said. "I'm sure your mom's still paying off your dad's medical bills, am I wrong?"

"No, you're right," Nash said. "She had to borrow money from my aunts."

"That's a tough situation," Alec said. "I know it well. My own sister had the cancer."

"She didn't make it?" Nash said.

"No, she died," Alec said, letting a little wobble into his voice.

"Sorry to hear that," Nash said.

"The card has been professionally verified three times," Alec said, steering the subject back to the rookie card. "The money could tide you and your family over till you get your first big contract. It's a win-win."

Nash drank from his pint of beer. "So what's the favor?" he said.

"Come back to my place and I'll ask you there," Alec said.

A silence hung between them, and then the kid said, "Jerry, are you gay?"

"Not in the least," Alec said. "No way. It's just something I can't ask you here. It's sort of top secret. You gotta trust me."

Alec bought three more cans of Coors Lights from the bartender, who arranged them in a paper sack, and then Alec asked him to call them a cab.

Twenty minutes later he and Nash LaMore were back at his Lake Street SRO. The armed security guard was playing gin rummy with the elderly Chinese front-desk clerk, and Alec and the kid walked right past them like two fun-loving guys about to go start their own late-night card game.

AND HERE THEY ARE, sitting across from each other in matching gruel-colored metal folding chairs. The mariner's clock, with its slightly crooked second hand, marks time at a muted clip. The Oxys combined with all those beers have made Alec feel even goofier than before. If only there was a radio in this shithole. To the right song—some Roy Orbison or REO Speedwagon or Boston—he might just get up and dance.

"So this favor," Nash says.

Alec can tell that the kid's a bit thrown by the sad little room, its transient simplicity, the blank, off-white walls, the colorless carpeting, the little lumpy bed—a glorified cot, really—wedged into the corner, and the small sink with its urine-yellow water stains, the floor-to-ceiling heating pipe, and this wobbly card table that might as well have a can of cold soup on it. Wouldn't a top scout for the Florida Marlins be staying in a Marriott or something? Alec considered this but knew the meager, low-tech digs would help him accomplish his mission. There wasn't a surveillance camera to be found in the place.

"First things first," Alec says, and sets the Mantle rookie card on the table before him. Also on the table are the postcards that his sister Myra Lee stupidly returned to him, several years ago, down in Eureka Springs, where he'd actually been trying to live a regular life, until she got his friend Lake locked up. The postcards are fanned out for the ritual like a winning hand of gin. This is Alec's version of his Last Supper, his twisted little Eucharist game.

Alec then reaches behind himself and into the tiny closet next to the transom-windowed entrance, where he retrieves Mantle's bat, whose yellow barrel has been wrapped in cellophane. Alec sets the bat carefully on the table before the kid. It rolls on its knob to and fro a few degrees and then comes to rest.

"That's really it?" Nash says.

"The one and only," Alec says.

Nash takes it in his hands and as he beholds the legendary implement a devious look—downright naughty, in fact—passes over his face. A door has opened in this kid's mind, a black hatch of negative space inviting him to some endless green pasture of velveteen greatness.

Oh, we're all so fucking stupid, Alec thinks. We're outfitted with piranha brains. We possess the intellects of catfish and crocodiles.

"So what do you want me to do for it?" Nash says, breaking a long silence.

"I'd like you to stove my head in," Alec says. He throws away the statement just so. It's as if he's asking the kid for a couple of bucks to buy a cup of coffee.

Nash laughs at the proposal. His face turns dumb when he laughs. He's seen too many movie stars laugh. Too many batting champions. "With the bat?" he says.

"With the bat, yes," Alec says.

"As in kill you?" Nash says, incredulously.

Alec nods three times, each nod deeply sincere and heavy.

"Jesus, Jerry," the kid says, his laughter all but gone now. "You're kidding, right?"

"I'm serious as a fucking ball-peen hammer," Alec says.

Nash's smile leaves his face. "But why?" he says. "That's crazy."

Alec opens one of the extra Coors Lights and takes a swig. "Some questions can't be answered," he says. "Let's just say it's an important action that must occur for the good of all things."

"You've done bad shit," the kid intuits.

"And not enough good shit to balance the ledger."

"What are those?" the kid asks, pointing at the postcards, a clear gambit to change the subject.

"I collect postcards," Alec says. "Every time I visit a new place. It's my little nerdy ritual."

"What's 'Saying Hello and Goodbye' mean?"

"It means hi and bye," Alec says matter-of-factly. "The greatest riddles are the simplest ones."

Nash squints at Alec as if unable to compute his response and shakes it off like a curveball he mistook for a fastball. He asks Alec if this is his first time in Elmira.

Alec nearly winces at the utterance of his hometown. His cheap dentures are starting to slip and slide around in his mouth and he has to clamp them together to reset them. "First and hopefully last," he says.

A moment passes. The air in the room starts to feel heavy, as if a cold front has settled over them.

"Why can't you just, like, hang yourself?" Nash says. "Or jump off a building?"

"Because I don't have the courage," Alec says. "You're in the privileged presence of a bona fide coward."

Nash grabs the beer, drinks.

Alec tells the kid that he's made it easy for him: the barrel of the bat is covered with cling wrap, and he'll be providing a pair of extra-large, fingerprint-proof rubber gloves, of the medical variety. There will be no trace of an assailant. He's already cased the place and there are no cameras, not an iota of surveillance. "Hell, they don't even make visitors sign in the stupid place," he adds. He then sets the rest of his cash on the table. "There's over six hundred dollars there," he says. "Think of it as a tip."

Nash stares at the wad of twenties.

"Go 'head," Alec says. "Put it in your pocket. It's yours."

Nash nods a few times, seemingly working out the logic.

"It should only take one or two good swings," Alec says, "possibly three. You walk out of here with six hundred bones, the Mantle rookie card, and his famous yellow bat. You sell the card, pull your family out of medical debt. Your mom dotes on you for the rest of your life. Maybe you even buy her a new house. A place where she can grow a little garden." He can see Nash working through the possibilities. He's definitely hooked the kid. "When you leave, turn right," he adds. "There's a back staircase."

Nash slowly reaches toward the cash, his hand like a giant, blond jungle spider, then snatches it and inserts it in the front pouch of his hoodie. "What if you start screaming or something?" he says.

From another pocket of his cargo shorts, Alec produces a roll of gauze, sets it on the table.

Nash squints, putting all the variables in order. "You're not gonna tell me what you did, are you?"

"I'd rather not," Alec says.

Nash then points to his own nose, signaling to Alec that something is wrong with his.

Alec brings his hand to his nose, which is bleeding. "Fucking nosebleeds," he says, bringing to the gauze to his face.

"You a cokehead?" Nash asks.

"Why, you got some?" Alec asks through the gauze, which is

thickening with the blood. "I'm kidding." He tends to his nose some more. These fucking nosebleeds.

"So long as this isn't about you going around messing with little girls," Nash says.

Alec senses an opening. "You got a fondness for little girls?" he says, pinching his nostrils together. He sets the wad of bloody gauze down beside the postcards.

"I have a sister, asshole."

"How old?"

"Seven."

"Seven," Alec says. "Nice."

Something shifts in Nash's face. A surprising bitterness turns his mouth small, like he's just swallowed a spoonful of lemon juice.

Alec releases his nostrils. The bleeding has ceased. He wipes his hand on his cargo shorts. "Does your sister come watch you play baseball?" he says. "After you jack a thunderous home run, does she give a standing O while her big bro is rounding the bases?"

"Stop it. Seriously, man."

"Does she do a little homer dance for her big studmuffin brother?"

"Fucking don't."

Alec is amused by the kid's familial valor. He's definitely poked the bear. He reaches into the pocket of his cargo shorts, fingers out another Oxy from the pill bottle, pops it in his mouth, and then takes the final three as well, because why the hell not, and washes them all down with the beer.

"I'm just trying to picture her," Alec says. "What's her name? Paige? Little blond-haired cutie-pie?"

Nash grips the bat handle, left fist over right. The veins in his hands are thick. The tendons in his forearms come alive like snakes.

"You can sleep with the thing," Alec says, tipping his head toward the bat. "Hang it on the wall, put it in plexiglas. It'll be your little lighting rod. Your good luck-charm. Sure, you're a bona fide talent, but you're gonna need more than your average rowboatful of luck to make it to the show. Even the best players at the major D-Ones need that."

"Are you really a scout?"

"Yes," Alec replies. "And I can assure you that an accurate and very favorable assessment of your talents has already been written up and sent to a certain member of the Marlins organization who will likely invite you to an upcoming free agent camp."

"Single or Double A?" Nash asks.

"Triple A," Alec says. "Only one set of monkey bars removed from the show." I am the world's greatest liar, he thinks. I'm like a villain in a movie. I'm like Darth Vader meets Willie Fucking Wonka.

Then the kid starts talking about his sister again. "She has Down's, okay?" Nash says, as if trying to appeal to some shred of decency in Alec, to ward off any further conversation.

"Little Paige?" Alec says. "As in the syndrome?"

"Yes, as in the fucking syndrome. Down's syndrome."

"Even better," Alec says, imagining the bucktoothed, sleepy-eyed brat. "A little blond retard girl. Hey, no shame, I got a retard sister, too."

Nash snaps his head toward Alec. The kid's piercing blue eyes are sickled now, reptilian.

"Does Paige have a middle name? What's her favorite color? Does she like Jell-O Pudding Pops?"

"Fucking pervert," Nash says.

Alec produces the aforementioned blue medical gloves, tosses them across the table. "Put 'em on," he says.

Nash stares at the gloves with an almost sickening intensity, as if putting them on will somehow make things irreversible.

"Look, I can promise you two things," Alec says. "One, you definitely got what it takes to make it to the show, and two, no one will ever know this happened. After you do the deed, just calmly walk out of here—take the back staircase—and head back to the bar. Don't take a cab. Pull your hoodie up over you pretty blond hair and walk there—it's only about a mile and a half. Strike up a conversation with the prettiest girl in the place, go home with her, fuck her brains out. Make her fall in love with you. She'll follow you around to all your games. She'll start packing your lunch and wax her pussy and get really good at giving you head. She might even turn you over and stick her tongue in your doody hole. It'll take about eight years before she gets fat and boring, but there are like umpteen thousand exercise programs to help her tighten things up again and you can always find a little piece on the side."

The kid stares at the bat, its cling wrap glistening.

"Put the fucking gloves on," Alec says. "Blow into 'em first."

The kid does exactly that, blowing into each glove and working his big blond paws into them.

From his cargo shorts Alec then produces a pair of handcuffs, rises, teeters a bit, pushes off the wall to balance himself, and comes around to the other side of the card table.

"Wait, what are you doing?" Nash says.

"You're gonna cuff me," Alec says, setting the cuffs on the table and joining his fists behind his back, facing the door now. He can practically feel the kid staring at the handcuffs. "Just do it, it'll make it easier, give you a cleaner shot. I won't be able to wave my arms around."

Nash takes the cuffs and manacles Alec's wrists behind his back, the left first, then the right. Alec drops to his knees. The blessed Oxy has made things considerably more forgiving. He normally wouldn't be able to kneel without a cushion.

"I'm gonna close my eyes," Alec slurs, his dentures all but loose inside his mouth now. "Three good shwings should do the trick."

Nash stands behind him, clutching the bat, Alec hopes.

"The better the shwings, the shooner this ends," Alec slurs. "You have elite bat shpeed, I've sheen it firsht-hand."

Alec giggles. He inhales and exhales through his nostrils, trying to luxuriate in the heavenly high of the pain pills, whose effect has seemingly doubled during the past thirty seconds. What's the word? *Elysian?* It's the one stupid thing he recalls from his high school English class. The Elysian Fields was like the afterlife, the place where all the Greek gods went to rest after they got sad or punished or lost their mojo.

"I thought you were gonna stuff that gauze in your mouth," Nash says.

"You're gonna have to do that for me," Alec says.

The kid reaches over, grabs the blob of bloody gauze and stuffs it into Alec's mouth. Alec can taste the metal of his own blood, the powdery latex of the rubber gloves. And then Nash grabs the bat and disappears behind him. Alec imagines him assuming a good batting stance, his feet shoulder-width apart, his hips lowered into a quarter squat.

"Jusht like Jimmy Jack taught you," he says through the gauze, high as a fucking kite now, giggling. He can feel himself grinning like a moron and has to stop for fear of losing the gauze. "Meashure it up real good now," he adds, knowing in his grisly, arthritic bones that Nash LaMore is doing exactly that. He can tell, just by the way the molecules are shifting behind his head, flooding the space around his ears. He can practically *see* the kid lining up the barrel with the sweet spot in back of his skull, where the brainstem meets the top of the spine.

Then Alec lifts his chin proudly and begins to count aloud, backwards from seventeen. He has no relationship to this number, it's a random integer, plucked from nothingness, like reaching your hand outside the window of a speeding car and catching a bug. It's a nowhere number perfectly assigned to the culmination of his nowhere life.

"Sixteen," he slurs, "fifteen, fourteen..."

He knows that this kid will respond to a countdown. After all, any athlete worth his salt will rise to the moment when time is on the line.

"Thirteen, twelve, eleven..."

Alec imagines his mother's nurse handing her the little burlap pouch from the mailbox.

"Ten, nine, eight..."

Ava Larkin opens the pouch to discover her son's rotten, discolored, foul-smelling teeth.

"Sheven, shix, five..."

Teeth befitting a catfish, or some bottom-feeding, half-decayed carp.

"Four, three, two…"

He is picturing her holding his teeth in her long, cupped, pterodactyl hand when the barrel of the bat strikes the floor-to-ceiling heating pipe.

"Yeah, get warmed up, shlugger!" Alec cries through the gauze. He snorts and laughs. *What a way to go! What a fucking joke on the world!*

But what's weird is that the kid just keeps hitting the pipe, over and over, and he's creating quite a racket. Alec twists around on his knees to face Nash. The cling wrap has freed itself from the bat's barrel and vectors of cheap yellow spray paint score the pipe.

"Hey!" Alec shouts. "*Me!* Hit *me!*"

But then Nash slings open the front door—the little doorstopper catches in the carpet—and starts screaming for help.

"Hey, fucktard!" Alec shouts again through the gauze, which muffles every word, making him sound like he's trapped in the trunk of a car.

A bolt of rage cuts through the Oxy fogging his brain and by sheer will, despite his hands being cuffed behind his back, he manages to get to his feet. His center of gravity seems to be stuck in his armpits. He wobbles, pushes off the closet with his shoulder, and accidentally kicks out a leg of the card table, which crashes to the floor. His collection of postcards tumbles toward the window.

And then, just as Alec is preparing to ram the kid with his head, Nash LaMore of Manteno, Illinois, wheels around and swings for the fences, striking him squarely across the jaw with the yellow bat. Alec's chin goes loose and his brain fills with lightning. His dentures shoot out of his mouth and ricochet off the wall, and the wad of bloody gauze plops to the carpet beside him. He centers his mind on the letter in his pocket, the letter from his sister Myra. This was the document of all documents, the passport to his salvation. Those six important words.

Now his center of gravity has dropped into his shins, his

ankles, and he can't quite make sense of his arms or legs, of how his hands are connected to his wrists. He emits a sound like some half-forgotten kitchen appliance going faulty and his right cheek becomes one with the carpeting. His hips are somehow jacked up way over his shoulders. He's gone ass over teakettle. He has been in his share of car crashes and this is way worse than any of those. He can smell all the years trapped in the carpet's short, dense pile: men's feet and spilled beer and cheap cigars and sex lubricants and clove cigarettes and third-rate Mexican food...One of his eyes is emptying out now, its humors dribbling down his cheek, filling his toothless mouth.

Alec manages to flip himself onto his back, the handcuffs cutting into his wrists. His body continues making that odd sound. He can still see through the other eye...If he could only reach the kid to make him stop screaming for help...He tries to wriggle onto his side but fails, thudding squarely onto his shoulder blades at the precise moment the security guard bursts through the half-opened door with his gun extended before him.

And though he engineered it himself, though he took such care and dealt with every detail, all Alec can think is: *It wasn't supposed to end this way, it wasn't supposed to end this way, it wasn't supposed to end this way...*

18

LOS ANGELES, CALIFORNIA
MAY 8, 2010

RONAN

A T THE CLINK OF the bat, Bruce Happ-Woods, Ronan's eleven-
year-old son, explodes out of the batter's box and sprints toward
first base without even taking a breath. Ronan can practically feel his
son's cleats digging into the dirt. The boy's feet are quick, his strides
somehow effortless, his natural speed almost breathtaking. The ball,
receding like a tiny thought sent out into the universe, is sailing over
the centerfielder's head. It's the bottom of the final inning of a tied
game, with two outs, and the bleachers rumble with the sudden ver-
ticality of parents. Popcorn flies. Drinks in plastic cups slop across
wrists. Fists are in the air. It was a hell of a hit and Ronan couldn't
be prouder. There is no fence, and he knows instantly this will be an
easy homer. It'll be his son's eighth dinger of the season, a mark that
leads the team and ranks second in the Eagle Rock Little League.
The one he hit two games ago was a nasty grounder that scooted
over the third base bag and kept going, and going, and going, taking a crazy "El Segundo hop," as his coach described it, evading the
left fielder, who didn't catch up to it until it rolled into a long strip
of johnsongrass designating the threshold of a tall, steep slope that
rises fifty feet or so up above the ball field and gives way to several
local hiking trails. Occasionally Ronan has seen the emaciated figure of a coyote peering down from the top of the escarpment, as if
homing in on prey, so still it looks like an effigy.
    That third-base foul-line hugger with the fortunate hop was a

cheap homer but the one Bruce just jacked is still sailing and the parents in the bleachers are squawking like mallards in heat. Henny, who makes a completely different noise—something akin to a teenage girl shrieking in a horror movie when she's fleeing from the invincible killer and the car won't start—is the loudest by far. Ronan remembers from his early baseball days that when you hit one like Bruce just did, when you really go center cut on it, it feels like nothing; it's just this perfect, inevitable absence. The fat part of the aluminum bat does all the work. The sound of contact is a separate musical note altogether, and Ronan is so glad for his son to have heard it today.

At eleven, Bruce is tall for his age, already 5'6", but also surprisingly coordinated. He has inherited his father's raw speed and is the fastest kid in Little League, even faster than all the twelve-year-olds. Rounding first base, he finally takes a breath—Ronan can see it, the anaerobic instinct of the sprinter at work—and his long thin legs seem to have an intelligence all their own.

But suddenly Bruce slows and comes to a full stop, simply staring up at the sky.

"What's he doing?" Henny says. "Why'd he stop?"

"Run!" one of the parents yells.

It's as if Bruce was mesmerized by the final flight of the ball, watching as it dropped into the outfield. He's never stopped running like this before. More parents are yelling now—"Run! Run! Run!"—but Bruce is stuck there, partway to second base, gazing skyward.

"Bruce!" his coach hollers from the dugout, to no avail.

Ronan can relate to the look on his son's face all too well. Is he having some sort of vision? This has been Ronan's growing concern lately, given his own mental health history. He looks for the coyote at the top of the slope, but it's not there.

For the past six months or so Ronan and Henny have seen subtle signs emerging in their son. Occasionally he'll just stare out the back-patio window of their house as if he's witnessing something materializing in the glass. Once he raised his hand like he was acknowledging someone or something in the backyard, but nothing was there. Other times it's subtler. He'll pause while eating dinner and stop blinking and his eyes will glaze over. "What is it?" they'll ask him, but he'll just shake his head and say, "It's nothing," and continue eating. Ronan has always felt that there is more to these moments than Bruce lets on. Before his correct drug therapy was administered—it took almost a year to get things calibrated correctly—Ronan felt during his own breaks with reality as if something in his head was dilating, like a portal was expanding behind his eyes, a gateway to some terrible, inevitable infinity.

At last Bruce returns from his reverie, taking off toward second, but now the ball comes sailing in from the outfield, and by the time he is nearing third the opposing shortstop has caught the ball and begun striding aggressively onto the infield dirt.

Bruce's third base coach has no choice but to hold him there. "You were the winning run," he says, shaking his head.

Bruce can only nod. He appears to be confused, and a little scared, as if he tried to hold his breath too long underwater and swallowed some of the ocean.

The other parents are beside themselves. A few of them glance at Ronan and Henny admonishingly, shaking their heads. It's as if Bruce has just pulled a fire alarm to disrupt the final performance of the spring play and they're to blame.

"What the heck happened?" the third base asks, a little too loudly, as if playing to the angry mob in the bleachers.

But Bruce can't answer. He seems utterly bewildered, if not stunned.

"Look at his face," Henny says. "Poor thing."

To makes matters worse, in the team's final at-bat, a teammate fouls out to the catcher, stranding Bruce at third base and ending the game in a tie.

LATER, AT CALIFORNIA PIZZA Kitchen, Henny asks Bruce why he stopped running. "Were you hurt?" she says.

"I saw something," Bruce says.

It's the first time he's revealed anything like this to his parents, and Ronan and Henny share a charged look.

"On the field?" Henny asks.

"In the sky," he says.

"What was it?" Ronan says.

"Coagulation," Bruce says. Off his mother's perplexed expression, he continues: "Today in biology class we talked about how the body changes blood from liquid to solid to protect itself from a fatal hemorrhaging. It was a lot of stuff about blood clots and activated platelets and vascular spasms and fibrin."

"Tell me about fibrin," says Henny, who is clearly disturbed and is trying to keep the conversation in a more scientific, practical vein.

"It's a protein that forms a mesh in order to stop the flow of blood," he says.

Bruce is in an advanced curriculum, with fewer than ten kids in each class. He is often bored by school, so this eruption of classroom knowledge is surprising, to say the least.

"The clouds were coagulating," he adds.

"They were red?" Ronan asks.

"Yeah," he says. "Mr. Prisby showed us a video."

Henny is wearing her 2008 Obama HOPE shirt, which is going a little loose in the collar. She has been teaching in UCLA's theater department since they moved to Los Angeles, three years ago, when Ronan was offered a TV-writing job that he simply couldn't refuse. He was going to make more money than the royalties for all of his plays combined, and Henny was able to swap her post at Columbia for UCLA. The television gig allowed them to have some space—a California ranch-style house in Los Feliz—and to live like normal people. It had been nearly impossible for three humans to co-exist in Henny's one-bedroom apartment on the Upper West Side, where they'd been living together since Henny returned from her professorship in Chicago. While the endless string of sunny days was a little strange at first—Ronan does miss New York City's surprising thunderstorms and heavy snowfalls and the changing leaves in the fall—he's come to appreciate the beautiful West Coast weather. They're only an hour from the Pacific Ocean, after all.

"Has this happened before?" Henny asks. "This seeing clouds go weird in the sky?"

"No," Bruce says, shaking his head carefully. "But they started turning into rabbits, too."

"The coagulating clouds?" Ronan says.

Bruce nods while taking another bite of pizza.

"Rabbits," Henny says.

"I could see their ears," Bruce says, talking through his food, "and their little pink eyes."

"Bruce, come on," says Henny, who hates it when he speaks with his mouth full.

He presses his lips together and chews dramatically.

"Actual rabbits, huh?" Ronan says.

Bruce nods, still chewing, and points to his mouth, as if to mock his own good behavior, then swallows. "You can use it on your show if you want," he jokes.

Ronan is one of the main writers on a popular premium cable series about a therapist and his crazy patients. The actor playing the therapist came over for dinner last week. After he left, Bruce remarked that the size of his head was way larger than it appears on TV.

Ronan and Henny share another look. The rabbits-in-the-sky is pretty alarming for someone Bruce's age. Ronan didn't start seeing things until his twenties.

"What?" Bruce says, taking a drink of Coke.

"It's nothing," Henny says, gently grabbing his chin between her thumb and forefinger.

Although Bruce still allows her this affection, something about the gesture reminds Ronan that soon his son will no longer be a boy. Somehow he knows deep in his bones that Bruce will wind up much taller than even his own 6'3" frame. But that's okay. Sons should surpass their fathers.

"Aside from the base-running mishap," Ronan says, "you really played a great game. That catch in the fourth inning was next level."

"Thank you," Bruce says.

Ronan is pleased at his son's good manners. The boy is humble and mostly keeps to himself, and despite Henny's mild concern that he might actually be antisocial, Ronan is secretly proud that Bruce doesn't belong to any clubs or cliques but is a bit of a lone wolf. Still, for the rest of their meal he can't turn his mind away from those rabbits and their worrying implication.

LATER, AT HOME, AFTER Ronan has taken his meds and said good night to Bruce, he checks on Henny, who has fallen asleep in their bed with the manuscript of one of her student's plays on her stomach. At times Ronan is almost stunned to realize that for all that has occurred, Henny has been in his life for almost twenty years now. For fear of waking her he resists the urge to kiss her, eases the door shut, and makes his way through the sliding patio doors and into the backyard, where he sits in one of their Adirondack chairs.

The air is light and cool. Even during the hottest days in Los Angeles, Ronan is surprised by how quickly the temperature drops after sundown. It is a desert, after all, and the humidity is never anything compared to July and August in New York City, or the mosquito-infested summers in Joliet for that matter. Recently this backyard idyll has become his evening ritual. He spends twenty, thirty, sometimes forty minutes here—whatever it takes to calm his mind—among the cool terra-cotta tiles and Henny's small, rectangular herb garden, before heading back in. He's found that it helps to let his mind wander, to not think about work. It's a kind of straightforward meditation, really. He simply sits and breathes.

The new neighbors planted mature jasmine bushes a few months ago and the backyard is now fragrant with their rich, floral scent. The smog-thickened sky doesn't have much to offer tonight and Ronan closes his eyes. Traffic sluices along Lyric Avenue. Insects hum in the neighborhood citrus trees.

After a few minutes he starts to envision his son in the future. He sees Bruce spending untold hours gazing up at the sky, waiting for those same rabbits from today to emerge. He is sixteen, eighteen, then thirty-five. A father himself now, with two children of his own. His wife is Scottish, a biologist from Glasgow, with a dramatic, Shakespearean accent and slate-colored eyes.

Sometimes the rabbits will appear to him and suddenly vanish, as if part of a fitful dream. Every so often they will remain in the sky for minutes at a time and Bruce will see new details: their little pink noses; the almost transparent fuzz in their ears; their giant, wondrous eyes...

Ronan is seized by the certainty that he will not become remote in his son's life. It's as if someone has handed him an important stone that he will keep in his pocket for the rest of his days. No matter what may become of Bruce Nehemiah Happ-Woods, Ronan vows never to allow himself to become a figment to his son.

Ronan thinks of his mother, gone almost ten years now, the care he received from her, a single mom, a career nurse, how she rarely missed one of his baseball games or track meets despite her need to take extra shifts at the hospital. He recalls the quiet, steady existence she found at the end of her life... the small house with its simple pleasures tucked away in the verdant hills of Vermont, her ancient calico sofa, her book collection, her love for hummingbirds...

And then he thinks of her brother, his uncle Alec, who currently sits on Death Row at Parchman Farm, the Mississippi State Penitentiary, in Sunflower County, convicted of the murder of three different boys. After he was apprehended in his hometown of Elmira, his postcards combined with a series of DNA tests linked him to the boys, whose bodies had been discovered in the back room of his small house on stilts in Tunica, crudely interred in three feet of cement. Ronan turned his seven postcards over to federal authorities as soon as Aunt Lexy called him about Uncle Alec's arrest in Elmira. From there DNA evidence further connected Alec to the bodies of numerous other boys from around the country, twenty-eight in total, none of them over the age of fourteen. Some people believe there are more; he hasn't confessed, and these are the ones that could be proven. Alec is in the final year of an appeals process destined to fail. Barring an unforeseen development he will have been put to death via lethal injection by this time next year. Alec Larkin. Now an infamous name.

Bruce could have been one of those boys. They were all like his son, a full life before them, but it was stolen by his uncle. The notion makes Ronan grimace. His mind is assaulted by a flash of that terrible night in London so many years ago, the grip of the knife in his hand, the certainty of its weight before he laid it down, the terror of what could have happened...

He pushes it all away, re-centers his thoughts.

Jasmine is sweet in the breeze.

He sees his father shuffling around the VA hospital in a pair of soft slippers, his eyes dulled by Thorazine, his face unresponsive to stimuli. His hand tentatively reaches toward one unmarked door, then another, then another. He is a man slowly turning into wood.

Ronan's mind then takes him back to college, a running track carved into one of the many surprising valleys of northeastern Iowa. A family of deer graze in the grass, beyond the long jumping pit. The smell of cinders hangs heavy in the air, like charcoal left at a campsite. He is doing wind sprints. Seventy meters at a time. He can feel a jolt in his calves, the wind in his hair. His running spikes dig into the cinders, that familiar hide of scoria from his youth in Illinois.

He is flying now...

Everyone else on the team has gone, but he's staying late, pushing himself. It's deep into spring and a rich sunset illuminates the clouds above him. As he jogs the curve of the track before starting another sprint, his mother's family, all those Larkins from life and from photographs—Aunt Lexy, Aunt Joan, Aunt Fiona, Uncle Alec, his mother, Grandpa Donald, and Grandma Ava—appear in the clouds, their figures as faint as faded tea stains. Ronan slows to a walk. After a few paces, he stops and simply looks up.

And now their faces form with astonishing clarity: garish, beautiful, bewildered, ancient, as if like some monument they have been permanently rendered in the marbling pastels of this vast Midwestern sky.

Somehow his life has doubled back on itself. He begins the next wind sprint. He is old and young, slow and fast, a husband, a father, a boy out of time, running for his life.

EPILOGUE

Tuesday, November 14, 2000

Dear Alec,

    By the time you receive this I will be dead.

    It's been over three years since I saw you. There was so much I wanted to say to you in Eureka Springs but unfortunately I wasn't able to. It turned out to be quite a shocking encounter for me. Since you'd left home I'd always wondered how you were, where you were, if you were okay. When it came to my only living brother, there has always been an ache, a sadness, which has never gone away.

    Unfortunately I left Eureka Springs with more questions than answers. I fear I was too overwhelmed by my declining health and my unsettling impression of you to say what I should have.

    Alec, I'm not going to deny that things were difficult when we were growing up. No one had it easy in that house, not even Joan, but Mom was especially hard on you, probably because she expected so much from her only son. She pushed you. She didn't allow mistakes. She expected perfection, which is unrealistic for any child. At times she was intolerant to a fault. But I fear that what is going on with you far exceeds the mistakes of a mother.

    Alec, I worry that something deep within you has shifted into a dark, untenable place.

    If you are hurting these boys you need to stop yourself.

    I implore you to take a long, hard look at your life.

    Please find whatever it is that might still be good in you, the smallest shred of dignity, and grab onto it. Seize it with all your might and cease this terrible cycle of behavior.

    Please make this thing inside you stop, Alec, at all costs, whatever it takes.

Your Loving Sister,
Myra Lee

ACKNOWLEDGMENTS

TK
  TK

ABOUT THE AUTHOR

An acclaimed filmmaker and playwright, Adam Rapp was a Pulitzer Prize finalist for his play *Red Light Winter* and is the recipient of the Benjamin H. Danks Award from the American Academy of Arts and Letters, among other honors. His work *The Sound Inside* was nominated for the Tony Award for Best Play. In addition to his numerous plays, he is the author of the novels *Know Your Beholder* and *The Year of Endless Sorrows* as well as several YA novels, including *Under the Wolf, Under the Dog*, a finalist for the *Los Angeles Times* Book Prize. Born in Chicago and raised in nearby Joliet, Illinois, Rapp now splits his time between New York City and upstate New York.